Circa 1740

T. O. Burnett

Copyright © 2023 by T. O. Burnett
All rights reserved.

Contents

Prologue: Naked and Afraid v

Chapter 1: Insane in The Brain 1
Chapter 2: Sounds of Blackness 11
Chapter 3: A Near Miss 21
Chapter 4: A Tie, A Guy, A Crucifix 32
Chapter 5: The Charity Game 40
Chapter 6: Positive Identification 48
Chapter 7: Terribly Wrong 56
Chapter 8: Fantastic Voyage 61
Chapter 9: Long, Sleepless Night 72
Chapter 10: The Awakening 81
Chapter 11: Object of Her Affection 96
Chapter 12: Don't Sleep 107
Chapter 13: Elizabeth's Sons 116
Chapter 14: Sarah, Smile 125
Chapter 15: A Last Gasp 133
Chapter 16: A Familiar Face 142
Chapter 17: The Uprising 150
Chapter 18: Old Friends 159
Chapter 19: Brunch Tales 169
Chapter 20: Tension 178
Chapter 21: Better Days 185
Chapter 22: Primal Man 193
Chapter 23: Showtime! 201
Chapter 24: Free 210
Chapter 25: Get Off Me 220

Chapter 26: The Golden Jubilee House 228
Chapter 27: Meet the Parents 237
Chapter 28: We Are Family.. 244
Chapter 29: Bradley's Big Day.. 250
Chapter 30: See You Next Lifetime 257

About the Author 263

Prologue

Naked and Afraid

July 2136

When Seth moved his hand from Daniel's wound, he released a crimson geyser that soaked his own upper body. He stifled a whimper. There was no time for self-pity, no time to cry. Daniel's chest rose and fell in a way that Seth knew was not conducive to him living much longer. That, along with his agonal breathing, foretold an abrupt end to a once promising life. As he looked at his blood-soaked hands, Seth found it hard to control his own breathing. His best friend lay dying in front of him, and the ones who had wounded him were still after them. He had a decision to make. Even *if* Daniel made it, they would both be caught and killed. If he left him to die, there was a chance that he could get away. A chance was better than nothing.

He stood. As he surveyed the landscape, he only knew in which direction he could not run. Bushes rustling in the distance told him that his pursuers were not far behind. Then, he realized that the sound of the approaching sentries was the only thing he could hear. He looked down at Daniel, whose unblinking eyes were looking back at him, whose chest was no longer rising and falling. He kneeled beside his friend, removed his wallet from his front pants pocket, and stuffed it into his own.

The state of Daniel's white tee shirt, which was now mostly red, angered Seth. They had all agreed to dress in all black. Even though his outer garments—his hooded sweatshirt, trousers, gloves, and shoes—were black, he had foolishly chosen to wear that white tee shirt underneath. The sentries had come quicker than they had estimated they would. Their sprint to freedom was longer than they had calculated it would be. That is what caused Daniel to unzip his hooded sweatshirt. He needed to breathe. He had lied to the others about his fitness regimen leading up to the event; it was apparent to Seth now. Even still, turning to look back was the action that caused Daniel's demise. The white tee shirt had illuminated their position through the darkness, and the capable marksman made him pay for that mistake. Only adrenalin carried him as far as he got, but not even that was enough. So, in an area too secretive to be named, Daniel Aikens died in an unremarkable patch of dirt in a wooded area. There would be nothing to mark his grave.

Seth turned away from Daniel's body and immediately tripped a wire as he tried to take a step. The signs they had seen at the perimeter of the property that read GOVERNMENT PROPERTY: KEEP OUT were suddenly at the forefront of his mind. He ran away from the approaching sentries and away from Daniel. The further away from them he got, the more he realized that he was going in a direction that was opposite from the way they had entered the grounds of the facility. He was lost; however, *he* had worked on his cardiovascular fitness in preparation of their mission, and they would have to work hard to catch him. As soon as the thought entered his mind, he heard the distinct sound of helicopter blades chopping air in the distance. It was coming from his front, so he stopped running. As the searchlight lit up the forest ahead of him, he observed a glimmer of hope. A flash of silver, outlining the top of a chain-link fence, appeared about fifty yards in front of him. He ran toward it.

As he increased the distance between him and his pursuers on the ground, the searchlight found him and tracked his every movement. Undaunted, he continued. He knew he could not outrun that, but *that* was not his goal. His first objective was to get to the other side of the fence. He needed to put a barrier between himself and the sentries. The fence was there for a reason, and he needed to see what was beyond it.

As he got closer, the helicopter hovered above the other side of the gate, at precisely the area he was running toward. It was as if the pilot knew exactly where Seth was trying to go. But then he turned the spotlight off. As a result, Seth's night vision was impaired, making it difficult for him to see anything at all. He eventually ran into the fence, which nearly knocked the wind out of him. With no time to spare, he scaled it and jumped down to the other side. Though he could not see anything, he felt concrete beneath his feet. The helicopter was close, so close that it drowned out all the other sounds around him. He could not hear himself breathe, nor could he hear the movement of the sentries he was sure were still following him.

He gathered himself and tried to take a step forward, but his clothing had gotten caught on top of the fence. As he reached back to untangle his sweatshirt, the pilot illuminated the area with the searchlight. The moment Seth freed himself, he saw that he was on the edge of a retaining wall, and the ground was more than thirty feet below him. He clutched the fence, which he did more from instinct than conscious thought. His body could not sustain a jump from that high up. As he looked side to side, he saw that there was a downward slope to the wall to his right. He turned his back to the helicopter and began to side-step left and toward the lower elevation, carefully.

Seth tried to mentally block out the presence of the helicopter—the fumes that emanated from it nearly overwhelmed him—and the fact that he was still being pursued as he focused on his footing. But then a violent distraction ripped through his shoulder. He yelled out in agony but held onto the fence. He had been shot. He gritted his teeth and quickened his pace. Another projectile creased the rail of the fence, sending a jolt of electricity through his body. He knew it was dangerous to keep going, but it was even more dangerous for him to just stand still. He moved even faster to decrease his elevation a little more, to gain a few more feet of safety. The next shot went through the back of his hand and eliminated the need for him to decide when and where to jump.

As he fell, he concentrated on landing in a way that he would sustain the least amount of damage to his body. Thinking quickly, he crossed his arms over his chest. A moment before impact, he was able to tuck his chin, narrowly avoiding hitting the back of his head on the hard concrete.

"Oof!"

Despite the considerable pain he felt, Seth knew he could not stay there. He had to move. He sat up. As he felt his warm blood streaming down his arm, he cradled his injured hand across his body. He winced as he stood, the spotlight from above reminding him that he was still in danger. As he began to walk, he saw a light in the distance—a service station. He estimated it to be a quarter mile away. He picked up his pace and jogged toward it. Then, the light from above went away and so did the helicopter.

Seth breathed a sigh of relief, but his heart rate quickened when he heard police sirens approaching from the other side of the service station. He increased his speed to a hampered sprint. He needed to beat them there. Even though it was after midnight, the service station was heavily occupied by civilian cars—some parked at the gas pumps and the others parked at the convenience store attached to it.

As he reached the outskirts of the service station, the first arriving police cars came into view. Seth began to remove his clothing as their cruisers screeched to a stop. He tossed Daniel's wallet down a sewer. As an officer approached with his service weapon drawn and pointed at him, he walked—naked and bloodied—onto the property of the well-lit service station, immediately drawing the attention of the already curious patrons. More police cars arrived on scene, carrying more motivated police officers.

"My name is Seth Tolliver; I'm a time traveler," he yelled to the surprised people in the parking lot. "Remember my name! You *see* me! I am twenty years old." He got down on both knees and placed his hands on top of his head. "I am not resisting. You are all witnesses to the fact that I have no weapons and was captured alive. I need medical attention."

As the onlookers obeyed the excited police officers' commands to back away, several of them kept their smartphones pointed at the incident, capturing video of it all. As the officers handcuffed him, Seth said his name repeatedly, echoed his outrageous claim, and continued to beg for medical attention.

Chapter 1

• • • ○ • • •

Insane in The Brain

75 years later.

"Eye in the sky, what's the score?" D'Quandray asked as he dribbled the basketball past halfcourt, his eyes focused on his eager defender.

"*The score is tied at eleven,*" the automated voice said from the speaker in the ceiling of the gymnasium.

"I'm scoring the next one on you, Maliq." He saw Bradley, his long-time friend and teammate, flash toward them out of the corner of his eye as he crossed half court. He was going to set a pick. D'Quandray began to dribble the ball in place to allow time for the play to develop. "Eye in the sky, give me a countdown from ten."

"*Ten, nine, eight, seven...*"

Bradley made his move and set the pick. With a crossover dribble, D'Quandray was at Bradley's back, shielded from the defender, who stepped shoulder first into the screen. Once clear, he released a form-perfect, uncontested jump shot from behind the three-point arc.

"*Three, two, one,*" the automated voice said as the ball left his hands. *"Ballgame,"* were its next words after the ball swished through the hoop.

D'Quandray turned around and threw his right elbow to the rear, then his left elbow, and then both together. With him, everyone in the gym, who wasn't on the opposing team, yelled, "Get off me!" They had gotten what they came to see. The hometown hero had saved the day again. Only this time, it wasn't the national championship game with their team down by one in the closing seconds. This was Saturday morning basketball at their local gymnasium, but it was no less intense. His team had won three games in a row, which was not an uncommon occurrence. D'Quandray was a ringer. Only a career ending knee injury in training camp stopped him from continuing his career in the top professional league. He had put on an extra fifteen pounds because of it, but he was still too good for the local competition, where his talent alone was too much. Although his competitive fire still burned, D'Quandray stayed out of local tournaments. He had lived out his dream and was not interested in destroying the fantasies of weekend warriors who never got the chance to realize their own. Therefore, he played to keep up his conditioning and because he loved the game.

Bradley approached him with his hand extended. "You just don't miss shots in crunch time, do you?"

"Not since the regionals in seventh grade." He shook Bradley's hand, and then he turned to his opponent. "Good game, man."

"Yeah, whatever." He waved off D'Quandray's handshake and walked off the court shaking his head.

D'Quandray laughed. "I'll see you at work Monday, Maliq."

"That guy just doesn't like you," Bradley said.

"Nah, he's cool. He just hates losing, especially to me. He'll get over it."

"I see your number one fan managed to make it again."

"Where is he?"

With his hands on his hips, Bradley used his eyes to point to the top row of the bleachers. "Right there."

As D'Quandray made eye contact with the clean-shaven old man, he was saluted with a wide smile and two jubilant fists, to which he responded with a simple head nod. It was enough for the old man, who turned to gather his things after being acknowledged.

D'Quandray had started playing organized basketball just before junior high school when he was still the same height as his classmates. Now at six feet, six inches tall, he was an athletic god. The old man had seen every game he had played in person. Every single one. Oftentimes, he was the only Black person besides D'Quandray in the arena. That was a change that occurred when he started getting recognition from major college scouts. The prestigious high school he attended and played for had plucked him away from the one on the south side of the city he had been zoned to attend. The old man had even been in the arena for his game winning buzzer beater in the national championship game. It was the shot that thrusted a precocious sophomore into superstardom, brought the Southside State University Cerulean Knights their first championship, and had kids all over the country mimicking his "get off me" celebration.

"D'Quandray 'The Stud' Tyson," is what the famous catch-phrase spewing, color commentator with the Southern drawl, Dick Rogers, had dubbed him at that moment, and the moniker stuck.

"Do you even know the guy's name?" Bradley asked.

"Nope. We've never spoken to each other. Not once."

"You don't think that's weird?"

"A little, but that's fans for you. It is short for fanatics, after all."

Bradley shrugged. "I guess you have a point there."

The crowd was still buzzing from his latest heroics. As he looked around the gym, he saw many of them re-enacting his signature celebration, happy that they had gotten a chance to see it in person. D'Quandray only brought it out in big moments. Most times, the games he played in the local gyms were blowouts. His knee had been bothering him that day, especially in the third game, so it was highly competitive. But he was not going to lose. Maliq had even outscored him, eight points to seven. D'Quandray had deferred to his teammates for most of the game. After he had scored ten points in the previous game, it was necessary.

Maliq had always played him tough. He had also been a division one college basketball player. At six feet, five inches tall, he was an undersized small forward, whereas D'Quandray was a large shooting guard. That made for competitive moments from time to time, but he was nowhere near as skilled or as athletic as D'Quandray. In some of their more heated encounters, he had made sure to point that out to Maliq.

"I'm going to the service desk to get the key from Imani," Bradley said. "Be right back."

"Yeah, good luck with that. I'll be waiting by the lockers."

"What is your deal? I think she's pretty for a Black girl."

"Pretty angry. I don't want her to bite my head off. She gave me the meanest look I've ever seen when she walked past me a few weeks ago, and that was after *she* was late opening the gym. Besides, the locks are a bit much for me. She looks like Super Sista."

Bradley shook his head and laughed as he walked away.

As D'Quandray walked off the court, he was greeted by a few fans, some with pen and paper in hand. As he signed autographs, the old man walked past him and gave a subdued fist pump. D'Quandray thought that for a man well into his nineties, he was still very handsome. Even with the thick-lensed eyeglasses he wore, his coal-black skin, cleft chin, and square jaw were attributes to be envied. And he always exuded dignity; that was what stood out most. He did not stop; he never did. It was as if he wanted D'Quandray to know he supported him but did not want to bother him at the same time. It worked for D'Quandray. Most fans were not as considerate, and he liked the fact that at least one person did not feel entitled to his time.

By the time he reached the lockers, the next game had already started. Maliq was apparently taking his frustrations out on his new opponents. His team was up five to nothing, and he had scored every point. Likely adding to Maliq's frustration was the fact that most of the two hundred or so spectators who were in attendance had started to leave. They knew what time D'Quandray played every Saturday, and, as usual, when he was done playing, they were done watching.

Bradley inserted the key into their locker, and they removed their things. The diner was a ten-minute walk away from the gym, and they were scheduled to meet Elijah there for lunch. D'Quandray put on his Southside State University tee shirt, of which he had an endless supply, and took off his basketball shoes. Then, he put his sweatpants on over his shorts. Next, he put on the slides, which were from a lifetime supply promised to him by the sneaker company that outfitted his alma mater. He placed his sneakers and the rest of his gear into his backpack and waved to the people as they left the gym.

"The Stud," a teenager walking through the front door from the parking lot said.

D'Quandray winked at him and made a peace sign with his fingers. They were thankful that the meteorologist had gotten it right for a change as they walked out into a sunny day. It had been rainy the past few weeks, so his promise of sunshine was met with heavy skepticism. The gym was in an affluent neighborhood, evidenced by the abundance of luxury electric cars in its parking lot. However, D'Quandray and Bradley were there free of charge. He had been given a lifetime pass by the owner, who was an alumnus of SSU, and Bradley was his one allowed guest. The only compromise was that Bradley was not allowed to wear his Ivy league paraphernalia while he was on the premises.

"You know, I realize you're a celebrity and everything, but it would be nice if someone acknowledged me, too, every once in a while."

"Have you ever tried speaking first? That might help."

Bradley shrugged. "Eh, you may have a point there."

"Which way is the diner again?"

"It's east of here. I think we have to walk past *Lord Leopold's* to get there."

"The insane asylum?" D'Quandray was incredulous. "All of a sudden, I'm regretting letting Elijah drop us off here. I should've driven. Besides, the other way is quicker."

"No, it's not. And what do you think is going to happen to you anyway? It's surrounded by an eight-foot tall, wrought iron gate. Nobody's getting out of or into that place unless they're authorized to do so. We'll be fine. You worry too much."

"I'm not a worrier, man. I'm just not a risk taker."

Bradley suddenly stopped walking, narrowed his eyes, and looked at D'Quandray as if he had said the most ridiculous thing he had ever heard.

"Well, maybe you have a point, BG. Let's go. We should've at least had Elijah come back for us, though."

"He wanted to make sure we got a table. It's not that far."

After about three minutes of walking, they reached the corner lot occupied by the *Lord Adoph Leopold Institution for the Criminally Insane*. They walked past the guard shack at the entrance of the asylum and continued toward Meridian Avenue, where the concrete pillar, to which the wrought iron gate was attached to two sides, was located. After turning right on Meridian Avenue, they continued toward the next pillar, which was a block away. They saw an old man and a younger woman standing near the portion of the gate they were about to pass.

D'Quandray concluded they were out on recreation time as he observed the various activities in which many of the others were engaged.

"You were right, BG; they look harmless enough. As a matter of fact, it looks like…"

"Bradley Gates!"

"There you go; somebody spoke to you first," D'Quandray said with a chuckle, having been interrupted.

"Excuse me?" Bradley furrowed his brow, stopped walking, and focused on the icy, blue eyes of the old man who had his face pressed between the bars of the wrought iron gate. "How do you know my name?"

The old man widened his eyes and tightened his grip on the bars as his caretaker reached for one of his arms. "That explains everything. I should've known."

"You should've known *what*?"

"Looks like you have an elderly admirer too, BG," D'Quandray said as he studied the name tag on the old man's shirt.

His caretaker pulled him away from the fence. "Come on, Mr. Tolliver. Don't bother these gentlemen. I'm sorry, guys; he thinks he knows *everyone*."

"That was a hell of a guess." Bradley was slack-jawed as he kept his unblinking eyes fixed on the old man. "I wonder who *he* is."

"Well, she said his last name, and he has Seth written on his shirt. If my deductive reasoning skills are up to par, there's a good chance his name is Seth Tolliver."

"Did you set that up, man? I mean, really? Stop pulling my leg."

D'Quandray brought his hands up to his chest with his palms facing Bradley. "It was your idea to come past here. I wanted to go a different way; remember? This is my first time ever seeing that man; I swear to God. People do that to me all the time, and you never seem to think it's strange."

"Are you kidding me, bro? You're D'Quandray 'The Stud' Tyson; everybody knows who you are."

"He didn't, but he damn sure knows you. Come on, let's hurry up and get to the diner. I'm starving."

"Sapien's where you're going," the old man yelled from several yards away as he was being ushered into the building. "Learn as much about the tech as you can. Learn it all!"

"Wow, is he still talking? Let it go, old man. I get it; you're crazy."

"Yeah, he's starting to creep me out now. Not only did he know your name, but it seems he knows you're a mechanical engineer, too. Why else would he mention tech?"

"You know, he might've seen that article they wrote on me in *Young Genius*. It had my picture in it. We have groupies sometimes, too, believe it or not."

"Yeah, but weren't you like seventeen when that issue was published?"

"Sixteen, but the fact remains, my picture was in it. He probably remembers it."

"Bro, that was like nine years ago. I barely remember it, and I'm your friend. Let's go."

As they started to walk, Bradley's gaze lingered on the door, his mind apparently still fixated on the peculiar exchange he had just had with the old man.

"Are you going to let that bother you all day?"

"That wouldn't freak you out?"

"Bro, I've been a household name since I was nineteen years old. I'm used to that type of stuff." He laughed. "Maybe I should be concerned about the fact that he *didn't* recognize me."

***

Despite having been delayed briefly at the asylum, D'Quandray and Bradley got to the diner on time. They walked inside to find Elijah already seated in a booth. He was wearing his lucky tee shirt, which had his favorite team's Irish logo on it, the same team that had drafted D'Quandray in the first-round. Hanging from a gold, rope necklace, and just below the crew neck collar of his shirt, was the crucifix pendant he always wore. His hair, as usual, was neatly trimmed, and he was clean shaven, as always. D'Quandray had often said that if anyone needed a picture-perfect example of a choir boy, Elijah would be their man.

D'Quandray was immediately bombarded with utterances of his nickname from a few excited people who were inside the diner. He smiled and waved his hand but did not look at any of them. He was adept at projecting friendliness while simultaneously giving the signal that he was not open to conversing with them. It was a skill he had developed after a few uncomfortable interactions with long-winded, overzealous sycophants.

Elijah stood to welcome them. "How's it going, guys?"

"Not too bad," D'Quandray said as he sat on the opposite side of the table.

After Elijah sat and scooted down the cushioned bench to make room for him, Bradley took a seat beside him. "Good. We're good," Bradley said. "I um...have you ordered anything yet?"

"Not yet." Elijah narrowed his eyes as he studied Bradley. Then, he turned his attention to D'Quandray. "Hey, don't forget we're getting together to play pool Friday night. Tiffany's going to be there, and you know how much you like brunettes."

D'Quandray smiled. "Yeah, I'm really looking forward to that. We might even be able to get BG some action." He and Elijah both laughed, but Bradley did not as he appeared to be preoccupied with his thoughts.

"Are you sure you're okay, BG?" Elijah asked.

"Tell him what happened, BG."

Elijah looked sideways at D'Quandray, then back to Bradley. "Yeah, tell me what happened, BG."

"You guys are comedians. It's nothing really; I just had a weird encounter with a guy we saw at *Lord Leopold's*."

"*Lord Leopold's*? Why'd you guys come that way?"

D'Quandray widened his eyes and nodded. "Thank you. That's exactly what I said."

"Shush it. It was quicker, trust me."

"Eh, that's debatable," Elijah said, "but continue."

"Well, anyway. We're walking past there to get here, and some old loon comes right up to the gate and yells my name like he's known me for years."

"Really?"

"Yes, really."

"Did he yell out D'Quandray's name, too?"

"Nope, acted like he didn't even see him. No 'The Stud' or anything. He was only interested in talking to me. Then, he yelled something about homo sapiens as the lady was pushing him into the building."

"No, BG, what he said was, 'Sapien's where you're going.' Then, he started babbling about some tech stuff."

"Wait...Sapien?" Elijah said.

"Yes," D'Quandray said.

"Well, he's exactly where he needs to be, because he's definitely crazy."

"What makes you say that?" Bradley asked.

Elijah looked back and forth from D'Quandray to Bradley, as if he was trying to decide whether he should even tell them what he knew. He sighed. "So, neither of you has heard of the fabled Sapien scrolls?"

D'Quandray shrugged his shoulders and shook his head.

"I haven't either," Bradley said.

"That's probably a good thing. At least there's some sanity left in this world. Anyway, there's a small—and I do mean small—segment of society who believes that all humans are descendants of aliens. They *think* we came here from another solar system, the Sapien solar system. They claim to have some ancient scrolls detailing our—and by *our*, I mean humanity's—pre-Earth existence. They're supposed to be locked away in some super-secret place."

"So, you don't think there's a chance of it being true?" Bradley asked.

"Heck no! If it isn't in the Bible, it didn't happen. I believe in Jesus Christ and creation. All that other stuff is just put out there to distract us from the truth. I'm a true Christ believer, man. You know that."

Bradley raised an eyebrow. "So, in your mind, we're all descendants of Adam and Eve?"

"Unless you have a better theory or explanation for us being here, yes. I'm talking actual proof, not some farfetched conspiracy theory you pulled off the dark web. Give me something as solid as Biblical text. Don't think too hard because there's no such thing."

Bradley rubbed his chin as he continued to look inward. His eyes, although wide open, were focused on nothing. "I don't know, man."

"You don't know *what*?" Elijah said.

"I don't know why some ninety-something-year-old man, whom I've never seen a day in my life, would know my name. That's what."

"Well, we can worry about that later," D'Quandray said as the waitress approached their table. "You know his name just like he knows yours."

"Yeah, I do, don't I?" Bradley's facial expression softened from the perplexed consternation it was showing to one of acceptance, otherwise inscrutable, as if he had had an epiphany. He nodded. "Indeed, I do."

D'Quandray turned his attention to the waitress, a green-eyed brunette, who had leant her hip against his side of the table and unlocked the screen of her order pad.

"What'll it be, gentlemen?" she asked as she winked at him.

D'Quandray smiled and placed his order. After that, he got her name and phone number.

Chapter 2

Sounds of Blackness

Monday morning.

D'Quandray walked into the office to find Maliq already deeply immersed in one of the multiple projects he was handling. His clean-shaven coworker was dressed in a dark suit, which was accented by a smart looking bow tie and matching pocket square. Their desks—two of three in the open office space—were near one another, and Maliq's was in the center of their workspace.

"Greetings, Black man," Maliq said as he briefly looked up.

D'Quandray grimaced and exhaled through his nostrils. To him, there was something performative about the salutation. Plus, the accompanying smirk always seemed contemptuous, like Maliq expected it to get under his skin. He stifled his emotions and relaxed his face. "Good morning, Maliq. How long did you stay at the gym Saturday?"

Maliq stopped what he was doing, leaned back in his chair, and looked directly at him. "I played two more games. One of the guys got hurt, so we shut it down." He paused to look at the row of open tabs on his computer screen, then turned his attention back to D'Quandray. "Listen, I know they like you around here, and that little nest egg you got from your settlement makes you feel like you don't need this job, but you have got to start pulling your weight."

"What are you talking about? I've made every benchmark they've set for me since I've been here."

"Barely. You've been doing just enough to get by. On top of that, they lowered the standard so you could meet it. It was much higher before you got here. Meanwhile, I've been shouldering the load for our whole department ever since. Don't let these people use you, brother."

"Use me? I'm confused."

"You really don't see it, do you?"

D'Quandray shrugged. "No, I don't. Explain yourself."

"How long have you been with this company?"

"This is my third year. I started right out of college."

"First job, right?"

"Yes. And?"

"And how did your interview process go?"

"There wasn't really an interview process," he admitted after taking a moment to think. "They requested my resume, I sent it to them, and then I came in to talk to HR." He shrugged his shoulders.

Maliq stood and faced him. "Exactly. I had to go through three rounds of interviews. I'm the only one in this department who had to do that, and I doubt Jason had to do as much as you did."

"His uncle is a VP; that's to be expected." D'Quandray paused, furrowed his brow, and shifted his eyes side to side. "Wait, are you saying they did me a favor?"

"No. I'm saying they're using you for your celebrity, Black man. Your interview was the national championship game. You think they take you on all those golf outings because you can play?" He laughed. "You're not half as good as I am. They take you with them to close deals; that's it. These people are treating you like the company mascot, Black man."

"Stop calling me that."

"Why?"

"You know why."

"No, I don't. Tell me why it bothers you so much when I call you Black man. Every time I say it, you contort your face into every expression but the right one."

"And what's the right one?"

"The one that shows appreciation for being addressed as who and what you are, Black man." He smiled, shook his head, and pointed a finger at D'Quandray's face. "See, there it is again. I've never seen your nostrils flare like that when they call you 'The Stud,' and that's one of the most disrespectful things they can say to you."

"Why are you attacking me?"

"Attacking you? *That's* how you see it?" Condescending laughter erupted from his mouth, followed quickly by an expression more serious than any look D'Quandray had ever seen on Maliq's face before. "Enlightenment always feels like an attack at first, but that's because it hits so close to home. When was the last time you got to work on time? As a matter of fact, when was the last time you stayed the whole day?"

"I don't know, Maliq. You tell me."

"I don't know either. All I know is I'm here before you arrive every day, and I'm still here long after you've left."

"I'm starting to think BG is right about you."

"You talking about your man who set that illegal pick on me Saturday? Let me guess, he told you I don't like you or something like that?"

"It must be true."

"The truth is, he feels threatened by me. He knows what I represent. He knows that if I enlighten you, you'll see him and your other *friends* for who they truly are."

"And what is that? *Enlighten* me."

"People who have no identities of their own and are seeking validation through their affiliation with you, 'The Stud.' How many Black friends do they have besides you?"

"They're not like that, man."

"Answer the question."

"I don't know; I haven't asked them."

"How many have you seen?"

"You got me there. None."

"And you don't think that's strange? When was the last time they all went out together without you?"

"How am I supposed to know that?"

"Okay, I'll give you that." Maliq put his hand on his chin and looked to the floor. Then his eyes brightened, and he smiled a toothy grin. "I'll tell you what—and here's your big chance to prove me wrong—the next time they suggest going somewhere, wait until the last minute and tell them you can't make it. Don't tell them beforehand because they'll make other plans. Tell them an hour before you're scheduled to go. I'll bet you my entire salary to a donut they won't go without you."

"You're that confident, huh?"

"Are you?"

He stared at Maliq. "This is ridiculous; I'm not playing your games."

"That's what I thought. You know I'm right."

"Whatever makes you feel good, man. I'm done with it." He turned away from Maliq and shook his head as his coworker mumbled a retort. He sat at his desk, checked his work emails, and listened to his phone messages. Then, he checked his personal emails and saw that he had received one from the *USA Men's National Team*. The subject field read *Reserves Needed*.

D'Quandray summarized the pertinent details about the invitation in an email he drafted to Greg, his company's general manager, and hit send. A few minutes later, he got a response saying that any leave he would need to play with the team was authorized as it would bring positive attention to *Turbo Boost Sports Agency*.

***

As D'Quandray walked away from the building and toward his high-end, electric sports car, Maliq's words echoed through his soul. For the first time in a long time, he waited until it was time to leave before he left work. His bosses had confided in him long ago that he was paid a higher salary than Maliq and one that was on par with Jason's, who had been with the company five years. Their rationale for it was that D'Quandray comported himself in a way that was representative of their ideals. He was never quite sure what they meant by that, but he was not going to question a mindset of which he was a well-paid beneficiary.

He got into his car. As he fastened his seatbelt and looked out over the sea of luxury cars in the parking lot, something occurred to him. Maliq was the best worker in the company, not just their department, and everyone knew it. He shook his head as he pushed the button to start the engine, thinking that his coworker would be in a much better position with the company if it were not for his militant beliefs. "Oh well," he said as he turned his music up, "better him than me." He shifted his car into drive and drove away.

Despite how much Maliq's words stung, D'Quandray felt that they always came from a good place. His position, though he never explained it to his confrontational coworker directly, was that Maliq was misguided but still a decent person. He had, however, stated that very thing to their employers multiple times. They, in turn, saw D'Quandray as a conduit between them and their abrasive taskmaster. On many occasions, he had delivered to Maliq—in his own words—messages that had come directly from the top. Most times, that included calls for Maliq to tone down his rhetoric, typically added as an aside to some inane message that masqueraded as the main topic.

He was on his way to the diner to surprise Katy, the waitress he had met after they played basketball on Saturday—the woman with whom he had spent that night and all of Sunday. It was not long before he found himself driving down Park Street and past the entrance to the *Lord Adolph Leopold Institution for the Criminally Insane*. He made the right turn on Meridian Avenue, taking note of the empty outside grounds as he passed the spot where the old man had shouted Bradley's name. An incoming call flashed on his dashboard as he pulled into the diner parking lot. He parked his car and answered it.

"What's up, BG?" He recoiled and winced because of Bradley's unusually loud and excited response. "Calm down," he said as he adjusted the volume on his speakers.

"Where are you, man?"

"I'm at the diner."

"Can you wait there for me? I'm not too far from there."

"Sure, I'll wait. See you soon." He pressed the end call button on his dashboard.

D'Quandray put his hand on the door handle to exit the car but released it when he saw Katy walking out of the diner, arm-in-arm, with a professional football player. He smiled. Then, he adjusted his seat to a reclined position and folded his arms across his chest.

He was awakened when Bradley tapped his window. "You got here fast," he said as he powered the window down.

"Yeah, let's get inside."

Before D'Quandray could answer, Bradley had already turned away from his car and was headed for the entrance to the diner. "What is up with this guy?" he said to himself as he watched his focused friend walk away with a manila folder tucked under his arm. He locked his car and walked into the diner. Bradley was already seated in a booth and had his eyes locked on him from the moment he entered. He raised his hand to acknowledge the few people who yelled "The Stud" as he walked toward the booth but kept his eyes focused on his destination.

"Man, you are going to freak when you hear this."

"Hello to you, too, BG."

"Yeah, hi. Anyway, I couldn't stop thinking about what happened at *Lord Leopold's* the other day, so I did a little research."

"You have got to be kidding me. You went back to that place?"

"Heck no. I went online and looked up Mr. Tolliver."

"What'd you find?"

"A lot! For starters, he showed up at a service station bloodied, naked, and claiming to be a time traveler about seventy-five years ago."

"Say *what*?"

"There were quite a few witnesses, one of whom was a young news reporter named Miles Jackson."

"Did he write something about it?"

"He sure did, but I noticed it was the bare minimum—like he intentionally left things out with the purpose of making you dig deeper. It was almost cryptic."

"So, I take it you dug deeper?"

"You know me well, my friend. He mentioned in his online article that he was also an adjunct at SSU. There was no reason for that information to be there other than to direct someone to go there, so I went to their library."

"And what did you find?"

"I'm telling you; this guy was smart. I found a more detailed article, and this was back in the days when they still printed newspapers. The college put out a weekly Op-Ed, and he hid this one by putting out an alternate one the same week as the real one. It never got published, but he clearly wanted this information to be documented, and he wanted it to be hidden from the government—or at least not searchable online.

It can only be found if you query his name, which is what I did, and then physically go through their archives. Searching for the incident itself gets you absolutely nowhere."

"What's in it?"

He slid the manila folder across the table to D'Quandray. "See for yourself. I scanned the article with my phone and left the original there."

He laughed. "So, you stole it."

"Semantics. Read it and tell me what you think."

He listened to the rhythmic drumbeat of Bradley's fingers as they danced on the tabletop while he silently read the article. When he finished, he looked up and into bright eyes that were filled with hopeful anticipation that D'Quandray had reached the same conclusion he had. "So, he actually interviewed Seth Tolliver about this alleged time travel adventure?"

"Yep. Did you read all of it?"

"I did."

"He took three others with him. One was murdered and two got away."

"Yeah, I saw that. Apparently, Richard W. Chester claims to have traveled to the future. Spooky stuff. I'm curious as to why he left one name out."

"My guess is that person was still alive at the time he wrote this article. He was protecting him."

"You got that from this?"

"Yes. Context clues matter. What's not said is as important as what is."

"So, I take it you want to visit the reporter's family?"

"Why would I do that? He's given us the breadcrumbs. We need to go to the Chester residence. If my gut is telling me right, his family will be expecting us."

"Us? Is there a mouse in your pocket?"

Bradley laughed. "Listen, you're D'Quandray 'The Stud' Tyson. If nothing else, they'll be nice to us. I'm betting at least one person there is a fan. That should be enough to get us in the door. I'll do the rest."

"Have you talked this over with Elijah?"

"Nope. I was just leaving the library when I called you. I wanted to see what you thought first."

"I think you're crazy."

"Come on, man. You don't think it's at least worth a try?"

"No, I don't. Some old, senile man recognizes your face from an obscure magazine article and you all of a sudden think you're the star of a *Twilight Zone* episode? Let it go."

"It wasn't obscure; it was from *Young Genius*. What do you have to lose by checking it out?"

"My reputation, that's what. I can't just go up to random people's homes and ask to be let in because one of my crazy friends had a strange encounter with some bozo."

"All you have to do is be with me. You don't have to say a word."

As he looked into Bradley's eyes, D'Quandray saw desperation. He shook his head. "The fact that something as trivial as this is so important to you troubles me. You need to get a grip."

"I'm going to call Elijah and run it by him."

"And I'm sure he'll say exactly what I just said. What do you hope to gain from this?"

"I honestly don't know, but the mere possibility that something so amazing could happen is intriguing to me."

"Possibility? So, this is not about finding out how the old man knows you? You really think you're going to click your heels together three times and end up somewhere else?" He decided to forgo further questioning on the matter when Bradley offered an embarrassed grin in lieu of a response to the question. "Unbelievable."

"Listen, man, I…"

"I'm done listening, BG. Change the subject."

"Alright, alright." Bradley leaned back in his seat, raising his hands in surrender. "My apologies. I didn't even ask what's going on with you. How are things in The Stud's world today?" He made air quotes with his fingers as he said D'Quandray's nickname.

"I'm good. I got an email from the *National Team* today. They're looking for reserves. Apparently, they're thin at the two spot."

"Are you going to do it?"

"I haven't decided. Beating up on you guys every Saturday isn't the same as playing against the best in the world."

"You're the best shooter in the world."

"Well *duh*, that's a given. I may as well be playing on my grandfather's left knee, though, for all the support—or lack thereof—that mine gives me. It doesn't matter if I'm the best shooter. I could be the greatest ever, but if I can't get my shot off, I'm no threat."

Bradley looked toward the door. "Speaking of shooting shots, Katy just walked in. Have you called her?"

D'Quandray looked over his shoulder at Katy, who was adjusting her uniform, and then out the window at the heavily tinted, luxury sport utility vehicle that was leaving the parking lot. "No. I decided against it; I don't think she's my type of girl."

"She sure seemed to be your type the other day."

"Eh," he replied with a shrug. "Things change."

"Well, you might want to put your game face on because she's coming this way."

"Hey, guys," she said as she approached their table. She put a hand on D'Quandray's shoulder. "I really want to thank you for..."

"Don't mention it. You earned that tip." He was looking directly into her eyes but offered no smile to soften the gaze. "By the way, I thought I just saw James 'Super Freak' Clayton in here. Did he leave?"

She furrowed her brow and held his gaze, but she removed her hand from his shoulder. "Yeah, he left. He's a pretty big tipper, too. In fact, he left a little more than you did." She raised an eyebrow. "What're you two having today?" She broke eye contact and looked at Bradley.

"Leftovers, apparently." D'Quandray kept his eyes on the menu when she looked his way.

Katy tucked her electronic order pad into her apron pocket. "You obviously need a little more time. I'll be back with your waters."

"What was that all about?" Bradley asked as she walked away.

"It's nothing, man. I just had unrealistic expectations for her. Not her fault. It's on me. I'll leave it at that. Besides, Tiffany is much hotter, and I can't wait to see her Friday night."

"You do have options; I'll give you that. So, when are the tryouts for the team?"

"Tryouts?" D'Quandray laughed. "The Stud doesn't *tryout*, bro. It's not like I'm vying for a starting position anyway. They need a specialist. All I have to do is show up in shape. I already know most of the sets.

Coach Stone was our offensive coordinator on the SSU national championship team. I'm sure he hasn't changed anything, especially since the plays worked so well."

"Are they going to pay you?"

"Of course. Well, it'll be a per diem, but what we'll get daily is probably more than the average person makes in a week for doing real work. They treat us like royalty. All that hard work in the gym is paying off."

"And that's exactly it, D'Quandray. If more African Americans were as hardworking as you, they'd be in a better position. I know this country has had its issues, but that was a few hundred years ago now."

"Yeah, I don't get it either. I just worry about D'Quandray Tyson; that's all I can do. I've never experienced any of the stuff they complain about most of the time. If there was less complaining and more doing, everyone would be alright."

Katy came back with their waters and set their glasses on the table. "Are we ready yet?" Her attitude had defaulted to a strictly professional one.

"Yes, I'll have a cheeseburger and some fries," D'Quandray said as he followed suit, playing the role of a typical customer. "No pickles or onions on the burger. And I'll take a diet cola to wash it down." He handed her his menu, which she took with the same smile one would offer any customer on any given day.

She received Bradley's order much in the same manner that she had taken his, professionally. She returned relatively quickly with their food, and they ate their meals. After signing a few autographs, D'Quandray left the diner and went home.

Chapter 3

A Near Miss

D'Quandray's wake-up alarm—which he had set to play a song that he loathed—blared through his surround sound speakers. It was 6 o'clock a.m. He stretched under his fluffy comforter and yawned. When he sat on the edge of his California King bed and put his feet flat on the floor, the music stopped. He got up and put on a pair of basketball shorts and running shoes. Then, he walked downstairs into his basement, which he had setup as a workout room, and got onto the elliptical machine.

"Housemate, turn on the television, mute the volume, and activate closed captioning."

"Good morning, D'Quandray. Is there anything else?" the artificial intelligence personality asked as it implemented his requests.

As his favorite entertainment news network appeared on the screen, he adjusted the speed on the elliptical machine to a faster setting. "Yes, play classic rock from the nineteen sixties." As the music played, he started his thirty-minute workout. The images depicted on the screen were of the latest tribal conflict between neighboring African countries. He shook his head as he read the statistics on Black-on-Black crime in America that scrolled across the chyron on the bottom of the screen. "They never learn." As the hosts transitioned to the topic of securing the US's southern border, D'Quandray focused on his workout. Within a few minutes, he had already worked up a sweat, and he felt like he could go forever. He was well conditioned, and his knee, though not perfect, felt better than it had in years.

D'Quandray finished his workout and walked back to his bedroom. He could smell the coffee brewing. The automatic timers in his home's smart technology helped to keep him on a tight schedule. The *Housemate* system was a luxury few could afford, so he appreciated the fact that he had it and made the most of it. The lights clicked on as he walked into the on-suite bathroom. He planted his hands on the counter of the double-sink vanity and looked at himself in the mirror. He smiled. His body was transforming back to what it looked like in his athletic prime, which was proof positive that his hard work was paying off.

It had been three years since his devastating knee injury. The surgeons had advised him to take his recovery slowly, so that's what he had done. After he had initially undergone weeks of grueling rehabilitation, he had hired a personal trainer to help with regaining his strength and muscle endurance and had done everything he had been asked to do. He was now on his own and being disciplined had brought him back to some semblance of his old self. He ran his hand under the faucet to activate the sensor, and the water started to flow. He brushed his teeth, and as he was finishing, the shower turned on.

After showering, getting dressed, and having a light breakfast, he drove out of the garage of his three-level home and toward the manned gate that opened from his neighborhood to the main road. It was now 8 o'clock. Work was a fifteen-minute drive away. Start time was also 8:00 a.m. He listened to a podcast as he drove, the topic: the effects of low-income subsidies on the nation's GDP. As he waited for the light to change, he thought it was somewhat ironic that he would see a Black woman with a child in her arms standing at the corner bus stop. He shook his head. "Choices."

D'Quandray arrived at work fifteen minutes later and drove around for an extra two minutes until he found an empty parking space. He took his time getting to the office. When he walked in, he saw the company's GM standing in front of Maliq's desk with his arms folded. Maliq was leaning back in his chair with an elbow dug into the armrest and his hand on his chin. His other arm was fully extended and controlling his mouse as he stared at the computer screen.

Greg glanced at D'Quandray. "Good morning." Then, he turned his attention back to Maliq. "I need that report by 10 o'clock, and it better not be late."

Maliq looked behind himself as if he was searching for the person to whom Greg must have been talking. Then he looked up and into his eyes. "Is your tone moderator broken?"

"Excuse me?"

"You heard what I said, Greg. Don't talk to me that way. I'll have your report ready."

Greg looked sideways at D'Quandray once more, then walked into his office and closed the door.

"What was that about?"

Maliq took his hand off the mouse and swiveled his chair around to face D'Quandray. "It was about the project you were supposed to have completed and submitted by close of business on Friday, Black man."

"I thought that was due today."

"Nope, it was due Friday."

"Why didn't you just tell him that I was the one responsible for it?"

"Because the assignment was given to our department, not to you specifically; therefore, we're all responsible. If one of us fails, we all fail. What did you think that little conversation was about on Friday?"

"I..." He put his hands on his hips and shook his head. Then, he ran a hand over his face. "I'm sorry, Maliq. I dropped the ball. What can I do to help?"

"Pull your weight, Black man. Pull your weight."

D'Quandray fought hard to control his facial expression, but unlike all the times in the past, Maliq did not focus on his face to see his reaction to being called "Black man." So, in addition to the normal emotions he felt from being called that, he felt guilty. He sat at his desk and logged into his computer.

Greg opened his door and looked out of his office. "Hey, Stud, we have a 1 o'clock golf appointment with a client. Victor wants you there."

"Count me in." He looked at Maliq after Greg closed his door. Maliq shook his head and looked back at his computer screen. D'Quandray sighed. As he glanced at his unread emails, deciding which one to open first, he was thinking Maliq could make things a lot easier for himself if only he would be less abrasive. That his counterpart was also a good golfer was not debatable; it was his attitude that kept him from being included on the outings. He thought back to the woman he had seen standing on the sidewalk on his drive to work. "Choices," he mumbled to himself.

"What's that?" Maliq said sharply.

Startled, D'Quandray turned to face him. "Oh, I was thinking about this lady I saw holding a baby on the sidewalk this morning. What set of circumstances puts a woman at a bus stop with a newborn at 8 AM?" he asked half rhetorically.

"Was she Black?"

"Yeah, but what does that have to do with anything?"

Maliq sighed and shook his head. "Of course, she was."

"What is that supposed to mean?"

Maliq stopped typing and turned to face him. "Did you think to ask her if she needed a ride?"

"*What?*" D'Quandray's impulse reaction was to recoil as if he was avoiding a punch. His lips were straight, and his eyebrows were pointed downward. "I was on my way to work."

"And you were late, as usual. What harm could a few more minutes have done?"

"You really expect me to put a complete stranger in my car and just..."

"Yes. That's exactly what I expect you to do. Never mind the fact that it was a Black woman—let's put race aside for a moment—it was a woman who clearly could've used a hand."

"She was the one who chose to have a child by a deadbeat."

Maliq's normally inscrutable face contorted into a snarl. "And you know that *how*? How do you know the circumstances surrounding her personal situation from a five second snapshot of her standing on a curb, Black man? That's awfully presumptuous of you."

"Listen, man, sometimes things just are what they are. Not everything is the result of some grand scheme to 'keep the Black man down.'" At that, he noticed another emotion on Maliq's face—sadness.

Maliq pointed to himself. "You see this look on my face? That's disappointment. You clearly have no idea what trauma the pathology of slavery has unleashed on our people."

D'Quandray leaned back in his chair and rolled his eyes. "Oh, give me a break." When he focused his eyes on Maliq again, he saw a third emotion, which he could not determine to be despondence or exasperation. Maliq was staring into nothing and shaking his head. "What?"

"Do you know what they call you in our community?"

D'Quandray shrugged. "The Stud."

"No, Black man, they call you The Coon Dray. And that's why."

D'Quandray waved his hand. "I don't believe that."

"Not surprising."

"You're telling me that something that ended," he turned to his desk and punched some numbers into his calculator, "three hundred forty-six years ago still affects you today?"

"Us. And that's exactly what I'm saying." He moved his chair closer to D'Quandray, leaned forward, put his elbows on his knees, and stared directly into his eyes. "Do you realize how valuable you could be to the Black kids in this town?" he whispered. "Do you know the *power* behind your name? Show your face from time to time. Immerse yourself into the community that carried you before it became obvious that you were going to be a big-time athlete. One thing history has taught me is that when the powers that be are done with prominent Black figures, they feed them to the wolves. Whether you know it or not, you have an expiration date, and the clock is ticking. When they let you go, where will you land?"

"On my own two feet, that's where," D'Quandray replied at his normal conversational volume.

"I get it. It's because you pulled yourself up by your own bootstraps, right?" Maliq said, matching his tone.

"Exactly. If I can make it, anyone can."

Maliq sighed, exasperation showing clearly on his face. "No. Not in the least, Black man." He paused and looked up as if he were searching through a mental rolodex. "Do you know who Tupac Shakur was?"

"No. Never heard of him."

"He was an icon. Tupac was a rapper in the late twentieth century. He made this song called *Troublesome '96*. The song is pure genius in that he managed to talk to two groups of people at the same time by using the same exact lyrics to send different messages. On the surface, it's pure gangster, and it spoke to this whole thug-life following he had created. But if you listen closer, you'll see that it's really his interpretation of *Mary Shelly's Frankenstein*. He implicitly equates the Black man in America to Frankenstein's monster, and that's what spoke to me. The point being that America created the Black man in our present form. Then, it quickly discovered that it couldn't control what it created and got scared. So, America's answer was to destroy us. Because they fear us. And they've been trying to get rid of us ever since."

"Maybe I'll listen to the song. What became of Shakur?"

"He was murdered. His last words were 'fuck you.'"

"Sounds like he kind of proved my point."

"Ironically, his untimely death proved his own point. *You* hit the genetic lottery, and the right people happened to be enamored with your athletic gifts. Because of that, you made it. Now, you're a celebrity, albeit a minor one." He smiled. "You're a novelty act. But the thing about novelty is it always wears off. You got put in a situation, and you were prepared. Kudos to you; I applaud you for that. One misstep and it'll go away. Landing on your own two feet is fine, but it does you no good if you break your legs. You're going to need someone there to catch you, and you're way too big for that to be one person."

"Too big literally or figuratively?"

"Does it matter?" Maliq slid his chair back to his desk and faced his computer. Then, he looked at D'Quandray again. "I'll tell you what, there's a charity game on the south side Friday night. It would be great if you came through. Show some love to *your* people for a change."

"I can't," he replied, ignoring the insinuation that he was not supportive of the Black community and resisting the temptation to express his thoughts on the matter. "I already have a commitment for Friday night."

"Hanging with your boys?"

"Yeah, why?"

"This is a good time to test my theory. Cancel that and come with me to the game."

"I'm not going to flake on my friends just to disprove some far-out theory you concocted in your head."

"Suit yourself." Maliq typed on his keyboard for a few seconds. "I just emailed you the address. Think about it. I'm getting back to this project that *we* didn't get done on Friday."

***

D'Quandray squatted behind the golf ball with two fingers on the ground, balancing on the balls of his feet as he looked at the lay of the land between it and the cup. Standing behind him were Greg and the CEO of their company, Victor Wainwright. On the other side of the hole were his opponents, their clients from *Exum Industries*—David Exum and his company's general manager. It was an eight-foot putt, it was for par, and it would send the match to extra holes if he made it. A miss would give their clients a one-stroke victory. He stood over the ball, widened his stance, and putted. The ball sailed two feet past the hole, missing the cup by less than half an inch.

"It's a good thing you don't shoot a basketball the way you putt," David said with a toothy grin as he walked toward him with his hand extended.

D'Quandray removed his glove and shook his hand. "I don't think there were enough people in the gallery," he said jokingly as he looked around the empty fairway. "Great game, sir."

"That's true," Greg said. "He seems to feed off the energy of the people. The arena was packed to capacity when he hit his famous shot. Speaking of clutch performances, his department tied a bow on your project this morning. They couldn't have done it without him."

"And a full three days ahead of schedule," David's general manager said. "Not bad."

"We aim to please," Victor said, seizing the opportunity to take over the conversation. "Which brings me to the reason we're here. We'd like a more permanent arrangement with your company. We've completed every project for you thus far and have beaten every deadline. I don't think a commitment is too much to ask."

"I can't argue those facts," David said as he extended his hand to Victor. "We have a deal. Send the contract to my people, and I'll have my lawyer look it over. Do you mind if we get a picture with The Stud before we head back to the clubhouse?"

"It would be my pleasure," D'Quandray said. He stood next to David, put his arm around his shoulders, and flashed a toothy smile. The *Exum Industries* general manager stood on the other side of D'Quandray, and they all posed as his caddie took a few pictures.

"Awesome," David said. "We'll see you back at the clubhouse." They got onto their golf cart, and he gave his general manager a high-five as they drove away.

"Good job, D'Quandray," Victor said as soon as they were out of earshot. "That miss was just close enough to be believable."

"I was afraid I was going to make it that time," D'Quandray said with a smile. "It's getting harder and harder to miss those. My muscle memory isn't programmed for that." He set another ball in the same spot from which he had just putted. Then, he stood over it, closed his eyes, and hit the ball. When he heard it hit the bottom of the cup, he opened his eyes and winked at Victor. "All net."

As the caddie drove them back to the clubhouse, D'Quandray checked his messages. He had texts from Bradley and Tiffany. He opened Tiffany's first. She apologized to him for not being able to make the outing they had planned for Friday night but offered to meet with him for dinner on Thursday instead, stating that she understood if he could not do it on such short notice. He gave a subdued fist pump. "Yes!" He liked the idea of being alone with her much more than in the group outing they had originally planned to attend. He responded that he could make it and was looking forward to seeing her.

They arrived at the clubhouse before he could open Bradley's text. As Victor walked inside, Greg stopped D'Quandray just before he walked through the door. They were alone. "Listen, this company's going to hit us with a lot of work and really fast. The truth is, we're probably the only option they have. They had no choice but to work with us. What I'm saying is this: This is a layup, and we can't afford to drop the ball. I'm going to give all the light stuff to you and Jason. The important ones must go to Maliq. That'll be one or two projects. All you and Jason need to do is act like what you're working on is as difficult as what we're giving to Maliq. We don't want him thinking he's being treated unfairly because we cannot afford to lose him. You think you can handle that?"

"Piece of cake. Don't worry about Maliq. As long as he's complaining, he's happy."

***

It was almost time for the basketball game to start. As D'Quandray watched the pregame show from his couch, his mind kept going back to the conversation he had had with Maliq earlier in the day. The part that was particularly interesting to him was his coworker's mention of the pathology of slavery. He felt Maliq was wrong about that, but he also realized that he was ill-prepared to refute his assertion, and that bothered him.

Start time for the game was still thirty minutes away. He got up from the couch, walked into his office, and turned on his desktop computer. Because he knew he would not have time to read them before the start of the game, he bookmarked several articles about the earliest slave plantations in America, the work the enslaved people were forced to do, and when slavery officially ended.

His cell phone rang. As he looked around his desk, he realized he had left it in the other room. After a few seconds, the call was relayed to his computer. An icon appeared on the screen, indicating a video chat request from Bradley. He clicked the receive button.

"What's up, BG?" he said as his friend's face appeared on his computer screen.

"Did you get my text earlier?"

"I did. Sorry about that. I was golfing with the bosses and forgot to respond. Is everything okay?"

"Yeah, everything is good. Listen, I know you said to drop it, but I talked to Elijah about the Seth Tolliver stuff."

D'Quandray rolled his eyes, put an elbow on his desk, and perched his chin on the palm of his hand. "I'm listening."

"Don't worry, he feels the same way you do about it, but he is willing to go to the house to see what happens. All we need is you."

D'Quandray sighed. "And just when are you guys supposed to be doing this?"

"I don't know. It's not like it's a time sensitive thing. Whenever you're ready, we'll go."

"And what if I'm never ready? What then? If it's that important to you two, you can go without me."

"Please? All you have to do is show up. You don't have to say a word. At worst, you'll have to sign a couple of autographs. Hell, you do that every day for nothing. Surely you can sign a few for your best friends. Come on, man. What's the worst that can happen?"

"You're not going to let it go, are you?"

"Honestly? No. I can't. The old man was too spot on for that to be a coincidence. I have to know how that happened. And you read the article yourself; you know there's something to it. You know it!"

"Alright, man, I'll do it. But it's not because I believe it; it's because I want you to shut up about it."

"So, when are we going?"

"Don't push it, BG. I just agreed to do it."

"I know, but the sooner we get it out the way, the faster I'll leave you alone about it. We're hanging out Friday, so it can't be then. You know Saturday is out because that's when we hoop. Elijah won't be available on Sunday because he'll be in church. I'm thinking Thursday evening is the best bet."

"Alright, we can do it then." As he watched Bradley smile, he remembered that he was supposed to go out with Tiffany on Thursday night. "Wait...no. I can't go Thursday." Bradley frowned. "Relax, I'm not canceling. That's just a bad day for me. What about Wednesday night?"

Bradley's eyes widened and he smiled. "That's even better. I'm going to go before you change your mind. I'll let Elijah know. Talk to you later."

D'Quandray smiled and shook his head as Bradley's image disappeared from the monitor. The signature theme music from the game telecast started playing on the television in his living room. He closed his computer browser, got up from his desk, and went to watch the game. It was the first televised preliminary game in which the pro league rookie-of-the-year—his ex-teammate from high school, Grayson Randolph—was going to play, and he had been looking forward to watching it. The game was pool play for the Americas. The outcome would determine the *USA National Team's* seeding in the *World Tournament*, which was scheduled to be played in an African country in the fall.

Chapter 4

A Tie, A Guy, A Crucifix

Wednesday

D'Quandray drove straight from work to Elijah's house. When he got there, they were waiting for him in Elijah's sport utility vehicle. Bradley was in the back seat.

"How's it going, guys?" D'Quandray asked as he got into the front passenger seat.

Bradley, who was wearing a crisp, white, button-down shirt and a red necktie, leaned forward, and put his face between the front seats. "Great, now that you're here."

Elijah looked at Bradley through his rearview mirror. "Sit back and put your seatbelt on, BG."

"Come on! You guys aren't excited? This is going to be amazing; I can feel it."

"I'm not driving until you sit back."

"Fine, I'll sit back." He moved to the seat position behind the driver's seat. "But I know you guys are excited, too. You just don't want to admit it."

"Seat belt on, too, BG."

Bradley fastened his seat belt. "Done. Can we go now?"

As Elijah backed out of the driveway, his car's GPS announced that they would reach their destination in twenty-five minutes. D'Quandray partially reclined his seat, folded his arms over his chest, and closed his eyes.

"Rough day at work, D'Quandray?" Elijah asked.

He looked at Elijah's undone top button, his dark blue tie (which was rolled up in a cupholder in the center console), and at the sweat stains in the armpits of his powder-blue shirt. "Looks like you've had a trying day yourself. Mine was long, not rough. I've been going at it with Maliq a lot lately. Nothing too bad, though."

"He thinks we're bad influences on D'Quandray," Bradley said.

"So says the guy who has me driving to a stranger's house because some old guy knew his name, and he now thinks we can time travel."

D'Quandray opened his eyes, looked at Bradley, and raised an eyebrow.

Bradley rolled his eyes and looked out the window. "Touché."

D'Quandray turned his attention back to Elijah. "How are things going at the youth outreach?"

"Fantastic. We visited an at-risk youth today. His teacher reached out to us because she was concerned about him. He lives with his grandmother over on the south side. She's on a fixed income, his father is incarcerated, and his mother is strung out on drugs. Really good kid, though. We took groceries to his family, and I was able to deliver the word while I was there. God was really in that place. He's going to start coming to Sunday school at our church. When I tell you that I am full, please believe it."

"That's awesome. You guys are doing good work. I'd be careful on the south side, though. You're a little pale to be over in the hood."

"Well, you may as well be pale, too," Bradley said. "When was the last time you were on the south side?"

"The last time I needed to be," D'Quandray said. "That was the regionals in high school. I scored fifty points that night. We had to get a police escort out of there. As far as going back, I didn't work this hard to get away from all that only to go back and risk my life just to prove something to somebody else."

"I travel with The Lord, D'Quandray," Elijah said, answering his question. "To be afraid is to not have faith, and I refuse to believe that God isn't looking out for one of his soldiers."

D'Quandray leaned forward and looked at Elijah's neck.

Elijah reached into his shirt and grabbed his crucifix pendant. "You looking for this? I never go anywhere without it." He smiled and gave it a loving pat but let it hang on the outside of his collar. "It's my physical reminder that the Lord is always with me."

For the rest of the trip to the Chester residence, they continued to talk about work. Bradley wowed them by telling them that, at the urging of one of his work mentors, he had incorporated. He had made a few gadgets at work that showed promise, and the idea was that he should be ready to make profits should he happen to invent something significant. D'Quandray thought that he had to be either very close to doing that or showing great promise and ingenuity for someone to suggest that.

They arrived at their destination—a ranch-style home with a two-car garage and a large front yard—a short time later. Elijah stopped at the beginning of the driveway and looked at D'Quandray.

"We're here now," D'Quandray said. "It's creepier to just sit here than it would be to drive up there. You might as well go."

Elijah nodded and drove forward. He stopped his front bumper just short of the sidewalk that led from the driveway to the front door. They all got out and walked to the door together. As Bradley—who was now in front—reached out to ring the doorbell, someone opened the door from inside the house.

"Can I help you?" the petite, thirty-something-year-old, blonde woman said.

Her cutoff shirt stopped well above her belly button, and the way her breasts moved underneath it left no doubt that she was not wearing a bra. The waist of her jean shorts was just low enough to reveal the fine hair that tickled the button on them and just high enough to cover the rest. The one plait she had hanging down the left side of her face made D'Quandray wonder if they had caught her in the middle of changing her hairstyle.

Bradley cleared his throat. "Yes, hello; my name is Bradley Gates. This is Elijah Soloman, and he's D—"

"I know who he is. Why are you here?"

"There was an article written by a man named Miles Jackson, and, in it, he named Richard W. Chester as someone who played a prominent role in an *incident*."

"Did this *incident* happen around seventy-five years ago?"

"Yes." Bradley grinned sheepishly.

"You're not the only ones to have come here about that article, but you're the right ones."

"And how do you know that?" Bradley asked.

"Because the right ones would have a sports star with them. Come in."

A chill went down D'Quandray's spine. She walked away from the door on her tiptoes, her bare feet making no sound as she glided across the hardwood floor. Bradley widened his eyes and looked directly at D'Quandray. His friend was giddy, and despite all the skepticism he had previously expressed, D'Quandray knew at that moment that something significant was about to happen. He lingered by the door as Bradley and Elijah walked in, wondering if he should wait in the car, especially since he had already served his purpose for being there. He decided that standing there in the doorway was no different than Elijah stopping the car at the end of the driveway, so, like he had advised his friend to do earlier, he moved forward, and he closed the door behind them.

"My name is Marissa Chester," she said as she split her attention between them and the notepad on which she was scribbling while standing in the center of the living room. "Richard W. Chester was my paternal grandfather. He left some information with my father, who is also deceased."

"You have our deepest condolences," Elijah said. "If this is too much for you, we can leave. We really don't want to cause you any more pain."

She smiled. "Thank you; you're good. In fact, it would be worse if I let you leave here without showing you this footage. He left it *for* you."

"Footage?" Bradley said, excitement in his voice.

"It's just a video of him talking. We've had to transfer it to different media a few times. Technology changes a lot over seventy-five years. Luckily for you, my dad had enough foresight to account for it." She put the notepad face down on the end table by the door, then turned and walked toward her home office. "What you're looking for is in here." She turned to face them when she got to her computer. "Let me warn you that what you're about to see is incredible, and I don't think you can be the same after viewing it. We can stop now if you like."

"No way," Bradley said. "Fire it up. I can't wait to see it."

"Okay." She flashed a closed-mouthed smile before turning around and booting up her computer. Then she uploaded the file and stepped to the side so they could view it.

"My name is Richard Wilbur Chester," the man said as his image appeared on the monitor. He paused as if he needed to compose himself.

D'Quandray looked over his shoulder as he heard the front door of the house open and close. Then, he looked at Marissa, who was standing there with her hand over her mouth and narrowed his eyes. Her gasp had drawn his attention. "Are you okay?" he asked as he watched her hand as it shook and her eyes gloss over with moisture. She said nothing but nodded, indicating that she was fine. He turned his attention back to the monitor.

Almost as if he had been waiting to regain the attention of everyone in the room, Richard cleared his throat and continued to speak. "If you do a little research, you'll find that my granddaughter, Marissa, was born two years after I passed away. Approximately seventy-five years ago, in the year twenty-one thirty-six, a group of friends and I traveled through time. We chose various destinations to visit. I chose the future, and I chose this town. In fact, in the chronology of events, today would mark the second day of my voyage. Your present and future are already my past.

"This time travel phenomenon is one that can only occur every seventy-five years. The opportunity is brought about by the arrival of Halley's comet. I was the one who alerted the others to this, and I got the information similarly to the way you're getting it now. I trust that one of you will do the same for someone else in the future. In fact, I'm certain of it." He smiled.

"I don't know where any of you will go; that business is your own. My job is to prepare you all for your journeys. That having been said, there are a few things that you should know. First, you have to go to specific coordinates within a certain window of time in order to make this voyage. My granddaughter will provide those coordinates to you. Secondly, your journey will require meditation. You must focus completely on the exact time and place to which you will travel for one minute. Lastly, this activity is monitored, and there are forces out there who wish to prevent you from doing this. They're called interdimensional sentries, or the IDS. You do not want to be captured by them. When you time travel, they are alerted to your presence. It takes them three minutes to get to your location. Don't worry, you can do it in that time, but you'll have to hurry.

"Seth Tolliver, whom you've met, and Daniel Aikens stayed behind too long. Unfortunately, Daniel was killed by the sentries. Seth was captured by the local police while we fled in another direction. What they didn't know at the time, is that he tossed Daniel's wallet down a sewer near the gas station at which he was apprehended. It should still be there.

"I suspect that you are skeptical right now and are wondering how this can be proven. I would be, too." He folded his arms and stoned his face. "There are three of you, two white men and one Black man. One of you is wearing a red tie, one of you is wearing a gold crucifix around his neck, and the other—the sports star—is six feet, six inches tall. That information I got from the note my granddaughter left at the front door. Safe travels, my friends."

"I'll stay here while you go look for the note," Marissa said when they all turned toward her after the video ended.

Bradley left the room and quickly returned. "It's gone. I-I can't believe it. That's amazing."

"I told you that you wouldn't be the same after viewing it." She wiped away a tear.

"Why are you sad?" D'Quandray asked.

"Because standing here and watching this monitor with you while knowing my grandfather—whom I've never seen alive—was just inside this house with me, was the hardest thing I've ever had to do."

***

D'Quandray stared at the computer monitor in his home office. He had been there for thirty minutes. All the articles he had bookmarked the day before were open and ready to be viewed, but he had not read one word of any of it. Marissa's warning that they would not be the same after viewing the footage had already proven to be more than prophetic. He had entertained the idea that the man on the video had seen them arrive at the home and recorded and sent the video while they were in the living room of the residence, but then he had to admit to himself that that would involve foreknowledge that they would be coming. Then there was the fact that the video had already started when he heard the front door of the residence open and close. The thought of that sent chills through his body. But the thing that bothered him most and had him sitting motionless in front of his computer was the raw emotion that came from Marissa. That was real, and that was what he found to be the scariest of it all.

He glanced at the clock on the corner of the screen. It was 9 o'clock p.m. If he was going to look at the files, he needed to get started. His thoughts had transitioned from merely learning the information with the purpose of being able to participate in an intelligent debate with Maliq to total immersion in the very thing that his counterpart had said was the bane of his people's existence. So, with that in mind, he focused all his efforts on learning everything he could about one Southern town during a particular pre-emancipation period.

D'Quandray also decided that part of his research would include observance of the supposed ramifications of slavery. That meant he had to get closer to the Black community. That also meant that he would go to Maliq's charity basketball game on Friday night. He had nothing to lose by going. Besides, he was going to see Tiffany on Thursday night anyway. To appease Maliq and to test his theory about Bradley and Elijah's motives, D'Quandray decided to follow his suggestion and not tell his friends until the last minute. He also decided that he would not tell Maliq he was going to attend. If he was going to go, he wanted it to be the same as it would have been had he not shown his face. In fact, he planned to arrive late so that Maliq would not know he was there until it was over.

D'Quandray took notes as he read through the various articles he had pulled up. He also created a file on his computer to consolidate all the pertinent information he could gather. He wanted to be prepared. As he jotted down notes, copied and pasted material, and saved files, he thought back to the ride to Elijah's house from the Chester residence. In all the years he had known Bradley, he had never seen him so quiet. He also found it interesting that Elijah had kept his right hand on his crucifix the entire time while he drove, and he had appeared to do so unknowingly, the same way anyone else would blink or perspire.

When he looked at the time again, it was 11 o'clock. He signed out of his computer, grabbed his cell phone, and walked to his bedroom. It occurred to him that he had not heard from Bradley or Elijah since they had parted ways. He looked at his phone to make sure it was functioning properly, checking to see if he had somehow mistakenly placed it in do not disturb mode or something like that. There was nothing wrong with his device. They simply had not tried to reach him, nor he them, and probably for the same reason.

By the time D'Quandray finished brushing his teeth and showering, it was 11:30. He put on his pajamas, got into bed, and stared at the ceiling for the next two and a half hours. He went to sleep knowing that the rest of his life—no matter how long or short it was going to be—would be vastly different from the life he had lived up to that point, and he did not know how he felt about that.

Chapter 5

The Charity Game

As he sat in the parking lot of the *Barack Hussein Obama Gymnasium* and watched the people as they poured inside, D'Quandray held his phone in his hand. It was 7 o'clock p.m., one hour before he was supposed to join Bradley and Elijah for a night out, and one hour before the charity basketball game was scheduled to start. He had positioned his car at the far edge of the parking lot; everything was in front of him. He was tired. The night with Tiffany had gone better than he had expected. She had left his house at 5 o'clock a.m., after a fun filled night in which neither of them got much sleep.

D'Quandray had spent Thursday at home. He could not make himself go to work after what he, Bradley, and Elijah had experienced on Wednesday night. He had, instead, spent the entire day reading the articles and notes that he had saved and had written the night before. Only the call from Tiffany took him away from that.

He scrolled through the contact list on his phone and stopped at Bradley Gates. Then he pressed the video call button. Bradley answered immediately.

"What's up, man? Are you on your way?"

D'Quandray shook his head as he looked at the screen. "I'm not going. Something came up, and I need to take care of it."

"Aw, come on! Everyone is going to be disappointed. They were looking forward to seeing you."

D'Quandray held back a frown. He thought that the appropriate response from Bradley should have been some form of concern for his well-being, especially since it was uncharacteristic of him to cancel so late, and he was vague about his reason for opting out of the outing. "Apologize to them for me. I'm sure I'll get around to seeing them all sooner or later. I'll see you at the gym tomorrow morning. Have fun." He pressed the button to end the call.

He set his phone alarm to go off in an hour and fifteen minutes, locked his car doors, and reclined his seat. When he closed his eyes, his mind went to slave plantations. He had consumed so much information in a short period of time that his thoughts were inundated with antebellum imagery.

D'Quandray opened his eyes and reached for his phone when the song he hated started playing. It was a quarter after 8 o'clock. There were more cars in the parking lot but less people outside. He popped a breath mint into his mouth and got out of the car. As he got close to the entrance, he noticed sharp looks and narrowing eyes from the people, and he saw some of them alerting others to his presence. There was no utterance of "The Stud" from anyone, he noticed. He nodded hello whenever he made eye contact with someone, and they politely nodded back.

He stopped at a donation table in the lobby. "Hi. I'd like to contribute to the cause."

"Oh my," the lady said as she looked up, "it's D'Quandray Tyson! Thank you for coming. She slid a piece of paper across the table. "Just scan the QR code on there with your phone and contribute what you like. Can I get a picture with you when you're done? My nephew is your biggest fan."

D'Quandray smiled. "It would be my pleasure, ma'am." He scanned the code and made a sizable donation to their cause. "Do you want me to come back there, or are you coming over here?"

"I'll come over there." She smiled, walked around to D'Quandray's side of the table, and handed her phone to the man beside whom she had been sitting. "Can you take this picture for me?" she asked as she slid her arm around D'Quandray's waist. The man agreed to take the picture as he accepted her phone.

After they posed for a few pictures, D'Quandray asked the man to switch the camera to video mode. Then he asked the lady what her nephew's name was. She told him. "Is it ready?" he asked the man as he looked into the camera.

"Yeah, go ahead," the man said.

D'Quandray flashed a broad smile. "Hey, Andre, your aunt tells me you're a big fan. Guess what, man? I'm a fan of yours, too. I wish you were here. I'm sending an autograph with your aunt to give to you. Be good, young man. Peace."

"Got it," the man said.

"That was so sweet of you," the woman said. "He is going to be so happy when he sees this. Thank you."

"You're welcome, ma'am. Have a good night."

He left the table and walked into the packed gymnasium. The bleachers were filled to capacity, and the area of the floor around the playing surface was standing room only. When he got close enough to the court to see the players, he saw that Maliq was one of them. They were involved in an intense game, and he could tell by the aggressiveness of the players that the referees were not officiating the game as strictly as he was accustomed to them being called when he played.

He took a moment to scan the crowd on the floor and noticed that many of the people were staring back at him. Then, he looked into the bleachers and locked eyes with the old man he had seen at all of his games, the one who, Bradley had said jokingly, was his number one fan. Imani was beside him, which he thought was odd. Seeing familiar faces brought a sense of calm to him. He was about to wave at them when he heard "The Coon Dray" uttered by someone close to him. It was not loud, but he could tell that the person who said it meant for him to hear it. He took his eyes off the old man and Imani and studied the faces of the people standing around him. None of them would make eye contact with him. When he turned his eyes back to the stands, the old man and Imani were gone.

Maliq's team won what turned out to be a nail-biter, 86 to 85. Afterward, the master of the ceremony gathered both teams at center court for the trophy presentation. The entire crowd was standing, and D'Quandray was happy to be taller than everyone who was in front of him.

"Before we wrap things up," the MC began, "I want to thank our sponsors." He smiled and nodded as the crowd applauded. "I also want to thank you. This could not have been possible without you. Our early numbers indicate that we have exceeded our goal by a few thousand dollars." Again, the crowd applauded. This time, it was louder and more sustained. "We also want to acknowledge that D'Quandray Tyson is in the building. Thank you for coming."

D'Quandray raised his hand, and all those who had not been alerted to his presence prior to then, looked his way. He received moderate applause.

"Thanks again, D'Quandray. It's important that our stars come back. We appreciate you, Black man. That having been said, this year's most valuable player is Maliq Godson." As he handed Maliq his MVP trophy, the crowd erupted with thunderous applause.

Maliq gave a gracious acceptance speech and thanked the crowd for coming and for supporting their cause.

It took over an hour for the crowd to thin out. D'Quandray signed more than a few autographs and posed for even more pictures. Still, there was no sign of the old man. He also noticed that he had not been referred to as "The Stud" once since he had been there, even though he included it with every autograph he signed. Finally, Maliq approached him with one of his teammates by his side, a man who happened to be one of the fewer than ten white people who had been in the building while the game was being played.

"I have to say I'm surprised you made it," Maliq said with a smile. "Thanks for coming out. This is going to be all over social media."

"Don't mention it. It was better than I thought it was going to be. I had fun. This place was electric."

"This game is like that every year. It's always intense, and it's always fun. By the way, this is Chad, my best friend."

D'Quandray raised his eyebrows but extended his hand. "Nice to meet you, Chad. I've heard *nothing* about you."

They all laughed.

"Nice to meet you, too, D'Quandray." Chad shook Maliq's hand and gave him a pat on his shoulder. "I'm going to leave you guys to it. I need to get going."

"Alright, brother, take it easy," Maliq said.

D'Quandray nodded to Chad in a mirrored response and turned to Maliq as he walked away. "Color me surprised."

Maliq furrowed his brow. "Surprised by what?"

"Surprised that your best friend is a white guy after all you've put me through about my friends."

Maliq turned the corners of his mouth downward and shook his head. "I've never in my life been anti-white. I'm pro-Black; there's a huge difference."

"I suppose you're right. My apologies."

"No worries. Let me introduce you to some people."

For the next hour, Maliq introduced D'Quandray to several important people, including the event organizer, the MC, a state congress person, some local athletes, and several community activists. When D'Quandray finally walked outside, he saw several citizens talking to police officers. Their cars had been broken into while they were inside watching the game. He stopped and looked across the parking lot at his car, even though he knew he could not see whether his windows had been broken from where he was.

"The Stud!" an officer whose name tag read P. Roberts said as D'Quandray walked past him. The officer winked and pointed at him, then turned his attention back to the citizen whose report he was taking, much to her chagrin.

D'Quandray walked around his car when he got to it, carefully inspecting the tires, windows, doors, and trunk. It had not been tampered with. He thought about calling Bradley when he got inside but did not want to have to explain to several people—that he knew would be around him—why he was not there, so he drove home instead. He was eager to get back to his computer to learn more about slavery. His perspective on things had not changed, but he thought that what he had experienced at the charity game was much different than what he had expected.

***

D'Quandray arrived at the gym Saturday morning to find a higher level of competition than usual. A few players from the *African Coalition Team* were in town and were looking for a good workout. So, rather than playing against each other, like they normally did, D'Quandray and Maliq decided to team up to take them on. Also on their team were Bradley and two other guys who, although they had never played basketball on the collegiate level, were good players. The crowd size was consistent with what he had seen since he started playing there.

They were moments away from starting the game. A few of the African players were still on the sideline removing their sweatsuits, tying their shoes, and hydrating. D'Quandray's team was already standing at mid-court. They decided to play two twenty-minute halves instead of going to a preset number. The gym's scoreboard had been turned on and was being operated by Mr. Lucas, the gym manager.

"How'd it go last night, BG?" D'Quandray asked. When he saw Maliq look at Bradley to wait for his answer, he was reminded of their wager about the motives of his friends.

"We decided not to go. It didn't seem right without you."

D'Quandray tried to ignore Maliq staring at him as he replied. "You were so excited about it, though. What happened?"

Bradley shrugged his shoulders. "After what happened Wednesday, I needed to be alone with my thoughts. You canceling on us turned out to be a good thing. It gave me time to think."

"I get that," D'Quandray said. As their opponents walked onto the court and started shaking hands with him and his teammates, he took a moment to look in the stands for the old man. He furrowed his brow as he looked at the spot where he usually sat and saw that it was occupied by someone else.

"Centers up," the official said as he held the basketball in the palm of his hand at center court.

D'Quandray and his teammates took their places around the jump circle as the referee prepared to start the game. Again, he found himself scanning the crowd for the old man. Again, he did not see him. The referee's whistle brought his attention back to the game, and his team got the first possession off the jump ball.

Despite a standout forty-point performance from one of the African players, the skillful combination of D'Quandray and Maliq was just too much for them to overcome. The game was competitive, and the African players comported themselves as true sportsmen throughout, but they lost by eight points. They thanked the American team for the workout and went on their way. Maliq also left immediately after the game concluded.

Like every other Saturday, the gym emptied of spectators as soon as D'Quandray was done playing. He sat on the bottom row of the bleachers with a towel over his head as he drank an electrolyte-rich beverage. Bradley sat beside him.

"I haven't seen your guy this morning, D'Quandray," Bradley said.

"Neither have I." He sat up and removed the towel from his head to take another look around the gym. "I didn't see him anywhere, but I definitely looked for him. Just when I was planning on talking to him, too. I hope nothing happened to him."

"He's probably okay." He smiled and playfully punched D'Quandray's shoulder. "He probably got tired of you ignoring him."

D'Quandray raised his eyebrows and shook his head as he thought back on his missed opportunity to speak to the old man the night before. "You kid, but there may be some truth to that."

"Oh, come on, man. I'm sure he's okay. He's probably doing some family stuff or something like that. I'm sure he has a ton of grandkids. They're probably keeping him busy."

"Eh, maybe you're right. I'm sure it's nothing. I'm probably a little shook-up still from watching what Marissa went through the other night."

"That was crazy, right?"

"It really was, or is, or whatever. This whole thing is nuts. Have you spoken to Elijah?"

"I talked to him for a few minutes after I talked to you last night. To be honest, I think he was kind of glad you canceled. He didn't seem like himself."

"Him too, huh?"

"And speaking of feeling uneasy, what do you think of Mr. Chester's mention of the IDS?"

"I think it's pretty scary. At the same time, it's intriguing."

Bradley smiled. "That's what I wanted to hear you say. I'm going to call Marissa and find out what she knows about them. Maybe her granddad gave her more than what we got on our video."

"Possibly. It seems weird to look at him as someone's grandfather. In that video he looked at least five years younger than us."

"I agree." Bradley stood up from the bleachers. "I'm going to get the locker key; I'll be right back."

D'Quandray leaned forward and rested his elbows on his knees. His muscles ached a little more than they usually did after his Saturday morning games. He also felt depleted. Regulation games were a lot different, he was reminded, than playing without a referee. He finished his power drink and took another look around the gym. He could not believe the old man was absent.

"No Imani today," Bradley said as he returned from the service desk with the key.

"Really?" D'Quandray stood, looked toward the desk, and squinted his eyes.

"Yeah. Mr. Lucas said she's on vacation. I think she figured she'd take a break before she had to hurt you. You're running everybody away." He laughed.

But D'Quandray did not think it was a laughing matter, and he could not reconcile the emotions he was suddenly experiencing with reality. He felt a void. There was something strange about him seeing the old man and Imani at the game together on Friday night, then not seeing either of them at the gym Saturday morning. Not lost on him was the fact that their absence coincided with his desire to speak to the old man.

As he and Bradley walked toward the lockers, D'Quandray was approached by a woman and a small boy. She wanted an autograph and a picture for her son. Bradley used her phone to take the pictures as D'Quandray posed with both, then the child alone, then her alone. It ended with her giving D'Quandray her phone number.

"You're like a brunette magnet," Bradley said as they watched the mother and child walk out of the gym.

D'Quandray smiled. "It's a good thing, too, because they're my favorite."

D'Quandray and Bradley parted ways when they got outside, each having driven his own car to the gym. He entertained the idea of stopping by the diner for lunch, but he decided the food was not good enough to offset the likelihood of tension between him and Katy if she was working, so he drove home instead.

Chapter 6

Positive Identification

D'Quandray quickly finished his meal, which consisted of a peanut butter and jelly sandwich, two boiled eggs, and a diet cola, the same thing he always ate when he made his own lunch. He missed the days when he could go to his parents' house and enjoy his mom's cooking. One of the bittersweet consequences of him becoming an overnight sensation was the unwanted attention it had brought to them. The fame was too much for his parents, and they retired to Florida shortly after his meteoric rise to stardom.

D'Quandray had already called Delores, the woman whose son he had posed for pictures with after the game, and he agreed to meet her for dinner later. She promised to cook for him and said they would watch movies after her son went to sleep, a routine with which he was all too familiar. He had yet to see the end of a movie in that scenario.

His phone rang; it was Albert, the front gate attendant, calling from the guard shack. When he answered it, he was told he had two visitors. The driver was Bradley Gates. He granted permission for them to enter the property, then he unlocked his front door and waited for his friends to get there.

"Bradley Gates and Marissa Chester have entered your home," the *Housemate* announced a few minutes later.

D'Quandray sprang from his couch. "I thought you had Elijah with you!"

"Hello to you, too, D'Quandray," Bradley said.

"Apologies. I didn't mean to be rude. Hi, Marissa. Nice to see you again."

She smiled. "Good to see you, too. Beautiful place you have here. Nice to see how the other side lives for a change."

"This is nothing," he replied with a smile. "Come in; have a seat. Can I get you something to drink?"

"No, I'm fine for now. Thanks."

"I called Marissa when we left the gym, and she agreed to meet with us to discuss things further. Elijah is on his way and should be here shortly. I hope we're not intruding."

"You're not. I wasn't doing anything anyway." His phone rang again, and again it was Albert. D'Quandray answered and told him to allow Elijah to enter.

"Have you started working on a game plan for your time travel event?" Marissa asked.

D'Quandray furrowed his brow. "Game plan? Who said I decided to go?"

"The universe did," she replied. "And it has told you so. Whether you know it or not, things have already been happening to prepare you for it."

"Things like what?"

"I don't know, and even if I did, I wouldn't tell you. Sorry, but that's how it is."

"She's right, D'Quandray. Besides, if we go through with it and nothing happens, what have we sacrificed?"

"Your 'what have you got to lose' tactic is starting to get old, BG." He excused himself when he heard Elijah's car pull into his driveway. He walked to the front door, opened it, and waited for him to walk in. When he saw the expression on Elijah's face, D'Quandray knew that he was not the only one who was perturbed by Bradley's infatuation with the idea of them traveling through time.

"*Elijah Solomon has entered...*"

"Shut up, *Housemate*," D'Quandray said.

"Hello, Marissa. Make this fast, BG; I've got a Sunday school lesson to prepare for tomorrow. Why are we here?"

"You know why you're here," Bradley said. "You both do, and the quicker you embrace the idea, the quicker we can get prepared for it. You saw the video like I did. Whether you want to or not, we're all going. That's a fact."

Elijah shook his head and sat on the living room couch. "If everything is already decided, why do we need to prepare?"

D'Quandray looked at Marissa and Bradley. "That's a really good question; why do we need to prepare?"

"You don't need to prepare for the event," Marissa said. "It's what's going to happen in the aftermath of the event that you need to be concerned about. The IDS are real, and they will be coming. Did you forget that part? You need a plan."

"That's exactly right," Bradley said.

D'Quandray waved a hand at him dismissively. "We're not listening to you, BG." He looked at Marissa and folded his arms across his chest. "Tell us what you know."

She shook her head. "I thought, after all you've seen, you'd be believers." She started pacing the living room floor. "I'll tell you this. In addition to leaving videos for my father and for me, my grandfather met with Miles Jackson after Jackson visited Seth Tolliver at *Lord Leopold's*. He had to work hard to convince Mr. Jackson that he had time traveled as well, but he finally did. After that, he was told some interesting things.

"Mr. Jackson said when the commotion died down at the service station seventy-five years ago, he walked into the woods and met with the IDS. He said they were there waiting, as if they knew he was coming. That's how we know who they are and what they do. They monitor those portals, and they're the only ones authorized to use them. Their job is to apprehend whoever time travels and to make sure they haven't altered fate. I know it sounds crazy, but it's true. Anyway, they wouldn't divulge their methods, which, to me, is the scary part. I don't know about you, but of all the people I've heard about being abducted by aliens, none of them volunteered to be probed."

"Your grandfather mentioned Daniel Aikens' wallet," Elijah said. "If this is true, his wallet should still be there, right?"

"Theoretically."

"That's a yes or no question," Elijah said.

"Then the answer is yes."

"If that's going to satisfy your uneasiness, we should go and get it," Bradley said.

"If you find the wallet, will you let me be part of everything?" Marissa asked. "I don't want to time travel, but you'll need someone to do the countdown while you focus on where you're going and to keep track of the time when you come back."

"Sure, why not?" D'Quandray said after Elijah, whose gaze seemed to seek permission to proceed, looked directly at him.

"Yes!" Bradley said.

D'Quandray waved his finger in Bradley's direction. "If we don't find that wallet, it's over."

"Come on; you can't be serious."

"But I am." He looked at Marissa. "If this is the universe at work, the wallet should one hundred percent be there—no doubt about it. And, BG, you're the one who's going into the sewer."

"And one more thing," Marissa said. "Halley's comet is in earth's orbit, but its cosmic effect will be at its most potent next week. I suggest you all get busy studying where exactly it is you want to go. Now, who's driving? We need to go get this wallet."

"I will," Elijah said. "My SUV is the only vehicle we have that's roomy enough for all of us."

***

"This is it," Marissa said from the rear passenger seat behind D'Quandray as Elijah pulled up to *Lucky's Service Station*, a charging station that had been a hybrid station seventy-five years prior. She pointed to a concrete retaining wall in the distance. "That's where the event occurred."

"Beyond that wall?" Bradley asked.

"Yes, in the woods."

Bradley shook his head. "That's a long way for him to run with fresh bullet wounds."

"They shot him, but it wasn't with bullets," Marissa said. "According to Mr. Jackson, the projectiles dissolved after a period of time, and they weren't able to recover them."

"Can we get this over with?" D'Quandray asked.

"Yeah, same," Elijah said. "I don't like the idea of just sitting here." He pulled his vehicle into the service station and parked.

"You guys have got to learn to appreciate life," Bradley said. "You're always so focused on the destination that you never appreciate the scenery while you're going."

"Well, make sure you take in all the scenery you can while you're in the sewer," D'Quandray said. "Get to it. I'll be right here."

"You're not getting out?" Bradley asked.

"No, BG, I'm not. You see those people over there?" He pointed to the few people who were charging their electric vehicles. "They'd recognize me in a second. You guys can handle it."

"He has a point," Elijah said. "Let's get it over with. Come on."

Marissa, Elijah, and Bradley got out and walked to the manhole cover that led to the sewer below. Bradley and Elijah lifted it as Marissa stood by. They all stood near the edge and looked down into the hole. Then, after they said a few words to one another, Bradley climbed down into it.

About three minutes passed before D'Quandray saw Bradley reach out of the hole and place something small and black on the ground between Elijah and Marissa. Then, he climbed out, dirty and wet. He had a huge smile on his face despite it. All D'Quandray could think about was how bad he would smell on the trip back and how happy he was that they had used Elijah's vehicle instead of his.

They replaced the manhole cover and walked back to Elijah's SUV together. Bradley clenched the item tightly in both hands. His eyes were bright, and he had a smile that stretched across his face.

As soon as they were all back inside the vehicle, D'Quandray looked back at Bradley. "Is that a wallet?"

"It sure is," Bradley said.

When everyone fastened their seatbelts, Elijah drove his vehicle away. After about a minute of driving, he powered the windows down.

"I'm hosing you down in the driveway, BG. There's no way you're coming into my house smelling like that. The *Housemate* will think I let a skunk in."

As they all laughed beneath the shirts they used to cover their noses, Bradley opened the wallet and started going through its contents. "Wow, this is like holding history in my hands. There's paper money in here."

"Really?" Elijah said. "I thought we had stopped using that by then."

"No, that happened in twenty-one forty," Marissa said. "Is his ID there?"

"It sure is," Bradley said.

Elijah immediately pulled his vehicle over to the side of the road and parked. Everyone turned to face Bradley. After taking a moment to look at it for himself, he handed the identification card to D'Quandray.

"There's your proof right there, Stud. Looks like we're going time traveling."

D'Quandray held the identification card mere inches away from his face. Though it was worn from years of being inside the sewer, the characters and image on it were still legible and visible. "Daniel Aikens, 3041 Womack Lane. Date of birth: November eleventh, twenty-one sixteen. Shit."

"Yes!" Bradley said as he and Marissa both raised their fists triumphantly.

D'Quandray handed the identification card to Elijah, who looked at it like it was an important note he was trying to memorize five minutes before an exam.

"What do you think?" Marissa asked as she received the identification card from Elijah.

Elijah shifted his vehicle into drive and pulled away. "I think we need to get to D'Quandray's house before Bradley ruins the fabric on my seats."

D'Quandray glanced to the left without moving his head. He had seen Elijah reach up out of the corner of his eye, and he wanted to confirm that he was caressing his crucifix pendant. He was. D'Quandray put his head on the headrest and closed his eyes. Everyone was quiet for the remainder of the ride to his house.

When they arrived, he gave Bradley a trash bag for his clothes. Bradley stripped down in the garage, put the clothes into the bag, and then used one of D'Quandray's guest bathrooms to shower. When he was done, he walked into the living room wearing an SSU tee-shirt, matching sweatpants, and a brand-new pair of slides from the sports apparel company that sponsored D'Quandray.

"The important thing to remember," Marissa said as if she was continuing a conversation, even though she only started speaking once Bradley walked back into the room, "is that you must get away quickly. The land belongs to the federal government. They have tripwires all over the grounds. It takes the IDS three minutes to reach the destination from the moment a portal is opened. That means after the countdown you'll have a head start."

"How long does it take to come back from the portal once you've gone inside?" Bradley asked.

"That varies. It has taken some people up to a minute, according to granddad. Anything longer than that would be cutting it extremely close, but you can still get away. You just have to be very fast. You also need to wear dark clothing. Daniel Aikens died because of a white tee-shirt. Stopping to assist him is likely the thing that got Seth Tolliver caught. You'll need backpacks. Fill them with flashlights, rope, and a change of clothes. The longest I'll wait after the event is two minutes and thirty seconds. You're on your own after that.

"Chances are, you already know where you need to go. Study it. Immerse yourself in that time and place and learn every single thing you can about it. It can make a difference in the quality of life you live while you're there."

"And how long will we be there?" Elijah asked.

"Until you die there."

"And then we just keep on living our lives here as if nothing has happened when we get back?" D'Quandray asked.

"Yes, that's exactly right."

He narrowed his eyes. Though Marissa had answered his question with a great deal of certainty, the idea that that was possible gave him pause. "And how much time do we lose in real life?"

"An instant—nothing more than a moment. In the blink of an eye, you'll gain more from another life than you've learned in the twenty-five years you've been in this one." She quietly studied each of their faces, yet her gaze was met with silence. "My advice is that you keep your destinations a secret. If you're going to travel to another time, and possibly another place, your objective should be to go through something that you are incapable of experiencing here, and you should do that alone."

"There's something that's been bothering me since we left your house, Marissa," D'Quandray said.

"Something else? What is it?"

"I'm having trouble wrapping my mind around how your grandfather got our descriptions onto that video in so little time."

"Ah, I see. I... I'll put it this way. When my grandfather came here, he didn't *stay* here."

"You mean he did a time travel *within* a time travel?" Bradley asked.

"Yes, that's why he chose this year. He met some other people, one of whom he had time travel back to their time. He gave that person the message I scribbled on the notepad, and that person, in turn, delivered the message to him. You'll recall that he said he got the information much in the same way that he was delivering it to you."

"I remember that," Bradley said.

"Well, there you have it."

"Fascinating," Elijah said. "Why don't you have a desire to go?"

"I don't need to. I'm fulfilling my destiny by doing this. Besides, for all you know, I could be in the midst of my own right now." She smiled. "But if I was, I wouldn't tell you."

Chapter 7

Terribly Wrong

D'Quandray waved at Albert, the ever-present daytime attendant seated inside the guard shack, as he drove past the security gate at the northern edge of his neighborhood. Saturday night with Delores had been no different than the nights he had spent with Katy and Tiffany. He had come to realize, however, that the women viewed him much in the same way that he viewed them, as a conquest. He got to have sex with women he found to be extremely attractive, and they got to put a celebrity notch on their belts. "Fair exchange is no robbery," he said aloud, but even as he did, he laughed to himself. He felt that he was getting the better end of the deal by far. Sunday had been a day filled with research. He had gotten so immersed in it that he had only stopped to eat and to shower. As a result, he felt tired. He drove onto the main road and continued his trek to work.

Before Marissa left his house on Saturday, they all agreed that the upcoming Sunday night going into Monday morning would be the perfect time for them to make their time travel attempt. The police would be busy with drunk drivers, wild parties, and everything else that came along with good weather weekends, especially on the south side where the portals would appear. Dealing with trespassers would certainly be a low priority. He had also decided to what place he wanted to travel and the exact time he wanted to arrive.

As he pulled up to the traffic light, he saw the same woman he had seen before standing at the bus stop. Again, she was holding her child. He thought back to what Maliq had said about offering her assistance when he had mentioned her in the office. He also thought of his counterpoint, which he still believed to be valid. "Hmph, choices," he said, shaking his head. When the driver behind him blew their horn, he looked forward and saw that the light was green. He raised an apologetic hand and drove through the intersection.

D'Quandray got to work at his normal time, and, as usual, it took him an extra two or three minutes to find a parking space. He walked into the office to find Maliq already at work. To his surprise, Jason, who usually worked remotely and rarely came into the building, was also in the office. He was sitting at his desk on the other side of the room. D'Quandray surmised that it had something to do with the conversation that he and Greg had had outside of the clubhouse at the conclusion of their golf outing. Though Maliq would be doing most of the hard work, they had to give the appearance that they were putting in an equal amount of effort on the new contract. He was certain that a similar conversation had been had with Jason.

"Good morning, guys."

"Good morning, D'Quandray," Jason said.

"Greetings, Black man. I hope you had a good weekend."

"I did. Thanks again for inviting me out to the charity game on Friday. I think I'll try to make a few more of those. I enjoyed myself."

"Good. That's good to hear." He removed his hands from his keyboard and swiveled his chair around so he could face D'Quandray. "Just giving you a heads-up, Greg is cracking the whip about this new contract. I know you're the golden child around here, but I don't want you to get in trouble for not completing your work."

Jason rolled his eyes and shook his head behind Maliq's back.

"I appreciate it," D'Quandray said, ignoring the not-so-veiled reference to slavery. He wondered how Maliq could equate what he was doing to something that was supposed to have been so bad when he was being paid so handsomely for his efforts. "Have they divided up the work yet?"

"As a matter of fact, they have. Your assignments should've been emailed to you." He turned back to his desk and started typing. "Did you ask your boys why they didn't go out Friday night?"

"You're not going to let that go, are you?"

"That's a funny way to say, 'you were right,' but I'll take it. I just hope you see the lesson in it; that's the main thing."

He chose to ignore the comment from Maliq and let him have his moment of glory. Although D'Quandray was sure Elijah and Bradley choosing not to go out had more to do with what they had experienced on Wednesday, Maliq's prediction was still true. They had decided to not go through with their plans only after he backed out at the last minute. He saw no need to argue with him about it or to retest his theory. He simply considered it a battle lost—a capitulation that was made easier because Maliq was not one to gloat excessively.

The rest of D'Quandray's workday was uneventful. In fact, his department was able to get a lot done. They ate lunch together at a nearby restaurant, and everyone stayed until the normal close of business. On his way home, he noticed the sign at the bus stop had been bent parallel to the ground, and he saw black car tire marks on both sides of it. When he approached the front gate of his community, he saw that there was a new attendant inside the guard shack. He stopped.

"Hello. Where's Albert? I've never seen anyone here in the daytime besides him."

The attendant looked down and shook his head for a few seconds. "He lost his wife and his youngest child today. She was standing at that bus stop just up the street this morning, and a drunk driver ran them over. It happened around eight thirty."

D'Quandray was crestfallen. "Thank you." He looked away from the attendant and at the road in front of him. He waved without looking at him and drove away, wondering if a simple act of kindness would have saved their lives. He knew that Albert, a Haitian immigrant, worked two jobs and allowed his brother-in-law to use his car for work. All that time, he thought she was an American Black. He had been wrong about the woman standing at the bus stop—terribly wrong.

***

After work the next day, D'Quandray stopped by a local hardware store to gather the materials he needed for the event. Marissa had been specific about the items they had to have, so he made sure to get everything that was on the list. After enduring a few predictable but corny jokes from the clerk about him planning a jewel heist, he made the purchase and drove home. As he passed by the guard shack, he winced. The sight of it was becoming a source of trauma. Every time he saw it, he thought of Albert. Every time he thought of Albert, he thought of his wife and child. Every time he thought of them, he thought of Maliq's admonishment of his behavior, and he felt guilty about his previous thoughts and his unwillingness to offer them assistance.

His evenings consisted of research through articles and documentaries about slavery. As he learned all he could, he still had a hard time accepting that it was possible to travel through time, but he was going to try. He remembered being told by his junior varsity coach that to properly evaluate a drill one must go through it precisely as it was intended to be done. That meant you had to commit to it with the belief that your efforts would achieve the desired results. If after all that, it did not work, then you knew it was because of a fault in the exercise and not due to your lack of effort while performing it. Therefore, he studied the material and prepared in good faith that it was indeed possible.

His workdays were each a carbon copy of the previous one. Jason was there every day. Maliq kept them on track with their projects, even though D'Quandray still arrived around fifteen to thirty minutes after he did each morning, and each day they ate lunch together. D'Quandray did, however, make it a point to stay there until it was time to leave each day. He felt it was the least he could do, especially with the knowledge that Maliq had been given the hardest projects to complete.

Peppered into the work sessions was the occasional barb from Maliq about D'Quandray's reluctance to fully embrace his Blackness. He noticed that he had not done it as fervently as he had in the past. He wondered if it was because he was showing him grace for attending the charity game or if it was because Jason was around them. He did not tell Maliq about Albert's wife and child. He could not bring himself to mention it, and he also wanted no parts of the backlash he would surely receive.

D'Quandray made it to work on time Friday morning, largely because he had chosen to forego exercising on his elliptical machine. That shortened his morning routine significantly. He was already well conditioned and thought that it was more important to have fresh legs for Saturday night. There were several available parking spaces when he got there, much to his satisfaction. He silenced the podcast he was listening to and took a moment to compose himself inside his car—to meditate. Then, he walked inside to start his day.

D'Quandray had not heard from Bradley or Elijah all week, but that did not alarm him. He figured they were preparing themselves, as he was, for the event. As the work hours crept by, he began to regret getting there on time. To him, it felt like time was standing still. Anticipation finally got the best of him, and he could not bring himself to stay another minute, so he left thirty minutes early. Maliq was still working when he walked out. Jason, who had been watching the clock as much as D'Quandray had, got up to leave, too.

He took the backway home and entered his community through the south gate instead of the north gate, where Albert's post was located. He simply could not bear to look at it. As he pulled into his driveway, his phone rang. It was Bradley, and he could hear the excitement in his voice as soon as he answered. He sat in his driveway as they discussed what time they would meet up and whether they had gotten all the items on their lists. They decided to forgo their normal Saturday morning basketball game to make sure they were able to properly prepare. Bradley had already called Elijah and Marissa before calling D'Quandray. Throughout the week, he had also gathered all the materials Marissa told them they would need.

That night, D'Quandray stayed up as long as he could, studying everything he could find about where he was going. He finally went to sleep around 4 o'clock a.m.

Chapter 8

Fantastic Voyage

The clock on D'Quandray's dashboard displayed 10 o'clock p.m., and the time had finally come. He had slept until the early afternoon and felt refreshed. He had his car's air conditioner set to 64 degrees and blowing at its highest setting as he sat in his driveway. Being dressed in black from head to toe on July 28th was not the best way to stay cool, but his focus was more on staying alive. Meeting the same fate as Daniel Aikens was not something that appealed to him.

He shifted his car into drive and exited his community through the south gate. The public parking garage at which they agreed to rendezvous was fifteen minutes away, located on the south side of town. That was only a few minutes' drive from the site of their planned time travel event.

He pulled into the parking garage and drove up to level B. Bradley and Marissa were already there, standing outside of their cars (which were parked next to each other), and dressed in black from head to toe, including knit skull caps. D'Quandray parked beside them and got out.

"Elijah's five minutes out," Bradley said as he extended a hand to greet him.

D'Quandray shook his hand and nodded to Marissa at the same time. "Do you have the timer?"

Marissa reached into her shirt through her neck hole and pulled out the black stopwatch she had hanging around her neck. "It's right here. We have everything. Do you?"

"I do," D'Quandray replied. "My backpack's in my car."

"Cell phones stay here," Marissa said. "We don't need to carry anything that will mark us there. We'll have enough problems with the IDS; we don't need the feds and the local cops on our tails, too."

"That's a fact," Bradley said.

They all turned toward the ramp that led to their level when they heard an engine roar and saw headlights illuminate the wall at the top of it. It was Elijah. He parked beside them and immediately got out. He, too, was dressed in black from head to toe.

"Hi, Elijah," Marissa said.

"Hi, Marissa." He nodded to D'Quandray and Bradley. "Guys."

D'Quandray and Bradley returned the gesture, and they all turned their attention to Marissa.

"Good, everyone's here on time," she said. "Roll your sleeves up." She walked to each of them and inspected their arms. "No one is wearing a watch. Great. We don't need any distractions when it's time for the event. One alarm or notification could ruin everything. My stopwatch is digital; you won't even hear it ticking. Check each other to make sure no one has anything on them."

D'Quandray performed a police style pat down on Bradley. Then Bradley checked him and Elijah both as Marissa watched. Then, at her request, they retrieved their backpacks and set them on the ground in front of them. She carefully inspected the contents of each one before loading them into the trunk of the heavily tinted, black SUV she had rented.

"Gather around and join hands, please," Elijah said. He bowed his head after they came together. "Let us pray. Father, we come to you with humble hearts. What we do tonight, we do not in defiance of your divine power, but in observance of your true omnipotence. We pray that your will be done, and we hope it is that we all return in one piece—mind, body, and spirit. Amen."

"Amen," D'Quandray said. He got into the front passenger seat of the rented SUV after Marissa got behind the wheel. Bradley and Elijah got in the back of it at the same time. As they drove down to the A level and out onto the street, he began to meditate on his destination.

The trip from the parking lot to the coordinates of the event was a blur.

"There's *Lucky's*," Marissa said. "Get ready."

D'Quandray sat up as they drove by the service station, taking a moment to glance at the sewer that had preserved the wallet that ultimately forced his commitment to the time travel event. Then, he focused on the large retaining wall in the distance. When they got to it, Marissa turned right and traveled a few hundred feet to the point where it sloped to meet the ground. The four-foot high, chain-link fence that ran atop the wall continued along the ground, and it separated the woods from the paved road.

She parked the SUV near the fence and away from the nearest streetlight, and they all got out and put their backpacks on. She placed the key fob under the driver's seat and closed the door, leaving it unlocked. Then, one by one, they scaled the fence as quietly as they could, ignoring the sign that read GOVERNMENT PROPERTY: KEEP OUT as they did. With a compass in hand, Marissa led the way. Bradley was right behind her and D'Quandray brought up the rear.

After they were a couple of hundred yards into the woods, D'Quandray's flesh began to tingle. He felt the same sensation he had felt just before the tipoff of the national championship game, when the referee was standing at center court and poised to toss the basketball skyward. Just as he accepted that it was a result of his nerves and adrenaline and nothing more, Bradley turned around.

"You guys feel that?" Bradley whispered.

"I do," Elijah replied.

D'Quandray said nothing but swallowed hard. He slowed down even more, even though they were already moving at a careful and measured pace, and he began to scan the area.

Marissa stopped at the perimeter of a clearing about the area of half of a basketball court. "This is it."

D'Quandray and the others joined her, standing shoulder to shoulder.

"We have to go to the center of it," she said. "D'Quandray, you and Bradley face one another. Elijah, you're going to have to face me. There needs to be room behind you. Leave your backpacks right here."

Without speaking, they did exactly as she said. They formed a diamond about six feet in diameter in the center of the clearing.

D'Quandray looked across at Bradley, to his right at Elijah, then to his left at Marissa. She was already holding the stopwatch in her hand with her thumb poised to press the start button.

"Ready?" Marissa asked. When they closed their eyes and lowered their heads, she began. "Fifty-nine, fifty-eight, fifty-seven..."

As the countdown continued, D'Quandray focused on his destination, immersing his mind in all that he had consumed over the past few days. After a few more seconds passed, he no longer heard the count, but the images of his destination were now so vivid that he felt like he could walk through them. He could feel his heart rate slowing. Then, there were no longer any images, and there was no sound, only calm. He was neither hot nor cold, but he felt like he was falling. With his eyes still closed, he took a step back to brace himself.

Compelled by a force he could not resist, D'Quandray turned around and opened his eyes. He instantly felt cold, as if he had walked out of the comfort of a fireplace warmed room and outside into a brisk autumn morning. He looked down and quickly realized that he was completely nude. Then he looked back to see if the others were experiencing the same thing. He was astonished to see that he was back-to-back with his own fully clothed body, which was still standing in the same position he was in when the countdown began. He surmised that his consciousness had been transferred from that body to whoever, or whatever, he was now.

D'Quandray faced forward and examined his hands, arms, legs, and all the other parts of his anatomy that he could see. Everything was familiar. The scar from his surgery was still on his left knee. He was himself, but he could not help but wonder who was behind him. Moments earlier, before they started the countdown, he was fully aware that he was standing still with his head down and focusing on where he wanted to go.

As he continued to examine his new body, he contemplated turning around and attempting to rejoin the vessel he had just left. Then, there was a glow that caught his attention. When he looked up, he saw a portal several yards in front of him, the inside of which was pitch black. Its appearance was accompanied by a tingling sensation, which he felt all through his body. It was reminiscent of the electrical stimulation treatment he had received on his knee during physical therapy, but it lasted less than five seconds. As he examined the passageway, only the red-orange ring that defined it was visible.

He began to walk toward it, and only then did he fully understand the moth's attraction to the flame. Each step he took was less voluntary than his last. Then, an image appeared inside the portal. As he looked through it, he saw daylight. Blue skies and green trees encased a red, dirt road that led directly from the portal into a meadow that formed the bottom half of a horizon. It resembled a portrait of a summer day, except for the breeze that moved the leaves.

His pace was quickened, by what—or how—he did not know. All he knew was that he was not in control of his body. D'Quandray entered the portal and immediately felt the warmth he had felt inside his own body before he separated from it. He took another step, and he was through to the other side. He stopped. The coldness had returned, and, this time, he began to shiver. Instead of being surrounded by the bright, summer day he had seen from outside the portal, he was back in the darkness. Though he had not turned around and had only been inside the portal for a moment, he saw the back of his own body—dressed in all black—standing a few yards in front of him and in the exact same position he had left it. Not only that, but he could also see his friends' bodies in the same position they were in when the countdown started.

Then, in the same exact way that D'Quandray had, Bradley emerged from his own portal, also fully nude. He looked on in astonishment as he watched Bradley reach up and grab his throat with both hands. Then, Bradley briefly looked back through the portal before quickly walking back toward his body. D'Quandray continued to watch Bradley as he touched the back of his sleeping body. The two became one, and his original self was reanimated.

D'Quandray looked to his right and saw a naked middle-aged man, who could pass for Elijah's father or uncle, walk out of the portal that was behind Elijah's resting body. Further scrutiny of the man's face revealed that it was indeed Elijah, only he was about thirty years older. He noticed that he also looked back toward his portal before proceeding, and much in the same way that Bradley had, Elijah rejoined his body.

As Bradley and Elijah looked at each other with bewilderment in their eyes, Marissa appeared to welcome them back. Then, she walked up to D'Quandray's sleeping body and started gently slapping his face, verbally imploring him to snap out of the trance as she did.

D'Quandray decided he should walk forward, like the others, to rejoin his body. He took a step and immediately felt pain. Every part of him ached, especially his head and back. He looked down at his skeleton thin hands and saw gray hairs on his knuckles. His muscle density had been significantly diminished as well, replaced by sagging, crepe paper looking skin that was leathery to the touch. He reached up to touch his head. He was completely bald, but in the center of his forehead was a hole that was big enough for him to insert the tip of his finger. His face had also been shaved.

He touched his back. As he ran his hand over the scars, he felt three different stages of damage. Some were completely healed, some had scabs, and some were fresh. He winced as he stuck the tips of his fingers into one of the unhealed wounds. It burned. He put his hand in front of his face and saw his own blood glistening on his fingertips. Then, he swept his thumbs across his heavily calloused palms, trying to imagine the amount of work that would have been required to leave them in such a state.

D'Quandray turned around—the same way Bradley and Elijah had—and looked back through his portal. Inside, it was raining. He saw several Black men, women, and children, dressed in attire befitting a bygone era, somberly walking away as two gravediggers shoveled dirt into a coffin-sized hole. There was no headstone. Close by was an eye-patch-wearing white man—who was unkempt and woefully underdressed for the occasion—with a rifle propped on his shoulder as he watched the others leave and the gravediggers work.

The portal went dark, so D'Quandray turned around. His intent was to hurry to rejoin his former self, but the limitations of his current body restrained him in ways no opponent ever had. As he watched Marissa continue her efforts to summon him back to consciousness, he tried desperately to get there quicker. His lungs burned, which he thought should not have been possible given his level of conditioning and the short distance he had walked. He began to breathe heavily and got concerned as Marissa appeared to abandon hope that he would return to consciousness.

He was ten steps away when Marissa waved for Bradley and Elijah to come along. As they were leaving, Bradley and Elijah stopped in front of D'Quandray's sleeping body to examine him. As they looked at his face, they appeared to be waiting for him to come back, not willing to give up on him so easily. When D'Quandray finally reached his body, he reached out and touched his back with his hand. His eyes involuntarily clamped shut, and he could feel himself being pulled forward. Warmth consumed him. He opened his eyes and took a deep breath, then several more.

D'Quandray brought his hands to his face; they were now young and full again. Then, he removed his knitted cap and ran them through his full head of hair. He touched his facial hair, which he had cut into a neatly trimmed beard. He looked behind him for the portal, but it was gone. When he faced forward and looked into the eyes of his friends, he saw expressions that reflected what he felt inside. No further confirmation was needed. That something supernatural had occurred was undeniable, but they had no time to discuss it. The interdimensional sentries would be there soon.

"Are you here?" Marissa asked as she tapped his chest with the palm of her hand.

Though all their lips had been moving since he rejoined his body, hers were the first words he could hear. "Yeah, I...I'm here."

"Good. Time is wasting, you guys. We need to move." Marissa put her arms through the straps of her backpack, turned away from them, and broke into a full sprint.

D'Quandray grabbed his backpack from the ground and immediately followed her. Bradley and Elijah were behind them; however, he was not going to look back to see if they were keeping up. As he ran, he focused on the matter at hand. They needed to get to safety. If it was true that they could travel through time, it was also true that the IDS would be coming to apprehend them. He was a believer now. He picked up his pace and passed Marissa, focused on reaching the retaining wall as quickly as possible.

The forest behind them lit up like a bonfire, and D'Quandray felt the same tinge of electricity surge through his body. Then, everything went black again. Though he did not look back, he knew the IDS had arrived. His aged, post-time-travel body had caused them to use too much time, leaving them with none to spare. He ran faster.

"They're here," Bradley said from behind.

"I know," D'Quandray said. "Keep running!"

D'Quandray and Marissa reached the fence at the same time. He pulled the backpack off Marissa's back and set it on the ground. "We can't risk running to the end; the thick brush will slow us down too much. We have got to climb down right here."

Marissa removed a knotted rope with a D-ring clip at the end from her backpack and handed it to D'Quandray. He promptly attached it to a link in the fence, locked it, and threw the rope to the ground below. He reached over the fence and gave the rope a tug to make sure it was securely attached. Then, he stepped aside.

D'Quandray waved Bradley and Elijah forward. "Let's go, guys; we don't have much time!"

They assisted Marissa over the fence, and she immediately scampered down the rope. Next was Elijah. Marissa was already on the ground before he got halfway down. She sprinted toward the SUV. Before Elijah reached the ground, Bradley climbed over the fence and stood on the ledge. D'Quandray grabbed all four backpacks and tossed them to the ground while Bradley rappelled down the wall.

D'Quandray put one leg over the fence, keeping his eyes on the woods behind him. When he raised his other foot, he felt resistance against his arch. Thinking he had gotten it tangled in some weeds, he thrusted it upward. When he looked down, he saw that it was a tripwire. He hurried to the other side. Then, he saw *them*. Less than one hundred yards away, a team of four, eight-foot-tall hominids appeared. Instead of running toward him, the stout framed sentries simply phased, two by two, in front of one another as if they were playing a game of cosmic leapfrog. They were unmistakably female, and they were beautiful. Their dark-blue, shoulder-length hair flowed as if they were completely submerged in water. The sentries' form-fitting uniforms were ivory colored, which D'Quandray found to be strange attire for beings whose purpose was supposedly to apprehend time travelers. It had done very little to conceal their presence. The contrast made their gray skin and red sclera stand out.

When they got to within fifty feet of him, two of them kneeled. They held their hands out in front of them—one more forward than the other—with their palms facing upward. Then a long, metallic object appeared in both of their hands out of thin air, and they were pointing them directly at him.

"Let's go, D'Quandray!" Bradley said from the ground.

Only then did he realize he had been locked in a trance. He hopped off the ledge and used the knots in the rope to control his descent as the toes of his shoes scraped the wall. He heard the car door slam behind him. Almost simultaneously, a projectile struck and rattled the entire fence, and it sent a jolt of electricity through the rope and his body. When he reached the ground, he hurried to Marissa's waiting SUV. As they drove away, he lowered the window a few inches and looked up at the ledge. The four Interdimensional Sentries were standing on the other side of the fence and looking down at them. One of them contorted her face into what he believed to be a smile before they all phased again. They were no longer there. D'Quandray looked at Bradley and Elijah. They were both focused on the road in front of them. No one else in the car had seen what he had.

"I tripped a wire," he said as they drove past *Lucky's Service Station*. "The police are probably on their way."

Marissa drove faster, and as she did, two helicopters flew over them and toward the retaining wall.

"No police cars," Bradley observed.

"That's the federal government," Marissa said as she leaned over the steering wheel and looked up to see the markings on the helicopters. "They don't want us; they want the IDS. Did anyone get a chance to see them?"

Before D'Quandray could speak, Bradley did. "No; we were too fast for them. We saw the glow, but we were gone before they appeared."

Marissa looked to her right and at D'Quandray.

"No. I didn't see anything at all." He did not understand why, but his instincts told him to lie.

It was just after midnight when they reached the parking garage. Marissa parked, and they all got out.

"That was too close for comfort," Marissa said. She looked up at D'Quandray. "What took you so long?"

His heart raced. He thought back to what he had seen as he stood on the edge of the retaining wall and started to shake his head, almost involuntarily. D'Quandray's conscience was about to betray his instincts. As the two battled inside him, the conflict forced him into paralysis outwardly.

"When we were standing in the clearing, what took you so long to come back?" she asked, rephrasing her question.

When he looked into her eyes, he saw that she was genuinely curious about what he had experienced and nothing more. She wanted intricate details about what had happened to him while he was absent from his body. He rolled his lips inward, closed his eyes, and exhaled through his nose. He felt his shoulders relax. For a moment, he allowed his head to droop. Then he looked up again. "I moved as fast as I could. I must've been a hundred years old." D'Quandray whispered his words, but his emotions would not allow him to raise his voice much higher. He remembered the pain. "I..." He looked away from Marissa and turned his eyes to Bradley and Elijah. "I just don't know, guys. I'm sorry."

From what he had experienced, he knew that he had indeed traveled through time. But the fact that he had no recollection of what transformed him from an elite athlete, who was in the prime of his life, to a feeble old man who could barely walk fifteen yards on his own without losing his breath, troubled him. He wondered if his memory had somehow been erased. He wondered if Bradley and Elijah had experienced the same things he had. He thought that he seemed to be the one who was most affected by the time travel event; however, he was also the only one who had seen the sentries. And they had seen him.

"We should probably get out of here," Elijah said. "Marissa, you get in with me; we're leaving your rental here for now." He looked at Bradley. "Can we meet at the diner in thirty minutes?"

"Sounds good to me," Bradley said. "There's a lot I want to talk about."

"We need to change first," Marissa said as she opened the passenger side door of her vehicle. She put her backpack on the seat and opened it. Then, she removed the black shirt she was wearing, revealing her bare-naked back, and pulled out a pink tank top. She barely had it past her chin when she turned around, her perky breasts jiggling from the quick movement. "Don't just stand there gawking at me," she said as she pulled it down to her waist, "get changed." She stuffed the rest of her belongings into her backpack and locked the rental car. She opened the passenger side door of Elijah's SUV, got inside, and placed the backpack on the floorboard between her feet. She took a pair of skimpy, white, jean shorts with frayed legs out of her backpack and kicked off her shoes, and after she raised her hips and slid her black pants to her knees, D'Quandray wondered if she owned any underwear at all. She put the shorts on, then closed the door.

D'Quandray, Elijah, and Bradley changed clothes inside their respective vehicles. Then, they all drove out of the parking garage and headed for the diner.

Chapter 9

Long, Sleepless Night

By 2 o'clock a.m. D'Quandray was already on his third cup of coffee. He was sitting across from Elijah, who had an elbow on the table and his other arm across the back of the bench as he talked to Marissa. She had her back to the wall and her arms folded across her chest. The air conditioning inside the diner was doing its best to convince them that it was not the middle of summer. He looked inward at Bradley, who was sitting next to him in the booth and had his head resting against the wall.

"If you're going to go to sleep, BG, you may as well go home," D'Quandray said.

"I'm tired, but I'm far from sleepy," Bradley replied. "I can't wrap my mind around this whole thing."

Marissa squared up to the table and looked directly at Bradley. "What do you mean?"

"I mean this is the most exciting thing I've ever experienced in my life, yet I have no recollection of where I went or how long I was there."

D'Quandray closed his eyes and sighed. Bradley's admission confirmed that he was not the only one to have had that specific experience.

"Maybe there was a glitch of some sort," Elijah said. "This isn't exactly documented science."

"It's not documented science *to us*," Marissa said, "but Miles Jackson did meet with the sentries and..."

"Did he describe them?" D'Quandray asked.

She looked at him and narrowed her eyes. "Are you sure you didn't get a glimpse of them?"

"No, I didn't. Why do you ask?"

"I ask because it took you a long time to get down that wall. Correction: it took you a long time to move from the ledge to the wall. It's like you were stuck."

"Stuck?" D'Quandray shifted in his seat but kept his eyes locked onto hers. "That's an interesting word to use. Why would you say that?"

She took a sip of her coffee, then set the cup down and put both elbows on the table. "Miles Jackson told my granddad that Daniel Aikens' white shirt had nothing to do with his death. It was the fact that he locked eyes with one of the sentries and couldn't look away that did him in. He was *stuck*, paralyzed by the sight of something so unusual, or phenomenal, that he simply could not look away."

"And how did Miles Jackson get that information?"

"He met with the sentries, remember? They told him."

D'Quandray shrugged. "Would they not know the exact reason someone couldn't look away from them?"

"I'm sure they do," Marissa said, "but they can only communicate with other beings according to the parameters of their own ability to understand. We teach babies one syllable words first, not paragraphs. I'm sure they took that same approach with Miles Jackson. I told you about the white tee-shirt because that was Seth Tolliver's understanding of what had happened, and that would be his perspective if he didn't get a chance to see the sentries."

"Lot's wife," Elijah said.

"Eh, probably more like Medusa," Marissa said, "but I get what you're saying."

Bradley sat up in his seat, seemingly energized by the conversation. "You're both wrong. They sound like sirens to me."

D'Quandray thought back to the ivory-colored uniforms the sentries had been wearing when he saw them. What Marissa said about Daniel's death made total sense; once they locked eyes with you, you were likely done. Camouflage was useless against them. He thought that a more accurate description of what had happened to him—and to Daniel Aikens—was more akin to what happens when a vampire locks eyes with the object of his desires. They become locked in a trance and fall under his spell. Goosebumps raised on his flesh as he thought about how close he had come to death. "I was trying to make sure the ground below me was clear; I didn't want to land on any of you. That's why I stayed there. I was also worried about the tripwire. I guess it scared me."

Marissa slowly turned her head away from him and back toward Elijah as she opened her body to her seatmate once again. Her eyes took a moment longer to make the journey. "Right," was her tight-lipped response.

"Can we talk about where we went now?" Bradley asked.

"I don't think that's a good idea," Marissa said. She pulled both her legs onto the bench. "Give it a few days. The comet is still at its perihelion, and I imagine whatever allowed you guys to go into the unconscious state you were in still has some sort of cosmic hold on you. Things may be back to normal for you once it's out of the sun's orbit. I'd wait until then."

"How long does that take?" D'Quandray asked.

"It stays in earth's orbit around six months, but the event is at its most potent, according to my granddad, for about a week—give or take a day or two."

"Well, can we at least discuss tonight's event?" Bradley pressed.

"I don't see any harm in that," Marissa replied. "What exactly is it that has you champing at the bit so aggressively?"

"The fact that I did see something." His eyes lit up and a broad smile flashed across his face. "I saw life inside the portal as I walked toward it. When I walked back from it, my throat hurt like I had been stabbed through my neck. I've never felt pain like that before. When I looked back, I saw something there. It was *different*, but it was still amazing. Maybe it's up to us to piece the rest of it together but *wow*. The fact of the matter is something happened. When I rejoined my body, the pain was gone."

"Your portal was gone, too," D'Quandray said.

Bradley turned his head toward D'Quandray. "That's exactly right. Did all three of us have the same experience?"

"It sounds that way," Elijah said. "What did you see, Marissa?"

She shrugged. "I saw three men fall asleep while they were standing up, then wake up confused as hell."

Elijah laughed. "Really? You didn't see anything that happened behind any of us?"

"No. Did either of you see anything behind D'Quandray once you woke up?"

Bradley shook his head. "No, I only saw him standing there. In fact, I didn't see either of their portals. I was the first one back."

"I saw you come out of yours, BG," D'Quandray said. "I saw you, too, Elijah. You guys got back so quickly you didn't notice anything else. I wasn't so lucky." He shook his head as he thought back on his walk from his portal to his resting body. He had been old, and he had felt the cumulative toll the years of abuse and hard labor had taken on his body, even though he had no recollection of it. "How'd you feel, Elijah?"

"I felt a little strange but not too different. Why do you ask?"

"Because you looked about thirty years older. BG, you looked exactly the same as you do now. That leads me to believe our duration of time away was maybe a little different."

"Sounds like it was a lot different to me," Elijah said. He reached up to his collar but flattened his hand on his chest when he found nothing there.

"It's in your cup holder," Marissa said. "Are you guys planning to stay here all morning? Don't you have to go to work?"

D'Quandray stood. "We do." He looked at his wrist for the nonexistent watch, then turned his eyes to the clock on the wall. "If I go home now, I might be able to get two hours of sleep." As Bradley slid down the bench toward him, D'Quandray stepped out of the way so he would have room to stand.

Elijah stood, extended a hand to Marissa, and assisted her out of the booth. She smiled.

"What now?" Bradley asked. "Do we just wait?"

Elijah looked at Marissa briefly then nodded. "Yeah, that's the plan; let's see what happens."

After agreeing that that was the best course of action to take, they embraced, paid their bill, and went their separate ways.

***

As D'Quandray lay still, staring at the ceiling, he regretted the multiple cups of coffee he had consumed at the diner. But he wondered if that was the only reason he could not sleep. What he had experienced was still at the forefront of his mind. He, in fact, had not been able to take his eyes off the sentry who had held his gaze, even though he was aware of the danger they posed to him. Their projectiles had barely missed him. If he had lingered there a moment longer, it would have been a moment too long. Bradley had called his name at precisely the right time, and the universe had granted him a stay of execution.

The *how* no longer mattered to him; it was the *why* that kept him awake. If the events taught him anything it was that everything was out of his control and that he was just a chess piece being moved by a master player. Never had he felt so insignificant and so powerful at the same time. He was a pawn poised to take the queen but limited by rules he did not make and vulnerable to every other piece around him.

The roar of the central air conditioning unit forced his eyes open. He glanced at the clock, which confirmed that he had only been asleep for a couple of minutes at the most. There was still an hour to go before he was scheduled to wake up for work. He sat up and rotated his feet to the floor.

He squinted to mitigate the brightness of the lights as they came on. After a few seconds, he got up and walked to the bathroom. When he crossed the threshold, the bathroom lights turned on, leaving him face to face with his reflection as he stood in front of the vanity. "Housemate, start my coffee."

D'Quandray decided he would not do his morning workout. His body was already under enough stress as it was, and he was thinking about the fatigue he would surely feel later in the day. He showered and cooked breakfast. He felt refreshed afterward. When he got dressed, he realized he was a full hour ahead of schedule. He went to the garage, unplugged his car, and got in. One benefit of leaving so early was he would catch the beginning of the podcast he normally listened to on his way to work.

He left his community through the south gate for two reasons: he had extra time to get to work, so taking the long way was okay, and he wanted to avoid having to look at the north gate. Moments after he got onto the highway that ran along the south end of his community, he saw a massive, automated billboard. On it were the images of him and the representatives from *Exum Industries*. It read "Don't be a dud, be like The Stud. Play with Exum." He smiled and accelerated, taking advantage of the lighter traffic he encountered because of his early commute.

"Oh shit!" he said when he saw the red and blue lights of the police cruiser as the officer sped from behind the billboard and got behind him. He pulled over to the right side of the road, powered his driver side window down, and placed his hands on the steering wheel.

"License and registration, please," the officer said after he positioned himself behind the B pillar of D'Quandray's car.

"They're in my center console. May I reach for them?"

"Sure; do it slowly."

D'Quandray retrieved the items and handed them to the officer.

"The Stud!" the officer said after he examined the driver's license and realized who he had stopped. "You're good, brother. Relax."

D'Quandray looked at the officer's name tag and then to his smiling face. It was Officer P. Roberts. He was the same one he had seen writing the report for a citizen after the charity game. "Oh, I remember you." He smiled. "Sorry I was going so fast. I'm not used to having this much open road in front of me."

"I get it. This is the new model you have here. That's a lot of horsepower." He nodded to D'Quandray's dashboard. "What are they talking about this morning? I don't get to listen while on duty because I have to pay attention to communications."

"They're talking about the new gun laws in California." He shook his head. "I don't see how anyone still lives there."

Officer Roberts gave D'Quandray a pat on the shoulder. "Neither do I."

"Did you happen to catch the episode I was on a few weeks back?"

"I did catch that, and I loved every minute of it."

"If they don't secure that southern border, we're going to be in trouble."

"That's right. You're a good man, Mr. Tyson. I'm not going to hold you. I'm sure you have somewhere to be and more important things to do. Nice talking to you. Be careful."

"Thank you, Officer Roberts. Have a nice day, sir." He powered his window up and shifted his car into drive as the officer walked back to his cruiser. As he pulled away, he paid close attention to the speedometer. Even when he was trying to control his speed, the smooth transitions his automatic transmission made from one gear to the next made it difficult to discern how fast he was going, especially with no other vehicles on the road for comparison.

When D'Quandray walked into the office, he encountered a true rarity. Maliq had not yet arrived. In fact, his entire department was still empty. He booted up his computer and walked to the break room, which was one floor below their office. There he encountered a few people from other departments who were having breakfast together. The people in his department, who were all former athletes (Jason had been a highly touted quarterback coming out of high school, but a mediocre one in college), referred to everyone else as regulars. He spoke to them and made himself a cup of coffee. Then he hurried out of the break room so they could finish their paused conversations. He walked back to his office and got to work on his *Exum Industries* projects.

"Greetings, Black man," Maliq said as he walked into the office.

He looked up at his coworker's smiling face. "Good morning, Maliq. Did you have a good weekend?"

"I did. It was nice playing *with* you for a change on Saturday. We make a pretty good team."

D'Quandray leaned back in his chair. "Yeah, that African player was something, though. Two more like him and we would've been in trouble."

"That was KB—Kofi Boateng. There're probably not two more players like him in the entire world, our pro league included. He is special."

"Then why doesn't he come here to play?"

"Already rich, that's why. He plays for country and for the love of the game. Kind of like you do every Saturday morning." He smiled. "That coalition team is going to be hard to beat with him on it."

"Anybody can be beaten."

"That's true, but if they lose to us, nobody cares. If our team loses to them, our country will go into depression and the guys on their team will probably be heroes. That's what's at stake for them. Those guys are on an American tour. They're here to get used to our style of play."

"You think so?"

"I know so." He sat down at his desk and turned on his computer. "Why are you here so early? This may be the first time you've ever beaten me to work."

"I couldn't sleep, so I figured I'd get an early start on things today." He chuckled. "I almost got a speeding ticket for my efforts."

"Let me guess, the officer was a fan?"

D'Quandray shrugged. "Hey, I don't make the rules, I just play the game. I can't help it if I play it better than everybody else."

"Be careful, Black man. The universe has ways of humbling you. That's been proven time and time again. As a Black man in America, you have got to be especially careful. The universe seeks balance, but white supremacy seeks to destroy you."

"We were doing so well. How did you manage to sneak *that* into our conversation?"

"I didn't *sneak* it anywhere. In fact, it's always at the forefront of my mind because I see evidence of their four-hundred-year head start all around me every day. And I see the four hundred years of trauma in our people. It's all about perspective, though. Colonizers and trespassers exist at a one-to-one ratio. How you see it depends on if you're the occupier or the occupied."

"It's not so black and white for everyone, Maliq."

"You're right." He swiveled his chair around to face D'Quandray. "I forgot about the people who are brainwashed by American exceptionalism propaganda."

"Why do you think everything is about race? Do you *really* believe it affects every aspect of our lives?"

"I do, Black man." He leaned back in his chair, folded his arms, and focused on D'Quandray's eyes. "Racism is like water. There's no crack it can't get into, no man it can't drown, and no mountain it can't erode. It's relentless, and it's powerful. But if you bring it into the open and shine as much light on it as you can, it will evaporate."

D'Quandray laughed. "And how do you evaporate an ocean?"

"With persistence. You do it one drop at a time and with a whole lot of light."

Chapter 10

The Awakening

D'Quandray normally went to sleep a few minutes before midnight, but his body simply would not allow him to stay up that long. So, at 9 o'clock p.m., he lay in bed in his silk pajamas. He had set his air conditioner to a brisk sixty-eight degrees when he got home. That was just cold enough for him to snuggle up in his duvet for warmth, which he loved to do. He had drunk his last cup of coffee just before 10 o'clock a.m. That was a switch from his normal routine, but he wanted to make sure he was ready to sleep whenever he chose to lie down.

D'Quandray had not heard from Bradley or Elijah all day, which was unusual, but it also did not surprise him. He figured they must have been just as confused about what had happened the night before as he was. Bradley had asked him what he had to lose prior to him agreeing to go along with their adventure. He was beginning to think that "nothing" weighed more than the emptiness it pretended to represent. Uncertainty about their experience, sleepiness, and frustration, stemming from his interactions with Maliq, had all combined to make him irritable. That culminated with him leaving work a full two hours early. He hoped that he would be able to put it all behind him with a good night's sleep.

"Housemate, lights."

***

As he looked out into a pasture through an open, front-facing window, D'Quandray focused his eyes on the rather large man who was walking toward the building. He was wearing tattered clothing. Striding wide with his arms crossing his body in an exaggerated way with each step, he looked like a prototypical basketball power forward, and considering his size, his fluidity of movement was something to be admired. Only when the man stopped, looked back, and waved his arm forward demonstratively did D'Quandray realize that he was urging two armed, white men to keep up with him.

Suddenly, he was aware of the stomping, clapping, and singing that was happening behind him. Boom clap, boom clap, boom-boom clap, boom clap, "O-oh Lordie," boom-boom clap, boom clap. He heard it over and over again, and in four-four time. D'Quandray turned away from the window and winced from the pain he felt in his feet resulting from the too-small boots he was wearing. In front of him was what first appeared to be a church praise break in full throat. But there was something more. The parishioners who were stomping, clapping, and singing were all women and children. Their clothing befitted a time more than four hundred years in the past. The people—every one of them Black—had their backs to him and to the entrance.

Even though the heat was suffocating, he felt a chill come over his body. Goosebumps covered his flesh. The realization that everything was tangible—the creaking floors, the people, and their sweaty bodies—had that effect on him. Also evident was their suffering; he could hear it in their voices. He knew exactly where he was—the time and the place. When he looked beyond them, he saw a bearded man who had his back to the pulpit. He was facing the others but looking down. He was sweating profusely and yelling words that D'Quandray could not hear. There was intensity in his glare. Directly in front of him, and kneeling, were men of varying ages, who were all focused on what the man was saying. Something important was happening.

D'Quandray took a step forward, and as he did, someone pushed the door open from the outside. A woman yelled, "Big Bartholomew," and the stomping, singing, clapping, and speaking all stopped at once. He looked back and saw the man he had seen walking across the pasture only seconds ago standing in the doorway with his hands on his hips and his eyes focused on the center of the sanctuary. When the intruder found who he was looking for, he smiled and walked out. When D'Quandray looked back at the parishioners, he saw fear on every one of their faces. Then their eyes turned away from the door and toward him, and their facial expressions transitioned from fear to anger.

"You was s'posed to be lookin' out fo' him," the same woman said, her subdued voice conveying a tone that was more sorrowful than accusatory. Despite the ravages of the Southern sun being apparent on her face, her body was strong. He estimated her to be about forty years old.

D'Quandray's heart raced. "I...," he began but hung his head instead of finishing the sentence.

Big Bartholomew walked back into the church—accompanied by Jethro McCoy and Silas Jones, the two men he had led there—with his finger already pointed in the direction of the speaker. "Yonder he is, suh. Mr. Joseph was the one doin' the talkin'. He the one showed up 'fore all them folks run off from them other plantations. I told you they was plannin' som'n."

He moved backward and centered himself one step behind Jethro and Silas, and though he towered above them, he seemed small. On his face was an expression that was all too familiar to D'Quandray. He had seen Grayson Randolph look that way one day at practice. The precocious sophomore had been called up to the varsity team at the end of the regular season during D'Quandray's senior year of high school. In his first scrimmage against the starters, Grayson scored forty points, which angered the varsity coach. The team had to run thirty suicides as a result. While the coach gave the team a tongue lashing, Grayson had stood just behind him, looking over his shoulder with that same expression. Selfish pride. Every part of his face smiled except his mouth. He had sacrificed the entire team for personal gain.

"Good work, boy," Jethro said, dark brown tobacco juice dripping down the front of his sun-damaged chin, the source of it packed into a wad in one side of his mouth. His eyes were hidden under the sweat-stained, khaki field hat he wore. "Run and tell Mr. John what you done found."

"Yessuh," Big Bartholomew said as he hurried out of the church.

D'Quandray looked out of the window. The speed at which Big Bartholomew ran left no doubt in his mind that he had made a terrible mistake, and he knew the consequences would be dire. He saw happiness in the man's carefree jaunt, which confirmed that he was right in his assessment of his expression. But the crying brought his attention back to the sanctuary. As the gun-toting slavers walked toward the speaker, the parishioners backed away. Joseph Freeman did not.

"I should shoot you right here, nigger," Jethro said.

D'Quandray's body tensed, and he stifled a gasp. The slaver's casual utterance of the N-word startled and infuriated him in proportionate amounts. He had never heard it directed toward someone as a pejorative. Every other iteration he had witnessed in his life had been something different, almost innocuous, but not this. This was spawned from pure evil. Equally startling and depressing to him was the lack of a reaction to it from anyone else in the church. That saddened him, and as all those emotions ran through him, he fought to maintain a neutral countenance so he would not draw more attention to himself.

Jethro moved the weapon from his shoulder to a ready position, the stock just beneath his armpit, the barrel pointed directly at Joseph's chest. "How dare you use the good Lord's house to corrupt these simple-minded folks—hard working folks." He spat tobacco juice on the floor and wiped his chin with his sleeve. "Bring yo' ass over here."

Joseph swallowed hard but kept his chin level, chest out, and shoulders back. He walked forward and directly into a backhanded slap across his face from Jethro. He flattened his lips into a straight line as his nostrils flared, his chest noticeably rising and falling; however, he kept his eyes fixed on his assailant.

"Mind how you look at me, boy."

His emphasis on the word boy made it sound more disrespectful than his use of the N-word. It was contemptuous, and it evoked two emotions from D'Quandray—rage and fear. He felt his legs trembling and his face tightening.

Jethro stepped aside to clear a path to the door, but he kept his eyes locked onto Joseph's. "Get outside." As Joseph walked past him, Jethro kicked him in his rear end. Then, he pointed his gun at his face when he turned around. "I wish you would. I'll splatter your brains all over this God damned floor. Now move. We 'bout to shave yo' face."

That, not the N-word, is what brought gasps from the parishioners. It also brought pleas for mercy from them, but not from Joseph

Freeman, who seemed to be accepting of his fate. He walked outside with his head held high, his heavy footsteps exposing every weakness in the poorly constructed floor as he moved. Jethro and Silas followed him closely with their weapons at the ready.

***

The white plantation-hands rounded up every enslaved person on the plantation and brought them to the redemption grounds. John Lester, overseer of the Lester Plantation, stood in front of Joseph Freeman with his bible in one hand and his flintlock pistol in the other. The slavers had stripped Joseph naked and tied him to a seven-foot-tall wooden post, one of twelve posts that had been arranged in a circle like the numbers on a clock. They had shaved his entire body, a Lester plantation custom established with the purpose of presenting souls to the afterlife in the same way they had entered the world.

D'Quandray marveled at how young and strong Joseph Freeman looked. The thick beard he had worn and the bushy hair he had had on his head were gone. They had hidden his facial features, and he was suddenly aware that these people were physically no different than he was, and that evolution moved much slower than the four hundred twenty-five years that separated them.

John raised his bible to eye level. "Ephesians 6:5 says, 'Servants, be obedient to them that are your masters according to the flesh, with fear and trembling, in singleness of your heart, as unto Christ.'" He turned his back to Joseph and faced the throngs of enslaved people who worked his plantation. "I am your earthly master, and I am the only one you will serve, for the bible says that you cannot serve two masters." He turned to face Joseph. "Out of the graciousness of my heart, I offer you an opportunity to redeem your soul, to seek salvation, so that you may inherit God's kingdom. What say you, boy?"

Joseph looked past the overseer and into the sorrowful eyes of those who had been forced to watch his lynching. He took a deep breath and raised his chin as high as he could. Then he turned his eyes back to John. "I don't believe in your bible, I don't believe in your Jesus, and I don't believe in your god, but on the off chance that heaven does exist, I look forward to what awaits me on the other side, because living here amongst you white folks has been nothing but pure hell."

It occurred to D'Quandray that despite having seen him talk to the others that was the first time he heard the man speak. What immediately stood out to him was how articulate he was, how measured his words were, and how little fear he had for his impending demise. For the first time in his life, he was witnessing real courage. As he tried to wrap his feelings around what was happening, the crackle of the gun jolted him from his thoughts. He drew a breath when he saw red mist explode from the back of Joseph's head. Between his eyes appeared a black hole, smaller than a dime. A single drop of blood trailed away from it, and Joseph's head drooped forward. When D'Quandray looked at John Lester, his arm was still fully extended, and he still had one eye closed as he pointed the weapon at Joseph. The puff of smoke that escaped the chamber of John's firearm still lingered in the air.

The surreal moment paralyzed D'Quandray. John lowered the weapon and walked away with his bible pressed against his chest with his non-shooting hand. His steps were steady and prideful, as if he had audaciously shown a rude guest out of his home to the delight of his frightened family. When Jethro and Silas followed John away from the redemption grounds, Big Bartholomew was close behind them. His shoulders were slumped, and he had his head hung low. D'Quandray thought that he saw sorrow and remorse on his face when he glanced over his shoulder; however, as he watched him walk away, he found it more telling that he had chosen to follow the slavers instead of staying back with the enslaved, even though he had received no orders to do either.

Several people hurried to untie Joseph's body. A sobbing woman sat on the ground and placed his head in her lap. She caressed his jaw with one hand and stared into his face as he lay dying in her arms. As he stood there watching the tragic events unfold, D'Quandray lowered his head and wiped away the tear that ran down his cheek. Fate had been unkind to him. He was angry that he had been transported at a moment that was most inopportune. The year he had chosen to arrive in Jamestown, Virginia was 1740. Abraham Lincoln had not yet been born, and the Emancipation Proclamation was still one hundred twenty-three years away.

He looked to the ground as more tears streamed down his face—too many to wipe away, in fact. It took every bit of self-control he had to stop himself from openly sobbing. He clenched his teeth, pounded his fist into his hand, and then thrusted both fists downward as he stomped his foot on the ground. As he listened to the voices of those who were grieving around him, he looked at the raggedy boots he wore and the dirty, tattered trousers that covered them. His feet hurt as much as his heart, and his heart was broken. He exhaled a laborious sigh.

"Leave him be, Horace; he need to thank about what he done," a woman said. Her tone was matter of fact and devoid of empathy. She was the same woman who had held him to account for allowing Big Bartholomew to barge in on them without warning.

"It's not his fault, Ms. Sarah," the man replied. His voice was calm, almost soothing. "Big Bartholomew must've seen Joseph when he came onto the plantation. He came into that church looking for him specifically."

The proximity of the male's voice caused D'Quandray to look up. When he did, he saw a man who—despite the obvious damage of the hard life he had lived—appeared to be about his age, standing about a foot away from him. Like Joseph Freeman, he, too, was well-spoken and bearded. In fact, he noticed that all the enslaved men were bearded. When the man placed a comforting hand on his arm, D'Quandray instinctively hugged him. Then, he bent over and shamelessly cried onto his shoulder.

"You have got to hold it together, or else this place will chew you up and spit you out," he said into D'Quandray's ear. "I've seen it too many times. This plantation isn't anything like the one they brought you from."

D'Quandray suddenly had a clue about the circumstances surrounding his existence there, but he needed to learn more. He had already unwittingly made a catastrophic mistake upon his awakening there, and he knew that he could not afford to make another. Other lives were at stake, and he surmised that the best thing he could do was assimilate into his environment. He would have to worry about making the most of his condition—their condition—later.

He had apparently been there long enough to supposedly know who Big Bartholomew was and long enough to be trusted to lookout for him. But he was not trusted enough to be included in whatever Joseph Freeman had been meeting with the other men about. From that, he deduced that he had been there a few weeks at best. It was with that understanding that he would attempt to navigate his way through the upcoming days.

Horace moved him out to arm's length by his shoulders. As D'Quandray looked down at him, he noticed how much taller than him he was. Except for Big Bartholomew, D'Quandray was taller than everyone he had seen so far.

Horace tilted his head toward the center of the circle. "Go on over there and have a seat on that stump."

D'Quandray nodded. He thought that even something as simple as speaking could be dangerous. If he put his words together too well or used some anachronistic word or phrase, he could expose himself to unwanted scrutiny. He also needed to absorb a few of their colloquialisms and to affect a Southern accent and dialect. D'Quandray walked over to the blood-stained tree stump, which was in the center of the makeshift death clock, and he took a seat. The other men worked cohesively to remove Joseph Freeman's body from the redemption grounds. Later that day, they buried him in an unmarked grave.

**

Night fell. As everyone else went their separate ways, D'Quandray stood at the edge of the village designated for the slave quarters, staring at the moon. He was alone, and as everyone else settled in for the night, he began to feel lonely. He was also afraid.

"They must've hit you over the head really hard," Horace said.

D'Quandray turned around, half embarrassed and half surprised to see the gentle man standing behind him. "What makes you say that?"

"You don't know where you're supposed to be right now."

"How'd you know?"

"I know because this is the third time since you've been here that I've had to show you."

D'Quandray sighed and decided to step out on faith. "How long have I been here?"

Horace smiled. "You've been here a month. That's my second time having to tell you that, too. Don't ask me what your name is because no one knows it."

For that, D'Quandray was thankful. He had wondered what they called him. His name was not one befitting the time they were in, and Horace's words proved to him that his decision to remain quiet was a wise one.

"Follow me; I'll show you where you're supposed to be." Horace turned and walked down the center of a dirt road that was lined on both sides with one-room cabins. They passed by several of them before stopping in front of one that was as simple as the rest. Two rickety steps led to an equally unsteady porch. The front door, which was made of wooden planks, was clearly there for privacy only. Anyone who wanted to get in would meet little resistance if they tried. "Normally, we get up before daylight, but they're going to want you ready for tomorrow evening, so they might let you sleep longer. They're bringing the folks from the other plantations here."

"For what?"

Horace looked at him and shook his head. "Go on and get some rest. You've been through enough today already."

As Horace walked away, D'Quandray made sure to watch where he went. He knew that he would have to lean heavily on him to learn the ways and customs of the plantation if he was going to live a life worth living while he was there. As he listened to the crickets chirping, watched the lightning bugs periodically show themselves, and heard the dogs barking as they scurried about, he was thankful that the moon was full. Otherwise, he would be standing in total darkness and even more lost than he already was.

Horace approached a cabin that was three down and across the road from where D'Quandray's was. It was no bigger than his, but on the porch with a candle in her hand was a woman who was dressed in a dingy frock. Standing beside her, with her arms wrapped around one of her legs, was a toddler. When Horace stepped onto the porch, he gave the woman a kiss and picked the child up. Then, they walked inside his shack together. And as he stood there watching, D'Quandray wondered how anyone could purposely bring a child into a world that treated them so cruelly.

The steps creaked under his body weight as he walked toward his front door. When he pushed it open, a rat ran out. He jumped back and nearly fell off the porch. It happened so quickly that he had no time to yell. He hated rats and was aware of the diseases they carried, even in his day. The thought of being touched by one now nearly sickened him. He stared at the door as it came to rest against the jamb, contemplating if he should go inside or sleep right there on the porch. He wondered if he would be able to sleep at all.

D'Quandray turned around and sat on his porch, his feet resting on the next step down. He examined his hands. They were calloused and rough, and he had scars on them, the causes of which he had no clue. He raised his left pant leg to look at his surgically repaired left knee. To his surprise, there was no scar. He was himself and not himself at the same time. He had read science fiction stories about parallel universes and multiverses, but he never imagined that any of it was possible. He wondered, as he rolled his pant leg down, how his scars could be left behind while his memories remained intact, and how he could have no recollection of what this version of him had been through in this life prior to his awakening inside the church.

After a few more minutes of introspection, he got up and walked into his cabin. Although it was pitch black, the sound his footsteps made as he walked across the floor told him that there was no furniture inside it. He was horrified to hear that there were more rats inside, however—two more by his estimation. He found a wall opposite of the one they were near and put his back against it. The rats stayed where they were; their odor did not.

He eventually slid down to the floor, pulled his knees to his chest, and wrapped his arms around his legs, the coarse wood pricking him as he pressed his back against it. Only a single layer of wood separated the inside of his home from the outside; it had no form of insulation whatsoever. Though it was the middle of summer, he already dreaded the winter. He closed his eyes and rested his forehead on his knees.

D'Qquandray was awakened by a crowing rooster. He also heard birds chirping. When he raised his head, he saw daylight creeping through the planks of his door. He noticed there was a loft at the back of the cabin with a wooden ladder propped against it. There was also a fireplace directly across from him. It was where the rats had been; he could tell by the droppings they had left behind. He was tempted to smile but would not allow himself to do it. Relief was what he felt, not happiness. It was morning. One day down, a lifetime to go.

***

It was late afternoon, nearly dusk. D'Quandray sat in a topless, horse-drawn, medium-sized delivery wagon as it was pulled across the pasture. His long-sleeve shirt and straw palmetto hat shielded him from what was left of the sun. With him were three other passengers, one man and two women. One of them was Horace's significant other, but Horace was not with them. Their destination was a large barn, which was several acres away from the main plantation where the big house and the slave quarters were located. They were being escorted by Jethro and Silas, who were both atop their own horses and both armed with rifles. The women were stoic, and both had glassy eyes, which, to D'Quandray, foreshadowed something upcoming that was at least unpleasant. He would not allow his mind to imagine the worst. The other person—a one-handed man, who was a few years younger than D'Quandray—was bright-eyed and sitting erect. Though his lips were flattened into a straight line, he appeared to be suppressing a smile.

D'Quandray's stomach was full. They had just eaten a stew that Ms. Sarah had prepared for everyone. The only ingredients he recognized in the meal were the yams and carrots. He thought that another might have been turnips, but he was not certain. The meat was good, but he decided against asking what it was due to the likelihood that finding out might have repulsed him. He had read enough about slave cuisine to know that they did not always have the pick of the best cuts of meat.

As they approached the barn, he saw two more men on horses, whose faces he had not yet seen, waiting out front. The way Jethro and Silas greeted them confirmed that they were not from the Lester Plantation. The coachman stopped the wagon and Jethro ordered the occupants out. He lined them up shoulder to shoulder, and both strangers walked in front of them, looking each one of them over from head to toe.

"I'll take this boy and that gal," the first man said, pointing to D'Quandray and to Horace's woman.

"He's dumb as a fence post," Jethro said about D'Quandray, "but he's built for studdin."

"I reckon I got this other gal and the one-handed boy," the other slaver said as he looked over the other two. "Let's get 'em inside and get it over with."

"You heard him," Silas said. "You wenches and studs get your asses on in there. Git!"

The one-handed man ran inside, and the women followed, though not enthusiastically. Because he did not want to invoke the ire of his handlers, D'Quandray kept pace. Once inside, he saw six more enslaved people—four men and two women—standing around. Big Bartholomew was among them. As he looked at them, he thought that all of them could be successful athletes in his time.

Four hay bales were evenly spaced around the dirt floor. Peering down from a catwalk one story above were several more slavers, including John Lester. A few feet away from him were a few white women who were attired in colorful antebellum dresses. His eyes were drawn to a brunette who was taller than the others. She had sharp facial features, and as he stared at the long spiral curls that draped over her bare shoulders, he thought he saw the beginnings of a smile on her face. When they made eye contact, he looked away, quickly turning his attention to John Lester. There were two other men beside the plantation owner, and they were dressed similarly to him and were about his age. He thought they all looked a bit formal, considering the heat; however, asking himself how else they would distinguish themselves from the lowly slave handlers removed the need to question their formal wear further. The way the slavers studied him and the other enslaved people who were with him reminded D'Quandray of the team owners who had assembled to discuss prospects as the athletes went through various drills at the pro basketball combine.

As Big Bartholomew and another rather large male stood off to the side, the slave handlers went about the business of coupling each male with a female, matching those who were brought to the barn with those who had already been there. D'Quandray noticed that the woman with whom they paired him was looking to the ground, not just waiting but existing. He looked around the barn for Horace's woman. When his eyes located her, he saw that her demeanor was no different than that of the woman who stood in front of him.

"Get to it." Jethro said.

Before D'Quandray had time to mentally process what he was seeing and experiencing, the woman pulled her one-piece frock up around her waist, exposing her naked lower body, and turned away from him. As she lay her upper torso flat on top of the hay bale, presenting her vagina to him, he stood motionless, mortified. The sounds of vigorous coitus immediately filled the barn. He knew that refusing to perform was not an option, so he grabbed the rope that held his trousers up. The woman stood as D'Quandray untied it. When he lowered his trousers, she grabbed his flaccid penis and pulled on it until it became engorged with blood and stiffened. Then she lay across the hay bale again. She had yet to look into his eyes.

As D'Quandray entered her, she gasped. With each thrust, she got louder, but he knew that she was deriving no pleasure from the experience. Neither was he. He simply wanted to finish quickly, and he did. After he was done, she faced him, lowered her frock, and stepped under the catwalk. D'Quandray pulled his trousers up and quickly tied the rope around his waist. Before long, the other woman, and the two men who had been there with her when they arrived, joined the woman he had mated with under the catwalk. The one-handed man who had accompanied D'Quandray's contingent to the barn was already standing by the door.

"Let's go. Get on over there, Ruth," Silas said as he stared at Horace's significant other.

That was D'Quandray's informal introduction to her. As he and the other woman who had arrived with them joined them at the door, he watched the plantation owners shake hands and the giggling, white women fan themselves. He felt sick. The fight between Big Bartholomew and the other enslaved man began just before they walked outside.

He winced as he heard the grunts coming from the men and the heavy blows they landed on one another, thankful that he was not a participant in that.

He stared into the distance as they rode the wagon back across the pasture to the main grounds, seeing nothing and hearing less. When the coachman stopped the wagon, he summoned his mind back to reality. Horace was standing on the ground with a hand extended upward toward Ruth. When her feet were flat on the ground, they embraced. Then they walked away, his arm around her shoulders, her arms around his waist.

D'Quandray moved quickly to the ground, not wanting to establish a pattern of being last to respond whenever action was required. He walked through the slave quarters and sat on his porch. It was getting darker. A few minutes later, Horace joined him. He sat beside D'Quandray and handed him a candle, a piece of flint, a piece of iron, and an apple. "You make fire with those. We call it a strike-a-light."

"Thank you."

Horace cut himself a slice of his own apple and ate it from the blade. "Charlotte is not my birth child—you've probably figured that out by now—but I'm her daddy, and I love Ruth. She's a good woman." *He kept his eyes forward as he spoke.*

"I understand." *D'Quandray took a bite of the apple, and thought it was the sweetest he had ever tasted.*

"I think you're starting to get it, sir." *Horace looked at him, finally.* "One-hand Moses—that fool they took to the sugar shack with you—looks forward to going there every time. Every time. He's even happier when he comes back, giving no care whatsoever to whatever woman he just defiled. He only cares about his manly desires. I watched you from my porch over there," *he pointed with his knife,* "and you look like you feel exactly the way you should. You're a good man, sir."

"You don't have to call me that."

"Oh, but I do, and it's as much for me as it is for you. It's important that we respect each other because they damn sure don't. We're not men to them. When you can remember your name, I'll call you that, but until then, I'll call you the most respectful thing I can." *He quietly ate the rest of his apple, then got up and walked away without saying another word.*

D'Quandray finished eating his apple and held the core in his hand, wondering what to do with it. He finally stood and faced his cabin, then threw the core over the roof and into the woods behind it. He set the candle on the porch and used the strike-a-light to light it. He walked inside to a different experience than the night before. He could see everything, and this time there were no rats. He climbed the ladder to the loft where he found an area just spacious enough to lie. It was dusty, but there were no critters up there. It was also hotter higher up, but he would take that in exchange for the peace of mind that came with knowing he would not be bitten by rats while he slept.

Though he was still far from knowing everything he was supposed to know, he had learned enough to make it through two days. That was a good enough start for him.

Chapter 11

Object of Her Affection

1745, 5 years later.

The day had been a long one. D'Quandray and Horace sat side by side on Horace's porch, eating apples and watching the children make use of the daylight they had left. Behind them, Ruth stood in the doorway. As she leaned against the frame, her four-year-old boy stood just behind her.

"Go on inside, Ruth," Horace said when he saw Big Bartholomew marching stridently down the middle of the road.

"Come on, Rufus," she said to the child as she stepped back and closed the door.

Horace stood and so did D'Quandray, their eyes fixed on the giant of a man as he made his way through the village. It was not long before he found Elizabeth, a twenty-three-year-old whose father's body had recently been deposited into one of the shallow graves of the redemption grounds, the same place the father of her two children had been buried two years before. He grabbed her by her arm. As he dragged her, kicking and screaming, through the village, Horace stepped into the middle of the road and blocked his path.

"It isn't right, Bartholomew. She doesn't want you. Leave her alone."

"You get out my way, Horace," he said, now using both hands to control the woman's wrist. "This ain't no business of yours."

Horace took a step forward, all five-foot-eight inches of him. "But it is, and you will leave her alone."

Big Bartholomew released Elizabeth, and as she ran down the middle of the road, he walked up to Horace. "Ain't you got no sense?" He grabbed Horace by the throat with a motion so sudden it resembled a punch, nearly knocking him off his feet. Then, he put one of his massive legs behind Horace's legs and swept him to the ground. As he lay supine, gasping for air, Horace wrapped both hands around Big Bartholomew's wrist. As he squirmed beneath him and tried to free himself, Big Bartholomew tightened his grip on his neck, drew back a fist, and punched him in his face. Horace's body went limp.

D'Quandray's heart raced. Without thinking, he jumped from the porch and ran toward them. In his best impersonation of an American football punter, he kicked Big Bartholomew's rib cage as hard as he could, sending him tumbling off Horace's body. The gargantuan assailant was wide-eyed as he lay on the ground, looking up and holding his ribs. He got up from the ground, using his other hand for support.

"Is you done lost yo' mind, stud boy?"

D'Quandray shifted in his stance as the bully walked toward him. Big Bartholomew's eyes widened. Then, he made a fist and reared back to throw a punch in a way that was so exaggerated that it almost seemed cartoonish to D'Quandray. He instinctively brought his left arm up to a high guard position as Big Bartholomew threw the haymaker toward his head, easily blocking the wild punch. D'Quandray stepped back and got into a fighting stance. Big Bartholomew furrowed his brow and looked at him as if he was both confused by what he was seeing and studying him.

He approached D'Quandray more cautiously than he did the first time. When he got close enough, he lunged for D'Quandray's legs, again in a telegraphed way. When Big Bartholomew ducked his head, D'Quandray wrapped his arms around his upper body, positioning his chin between his attacker's shoulder blades. Then, he sprawled his legs to break the grip Big Bartholomew had around them and to prevent himself from being tossed. Once he steadied himself, D'Quandray delivered an explosive knee strike to his abdominal region to soften him up. After that, he quickly got behind Big Bartholomew and fell backward with him in his grasp. He applied a rear naked choke hold to his neck. Then, he wrapped his legs around his waist from behind and locked his ankles together in front of him. As Big Bartholomew fought to free himself, D'Quandray tightened his grip. Big Bartholomew grabbed D'Quandray's arm with both hands and nearly pulled it away from his neck; however, with each passing second, the bully's power faded more and more. Thirty seconds later, Big Bartholomew was unconscious.

D'Quandray pushed his massive body aside, got up, and kneeled beside Horace. When he looked up again, the entire village was standing around them. As Horace began to blink to awareness, D'Quandray stood. Ruth emerged from the crowd of onlookers and kneeled beside her man, quickly cradling his head against her bosom.

There was silence. D'Quandray knew not what to make of the looks he saw on the faces of the villagers as he stood there, but this time he saw neither disappointment nor rage. For the second time since he had been there, he had done something to cause all their attention to be on him. He was fearful that he had shown them too much, but he was also confident that he had done the right thing.

"You done good, Sir," Ms. Sarah said. "But don't you go whoopin' Big Bartholomew in front those white folks. They gon' make you fight fo' yo' food if'n you does."

D'Quandray nodded. "Yes, ma'am."

Sarah turned to address the rest of the villagers. "Y'all get on 'way from here. Don't nobody wanna be 'round when this no count wakes up."

The villagers dispersed with haste and disappeared into their respective dwellings. From behind his partially opened cabin door, D'Quandray kept his eyes focused on Big Bartholomew. After some time, the behemoth slowly began to stir. Suddenly, as if he realized he had overslept and was late for an important appointment, he sprang to an upright seated position. For a few moments, he looked around with his mouth open and his eyes wide. Still dazed and confused, he stood. He ran up the road and out of the village, struggling to maintain his balance as he did.

***

Circa 1740

The rooster was on time, as usual. As the morning light crept through the slats of his cabin door, D'Quandray willed his body to action. He winced as he began to move. His arm and leg muscles were aching from his entanglement with Big Bartholomew the night before. Being a lifelong mixed martial arts fan had finally paid off. All the televised events he had purchased and the tournaments he had attended as a spectator, had given him just enough knowledge to know how to defeat a complete novice. Though he was powerful, Big Bartholomew was woefully unskilled as a fighter, a weakness D'Quandray was able to exploit.

There was a gentle rapping at his door, so he scurried down the ladder that led to his loft to see who it was. When he opened the door, he saw Elizabeth standing there. She was holding an apple. She smiled and handed it to him.

"Mornin,' Sir."

"Thank you, Elizabeth. Good morning to you, too. Are you okay?"

She nodded through a tearful smile, then waved goodbye. He took a bite of the apple and stepped out onto his porch to watch her as she walked away. When she got halfway to her own cabin, she looked over her shoulder at him. Again, she smiled. D'Quandray waved and turned his attention to the horses and wagons that were coming down the road to fetch the field hands who had already assembled near the edge of the village.

"Get down here, stud," Jethro yelled from atop one of the unattached horses. D'Quandray ran toward him, stopped a few feet short of his horse, and looked up. "Get on the back o' that there wagon right yonder. Ms. Rebecca got some work for you to do 'round the big house."

"Yessuh," D'Quandray said, nodding demonstratively to show subservience. He got in the back of one of the wagons and waited for the field hands to get in.

The big house was two acres from the village but between it and the fields. D'Quandray knew the routine. He had been called on to do work at the big house on several occasions by Ms. Rebecca since she had first laid her eyes on him from the catwalk inside the sugar shack.

The wagon slowed just enough for him to jump off. He hurried to the back door and stood near it, trying to ignore the envious glares of the field hands as they disappeared into the distance. The door opened.

"Come in here," Ms. Rebecca said, her jet black, spiral curls bouncing on her bare shoulders as she turned away from him.

D'Quandray walked in and closed the door behind him, making sure it was locked. The back room they were in resembled a shed more than anything else. In the corner, a palate. On it was Ms. Rebecca's dress, and she stood naked before him.

"I've been thinking about you all night, stud. Take those rags off and get on in that tub over there."

D'Quandray removed his boots, trousers, and shirt. Then, he stepped into the tin tub of lukewarm water. Rebecca walked over to him and submerged a cloth into the bath. Then, she commenced to wash his flaccid penis as he stood motionless. He had long been repulsed by the sight of her. Her stained teeth, thick pubic hair, and malodorous vagina had nearly forced him to vomit on several occasions in the past.

She pulled on his member longer than she needed to for it to be cleaned. "What's the matter; you don't like me anymore?"

"Yes, ma'am, I does," he lied, avoiding eye contact with her as he did.

She smiled, and then she reached up and touched his chin with two fingers, directing his gaze toward her eyes. "You don't want to hurt my feelings, do you?"

D'Quandray detected something sinister behind her smile—something that betrayed the soft tone with which she spoke and promised retribution if she was rebuffed in any way. "No, ma'am. I'm just a little nervous is all." He took the rag from her hands and started the process of washing the rest of his body, mentally going through the archives of his real-life sexual escapades for inspiration as he did. When he stepped out of the tub, he grabbed her forcefully.

"Ooh!" She smiled and grabbed his engorged penis. "There it is," she whispered.

D'Quandray grabbed her rear end with both hands and forced his lips onto hers, and she kissed him back. Then, he carried her to the palate and positioned her on her hands and knees. He grabbed a handful of her spiral curls and took her from behind, making sure to finish inside her, but not in her vagina.

As he made the long walk back to the village, the old saying "no good deed goes unpunished" entered his mind. He had contemplated, on many occasions, impregnating her. He wanted to expose her for what she truly was and bring shame to the Lester family all at once. After all, the walk he had taken from his portal on July 28th, 2211, had told him that death would not come to him because of it. However, he could not predict the horrors the rest of the villagers would endure because of his selfish act. For their sake, he showed restraint.

It occurred to him that the spectators who visited the sugar shack during the mating sessions were nothing more than pornography addicts who were satisfying their perversions while masquerading as professional breeders. Rebecca Lester's fascination with him could be attributed to her fetishizing him. He wondered if she had told the other women about their escapades and if that was their culture, meaning the other women probably had favorite studs of their own. One-hand Moses's enthusiasm to breed told D'Quandray that he was not a candidate for such a thing, just a big strapping buck who had useful genetics. The likely scenario was that there were only one or two per plantation who filled that role, and D'Quandray Tyson—or Sir, or boy, or stud, as they called him—was the unlucky candidate for the Lester plantation, the object of Ms. Rebecca's affection.

***

D'Quandray never thought that he would enjoy 'possum stew, never mind standing in line for a second serving of it, yet there he was. As Ms. Sarah scooped helpings into the bowls of those who were in line in front of him, he waited patiently, hoping that there would be enough for him when he got there. The field hands always got the most, and everyone else simply got enough. One-hand Moses was directly in front of him, vying for a third helping.

"Only enough for one o' ya," Ms. Sarah said when they approached. "Get out the way, Moses. Come on up here and eat, Sir."

D'Quandray walked forward as One-hand Moses begrudgingly stepped aside. He could feel him glaring at him as he extended his bowl toward Sarah, who unapologetically filled it with enough stew to feed two people. D'Quandray scooped the excess into his mouth to prevent it from spilling out of the bowl as she did, also unapologetically. One-hand Moses scowled as he turned to walk away. Ms. Sarah smiled sheepishly.

"Thank you, Ms. Sarah."

"There's enough in there for two. I don't think Lizzy et nothin' yet. She's right over yonder." She nodded in Elizabeth's direction.

"Yes, ma'am. Do you have an extra bowl?"

Sarah handed him an extra spoon. "Go on over there."

D'Quandray's day had started with Elizabeth giving him an apple and a smile. He felt it was only right that he returned the favor. In a place where everyone had it bad, she had endured an especially tough time. Her two boys were still too small to assist her with any chores or to protect her. Though she appeared to be looking his way as he approached her, he could tell that she did not see him. Only when he stood three feet in front of her did she look up from the tree stump on which she sat.

D'Quandray extended a spoon to her. "Is there enough room for me?"

She accepted the spoon, smiled, and moved to the edge of the stump, leaving him enough room to sit beside her. He sat and moved the bowl to his inside hand, and she immediately began to eat.

When the stew was half gone, she removed her spoon and wiped her mouth with her sleeve. "Big Bartholomew ain't been 'round here all day. I reckon he tryin' to find a way to tell on you without sayin' he got whooped."

"You really think so?"

She shrugged. "I reckon." She put both hands in her lap, leaned forward, and looked up into his eyes as he ate. "You really don't know yo' name?"

"I don't." He placed the spoon in the bowl and sighed. "I don't remember anything before five years ago, including my name, my age, or where I'm from."

"You don't know yo' mama and daddy either?"

He shook his head. "It's probably best if I don't remember them. Knowing everything I do know is painful enough."

"And who taught you how to talk so good?"

He looked at her and smiled. "Again, I don't remember. I wish I could tell you." He stopped talking when he saw Horace running toward them. He handed the bowl to Elizabeth and stood.

"Bartholomew is coming, and he has Jethro and Silas with him. He's in the back of the wagon."

"The wagon?" D'Quandray turned to Elizabeth. "They're coming for you. Go hide down there by the river. We'll come and get you when they leave. Hurry up. Go!"

As Jethro, and Silas brought the wagon to a stop, Big Bartholomew jumped out. D'Quandray and Horace walked toward them.

"Remember what I done told ya," Ms. Sarah said, reminding D'Quandray not to best Big Bartholomew in front of the slavers.

When Big Bartholomew saw D'Quandray approaching, he stopped and allowed Jethro and Silas to walk ahead of him. He stood tall behind them, his eyes darting to and fro as he craned his neck to see the fringes of the assembled villagers.

"Sarah, you get on the back of that there wagon," Jethro said. "You studs get on in there, too."

D'Quandray looked at Ms. Sarah, then at Big Bartholomew. The troublemaker looked away and moved closer to Jethro.

"If you let them see you get angry, they'll know you aren't afraid of them," Horace whispered. "Take your emotions out of it. Ms. Sarah understands. She isn't going to hold it against you."

D'Quandray nodded and walked toward the wagon. One-hand Moses was already seated inside, his eyes suddenly much brighter than they had been moments ago.

"Where's that other gal you was talkin' bout?" Jethro asked.

"I don't see her, Mr. Jethro," Big Bartholomew said. "She done run off somewhere."

"It don't matter," Jethro said. "We got who we come for."

Jethro and Silas left Big Bartholomew behind with the villagers as they took D'Quandray, One-hand Moses, and Ms. Sarah to the sugar shack. When they got there, no one else was inside. As Sarah and One-hand Moses both removed their clothing, D'Quandray questioned—in his mind—the purpose of the non-sanctioned event, and the answered he arrived at angered him.

"Get out them clothes, stud!" Silas said.

D'Quandray directed an icy glare at the rifle-wielding slaver as he loosened the rope at the waist of his trousers and let them drop to his ankles. Sarah lay her upper torso on the hay bale. As D'Quandray stood behind her, he kept his eyes fixed on Silas.

"Get yo' eyes off me and start workin, boy!"

Sarah stood and grabbed D'Quandray's flaccid penis. "It's alright. Don't get yo'self in trouble on my account."

D'Quandray pushed her hand away, stepped back, and pulled his trousers up, keeping his eyes fixed on Silas the entire time. "You gon' have to shoot me."

The slaver gritted his teeth and pointed the barrel of his rifle toward D'Quandray's face.

Jethro stepped in front of D'Quandray with his hands on his hips. "That's alright, you ain't got to do nothin; but you will pay." He turned around. "One-hand Moses, get over here and give it to her good, you hear me?"

"Yessuh, Mr. Jethro." He mounted Sarah and immediately began to take her.

A session that usually took seconds to complete lasted several minutes, and it was hellacious. Ms. Sarah barely made a sound at the beginning. In pure defiance of her violator and his evil masters, she gritted her teeth and took it. But as the ordeal continued, the brutality of the assault produced the desired effect, reducing her to tears as she begged for One-hand Moses to stop. He continued until he finished, collapsing on her back in the end. When it was over, D'Quandray turned and walked out of the barn, ignoring Silas's rifle being pointed at his face the entire way, and seething at the ferocity of One-hand Moses's efforts. He was already in the wagon when the others walked out.

"Get yo' ass down from there," Jethro said. "You gon' walk back. Good luck findin' yo' way through the snakes in the pitch-black darkness, boy."

D'Quandray got down from the wagon and assisted Ms. Sarah into it. He directed an unreturned glare at One-hand Moses as he got into the wagon. He stood beside the barn as they pulled away, watching them until their swaying lanterns disappeared into the night. He contemplated staying there for the night. It was already darker than dusk, and visibility was lessening more and more with each passing minute. He waited about thirty minutes after they were gone before he moved. He wanted his eyes to adjust to the darkness as much as they could. He grabbed a shovel from against the barn and used it to probe the ground in front of him as he made his way.

D'Quandray had seen signs of Jethro's contempt for Ms. Sarah in the past. It was increasingly evident every time he looked at her. As much as she had tried to mute herself in the presence of the slavers, the fact that she was the matriarch of the village was a poorly kept secret, likely disclosed by either Big Bartholomew or One-hand Moses, or both. Jethro and Silas wanted to humiliate her. They hoped that having her taken in that manor would diminish her in the eyes of the villagers. He was certain of that, and he was glad that he had defied their orders. Even still, his heart ached as he thought of what the villagers might be going through because of his actions. Whatever was happening, he could not be there to stop it.

As fireflies occasionally crossed his line of sight, he tracked them with his eyes to see if he could catch a glimpse of what lay yards ahead of him. During his five years stay in Jamestown, he had already had a few too many encounters with timber rattlesnakes, which were hard enough to see in the daylight. He took comfort in knowing that their rattles were a warning and they rarely struck without first giving notice. For that reason, he moved with a lack of haste.

In the distance, he saw more fireflies—more than he had ever seen together before. As he continued to walk, their numbers grew. Then, he noticed something peculiar. Their movements were too steady—too uniform. As he moved closer to them, they moved closer to him. Then, he heard the voices. He stopped to listen.

"Sir," they yelled. "Sir! Sir!"

As he choked back tears, he resisted the temptation to run toward them. "I'm here," he said when his voice was steady enough to carry over the chirping crickets and croaking bullfrogs. "I'm right over here."

The villagers had come for him. When they finally reached him, Horace and Ms. Sarah were leading the way. One-hand Moses was nowhere to be found, and neither was Big Bartholomew.

"I'm alright," Ms. Sarah said as she wrapped an arm around his waist and handed him a candle. "Dry yo' tears. Don't you go worrying 'bout me."

When they got back to the village, Jethro and Silas were waiting. They tied D'Quandray, shirtless, to a tree. As fire ants ravaged his body, he received twenty lashes across his back with a whip. They kept him there all night. The next morning, the villagers found Elizabeth lying face down in the river, her lifeless body battered and bruised.

***

Jealousy is a powerful emotion—born from the union of desire and proximity, reared in captivity, and released through rage—to which no soul is impervious. Its rival is vengeance, which can only be satisfied if exacted in equal proportion or greater, though excess is the expectation. But wrath is altogether different. It exists on a tier of its own. When word got back to Rebecca Lester that Jethro and Silas had attempted to pair her stud with a slave who was incapable of bearing children, she was incensed. When she learned that the wounds from his subsequent beating were so severe that it would take him weeks to heal, she was moved to act on his behalf. By dusk the next day, both men had been relieved of their duties as slave handlers on the Lester plantation and unceremoniously escorted off the property. To further add to their troubles, John Lester made sure that they would find no work with any of the other plantation owners who knew his name, and there were many. A year later, Jethro and Silas were both shot and killed, along with two other horse thieves, on a plantation in the neighboring county.

Chapter 12

Don't Sleep

D'Quandray lay still, thinking about the chores he had to complete and wondering why the rooster had yet to crow. He opened his eyes when the song he hated blared through his house speakers. He sprang up to a seated position and took a deep breath to fill his nose with the scent of the vanilla air fresheners he used to make his home smell pleasant. He was back in his bedroom. He got out of bed, and when his feet hit the floor, the music stopped, and his bedroom lights came on. He grabbed his phone from the dresser and pressed the button on the side, and as the screen lit up, he focused on the date and time. The display read Tuesday, July 30, 2211…6 o'clock a.m. He set it down and placed both hands on the crown of his head. With his mouth wide open, he kept his eyes fixed on the phone and slowly backed away from the dresser until he bumped into his bed. Then, he sat and started to weep. He was home, and *that* had really happened.

As his tears continued to flow, he made no effort to wipe them away. While he was away, he had reached a mature forty-five years of age. For twenty long years, he had lived in the worst conditions imaginable, and he had felt every excruciating hour of each oppressive day.

He had given up on the thought that it was just a dream within two hours of his arrival at Jamestown, Virginia. The events of that day were all too real, and they had dictated the conditions of his acceptance by the other enslaved people who were there. If not for the grace that had been shown to him by Horace, he would surely have suffered a much crueler ordeal than what he had endured. Even still, it took him years to assimilate into their community and to be accepted fully by them.

The slavers' lynching of Joseph Freeman had dealt the villagers of the Lester plantation a heavy blow.

D'Quandray had sired more than twenty children—none of whom called him father, though there were others who did—in another life. Although he had helped with other menial tasks around the plantation, studding had been his primary function. His size and strength had made him an asset to the slavers, and they had regularly mated him with prolific breeders from other plantations.

D'Quandray lay back in his bed and ran his hands over the soft sheets. The firm mattress felt amazing against his back, a vast improvement from the lumpy, hay-cushioned palate he had been sleeping on in Jamestown. His phone rang. It was a video call from Bradley. He wiped his tears away, sat on the edge of the bed, and answered it.

"What's up, BG?"

"Tell me it wasn't just a dream. Tell me the same thing that happened to me happened to you."

"It wasn't a dream, BG. How long were you there?"

"Two days! How about you?"

"Twenty years." D'Quandray shook his head. "I think what Marissa said about the cosmic effects of the comet was true." His walk back from the portal to his body flashed in his mind. By his own estimation, he was a one-hundred-year-old man at that time. That meant he still had at least fifty years left to live in slavery.

"What's wrong, man?" Bradley asked. "You look like you just got some horrible news?"

"I think I did, BG." He ran a hand over his face and sighed. "Have you spoken to Elijah?"

"Not yet; I called you first. Are you okay?"

"I think so. I...I don't know. I just need to sort a few things out in my mind, that's all. Go ahead and call Elijah. I'll be here. I don't think I'm going to work today."

"I'll do that. I'll check back with you in a few. Talk to you soon."

D'Quandray pressed the button to end the call and placed his phone on the nightstand. Bradley had only been away for two days during his first night of sleep, which explained why he still looked like himself when he walked out of his portal. He was going to die quickly at whatever place he had time traveled to.

D'Quandray went to his office and sent an email to Greg stating that he did not feel well and would not be coming to work. He stayed in his comfortable chair and stared at the computer screen, marveling at the complexity involved in what he had just done. In an instant, his message would be received by someone who was miles away. That would have taken days to consummate where he had just been. He used his feet to slowly swivel his chair around in a circle as he took in all the luxuries he had acquired, from the carefully selected cerulean paint on his wall to the plush fabric on the futon he had behind him.

"From absolute squalor to this. Unbelievable." He stood and turned around once more, again taking it all in. Then, he walked back to his bedroom and took off his silk pajamas. He walked into his bathroom and got in the shower. D'Quandray stared at the shower floor with the palms of his hands pressed against the wall as the hot water that rained down on him massaged his body. He stayed there for thirty minutes. When he walked into his kitchen to make breakfast, the aroma of freshly brewed coffee filled his nostrils. He poured himself a cup, took a sip, and then placed it on the counter.

For breakfast, he had salmon croquettes, biscuits from a can, and scrambled eggs. Two tablespoons of sugar-free syrup accompanied the meal. He ate slowly so that he could savor the food and savor it he did. It was a far cry from the meals they had been forced to create out of leftover pig and chicken parts on the plantation. In fact, the meal he had just eaten was even better than the so-called gourmet feasts his masters had enjoyed daily. Then it occurred to him that John Lester had been dead a long time by now, and that racist slave owner had never enjoyed the lifestyle that he was now living. Before he could smile about that, the thought occurred to him that that was the issue with inequality. It mattered not that the enslaved people made the most of what they had. What mattered is that they were denied the opportunity to live as others did. So, from John Lester's perspective, it would have made no difference that D'Quandray now enjoyed better amenities than he did when he was alive. What mattered was when they were in the presence of one another, D'Quandray was beneath him. He pounded a fist into his hand, stood from the kitchen table, and walked back to his bedroom with his head down.

D'Quandray had received a text message from Maliq inquiring about his welfare, to which he responded that he was okay and just needed a personal day. Then, he got back into bed. As he lay there, he felt his eyes getting heavy and nearly jumped out of bed. "No!" D'Quandray paced the floor between his bed and dresser. He looked at the clock and saw that he had been up for two hours already. He walked back to the kitchen and made himself a double espresso, which he consumed quickly.

D'Quandray went to the bathroom to search his medicine cabinet for over-the-counter stimulants. There were none. Then, he checked his workout supplements for anything that contained a trace of ephedra. He found two pills, which he quickly ingested. He decided he needed more. He got dressed, got into his car, and headed to the nearest sports nutrition store, making sure to slow down as he passed the billboard with his image on it. He looked behind it as he passed by and saw a marked police cruiser, which was poised to pounce on unsuspecting speeders.

D'Quandray walked into the nutrition store in search of pre-workout supplements. After a few minutes, he walked to the counter holding two containers of the one that claimed to be the best on the market and stood behind two white men who were already in line. His ears perked up when he heard the clerk say "sir" to the customer he was serving. He smiled as he repeated the pleasantry to the next man, and he stepped up when it was his turn to be served.

"The Stud," the bright-eyed clerk said when they made eye contact with one another.

D'Quandray simply looked at him for a moment, studying his face while he fought to control his own expression. "Good morning," he said after detecting no ill intent from the clerk. "Is this really the best one, or do you have something more powerful?"

"That's the best," the clerk confirmed. "Two scoops of that will have you breaking PRs like it's nobody's business. The pro bodybuilders who come in here love it."

"Thanks, I'll take both." He grabbed a bottle of water from the small cooler beside the counter. "Add this with it, please."

The clerk rang up the purchase and placed both containers in a large bag. D'Quandray unlocked his phone and passed it under the sensor to pay for everything. He thanked the clerk and went on his way. Once he was back inside his car, he opened the bottle and carefully poured two scoops of the pre-workout powder into it, using his receipt as a funnel. Then, he shook it up to mix it with the water and drank it.

He decided against going straight home. Instead, he drove to a local park and went for a walk. After about an hour there, he found a bench under a large tree and took a seat. It was almost noon. He watched the kids as they played various sports. The basketball court and soccer field were both full.

He started to perspire, so he got up and walked to his car. After he turned it on, he put the air conditioner at its lowest temperature and set the fan to blow from its highest setting. When he put his face close to the vents, his phone rang. Again, it was Bradley.

"Just checking on you, man. How are you doing?"

"I'm okay. I'm about to get lunch soon. Have you talked to Elijah?"

"I have. He said he was away for six years when he went to sleep. How old did you say he looked when you saw him come from his portal?"

"He looked about fifty-five or sixty years old."

"Do you see what's happening?"

"I think I do. The event might be spread-loading our time away over the days the comet is at its most potent. If I'm thinking right, we have about four more nights of this."

"That's exactly what I'm thinking. This is exciting, man! I can't wait to go to sleep tonight. I might just take a nap in a few minutes."

"Whatever suits you, BG. I'm about to get moving. I came to the park to get some fresh air and think about things. I need to eat now."

As he ended the call, he put his head on the headrest and stared into the distance. After a few seconds, he had to remind himself to blink. It was then that he noticed his heart rate had increased, and, even if he tried, he would struggle to get to sleep. He shook his head side to side vigorously. His hands were shaking, and he felt jittery as he pulled out of the parking space and oriented his vehicle toward the main road. He breathed in deeply and exhaled several times before driving away.

***

D'Quandray made his usual peanut butter and jelly sandwich for lunch when he got home. He sat in the living room to watch television while he ate. With it, he had a diet soft drink. By the time he was done eating he had started to develop a headache. He put his right hand over his chest and looked at his watch for thirty seconds. Sixty was significantly more beats than his normal resting heart rate. Again, he closed his eyes and took several deep breaths, exhaling slowly after each one. He started to sweat again, and his hands continued to shake as he rested them on his knees.

He stood to stop his legs from bouncing up and down. "Housemate, set the air conditioner to sixty-four degrees." As the furnace roared to life, he stood in front of the television with his hands on his hips. The topic of conversation on the show he was watching was doing nothing to slow his heart rate.

D'Quandray walked to his room and grabbed a pair of SSU basketball shorts and a matching tee shirt. He got undressed and put those on, and he put on a pair of his free sneakers. He needed to calm down, so he grabbed a bottle of water and walked outside to take a rare stroll through his neighborhood. As he got halfway down the block, he saw Deidre, a friendly neighbor, standing at her mailbox and shuffling through letters.

"D'Quandray! D'Quandray, wake up, buddy. D'Quandray, can you hear me?"

D'Quandray opened his eyes to two paramedics leaning over him. He squinted to minimize the intensity of the bright light that was over their heads.

"He's conscious," one of them said. "Let's get him to the hospital."

D'Quandray tried to sit up but could not, and he quickly realized that he was strapped to a stretcher in the back of an ambulance. He also had an oxygen mask over his nose and an intravenous needle in his arm.

"Relax, buddy," the emergency medical technician said. "You're going to be okay. Just try to take it easy for me."

D'Quandray put his head back and nodded.

"He's responsive," the EMT said.

As the ambulance's engine roared and monitors beeped around him, D'Quandray started taking in deep breaths again. He focused on keeping his eyes open. Then, the pain from his forehead hit him. He winced, and even though he could not touch it with his hands, he could feel the sizable lump on it. His lips were also swollen. He ran his tongue over his teeth and breathed a sigh of relief when he felt no chips.

The EMT's moved at a frenetic pace once they got him to the ER, and within minutes he was in a private room. A doctor came in and removed the clipboard from the end of his bed.

"Thumbs up if you can understand me, Mr. Tyson."

D'Quandray lethargically raised his right hand and gave the thumbs-up to the doctor.

"Good. It seems you took a nasty spill out there. Here's where we are. We had to give you something to counteract all the stimulants you have in your system. Your heart rate was not going to come down on its own. In fact, going for that walk probably exacerbated it. It's a good thing your neighbor was there." He walked closer to the bed, lifted the bandage from D'Quandray's head, and gently palpated the bruise with his index and middle fingers. "You have a sizable scalp hematoma. We're going to do a CT scan to make sure there's no bleeding on your brain or anything like that. There's a slight abrasion on it as well. Other than that, you're fine. Your vitals are good. You're pretty healthy, in fact. It looks like you've been taking care of yourself."

D'Quandray nodded.

"The technicians will be here soon to take you for your CT scan and your x-ray. There's a buzzer over there." He nodded to the cord that was tethered to his bed. "If you need anything, just press it and the nurse will come. Okay?"

Again, D'Quandray nodded.

"Good. Don't worry, Mr. Tyson, we'll get you back to draining clutch three-pointers in no time."

He smiled as the doctor left his room.

***

D'Quandray sat up as Bradley, Elijah, and Marissa walked into his room. He was no longer wearing the oxygen mask, but he still had a massive headache. He grimaced as he forced a smile.

"Take it easy, man," Bradley said. "We came as soon as we heard."

"How'd you hear about it?"

"I called you a few times. When I couldn't get you, I drove to your community. The guy in the guard shack said they took you away in an ambulance. We called all the local hospitals until we found the one you were at. I'm your brother, by the way." He grinned sheepishly.

D'Quandray smiled. "Thanks for coming. I don't know what happened. One second, I'm on a leisurely stroll and the next I have some guy rubbing his knuckles up and down my chest and calling my name."

"What do you think caused it?" Elijah asked. "Do you think it's related to the event?"

"Partially," D'Quandray said before averting his eyes and then looking back at Elijah. He furrowed his brow when he saw Bradley try to make eye contact with Elijah without him seeing it. "What?"

Elijah sighed. "Were you trying to avoid going to sleep?" He stepped closer to the bed and put his hand on D'Quandray's hand. "You know that's impossible, right?"

As a tear rolled down his cheek, D'Quandray looked away from them and at the bag of saline solution that hung beside his bed, trying to focus on the drip of liquid instead of answering the question.

"Listen, man," Bradley said, "you said you must've been close to one hundred years old when you walked out of your portal. It sounds like you were the only one lucky enough to die of old age."

D'Quandray looked away from the bag and directly into Bradley's eyes. He felt his face as it began to tremble, and his nostrils started to flare.

"Unclench your fist, D'Quandray. Bradley didn't mean anything by it. Don't upset yourself."

He looked away from Bradley and transferred the icy glare directly to Elijah, who immediately released his hand. D'Quandray then stretched his hand open and placed it on his stomach, leaving a crumpled-up bed sheet where it had been. Then, he took several deep breaths, the distance between each growing the longer he did it. "I'm sorry," he said once his breathing was back to normal. "Twenty years is a long time to be away from you guys. I shouldn't have agreed to do this."

"You say that now," Bradley said, "but it'll be over in five days."

"You were only gone for two days, BG! That's nothing!"

"D'Quandray, please calm down," Elijah said. "He's right, Bradley. It's a lot harder when you're gone for years instead of days. I'm not exactly anxious to go back to sleep either, but my experience wasn't bad. Maybe his experience was different."

The nurse knocked and entered the room. "Is everything okay? I heard elevated voices. The doctor doesn't want anyone to upset him."

"We apologize, ma'am," Elijah said. "We'll keep it down."

When the nurse looked at D'Quandray for confirmation, he simply nodded. She followed his cue and backed out of the room, closing the door behind her.

"I think we should go," Marissa said. D'Quandray offered no protest to the suggestion. As Bradley and Elijah walked toward the door, she remained. "Remember what your purpose is. You all were supposed to choose times and destinations that would enrich you with useful knowledge that you could not obtain here. Lessons rarely come gift wrapped. They come with bruises, scars, and pain. If you were able to experience that much in the twenty or so years that you were away, imagine what the next fifty will bring."

His heart rate sped up again, and as he felt his face begin to contort into a scowl, he looked away. "No human was meant to endure this much pain."

Chapter 13

Elizabeth's Sons

Jamestown, Virginia - 1760

The cock-a-doodle-doo of the rooster forced D'Quandray's eyes open, and the mustiness of the dank cabin assaulted his sense of smell. He touched his face. There was no lump on his forehead, and his lips were their normal size. He sighed. Then, he sat up, yawned, and attempted to stretch away the aches and pains that came with being a forty-five-year-old, enslaved man. He made his way down the ladder, cursing the fact that in a blink of an eye he had been physically transformed, and cosmically transported, yet again, to hell.

As his feet hit the ground, he wondered how many years he would be in Jamestown this time. He opened his door and walked outside to find his adopted sons—George and Isiah—standing on his porch and holding fresh apples. Elizabeth's boys had grown to be strong young men, the oldest now five years younger than she had been when Horace stopped Big Bartholomew from dragging her down the very road they had walked to get to his cabin. They were on their way to the field, as usual, and as usual they made sure to check in with D'Quandray—or Sir—before they started their day. He accepted the apples from them and wished them well, compartmentalizing the emotions he felt, which were attached to the knowledge that they were born enslaved, and he knew that unless they lived to be well over one hundred years old, neither of them would ever taste freedom. But their grandchildren would. And their grandchildren's grandchildren would reap the benefits of their desire to simply survive—to live.

In this time and place, he was one day removed from yet another rendezvous with Rebecca, which was now, through no fault of his own, a poorly kept secret. Her lustful gazes had long ago given John Lester more than enough evidence to convict, but the plantation owner's desire to please his eldest daughter and to protect his own reputation resulted in D'Quandray being shown grace. Yet while they all veiled themselves in plausible deniability—one of the reasons neither he nor John had ever spoken a word of it to anyone—everyone knew. They all knew.

For fifteen years, D'Quandray had raised two boys, who were not biologically his own, while he had no connection to the faceless offspring of mothers whose names he had never learned. At last count, there were more than twenty of them. That was the way of the village, no different than the behavior of Horace or any of the other fathers who helped to raise the children around them. He protected and cared for George and Isiah as if they were his own, and they were as far as he was concerned. He was the closest thing to a father they had ever known. As for Elizabeth, George barely remembered her, and Isiah had no recollection of his mother at all. What they knew about her, they got from D'Quandray and the other villagers. They knew she had been a shy woman, that she had been a good-natured woman, that she had had a great smile, and that, despite all of that, Big Bartholomew had raped and killed her.

As he watched his sons get on the wagon with the others, he smiled—something he had refused to allow himself to do for the first five years that he had been in Jamestown. They were unaware of what they did not know, and he was not going to ruin that for them. They had hope, and it was hope that kept them going each day. Hope brought him apples each morning, and hope was moving Black people toward equality at a glacial pace. It was all necessary, and the soldiers in the army of hope were going to battle on the back of a wagon full of field niggers.

D'Quandray moved from the porch to the ground to meet Horace in the center of the road. He wondered, as he looked at him, if the twenty years he had spent on the Lester plantation had been as harsh to him as they had to his friend. Horace, now balding and with traces of gray in his beard, looked years older than his actual age. Though he had managed to stay out of the fields—he was a hostler by trade—the stress of plantation life was clearly eating away at him. D'Quandray felt especially bad for Horace because, unlike most of the others, he was highly intelligent. He viewed him as an anachronism and felt it a travesty that the universe had placed him there and had placed him then.

The wagons to the stables came about an hour after the field hands were picked up each morning, which gave them time to talk to one another. Horace's daughter, Charlotte, now had her own family, and his son, Rufus, worked the stables with him every day. Ruth, his wife, was no longer a candidate to bear children for other plantation owners. Though she had given birth to eight children—one of whom died at birth—she was only allowed to keep two, Charlotte and Rufus.

After a brief conversation, they separated. They normally talked for as long as they could, but the appearance of Big Bartholomew usually meant trouble. He was carrying a fishing pole. At fifty-one years of age, he was now too old and too hampered by injuries to ply his trade as a fighter for the plantation. That duty now belonged to a thirty-year-old man who had apparently been a more than capable replacement; he was an upgrade. Being relieved of his duties made Big Bartholomew desperate to prove his worth in other ways, and the easiest was being an informant for the masters of the Lester plantation. Only he could make stolen apples an offense worthy of a man, too old to work the fields, losing a hand.

Big Bartholomew kept his eyes forward as he limped by D'Quandray but cast a scornful look at Horace when the opportunity presented itself; however, he said nothing. As he made his way toward the edge of the village, the women and children began to exit their cabins. D'Quandray and Horace reconvened in the center of the road.

"He hasn't gotten over you whipping his butt three times," Horace said. "Before you got here, he was even worse than he is now."

D'Quandray was thankful that Ms. Sarah had warned him never to defeat Big Bartholomew in front of the slavers after their first fight. Though that meant he had to bite his tongue on several occasions and back down on others, it had proven to be sage advice. The villagers all knew they had at least one protector from the brute; what the slavers thought did not matter. "What he hasn't gotten over is everybody knowing about it. He's not used to being controlled, not by Black men anyway. He'd touch the moon if John Lester told him to jump and stay in the sky."

Horace smiled, and as D'Quandray looked at him, he felt an odd sensation. Though it was fleeting, it was distinct.

Horace narrowed his eyes. "Is everything alright?"

D'Quandray paused before he spoke again, not certain if déjà vu was a term that had been used by the seventeen sixties. "Something felt strange for a second. I don't know what it is, but this moment feels familiar. I'm sorry. I don't mean to talk crazy, but it just seems weird."

Horace shook his head. "I don't know either, Sir. I don't know either."

They shook hands, and Horace headed to the pick-up point, where Rufus was waiting. D'Quandray sat on his porch and sighed, lamenting the idea that yet another day of his life would be wasted.

***

D'Quandray knew he was certain to see at least one fiftieth birthday in his two lifetimes, but he had not planned a celebration for it. The year was 1765, and he had been in Jamestown, Virginia for twenty-five of them. It occurred to him that they only celebrated births on the plantation, not the meaningless anniversaries of them. He was not supposed to know when his birthday was anyway, or where he was born for that matter.

The day had been a long one. George and Isiah walked down the road toward him, having just completed another day of days that would never end. They were now fully matured men, both over six feet tall and over two hundred pounds, George now the same age Elizabeth had been when she was murdered. As he watched them, he thought that their days in the field might be numbered, and they would probably be making visits to the sugar shack soon. They were headed for the chow line, but they were making their usual stop to see their father beforehand. As they approached, he detected something different in them. Their body language and facial expressions combined to present to him something he had never seen from either of them before. He stood.

"My sons, what's wrong?"

Isiah glanced sideways at George, then raised his chin. George looked toward the end of the road, at where the woods began, and beyond which the riverbed lay. Then, he looked at D'Quandray.

"Has anyone gone fishing today?" George asked.

D'Quandray folded his arms across his chest and narrowed his eyes. "I saw Big Bartholomew go that way earlier." He knew they were aware that the ogre of a man liked to fish every day. He could no longer fight other slaves for a living, and that was how he chose to spend his time. "One-hand Moses went, too, but they weren't together. I think some young boys might've gone as well."

"Can we go fishing?" George asked.

D'Quandray unfolded his arms, placed his hands on his hips, looked at Isiah, and then looked back at George. "Is it permission you seek?"

"It is," George said.

"Then go."

George nodded. "Thanks, father. Let's go, Isiah." He turned to walk away, then stopped. He walked back up to D'Quandray and hugged him.

As D'Quandray turned his head toward Isiah, he almost recoiled when he, too, wrapped his arms around him. After a few seconds, they both released him and walked down the road. D'Quandray simply watched them, quarreling with the fact that their hellos felt like a unified goodbye. His instincts as their protector were at war with his willingness to let them be men and his knowledge that they were fully aware of the consequences of their actions.

"They seem affectionate today," Horace said as he approached. He had been watching them from the porch of his cabin across the road.

"They do, don't they?" D'Quandray turned to face his long-time friend. "I didn't hear you walk up. The boys were just telling me how much they appreciate me." He shook his head. "I should be telling them that; they made me a man." He turned his attention back to his boys and watched as they walked away.

"Are you going to get something to eat?" Horace asked.

"No, I'm not hungry today." He answered the question but did not look away from his sons. Even when Horace placed a hand on his shoulder and turned to walk back toward his cabin, D'Quandray still kept his eyes on them. As they disappeared from his sight, he sat on his porch. Twenty minutes later, One-hand Moses and the boys, who had gone to the river with him and Big Bartholomew earlier, walked up the road with their fishing poles. One-hand Moses had his hand wrapped around two of them. He had only carried one—his own—when he walked to the river earlier.

D'Quandray had an odd feeling in the pit of his stomach, and it compelled him to confirm his suspicion. He made the five-minute walk to the area where the food was being served. When he got there, he walked up to Ms. Sarah.

"Have my boys eaten yet?"

"I ain't seen a one of 'em. Thought maybe you had 'em doin' somethin' or other. Tell 'em to hurr' up if they want som'n t'eat; it's goin' fast. I'll save some for 'em."

"No, don't do that. They won't be coming today. I'll see you later."

"Is you okay?" she asked.

"Yes, ma'am." He looked into her eyes. "Everything is just fine, Ms. Sarah." And as he walked away from her and toward the river beyond the woods at the end of the road, he knew exactly what he would find.

The daylight was making its transition to dusk, and that was the only thing that hastened his pace. Elizabeth's boys needed time. He reached the end of the road and started through the woods. It was not long before he heard the sloshing of water in the distance. When he finally reached the river, his suspicions were confirmed. George was on his knees in the river and his hands were in the water. They were on Big Bartholomew's back, and his brother was beside him, holding Bartholomew's legs.

George briefly looked up and directly into D'Quandray's eyes. Then, he looked down and applied more pressure. His face was devoid of emotion, yet his arms were straight, and his chest and shoulder muscles were flexed to their rigid and dense capacities. D'Quandray turned and walked back through the woods, leaving his sons to finish the job of avenging their mother's death. He smiled, even though he knew the cost for ridding the village of the master's snitch would be expensive.

The sun had set by the time George and Isiah made it back, and the entire village was waiting for them in the middle of the road. The boys said nothing as they walked through them. The villagers parted for them, using their candles to look upon their faces as they passed them by. D'Quandray stepped down from his porch and waited for them. Horace was by his side.

D'Quandray pulled them both into his arms when they got to him. "I don't know who told it, but all the villagers know. There will be consequences."

"We didn't do this without consideration of that fact," Isiah said. "We're prepared for whatever comes our way."

He broke his embrace and moved George out to arms' length by his shoulders. "Get some rest tonight—both of you. Tomorrow is going to be a long day."

***

At dusk the next day, and after a long day of work, John Lester stood beside the blood-stained stump in the center of the redemption grounds with his bible in hand. It was on that stump that they had removed the appendages of many past violators of plantation rules. Behind him stood his eldest son, Willie Lester; he was holding an ax. At seventy-five years of age, John had grown too old to do the deed himself. On the other side of the stump were George and Isiah. It did not take long for word to get to the Lesters that Big Bartholomew had been killed and that the brothers—the orphaned sons of Elizabeth—had done it.

D'Quandray stood at the innermost layer of the circle of villagers, just outside the makeshift death clock. He scanned the faces of each one of them, and when he looked into One-hand Moses's eyes, One-hand Moses looked to the ground. And he kept his head down, and his shoulders slumped, and his mouth closed.

For all Big Bartholomew had done for them, the cost to redeem his life was going to be two severed hands, one from each of Elizabeth's sons. George and Isiah were shirtless, and they stood side by side with their chins level, and their eyes burrowing through One-hand Moses. Their broad shoulders and striated muscles were the result of superior genetics honed to their magnificent best through years of hard labor. Big Bartholomew never stood a chance.

John opened his bible and turned to face the other villagers, who had gotten accustomed to his routine long ago. He rarely came out of the big house to address them, but when he did, it was typically from the redemption grounds. He stood tall and extended his bible out to an arm's length in front of his face. "Exodus, chapter twenty-one, verses twenty-three through twenty-four, says, and I quote, 'And if any mischief follow, then thou shalt give life for life, eye for eye, tooth for tooth, hand for hand, foot for foot, burning for burning, wound for wound, stripe for stripe.'" He lowered the Bible. "I have been wounded. Big Bartholomew was my property to do with as I please." He turned to George and Isiah. "Since you are both my property, and the Bible says I must, I will take the very hands that carried out this transgression. George, lay yo' arm on that stump."

George kneeled and put his forearm on the stump, keeping his eyes locked on John Lester's face the whole time. As his chest rose and fell, he refused to show emotion. He looked at his hand, opened his fist, and lay his palm flat on the stump. Willie Lester stepped forward.

As D'Quandray looked upon them and listened to John Lester talk, his walk back from the portal flashed through his mind. Though he had been old and had suffered tremendously, he had been a whole man. "Wait!" He stepped forward with his hands out and in a halting gesture. "I can't let them boys get punished fo' what I done. I was the one what killed Big Bartholomew."

John Lester looked at One-hand Moses, then looked back at D'Quandray. "There is no way you were able to whoop Big Bartholomew. You're lying to protect those boys, stud."

"I did, too, whoop him. Ask One-hand Moses; he'll tell you how many times I done it."

John turned to One-hand Moses. "Is that true, Moses? This boy beat Big Bartholomew?"

"Three-fo' times, Mr. John," One-hand Moses admitted. "Big Bartholomew was 'fraid of him."

John Lester's eyes widened, and his mouth was wide open. He kept that same expression on his face as he turned to face D'Quandray. "All those years I could've made money off fightin' you instead of Big Bartholomew, and you just let it happen?" He turned to face One-hand Moses. "And why was I told with so much certainty that those boys were the ones who killed Big Bartholomew?" One-hand Moses said nothing. John Lester turned to face D'Quandray yet again. "And why, boy, did you kill Big Bartholomew?"

"I seed how he was lookin' at Ms. Rebecca—same way he liked to look at them young gals. He 'bout scared her half to death. She run off cryin,' and I got powerful mad 'bout it. I seed him down by the river with the boys and made them come back. I left him by the big tree. Now, only the person what done it could've knowed that."

John closed his Bible and waved Willie away from the stump. D'Quandray had said the one thing he knew the prideful plantation owner would not dare to explore deeper in front of everyone else. He stared into D'Quandray's eyes. "That's going to cost you thirty lashes." His voice trembled as he said those words. "Get up from there, George. You and your brother start studdin' tomorrow. If I can't have Big Bartholomew, I'll make ten more. Moses, bring yo' ass to the big house."

***

The next morning, before the rooster had an opportunity to crow, there was a knock on D'Quandray's cabin door. He raised up to his elbows from his stomach and made his way down the loft ladder. He winced from the sting of the sweat that entered the open wounds on his back and cursed the slaver's whip with each arduous step he took toward the door. When he opened it, he saw throngs of villagers standing in the road and a tin pail filled with apples on his porch.

Chapter 14

Sarah, Smile

When D'Quandray opened his eyes, he saw the doctor standing at the foot of his bed, studying his chart on the clipboard. He put his forearm over his eyes to shield them from the bright lights, and he winced when his hand hit the bruise on his forehead.

"You're awake," the doctor said. "How do you feel?"

He reached for the sheet, put his arms under it, and pulled it up to his neck. "I'm okay," he said through chattering teeth. "It's cold in here; can they set the temperature higher?"

"I'm afraid not. The hospital thermostat must stay at a certain setting; however, we *can* get you some blankets. Not that you'll be here much longer." He put the clipboard into the slot at the end of the bed. "Everything looks good, but we want to keep you here until about noon, just to be certain."

D'Quandray shivered beneath the sheet and started to take deep breaths. "That's fine. How long was I out?"

"You can ask your nurse when she comes in with your blankets. She'll have access to the logs. Okay?" He stood there until he got a head nod from D'Quandray. "Good. I'll be back when it's time for you to be discharged, Mr. Tyson." He smiled and left the room.

D'Quandray put his head back on the pillow and stared at the ceiling, his eyes now adjusted to the light. As he lay there, it occurred to him that he felt vastly different emotionally than he had the day before. Presently, he was a twenty-five-year-old man with all the sensibilities and life experiences of a sixty-five-year-old man who had endured the worst that life had to offer. But, in many ways, he had also experienced the best that life had to offer. He felt conflicted about the fact that he could not wait to get back to his sons, George and Isiah, who both had families of their own there. He had spent another twenty years in Jamestown, bringing his total time there to forty years, and he realized the biggest sin of slavery was not its brutality and inhumanity but the fact that its victims could adjust to it, and adjust he had.

"Good morning, Mr. Tyson," the nurse said as she walked in carrying blankets. "How are we feeling today?"

He sat up and smiled. "Good morning. I feel pretty good, thanks."

"Okay, so I looked at your chart. The night log says that you were asleep by 9 o'clock."

He looked at the clock on the wall. It was now 8 o'clock. "I need to make a call. Does that phone go out?"

"It sure does. Just press nine, then dial the number." She unfurled one of the blankets over his body and placed the other one in the chair beside his bed. "I'll be right back with your breakfast."

After the nurse walked out, he picked up the phone and called his job. He told the receptionist that he was in the hospital and would be out at least one more day. He also gave her his room number. He thanked her for her well wishes and ended the call. The nurse walked back into the room pushing his breakfast cart. He had failed to notice that she was a brunette when she had been in his room the first time. She was also pretty, but when he saw the tell-tale gleam in her eyes that said she was open to getting to know him on a more intimate level, he felt repulsed; however, years of experience in masking his true feelings had conditioned him to project outwardly the exact opposite of what he was feeling inside, so he smiled. She blushed.

"Mr. Tyson, you must have *all* the ladies going crazy."

Again, he simply smiled. And he watched with great amusement as the smile on her face transitioned to a different type without her expression changing. Her hope for a chance of anything intimate happening between them seemed to disappear.

"Well, I'll give you some privacy," she said, turning away. "Just press the button if you need me for anything."

"I will. Thanks."

He quickly devoured his breakfast, which, even after forty years of table scraps and thrown together meals, was not that good. Then, he grabbed the other blanket from the chair and added another layer of warmth to his body. It was not too long after that that he dozed off.

D'Quandray sprang to a seated position when he heard movement around him. The nurse and doctor were back. He looked at the clock. It was a few minutes before noon. He had been asleep for a little over three hours but had not gone back to Jamestown.

"We didn't mean to startle you, Mr. Tyson," the doctor said. "I apologize."

"It's okay," D'Quandray said. "Is it that time?"

"It is. Your co-worker, Maliq Godson, is waiting for you in the lobby. He's been here for about two hours."

D'Quandray smiled. Then, he rotated his feet to the floor. "Thanks. I'm sure there's some paperwork for me to sign?"

He handed D'Quandray a clipboard with his discharge papers on it and a pen attached. "There is, along with some instructions and a couple of prescriptions." He was quiet as D'Quandray read over them. "Any questions?" the doctor asked once he looked up.

"No. It seems to be pretty simple; don't hit my head again." That brought a laugh from the doctor. D'Quandray signed the papers and gave them to him.

"That's correct. I wish I could've met you under better circumstances, Mr. Tyson, but I'm glad we were able to take care of you." He handed D'Quandray his copy of the paperwork.

"Thanks, doc."

The doctor nodded and left the room. The nurse placed a bag containing the clothes D'Quandray had been wearing when he was admitted to the hospital on the foot of the bed. She also gave him a disposable toothbrush with some toothpaste and a travel-size bottle of mouthwash.

"I'll give you a few minutes to get dressed," she said, though she lingered by the door as if she expected another request from him.

"Okay," D'Quandray said in the most matter-of-fact tone he could muster.

She smiled, nodded, and walked out. D'Quandray got dressed and brushed his teeth. A few minutes later, he walked into the lobby, which he thought was quite busy for a Wednesday morning. Maliq was sitting in a far corner but stood when he saw D'Quandray walking toward him.

He extended his hand. "Greetings, Black man."

D'Quandray saw Maliq's eyes light up when he did not react negatively to his greeting. In fact, he was happy to hear it. He pushed his hand away and hugged him. A few seconds into the embrace, Maliq gently patted his upper back but did not pull away. D'Quandray was tearful when he finally broke the embrace.

Maliq nodded. "I'm parked in the visitor lot; let's go."

Maliq's midsize car was clean and equipped with all the modern amenities. The color was a sensible navy blue. They spoke very little on the ride from the hospital to D'Quandray's side of town. His mind was focused on the fact that he had not traveled through time while he was napping. He also tried to reconcile the fact that he did not know if he was happy or sad about that. As they turned onto the street that led to the northern entrance of his community, they found themselves first at the traffic light.

"Is that the bus stop you saw the lady and her child standing at?" Maliq asked as he looked at the downed sign and the tire marks that surrounded it.

"It is," he replied, refusing to look at the crime scene.

"What happened there?"

D'Quandray let out a deep sigh. "The woman and child were killed by a drunk driver." He kept his eyes forward but saw Maliq looking at him out of his peripheral vision.

The light changed, and Maliq drove forward. A short time later, they turned into D'Quandray's neighborhood. Maliq stopped at the guard shack. The attendant walked out and up to the driver side window.

"Good afternoon, sir," he said. "Who are you visiting today?"

Recognizing his voice, D'Quandray leaned over just enough for him to see his face. "He's with me, Albert. Welcome back."

Albert's eyes lit up. "Mr. D'Quandray, it's so good to see you!" His face immediately went from happiness to pain. "I lost my wife, Mr. D'Quandray. A man hit them with his car the other morning."

"I know, Albert. The other attendant told me. So sorry to hear that. If there's anything I can do for you—anything at all—don't hesitate to ask."

"Thank you, Mr. D'Quandray." He nodded. "I'll open the gate."

When the arm raised, Maliq drove his car forward. "It's not your fault, brother."

"I appreciate that, Maliq, but it is." He looked directly at his coworker. "We're all in this together; I know that now. It was exactly my job to help her, and I failed. I should've listened when you told me that."

As they continued to his house, D'Quandray was appreciative of the fact that Maliq said nothing to soften his contrite admission, allowing him to take full responsibility for his actions, or lack thereof.

Maliq kept his car running after they pulled into the driveway.

"Any word from the bosses?" D'Quandray asked.

"Yes. They had a lot to say, but I'm not their messenger. That's a control technique, often used to divide-and-conquer. If you want your marching orders, you'll have to get them directly from them."

"Thanks; I will." D'Quandray extended his hand, which Maliq accepted. "Thanks for being a good friend. I'll try to be a better one to you."

"No worries. Get you some rest, Black man. I'll see you when I see you."

D'Quandray smiled. Maliq nodded. No other words were spoken between them. He got out of the car and walked into a nearly frigid house.

"Housemate, set the air conditioner to seventy-two degrees."

A moment later, the air stopped blowing. He walked into the bathroom and turned on the shower. As he stood under the water, his thoughts were in Jamestown. The only thing that mattered to him was the community of villagers who had become his family. They were real. In whatever parallel universe or dimension, they existed, they were real; and Horace—his best friend in any life—lived there.

After showering, D'Quandray made lunch. He sat on his living room couch and turned on the television, but it was not long before he had to find another channel. The victim-blaming on the show he was watching was simply too much for him to bear. He shook his head as he searched the other channels for something more suitable to watch, disgusted with himself for ever having enjoyed or bought into the content the former was delivering to the masses. Flipping through channel after channel, he began to scoff at the lack of representation from ethnicities other than the various ones that made up the population of whites in America. Finally, he decided that he would not watch anything at all.

It occurred to him that he could research the Lester plantation online, and that a simple inquiry could give him some insight into their plight after his departure. The idea intrigued him so much that he sat up, energized by the mere thought of it. But as it registered to him that his position amongst the villagers in Jamestown had been established by the parameters of what he knew when he came to them, he decided against changing the rules. He would not do any further research, not now.

As the minutes passed by, it became harder and harder for him not to call Bradley or Elijah. They were collectively almost at the halfway point of their journeys, and he was sure that each of them had assimilated to their new worlds by now. Or had they? He thought back to how clueless he had been about everything after his first two days in Jamestown. If Bradley's pattern of days away remained consistent, he would only be where he traveled to for ten days. Based on that assumption, his youthful appearance as he walked out of his portal made sense. Making a mistake that could cost you your life in an unfamiliar environment, was not hard to do.

He picked up his phone and called Greg. They exchanged pleasantries, and his boss inquired about his well-being. He eventually told D'Quandray that he should take Thursday off as well, but he wanted him to come in for the meet-and-greet at their annual convention on Friday. They settled on a time, and they ended the phone call.

D'Quandray spent the rest of the day relaxing; he felt he had earned it. He turned his television off and raised the volume of his music to a level that all the instruments could be heard in the way that they were intended. He also snacked throughout the evening, shamelessly indulging himself in all the creature-comforts of his lavish home.

***

Jamestown, 1785

At eighty-five years of age, Sarah was given the best gift anyone in her position could ever hope for. She died from no known physical ailments. She went to sleep one night and simply refused to wake up the next morning. That was the way D'Quandray saw it. In life, she had simply been too strong willed for it to be perceived any other way. Death, as punctual, persistent, and pushy as it is, could not dictate its terms to her. She told death when she was ready, and death obeyed. He hoped that Rebecca Lester would be so bold.

Presently, D'Quandray was five years into his most recent stint in Jamestown. At seventy years old, he himself was an old man. The Lester plantation had seen better days. Many of the slavers had been called upon to fight for the United Colonies against the British invasion. As a result, inexperienced handlers were brought on to manage the plantation's enslaved people. With John Lester being an old man, and Willie Lester having been killed in the war, the system they had in place—which would have been self-perpetuating had the enslaved people chosen to cooperate—had fallen apart.

The youngest Lester, Elroy, was now the overseer of the plantation. In his zest to prove himself a worthy replacement to his father, he was as brutal to his slaves as John Lester had been on his worst days and half as kind as he had been in the opposite direction. He lacked balance, which showed up as an absence of sophistication, something that extended to his personal life. For that reason, what they produced from the plantation was often overlooked for products of lesser quality from merchants who had better reputations and more social etiquette. The once respected Lester plantation had become a joke.

Despite the vibrant colors of the leaves, the dark skies and heavy rain combined to turn the autumn day gray. The villagers grieved as Ms. Sarah's body was interred into its final resting place, sans a coffin. A long-discarded gown from a bygone era was the only barrier between her body and the soil that surrounded it. Her inability to bear children had simultaneously been her personal curse and a gift to the rest of the villagers, so the memories of those in attendance would be the only evidence that their matriarch had ever existed at all.

Until that day, D'Quandray had never seen Horace shed tears. Even through the rain, he could see them. And as he looked upon his face, he, too, felt the gravity of the loss. Ms. Sarah had given them all of herself for her entire life, selflessly guiding a village of enslaved people through rough waters with no promise of ever seeing land. So, as D'Quandray stood there wallowing in his pain, he knew that Horace—as intelligent as he was—cried for them, and, somewhere in his heart, rejoiced because Ms. Sarah was free.

Like soldiers given the command of about face by the strictest drill sergeant, they all turned away when the gravedigger shoveled the first bit of dirt onto her body. A day of mourning had begun, and, despite Elroy Lester's orders to the contrary, there would be no work done that day.

Three years later, at ninety-one years of age, John Lester also died.

Chapter 15

A Last Gasp

Two more nights. That was what D'Quandray thought to himself as he lay still and listened to the song that he had loathed only days ago. Now? Not so much. It was already on its second play and was about to end and repeat again when he sat up and placed his feet on the floor. The music stopped, the lights came on, and the ambient noises of his home replaced the music. He marveled at all the sounds he had failed to notice in the past. Only now did he realize that light bulbs buzzed when they were turned on, and he could hear the hum of his refrigerator from his bedroom. As his air conditioner roared to life, he thought that maybe those sounds had been drowned out by it all that time. But the truth was he had just never noticed them, a fact that he accepted with scornful self-reflection. That criticism, ironically, was not too different in sentiment than the first words Ms. Sarah had spoken to him inside the church during his first moments in Jamestown. In life, he had been too busy listening to everyone else around him instead of seeing and hearing everything around him, and it had been his lack of awareness that had robbed Joseph Freeman of his life.

D'Quandray appreciated his fluidity of movement, which was vastly different from the motor functions of the seventy-five-year-old he had become in Jamestown; he had only spent ten years there this time. There he was already twenty-five years older than his real-life parents and the same age as his maternal grandmother, his only living grandparent. As he moved, he could feel the resilience in his muscles. What he did not feel was the taxing pain associated with every little movement he made, movements he did not have to think about in this life, unlike in Virginia.

While in Jamestown, he had been lucky to get a bath biweekly, and every bath he got had been attached to the trauma of having to pleasure Rebecca Lester immediately afterward. Clean on the outside, dirty on the inside. Defiled. So, his morning showers were something he looked forward to with great anticipation each day he awoke at home. Two more days.

D'Quandray positioned the shower knob to its hottest setting and let the water run while he brushed his teeth. When the bathroom mirror was completely covered by steam, he got in. As he stood beneath the water, he thought that he would never complain about it being too hot again. He stayed there for twenty minutes.

After breakfast, he watched a cult classic science fiction movie—*Rod Apocalypse and The Galactic Trackers*. He needed to detach himself from reality, and the adventures of a space, bounty hunter, who possessed special abilities, was the perfect thing to entertain him. It was his favorite movie franchise, as well as Bradley's, and he could think of no better way to pass three hours. The two of them had bonded over conversations about the comic books featuring the cosmic swashbuckler when they were teenagers. Their friendship, and their passion for the stories they read, grew from there.

The movie served its purpose. When it was over, he picked up his phone. There were two new notifications—an email and a text message. The former was from the *USA National Team* coordinator, and the latter was from Marissa. He opened and read Marissa's text message first, and in it she mentioned that she had observed a change in Elijah's behavior. Three thoughts immediately entered his mind, the first being that his friend must have experienced something significant for a change in him to be observable so quickly. The second thing he thought was that Marissa must have spent a great deal of time with him to have noticed that. The third was that the change was so dramatic that she felt the need to reach out to at least one of his friends about it. Curious.

The email from the *USA National Team* coordinator included an itinerary and highlighted some media commitments that were intended to increase the profile of the team. The roster was sure to consist of a who's who of American basketball players, and he looked forward to reuniting with some of them and meeting the others. He especially looked forward to reuniting with his former coach. The email required no response.

D'Quandray video called Marissa.

"Hi, D'Quandray. I'm concerned about him," she said as soon as her face appeared on the screen.

"Why? What's wrong?"

"He hasn't eaten anything, and he's been locked in his bedroom all day. He's barely said two words to me."

So, she's at his house. "How long has this been going on?"

"Just today. He was fine yesterday. In fact, he was in a pretty good mood."

D'Quandray narrowed his eyes. *She spent the night with him.* "Did he sleep okay?"

"Like a rock. He didn't move a muscle all night."

"Listen, Marissa, this may be hard for you to hear, and—at the risk of sounding insensitive—he's going to have to deal with it. We're over halfway through this thing, and we couldn't stop it now if we tried. Do I have to remind you of what I just went through?"

Her shoulders slumped, and she shook her head. "No, you don't. I guess I just wanted someone to know what was happening. Sorry to bother you."

"It'll be over soon. Try to make him eat something. Other than that, there's really nothing that can be done. He's gotta ride it out."

She looked down briefly, then leveled her chin. "I understand. Thanks for listening. I'll talk to you on Saturday. Goodbye."

As curt as it was, D'Quandray felt Marissa's adieu was appropriate, and he attributed no ill-intent to it. She was emotional, but Elijah's reaction to his time away, though interesting, was not surprising. He looked forward to hearing exactly what triggered that response. On the other hand, it was becoming increasingly apparent that Bradley's death was going to come as a surprise, all things considered. They would all have stories to tell.

D'Quandray started to feel sleepy, and though he was no longer fearful of napping, he did not want to chance doing anything that would interfere with his sleep later. He decided to go for a drive to help stave off the impending slumber. As he pulled out of his garage, he opted for the south gate of his community. As he approached Deidre's residence, he saw her standing in her driveway. When he pulled over and lowered his passenger side window, she walked toward his car.

"How are you feeling?" she asked as she placed her forearms on his door and leaned inside his car.

"A little battered and bruised, but I'm okay." He smiled as she focused on the lump on his forehead. "I want to thank you for calling the ambulance for me. It's a good thing you were out here."

"Don't mention it; it was the neighborly thing to do. Besides, you would have done the same thing for me."

"I sure would have."

She narrowed her eyes, still focusing on the lump. "That street got you pretty good. You 'bout scared the life out of me when it happened."

"Scared *you*?" He laughed. "Try waking up in an ambulance to some strange guy breathing hot coffee breath in your face. I didn't know *what* to think."

"I imagine that would do it," she said with a smile. "I'm not going to hold you, sweetie. It's good to see you back and in good spirits."

"Thank you." He waved goodbye to her as she stepped back and onto the curb. Then he powered his window up and drove away.

It was late afternoon, and he was hungry again. His favorite restaurant was in the closest shopping center to his community, so he decided he would go there and have a meal.

As he pulled into the parking lot of *The Ultimate American Grill*, he was delighted to see that it was only half full. He found a parking spot close to the entrance and waited for the song that was playing on the radio to end. He also took that time to mentally prepare himself for the fact that he would be pelted with salutations of "the Stud" when he walked in, like all the other times it had happened when he entered the restaurant in the past. Maliq had once told him that that was the most disrespectful thing he could be called, he remembered. "Truer words have never been spoken," he said as he thought aloud and shook his head.

The song ended and he turned the car off. Then, he walked into the restaurant. "The Stud," a blond-haired, blue-eyed man, who looked to be about fifty years old, said, much to the embarrassment of his mulatto daughter, who—D'Quandray noticed—looked away and shook her head. Her mother—his wife—smiled and nodded. D'Quandray forced a smile and nodded as he walked by them.

"I can't believe we just saw the Stud," he heard the woman whisper. "He's so tall."

D'Quandray stopped, closed his eyes, and exhaled through his nose. Then, he opened them and continued to walk. He found a small table that was only big enough for two people. After he sat, he opened the menu and held it in front of his face, a tactic he used to avoid making eye contact with other customers. He already knew exactly what he was going to order.

"Good afternoon, sir," a soft voice said. "May I interest you in our special?"

D'Quandray smiled and looked up into the eyes of a waitress he had never seen before. "Hello, I would like…"

"Oh my God, The Stud! I can't believe it." Her eyes lit up, and she shook her hands as if she were trying to dry her fingernails after a manicure.

D'Quandray placed his menu on the table and leaned back in his chair, his face a picture of nothingness as he waited for her histrionics to cease. "Are you done?" His words sounded colder than he had intended, but as the joy left her face, he took solace in the fact that his penalty was not equal to her infraction and felt no remorse. "My name is Mr. Tyson, and I'll have a cheeseburger—cooked medium rare, an order of fries, and a diet cola." He handed her the menu, smiled, and looked at her name tag. "Thank you, Chloe."

"You're welcome," she said without an apology. "I'll be right back with your order."

As she walked away, he folded his arms across his chest and began to scan the restaurant, no longer having the menu to shield him from the gawking eyes of onlookers. What he noticed right away was that most of the customers were white. Looking at the restaurant staff, he noticed that the people bussing the tables were either Black or Hispanic. Everyone who was in position to interact with the customers was white, including Chloe. He shook his head, disgusted with the fact that he had never noticed that before.

This was only a local restaurant, not a place of worship, not a *Fortune 500* company, and not a business that would cause a ripple in history if, at that moment, it ceased to exist, yet interwoven into its hiring practices was the very pathology about which Maliq had spoken so adamantly. Not even on a restaurant staff did a true meritocracy exist. Nor did it exist in sports, where he had gained his fame and notoriety, and where coach's sons often held positions that should be occupied by more talented athletes. He had simply been too good to keep off the court, just like Grayson Randolph; however, when D'Quandray's left knee was done, so was he. He was lucky to have parents who had been smart enough to invest in the insurance policy that now afforded him the life he lived. He knew now just how fortunate he was.

When the waitress returned with his food, he saw the same smile on her face that he had seen on the nurse's face the day before, after she realized that there would be no love connection between the two of them. That type of smile was so easily detectable now, and he wondered how many times he had mistaken it for something innocent in the past. Underneath the trojan horse of pleasantry was a furious assassin, dying to break through and unleash its wrath, yet held in check by capitalism.

D'Quandray thanked her, and she nodded to acknowledge it and walked to another table. He took his time eating his meal, which he enjoyed immensely. Then, he left the restaurant after leaving exactly fifteen percent of the cost of his meal on the table for the waitress, significantly less than the fifty percent he typically left behind.

He drove home through rush hour traffic, looking at familiar surroundings with alien eyes. In many ways, he was now collecting data at home in a manner not unlike the way he had collected it in Jamestown during his first few days there. Ironic. It took him over seventy-five years of living in another place and time to realize that he had wasted twenty-five at home.

When he got to his house, he took a sleep aid and got dressed in his pajamas. After watching a few mindless, non-political shows on his television, he went to bed. Not long after, he was asleep.

Jamestown, 1800

It was not often that D'Quandray found himself inside the big house, but this time he had been summoned by the overseer himself, Elroy Lester. The head house servant escorted him up to the second floor and told him to wait outside of Rebecca's room. She wanted to see him one last time. The door opened and the preacher man walked out, casting a look toward him that would have struck him dead right then and there if it had fulfilled its promise. D'Quandray mirrored the expression until the Bible-carrying thug looked away with a huff.

Then, Elroy Lester walked out of the room with the doctor in tow. The look in the plantation master's eyes was that of a man who had come face-to-face with the inevitable and submitted to its will. "You can go on in and say goodbye. We'll give you a few minutes."

D'Quandray nodded and walked into the room. As the door closed behind him, he found himself in a familiar position—alone with Rebecca. The difference was that this time they were not meeting in secret. In fact, it had been over fifteen years since they had had sex. Her desires had long ago shifted from those of a carnal nature to soft kisses and warm embraces, accented with coerced proclamations of love from the subjugated object of her desires.

Rebecca was barely conscious as she lay there. Her once jet-black hair, now filled with streaks of gray, was splayed out over the white pillow on which her head rested. The softness that used to be evident in her face had all but disappeared. Her cheekbones were sharp, her pink lips were cracked, and the tissue around her bulging eyes was recessed. The covers were pulled to her neckline, and her skinny, pale arms were on top with her hands resting on one another near her waistline. For a moment, she opened her eyes wide—as if she could sense his presence in the room, and then she slowly closed them.

"Come here," she whispered. The illness that ravaged her body had bifurcated her voice into a raspy mess and the softness he was accustomed to hearing from her.

D'Quandray said nothing but walked slowly toward the bed. He leaned close to her, placed a hand over hers, and gently pressed his lips to her ear. He could smell the rose scented soap they had used to clean her, and he felt her cold hands as they started to shake beneath his.

Her breaths came quicker and got shallower. He could feel her fighting to stay alive, but he could sense that she did not have long to live. Emotions began to take over his body, so he responded to them, and to her, in a way that he felt would give him the most closure.

"Die, you nasty bitch," he hissed through clenched teeth.

She gasped, her body seized, and she opened her eyes all at once. A moment later, her hands stopped moving and her body relaxed completely, expelling her last breath as it did. D'Quandray smiled as her eyes closed for good, then watched her chest to make sure she was not still breathing. He spent the next minute manufacturing tears, and when he had harvested enough, he opened the door and walked out into the hallway.

"Oh Lawd, she done gone on t'glory. What is I's gon' do?" He went down to both knees, looked to the floor, and wrapped his arms around himself as the doctor and Elroy looked on.

"She loved herself some you," Elroy said as he put a hand on his shoulder. "I'll make sure you ain't stressed out too much; that's the best I can do. She would've wanted that." He and the doctor walked back into the room.

When the door closed behind them, D'Quandray hoisted himself up to his feet and smiled, much to the displeasure of the house servant who had watched the entire thing unfold. He leveled his chin, rolled his shoulders back, stuck out his chest, and walked out of the big house for the last time.

***

In the wake of Rebecca Lester's death, a Sunday meeting was called by George's eldest son, Charles. He requested that all the adults in the village be present except for three: One-hand Moses and the young women who were tasked with the duty of keeping him occupied. The village children were being watched by the teenagers. D'Quandray and Horace, now both village elders, sat together in the pulpit of the church as Charles addressed the men who kneeled in front of him. The Lester plantation, in their eyes, had become susceptible to an uprising.

Charles warned that it would require meticulous planning, and would possibly take years to accomplish, but a revolt was necessary. Neither D'Quandray nor Horace disagreed.

As he watched his grandson command the room, a warm feeling came over his body. He looked at Horace, who smiled and nodded back at him. Again, déjà vu. This time, however, D'Quandray controlled his own expression, realizing now that the feeling had been triggered by Horace's smile—the expression that seemed to separate itself from the rest of his bearded face more and more each time he made it. But, again, it was fleeting.

D'Quandray's arrival in Jamestown back in 1740 signified a time of change on the Lester plantation. Though it had been slow, it was steady, and it had begun the exact moment he had awakened in the same church they were in today. The children were no longer allowed in the meetings. They were too easily conned by the slavers into divulging the villagers' secrets. A slice of cake or the promise of a night of warmth inside the big house were simply too much for them to resist.

The tactic of disguising their meetings with singing, stomping, and clapping had also proven to be ineffective, as it had become as much a distraction to the villagers as it had been subterfuge for them. So, they posted two gossiping women outside the entrance of the church to keep watch instead. That worked. Not since that day had they been intruded upon unexpectedly by unwanted guests, though many attempts were made. Another safety measure they implemented was strategically allowing One-hand Moses to overhear incorrect information from time to time, a tactic that never failed to bear fruit.

They agreed that moving forward their suits of armor would be silence, obedience, and feigned ignorance. The more docile, controllable, and dumb the slaves appeared to be, the more comfortable the slave masters would become. The slavers' insistence that their slaves had to learn and obey Christianity was the one thing that allowed the villagers to congregate for more than a few minutes, so they took full advantage of the opportunities they were given—in the name of the Lord.

Chapter 16

A Familiar Face

D'Quandray was beginning to love the wake-up song that blared through his surround-sound speakers each morning. He smiled as he basked in the comfort of his king-sized bed, even singing along with the chorus as it played. He had survived yet another ten long years in Jamestown, and he was certain that he had fewer than fifteen years remaining there. The level to which Maliq had been correct about the ugliness of slavery could not be overstated. D'Quandray knew now that it would take centuries to undo the trauma caused by the devastation it unleashed upon the collective psyche of Black people, and it all stemmed from that time. He wondered how he could have been so naive about that; the signs had been all around him for twenty-five long years.

After listening to the song three times, he sat on the edge of his bed. When his feet hit the floor, his bedroom lights turned on and the music stopped. Unlike all his other post time travel mornings, he had to get ready for work. Waiting for him there was the meet-and-greet that Greg had asked him to attend, and he was not looking forward to it. Another song and dance routine for another set of unworthy suits; that's how he viewed it.

He decided he would not be late getting to work this time. Life had taught him that the more activity you filled a day with, the more quickly the hours seemed to pass. He wanted his day to be over as soon as possible. His last years of life in Jamestown were ahead of him, and he looked forward to dying.

After an expedited morning routine, and after a brief but cordial conversation with Albert at the guard shack, D'Quandray drove onto the main road. Instead of averting his eyes, he studied the aftermath of the tragedy that had occurred at the bus stop as he drove by it. The yet to be replaced sign was still bent parallel to the ground and the tire marks on each side of it were still dark. What had once tormented him was now a reminder of who he used to be, and the fact that he *used to* be that person was now a source of pride. Understanding. Growth. Empathy.

D'Quandray arrived at work to find a nearly empty parking lot. He parked, went into the building, and walked straight to the office. Once inside, he logged onto his computer and checked his emails. He had gone through nearly a hundred of them when Maliq walked into the office.

"Greetings, Black man."

He looked up from his computer and smiled. "Good morning, Maliq."

Maliq stopped where he stood. "Good morning." He nodded as if he were a math teacher looking at a prized pupil who had just solved an unsolvable equation. "Good morning," he repeated. Only this time his tone was slightly different. It was lighter and almost sounded appreciative. "Welcome back."

D'Quandray stood, walked over to him, and shook his hand. "It's good to be back, all the way back."

Maliq kept his gaze as he shook his hand. "I believe you."

As D'Quandray walked back to his desk, he felt that what had just occurred was a transcendent moment. Maliq had no way of knowing what he was going through. But Maliq had a profound understanding of pain. Maliq understood men. And Maliq understood that D'Quandray was a changed man. He felt it.

"Tell me something, Maliq. Is Godson your birth name, or did you change it to that?"

"It's the name I've always had." He sat at his desk and turned his computer on. His behavior was that of a man who had always expected that very question and was neither offended nor surprised by being asked it.

D'Quandray shook his head, amazed by what the universe had done. "God's son indeed. You're an amazing man, Maliq. I appreciate you."

Maliq looked at him and smiled. "You must've hit your head pretty hard."

"Just hard enough," he replied.

They both looked up when they heard the office door split from the jamb. Greg and Victor walked in together.

"Stud! Welcome back," Victor said. "I heard you took a nasty spill. How are you feeling?"

D'Quandray felt his face contort into something that he did not want to show his bosses. Although he could not convert it into a smile, he forced it into what he felt was something neutral. "I'm good. I feel a little banged up still, but I'm alright." He nodded to his GM. "Greg."

"What's wrong?" Greg asked.

"What do you mean?"

"Well, I don't know." He narrowed his gaze. "You seem *different*. I can't put my finger on it, though. Are you up for the meet-and-greet? Our shuttle should be here a little before lunch."

D'Quandray shrugged. "That's why I'm here, right?"

"Yeah, that's exactly right." As Greg nodded his head, he appeared to be holding onto the notion that D'Quandray was not himself.

For his part, D'Quandray was not interested in satisfying Greg's curiosity. His only obligation to the company was what they were paying him to do, nothing more.

As Greg and Victor disappeared into their respective offices, Maliq swiveled his chair around to face D'Quandray. "If you keep that up, they're going to think I'm recruiting you."

"Let them. I should've been on your team a long time ago."

***

At noon, D'Quandray, Greg, Victor, and Maliq walked into the *Downtown Ballroom* for the meet-and-greet that preceded the seminar. In attendance were potential clients from all over the world.

Maliq was scheduled to give the company's presentation an hour after the pleasantries were exchanged. His tailored, navy-blue suit, crisp white shirt, and neat bowtie were accented perfectly by his whiskey-colored wingtip shoes, signifying that he was prepared to present their company in the best possible light. D'Quandray's purpose for being there was to bring clients under the tent, and Maliq's job was to sell them on *Turbo Boost Sports Agency* at the end. Greg and Victor would work on the details in between.

This appearance was D'Quandray's third. He remembered the first as a pleasurable experience. Of all the important people who had been in the room that day, it was he who had attracted the most attention. Several important contacts had been made by the end of the event, and they had acquired a few lucrative contracts as a result. The second time was one he had looked forward to because of his experience at the first, but by the time that one was over, the novelty of the event had worn off. He lost count of the number of pictures he had taken and the number of smiles he had forced. This year's event was not one he looked forward to at all, especially given what he had endured all week.

They positioned themselves in the center of the main ballroom floor. Slowly, the room began to fill, and it did not take long for it to reach its five-hundred-person capacity. For a solid hour, D'Quandray shook hands, posed for pictures, and smiled, which was particularly hard for him given his newfound understanding of the meaning and significance of the word stud.

At precisely 2 o'clock p.m., the event coordinator announced through the ballroom speakers that the seminar was going to start in fifteen minutes. Maliq had already left to prepare for his presentation a half hour earlier. When they walked into the auditorium, they quickly found their assigned seats. D'Quandray's was between Victor's and Greg's. The auditorium quickly filled, and Maliq started his presentation shortly thereafter.

Victor leaned close to D'Quandray, and, as he did, Greg did the same from the other side. D'Quandray turned his head slightly so that he could focus on his CEO's lips as he spoke.

"We can't afford to lose him," Victor said about Maliq, who had already taken command of the room.

"Then why don't you pay him like it?" D'Quandray asked the question before he had a chance to assess the potential repercussions of doing so. Victor recoiled slightly and D'Quandray could feel Greg leaning closer from the other side. But instead of retracting his question, he decided to double down on the sentiment. "It makes no sense for someone who means as much to *Turbo* as Maliq does to be treated the way he's been treated."

"That's not fair, D'Quandray," Greg said, coming to the defense of his boss.

D'Quandray snapped his face toward him. "It's not? Tell me how it is fair, Greg. He does the best work, has the most time on the job of anyone in our department, and is the lowest paid. Hell, Jason isn't even here, and he gets paid more than *both* of us."

"Where is all this coming from?" Greg asked. "Victor was just saying..."

"I know what Victor was *just* saying; he's sitting right beside me. I heard him loud and clear."

"Clearly there's something bubbling underneath the surface here," Victor said. "Why don't we table this discussion for later?"

D'Quandray looked forward and onto the stage at Maliq. "I think that's a very good idea."

***

D'Quandray had done his fair share of smiling and glad-handing at the convention, so he intentionally stored his gregarious personality away for the next time it would be required. As a result, the shuttle ride back to the office was a quiet one. Victor's face was beet red as he sat behind the driver, and he kept his arms folded across his chest the entire way. Greg spent much of the ride staring at the CEO as if he could put him in a better mood by doing so. D'Quandray split his attention between the scenery outside the shuttle van and the occupants inside it. As the tension grew, he was fully aware that he was the source of it.

They walked into the office to find Jason leaned back in his chair with his feet crossed on his desk. He was asleep.

"For God's sake, could you at least act like you're working?" Victor said. A vein appeared in the center of his forehead as wide and long as a finger.

Jason sat up, knocking several folders filled with paper onto the floor as he did. "I'm sorry, Mr. Wainwright, I wasn't expecting you all to be back so soon." He gathered the papers from the floor, placed them on his desk, and stood up. "How'd it go?"

"If you're that concerned about it, you should've been there," Victor said on the way to his office.

"What's wrong with him?" Jason asked after Victor slammed his door shut.

"For crying out loud, Jason, you're on company time," Greg said. "You can't let the CEO walk in and see you with your feet propped up on your desk."

"Greg, I do that all the time. You've never said anything about it before."

Greg's eyes widened. Then, he briefly looked at Maliq, who folded his arms across his chest as he stared back at him. Greg looked back at Jason, shook his head, and walked into his office.

Jason turned to Maliq and D'Quandray with his eyes wide, eyebrows raised, and the palms of his hands facing upward at shoulder level. "Am I wrong?"

"That's not for me to say," Maliq said. "I'm not your boss."

***

When D'Quandray got home from work, his attention was divided. As much as he wanted to focus on what was to come in Jamestown, the events of the day kept tugging away at his mind. If his years in slavery had taught him anything it was that there would be consequences for what had occurred earlier. Victor and Greg had been caught off-guard by his behavior, embarrassed even; and he could tell they were not happy. He knew that once they had time to assess what happened, they would formulate a plan and respond. Too many times in Jamestown, he had seen the same looks on the faces of the plantation-hands that he saw on the faces of Victor and Greg. There was going to be a punitive measure exacted upon him. Unlike the slavers, however, subtlety was required with them. They would need to disguise it as something else and mask what motivated them. Their displeasure had already shown itself when they lashed out at Jason for doing something they had overlooked many times in the past.

His phone rang. It was a call from Bradley.

"What's up, BG?" he said as he accepted the call and his friend's face appeared on the screen of his smartphone.

"I'm scared, man."

D'Quandray furrowed his brow. "Scared of what?"

"I'm scared of being murdered. I've been away for eight days over four nights. If that holds up, I only have two days left to live there, which means I'm not dying of old age."

As D'Quandray looked at him, he found it hard to come up with words of comfort. Bradley was right, he was likely going to be murdered. But D'Quandray felt no sympathy for him. There was a good chance that that would also be his own fate, except his end would be the period to a life sentence of pain; therefore, his perspective on it was different. In addition to that, it was on Bradley's insistence that they all partook in the adventure in the first place. His trauma would be his to bear alone.

"I don't know what to tell you, BG, except I hope it's quick."

There was silence as they stared at one another—the same expressions, born of completely different emotions. The chasm between helplessness and indifference was never as wide as it was in that moment. And as he looked at his friend, D'Quandray realized how devastating it was for Bradley to endure for one minute what he, and all the people who had experienced the hell of slavery, had endured for a lifetime. Indifferent was absolutely an appropriate description of how he felt. Helplessness either built character or revealed it, and Bradley was receiving a healthy dose.

"You've changed, D'Quandray."

"That was the whole point of us doing this, was it not?"

"Yeah, I guess it was. You're right. We'll all have to face something traumatic tonight; I'll deal with it. It was selfish of me to forget that you're going through something yourself. I'll see you tomorrow."

D'Quandray nodded. "I'll see you tomorrow, BG."

When they ended their call, D'Quandray took a moment to reflect. Bradley was right; he had changed. How could gaining the life experiences of an eighty-five-year-old man not change a person? When you add the fact that he had been enslaved for sixty of those years, change was inevitable. It had shown him the height of love and the depths of hate, both in their purest forms. For that, he was thankful. The life perspective he gained from that was invaluable.

"You're goddamn right I've changed," he said as he walked to his kitchen to prepare dinner.

An hour later, he was enjoying a meal consisting of a pan seared rib-eye steak, cooked medium rare, with green beans, and a sweet potato, topped with brown sugar and butter. He ate slowly and savored each succulent bite. When he was done, he cleaned his dishes, then showered and went to bed. Twenty minutes later, he was asleep.

Chapter 17

The Uprising

Jamestown, 1810

Under a full moon, two old friends stood shoulder to shoulder on Horace's porch. It took ten long years of secret planning, but the time had come. They were on the eve of an uprising, and the slavers who ran the Lester plantation could not be more unprepared for what was about to happen. The villagers' obedience through the years had lulled Elroy Lester into a false sense of security. As a result, he had reduced his staff of handlers by half, convinced that his slaves were too docile to cause any trouble. He thought they had been broken. The move had also been made to offset the losses he had incurred because of his diminished social standing among the rest of the plantation owners.

Every aspect of Elroy Lester's plantation had suffered a loss in quality, except the big house, which was well maintained and had been run with peak efficiency throughout. His unwillingness to sacrifice his own comfort for the good of the plantation was about to come home to roost.

"We did it right, you and I," Horace said as he looked up at the moon, squinting his eyes.

"We did, didn't we?" D'Quandray replied. "There's going to be a lot of bloodshed these next few days." Out of the corner of his eye, he saw Horace look his way. "But dying is better than being a slave." He looked at his friend just in time to see that familiar smile fade from his face, and, again, it triggered the exact same feeling it had the last few times he had seen it. D'Quandray thought that somewhere under that thick, scruffy beard was possibly a handsome man. He imagined that he himself looked just as haggard, that all the years of slavery had been just as harsh to him as they had been to Horace.

"I don't smile much these days," Horace said. "The last few times I felt a want to do that have been in your presence. For that, I thank you. You're a good man, Sir."

"And you're a good man, Horace. If I had some of that whiskey from the big house, I'd drink a glass with you." He smiled. "And maybe have a cigar, too."

"That would be nice," Horace said.

Like a fog rolling over the sea, a horde of adult, male villagers came walking down the center of the road. Charles, D'Quandray's grandson, was leading the way. Now in his fifties, he had grandchildren of his own. His father, George, who had once escaped the wrath of John Lester, had been—along with his brother, Isaiah—among the first casualties of Elroy's tenure as plantation overseer. He stopped at Horace's cabin.

"Grandfather. Mr. Horace," he said, acknowledging them both as he approached. "Are you sure you want to stay?"

"We've lived long lives," Horace said. "We'd do nothing but slow you down. We're alright with what's going to happen to us. Don't you worry."

When Charles looked away from Horace and at him, D'Quandray flashed him a reassuring smile, and with that, his grandson continued to the other end of the village. They stopped at One-arm Moses's cabin, dragged him into the middle of the road, and promptly beat him to death. It had begun. After that, they gathered all the women and children in the village and led them to the river. The freedom-seeking escapees would use it as a guide as they traveled north throughout the night. While the able-bodied men chose to stay and fight, they allowed five young men to go with the women and children for protection.

***

D'Quandray had already been in his loft—for what he thought would possibly be his last night of sleep in Jamestown—for hours, and when he woke, he could smell wood burning. It was just before dawn. It was only after he heard a gunshot that he felt compelled to get up. He moved to the door as fast as he could, and when he got outside, he saw that Horace was already on his porch. He walked across the road and joined him there. In the middle of the night, while everyone in the big house was sound asleep, Charles and his men had gone across the pasture with torches in hand. By the time D'Quandray and Horace looked at it, the house was already engulfed in flames.

Down the road came a wagon drawn by two horses. Its coachman was one of the field hands who had ridden in the back of it every morning of his working life. He stopped the wagon in the middle of the road, a rifle across his lap.

"You ol' mens get on in here," he said. "We's 'bout to be free."

D'Quandray shook his head. As he looked at him, he knew the young man was not going to get the type of freedom he sought. Earthly freedom was not his to gain, but eternal freedom was at his doorstep and waiting to be let in. "Mr. Horace and I are staying. We're going to die here. You go on without us. Save anybody who wants to go. Save yourself if you can, but we're not going."

"They gon' whoop you 'til you tell."

"And they'll do so in vain," Horace said. "We know exactly what we're up against, and we're prepared for it. We've been preparing for it for ten years now. Besides, I can barely make out your face from here. There's no way these bad, old eyes will get me through unfamiliar land."

"Alright," he said as he gathered the reins of the horses. "We's comin' back fo' ya. If you still alive, we gon' get ya."

"We won't be," D'Quandray said with a smile. "Once you get away from here, just head north and keep going. Just keep going."

The young man tipped his hat, and then he snapped the reins. "Ya!" With that, he was gone.

In the distance, the gunshots, screams, and neighing horses combined to create an eerie soundtrack to the surreal picture created by the combination of a smoky landscape and a predawn sky. Charles and his men had succeeded in phase one of their plan. D'Quandray wondered how many, if any, inside the big house had survived. Not long after that, a single rider came down the center of the road with his horse at a full gallop. He was raised up off his saddle with the reins in one hand and a rifle in the other. Extending backward from the saddle was a taut rope. Tied to it by the ankles was the body of Elroy Lester. He was naked, bloodied, bruised, and he was dead.

***

It was almost noon before word of the uprising reached the other plantations. It did not take long for a heavily armed mob of angry, white men to arrive at the Lester plantation seeking answers, seeking retribution. As he listened to the horses stir on the road outside, D'Quandray knew the hour of reckoning had come. Cabin by cabin, they kicked in doors as they searched for those who were responsible. So, he stood underneath his loft bed with his back against the wall, waiting. His door splintered inward, causing D'Quandray to flinch. His heart raced as he looked into the rage-filled eyes of three men he had never seen before.

"Get yo' old ass out here, nigger!" the one in front wearing an eyepatch said. He was a tall man, and his frame was densely packed with hard muscle.

D'Quandray moved toward the door as quickly as he could, but that was not quick enough. The man met him halfway, grabbed a fist full of his shirt, and dragged him the rest of the way out of his cabin. Once they were outside, he heaved D'Quandray into the middle of the road. He landed on his stomach and was almost face to face with Horace, whose thick beard was already soaked with blood.

"Man is to be free." Horace forced the words out of his mouth through a pained expression.

Though incomplete, D'Quandray thought the sentence poetic, yet it spoke to just how much pain his friend was feeling. Horace had been the most articulate man he had known in any life. So, whether he was trying to say "man is going to be free" or "man is meant to be free" did not matter. He managed to get the important words out. "Man is to be free" was the most beautiful thing he had ever heard. Before he could respond to his friend, a man kicked D'Quandray in his mouth. He felt his remaining teeth break and his mouth fill with blood. Instinctively, he spat them out, and the pain was already worse than anything he had ever felt.

The mob's continued search of the villagers' cabins produced the same result. The only slaves they found were men who were far too old to fight. In all there were ten—ten men who knew they would not live past that day. When they pulled the last of them out of his cabin, they brought him up to the others. The man wearing the eye patch—the same man who had kicked D'Quandray's door open, tossed him into the middle of the road, and kicked his teeth out—held the old man by his upper arm and placed the muzzle of his rifle under his chin.

"You niggers get yo' eyes up here!" He scanned the faces of the men who lay on the ground before turning his attention back to the one he was holding. "They call me the slave breaker. You ain't never seen a slaver worse than me in yo' nigger lives." He looked the old man standing beside him in his eyes. "I'm 'o give you one chance to save yo' worthless soul, boy. Who is responsible fo' this?"

"I swear I don't know..."

Bang!

Red mist filled the air as his brains left the back of his head and the single shot echoed through the village. His body crumpled to the ground in a heap.

"That ain't the way we do thangs here," one of the Lester plantation-hands protested. "Anybody dies here, they do it at the redemption grounds."

"If we did thangs y'all's way, these niggers would be runnin' free like the animals they is. They know I mean business now." He turned to the mob of men who were with him. "Get 'em up. Take their asses 'way from here and make 'em talk. They'll be lucky if they make it to those goddamn redemption grounds. Move!"

***

An hour later, D'Quandray, tied to a tree, had been whipped mercilessly. He was already six lashes into his beating, and the slave breaker had yet to question him. Every time he thought his body had reached the threshold of its pain tolerance the limit was increased. He wanted to pass out. He wanted to die. The slave breaker simply would not allow him to do either. After ten painful lashes, the whip-wielding slaver walked up to the tree.

"Tell me who done it and where they is, boy."

D'Quandray closed his eyes and whispered, "I don't know," so he would not agitate his aching mouth.

The slave breaker walked away. "Yo' ass is lyin,' nigger."

The sound of his voice told D'Quandray that he was back in position to deliver more lashes. He braced himself, and the beating continued. The slaver maliciously put enough time between each strike for the last one to sting as long as it possibly could before he delivered the next one. It was apparent that this slaver was no stranger to torturing men, and he was as vicious with his words as he was with his whip.

After another ten lashes, he approached again. As he demanded to be told the whereabouts of the architects of the uprising, D'Quandray entertained the thought of spitting in his face. He refrained. He knew that a man so composed and eager to abuse would welcome an excuse to be more violent. The slave breaker would never offer him an easy way out, and death would have been just that.

"You's a tough som'bitch, I'll give you that. But niggers don't break me; I break niggers." He got back into position. "I'll see if you feel like talkin' after ten mo."

D'Quandray winced. Hearing the number of lashes he was about to receive was almost as painful as feeling one of them. After the first two, another slaver arrived on horseback.

"He ain't talked yet?"

"Nope. He's a tough one."

"In that case, the Lester hand wants you to brang him to them redemption grounds up yonder," the man said.

"I'll brang 'im right after I give his ass these other eight."

"Don't take too long." He turned his horse in the other direction. "And he also wants you to shave his head and face befo' you get there."

"I got it—shave the nigger." He waited for the horseman to be gone before addressing D'Quandray again. "I must admit, I ain't never had to whoop nobody this long. I almost believe you don't know nothin." He cracked the whip on D'Quandray's back again. "Almost."

D'Quandray's body went limp as the contents of his bladder were released. When he felt endorphins all through his body and euphoria start to set in, he knew he was close to death. Just before he lost consciousness, the slaver's whip overrode his pain inhibitors once more. He wailed as he opened his eyes. His body began to tremble, the pain no longer bearable.

***

D'Quandray was the eighth man to be brought to the redemption grounds. As they tied him to one of the twelve posts in the death clock, he scanned the faces of the doomed men who were already there, searching for Horace. They were all naked, shaved, bloodied, and teetering on the brink of death. In the center was the blood-stained stump they had used to remove appendages of unruly slaves. He felt rage surge through his body when he saw the head house slave, who had escorted him to see Rebecca Lester for the last time, standing behind the white men on the outside of the clock and in the innermost layer of the circle of spectators. His posture reminded him of the way Big Bartholomew used to stand behind Jethro and Silas. As he looked at his smiling face, he knew exactly who had told the other plantation owners about the uprising. He thought that had it not been for the abundance of traitors among them, the enslaved people would have taken their freedom at least one hundred years before Abraham Lincoln was forced to emancipate them.

The expressions on the faces of the other house slaves told a different story. They were despondent and had been assembled against their will. D'Quandray saw uncertainty on their faces and uneasiness in their body language. They were scared. The old expression "the devil you know is better than the devil you don't know" came to mind. As evil as he had been, they had adjusted to Elroy Lester's methods. They had also been shielded from the brutality of what went on with the villagers—the back breaking work, the poor living conditions, and the brutality inflicted upon them by the plantation-hands—daily. Happy house slaves made for happy masters. But not today. Today they would see the horrors of slavery in full—unfiltered and devoid of pretense. Pure evil.

As the slave breaker stood near the stump with his rifle in hand, there was movement to D'Quandray's left. Another man had been brought to the redemption grounds and was being tied to the post beside him, also naked and completely shaved. Prior to that, only Horace had been missing from the circle. D'Quandray studied his face. His heart began to race, and he felt a surge of adrenalin stronger than he had ever felt at any other time in his life. When the man squinted and smiled at him, it was confirmed. It was Horace; he was alive. D'Quandray gasped. Suddenly, the feeling he had experienced time and time again made perfect sense, but it had never been what he thought it was. It had been familiarity, not déjà vu. The man's strong jawline and cleft chin, sans his thick beard, were now prominent. How could he not have seen it all those years? Horace had always been that old man who had come to see every basketball game D'Quandray had played since he was thirteen years old, and he had been with him every day of his life in Jamestown.

The thoughts that went through D'Quandray's mind started to keep pace with his rapid heart rate. There were questions he wanted answered, but he had no time to ask them. He simply stared at Horace in disbelief, and despite all the obvious pain he was feeling, his best friend continued to smile back at him. Horace had no way of knowing that D'Quandray was from his time, but the expression on his face said that he knew that he himself was not a prisoner of the life they were in presently, and he was about to be set free. D'Quandray knew that he had to let him know some way, somehow, exactly who he was and that he would be joining him in their other life.

The slave breaker raised his weapon as the Lester plantation-hand quoted scripture. He fired his first shot, killing a man instantly. As the bound men who were still among the living remained stoic, unshaken, and resigned to their fates, wailing cries from the horrified house slaves filled the air. He calmly loaded another round and aimed the weapon at the next man, a man who had his unblinking eyes fixed on a sociopath. Another shot, another kill. He was systematically and chronologically working his way around the clock, which meant that D'Quandray would be shot before Horace. If the first man he killed was high noon, D'Quandray was 7 o'clock. Eventually, he shot and killed the man to his immediate right. As the slaver reloaded his weapon, D'Quandray felt a sense of calm. It was all about to be over. It was time. The slaver raised the weapon, and D'Quandray found himself looking beyond the barrel and into the steely eye of his judge, jury, and executioner.

He took a deep breath, and he yelled his final words. "My name is D'Quandray!"

The last thing he heard in his life as an enslaved man was the pop of the slave breaker's rifle. So, on July 28th, in the year of 1810, the man the villagers called Sir died in Jamestown, Virginia at ninety-five years of age.

Chapter 18

Old Friends

D'Quandray opened his eyes with a gasp and sprang up to a seated position in his bed. He was sweating, he was breathing rapidly as if he had been sprinting, and he could feel his heart pounding inside his chest. It was really over, and he had lived a lifetime in slavery. He took in deep breaths and exhaled slowly. The last thing he wanted to do was end up in the hospital again. His urge was to leap from his bed and drive directly to the gym; however, it was still dark outside, which meant he still had a few hours to go before it opened.

He lay back as he tried to process everything he had gone through. He wanted badly to see Horace, whom he had last seen at the charity game he had reluctantly attended. In retrospect, D'Quandray thought that when the old man had failed to come to the gym to see him play the next morning, which was the first time he had not been present for one of his games in years, he should have suspected something. But how could he have known? At that time, he had not experienced the event, and he, therefore, had no cause to suspect that Horace had been a part of the quartet that had traveled through time in the year 2136.

What if he was sick? What if he *died*? The mere thought that something had possibly happened to him nearly brought tears to D'Quandray's eyes. "Man is to be free." He repeated aloud the last words his friend had said to him. Then, a tear did fall. "You were trying to give me hope," he said, his voice shaking. "You were trying to let me know that our people were going to be free. *Going*; that was the word."

D'Quandray sat on the edge of his bed and placed his feet flat on the floor. The lights turned on. He took another deep breath and exhaled as if he was releasing seventy years of pain. He shook his head, thinking that indifference to the suffering of another human being was nothing short of a crime. Denial of an attempted genocide was so insidious that the depths of its depravity defied description, yet he had held that very position only one week ago—a goddamn fool.

He looked at the clock on his dresser. It was a few minutes before 7 o'clock a.m. "Housemate, set my alarm song to play on weekends." No longer was it enough for him to wake up to the song on weekdays; he wanted to hear it every morning for the rest of his natural life. He had grown to love it.

D'Quandray grabbed his phone from the dresser and walked to the kitchen to make breakfast. He expected to hear from Bradley and Elijah soon. That was, of course, after they dealt with whatever emotions they were feeling resulting from the conclusions of their own time travel experiences. He was in no rush to call them because he was still processing his own. Where did they go? What did they do? Only now did he allow his mind to go there. Only now *could* he allow his mind to go there. He had simply been too immersed in his own pain to focus on what they were dealing with. It was necessary for his survival. Not his physical survival (his walk back from the portal told him that that was preordained), but his mental acuity, given what he had gone through, had to be handled with care. Marissa had given them good advice. Waiting until it was over to discuss where they went, or why they chose to go there, was a great idea.

D'Quandray cooked and ate his breakfast. Then, he showered. When he was done, he had a decision to make. It was not a major one but a decision, nonetheless. Except for the most recent one, he had played basketball every Saturday morning since he had healed enough from his knee surgery to do so. It did not feel like the right thing for him to do today; however, going to the gym to locate Horace was an absolute must. That, he decided, had to happen.

His phone signaled an incoming video call. It was Elijah. "And so, it begins." He pressed the button to answer the call.

Elijah was smiling. "Good morning, D'Quandray. We made it."

"That, we did. Seems like you're in good spirits."

"I am. I'm happy it's over. This was a really good idea. I've talked to BG already. We want to meet for brunch tomorrow if that's okay with you."

"That's fine—sounds like a good idea. Have you guys decided where?"

"Yes, Marissa knows a place."

D'Quandray nodded and smiled. "I bet she does. Just text me the particulars, and I'll be there. Take care."

"You too, D'Quandray. Talk to you soon. Goodbye now."

***

D'Quandray arrived at the gym thirty minutes before it was scheduled to open. He simply could not wait any longer. To his surprise, there was already a car in the parking lot, and it was parked near the entrance. The lights inside the gym were on. He parked beside the other car, got out, and walked to the front door. He was wearing an SSU track suit and a brand-new pair of running shoes that had been comped to him by the sports apparel company that sponsored him.

He pulled the door handle, but it was locked, which was what he half expected. Instead of getting back into his car, he waited. A few seconds later, he saw Imani walking toward the front door. She was smiling and holding an envelope in her hand. She unlocked and opened the door.

"Good morning, D'Quandray. Mr. Goodman told me to give this to you."

"Mr. *who*?"

"Horace. He said you would come looking for him."

"Good morning." D'Quandray smiled as he accepted the envelope, but instead of looking at it, he kept his eyes focused on her. Apparently, her beauty was another thing to which he had been completely blind.

"He also said you probably wouldn't be playing ball today. How he knew that I don't know. I'll see you next week?"

"You most definitely will." He held the envelope up and shook it. "Thank you, Imani."

"You're welcome." She closed the door, locked it, and walked toward the service desk.

"Of course, his last name is Goodman," he said as he walked back to his car. "Of course, it is." He laughed. He sat in the driver's seat and opened the envelope. There was a handwritten message inside.

Good morning, old friend, and welcome back. I can't wait to see you. I would love for you to join me and my family for dinner tonight. We have a lot of catching up to do.

Your friend,

Horace

Behind the handwritten note was a flier with a picture of Horace's home on it, his address, and the time dinner was scheduled to start. He placed the flier into the center console of his car and studied the letter. As he looked at the neat penmanship and the succinctness of the message, he thought that it was Horace through and through—dignified yet simplistic. He smiled and wiped away a tear. He folded the letter and placed it back into the envelope. After looking at the gym entrance once more, he drove away.

***

D'Quandray parked his car in Horace's driveway at exactly the time the flier said to be there. He had arrived thirty minutes early but chose to park on a street two blocks away and wait. On his passenger seat was a gift he had purchased after leaving the gym. He grabbed the package and walked to the front door. A woman wearing a maid's uniform opened the door before he could push the doorbell.

"Welcome, Mr. Tyson. Come in; Mr. Goodman is expecting you."

D'Quandray walked into the foyer, which was vast and bright and had a grand staircase, which, despite being offset to one side, did not upset the symmetry of the space. "Thank you."

She nodded toward the package he was holding. "Do you mind if I take that for you?"

"No; not at all. Please do." He handed the gift to her. "Could you bring that to us after dinner?"

"Yes, sir. I will do that."

"Thank you very much."

"Follow me, please." She walked out of the foyer, down an adjoining hallway, and stopped by a study. "You can have a seat here. He'll be with you shortly."

He thanked her again and sat in a comfortable leather chair. The room featured a floor to ceiling bookcase on the wall opposite its entrance. Three more chairs, that looked as comfortable as the one in which he was sitting, were evenly spaced about the room. He had thought the marble floors in the foyer were Horace's attempt at putting his best foot forward for guests to see, but from what he had seen so far in the study, the entrance was somewhat understated. Horace had done well for himself.

D'Quandray sat up when he heard voices coming down the hall. It sounded like ten or more people. When he looked at the door, he saw them gathering on both sides of it. He stood, and then Horace walked into the room from the hallway, showcasing that smile that had become so familiar to him.

They embraced. For a full minute they held onto one another, until tears were streaming down both their faces, and the people standing around them started to clap. When they separated, a woman about Horace's age handed them both tissues. She was smiling.

"My apologies, everyone," D'Quandray said with an embarrassed chuckle. "My name is D'Quandray Tyson." They all laughed, which made him laugh as well.

"We know who you are, young man," the woman said. "Horace has been ranting and raving about you for twelve years. My name is Janice; I'm his wife."

He walked to her and hugged her, too. "It's a pleasure to meet you, Mrs. Goodman."

She turned to the others after their embrace. These are our grandchildren and great grandchildren. Horace talks about you so much that they wanted to meet you, too."

Horace's great grandchildren were close to D'Quandray's age. He asked everyone their names, where they fell in the family tree, and what they did for a living. They were all college educated and had fulfilling careers.

"That's enough of that," Janice said. "We'll let you and Horace catch up. We should be ready to eat in about thirty minutes."

"Have a seat, old man," Horace said once the others were gone.

D'Quandray sat back in his original seat and started shaking his head as he looked at Horace. "You knew all this time and didn't say anything. That takes a lot of self-discipline."

Horace lowered himself into the seat directly across from D'Quandray. "Self-discipline, respect, and love to be exact." He crossed his legs. "You want to hear something funny?" He shrugged his shoulders and laughed. "I don't even like sports."

D'Quandray laughed. "You could've fooled me."

"It's true. I went to a basketball tournament on the south side to see one of my great granddaughters play twelve years ago, and I got there early. Her game was the one after yours." He got a blank look on his face and started shaking his head. "When that announcer said, 'at center, D'Quandray Tyson,' every hair on my body stood up. I had only heard that name one other time before, and that was one second before that racist slaver put a bullet through my best friend's head." He removed his glasses, used his thumb and index finger to wipe the moisture away from his eyes, and shook away the painful memory. Then, he put his glasses back on and looked at D'Quandray. "I got up from those bleachers, walked all the way to the edge of the court, and stood about five feet away from you. I had to confirm my suspicions, and damn if it wasn't you. That thirteen-year-old boy had every one of your mannerisms and facial expressions. You can imagine how I felt that day. I didn't sleep a wink that night. The next comet wouldn't be around until this year, and I just had to wait. In the meantime, I was not going to lose track of you. I would've followed you to the end of the earth if you were playing there. You needed to see my face everywhere you went." He shook his finger at him. "You're a smart man, D'Quandray Tyson. I'm so grateful that you yelled your name at that moment. It never made sense to me until I saw you twelve years ago. That's when it all came together."

"I was desperate, and I had to do something. Once they shaved your face, I knew it was you. I *knew* it was you. The only thing I could think to do was to yell my name." He laughed. "If my parents had named me James or John, we probably wouldn't be having this conversation right now." That brought a smile to Horace's face. "I saw you and Imani at the charity game. Why'd you disappear?"

"Because I couldn't take the chance of you wanting to talk to me. I kept my voice from you all that time for a reason. If you had recognized me when you first got to Jamestown, it might've changed everything for you and for me. There's no telling what knowing I had a fellow time traveler there with me would've done to me. I'm glad I didn't know. You needed to go through exactly what you went through, and so did I.

"When my friends and I time traveled, one of them went to the future. He was the one you saw on the video at his granddaughter's house. He came to visit me not too long before you saw me at the gym. He went to see Seth, too. Once that happened, I knew you were on your way. I didn't want to blow it at the last minute."

"I understand." He swept his eyes around the room. "What did you do for a living? This place is amazing."

"You mean what do I do? I'm the president of Kelser University. I've been a professor nearly all my professional life—a history professor, to be exact. And it's Dr. Goodman, thank you very much."

"I should've known." He smiled, but then he changed his expression as he became pensive. He briefly looked at the floor, then looked back at Horace. "How long were you there in Jamestown?"

"Seventy-five years. I had already been at the Lester plantation for five years when you got there. I came into awareness at a slave auction. The Lesters bought me because I knew how to work with horses. What about you? At which moment did you arrive?"

"It was the minute before Big Bartholomew barged into the church and pointed his finger at Joseph Freeman." His face got warm, and he felt his eyes fill with tears. "I felt horrible," he said through clenched teeth. "I felt like I let all of you down."

Horace nodded. "That makes sense. I knew it had to be sometime around those days once I thought about it."

D'Quandray wiped his eyes and furrowed his brow. "You time traveled in twenty-one thirty-six," he stated.

"Yes, seventy-five years before you did."

"Yet we were there at the same time. That's incredible."

"Is it?" Horace asked. "I mean, does time *really* exist? I don't think so. We exist; time does not. The universe places us where it needs us to be. I know that now. I came back here at twenty years old, and I have not been afraid of death since I opened my eyes in my dormitory room."

"That's an interesting perspective," D'Quandray said, thoughtfully.

Horace uncrossed his legs and moved to the edge of his chair. "That's reality. All those beatings we took, all that manual labor we did from sun-up to sundown, and even the bullets you and I took from that self-proclaimed slave breaker's rifle, were all real, and yet we didn't bring one physical scar back with us." He pointed to the crown of his head. "It's all up here, but that doesn't mean it didn't happen. It just happened somewhere else."

"So, what does that say about us?"

Horace shrugged. "It says to me that this package we're wrapped in is nothing more than a way to make us distinguishable from one another."

"Or recognizable *to* one another."

"That's right! There's a good chance that once we've been released from this," he extended his arms and hands in front of him and looked at them, "*vessel*, we'll exist in another form and in another place entirely. The only thing is we may not have any recollection of our time here, but if we do..." He shook his head and smiled. "If we do, there truly is a heaven."

The maid walked through the doorway. "Please pardon the interruption, gentlemen. Dinner is ready, Mr. Goodman."

Horace rose to his feet. "Thank you, Mary." He looked at D'Quandray. "Let's go eat like the kings we are."

D'Quandray laughed. "You'll get no protest from me. Lead the way, my friend."

Horace reached out, grabbed his hand, and gave it a gentle tap. "No, let's walk together."

And they walked out of the study hand in hand.

After what D'Quandray could only describe as the best meal he had ever eaten, they came back to the study. He found Horace's family to be a delightful group of people. He thought that Maliq would have enjoyed the conversation they had at the table and wished he could have been there to experience it. Every topic they discussed came back to how each of them could do something to make life better for Black people, as if they had all taken it as a personal challenge to be the one who would make the difference.

As they both settled into their chairs, Mary pushed a cart with two dinner trays on top of it into the room. She raised the lid off the first tray revealing two, shiny, red apples. "A gift from your host," she said with a smile. Then she turned toward Horace and removed the other lid. "And for you, Mr. Goodman."

Horace walked over to the cart. On the tray were two drink glasses, a bottle of whiskey, and two cigars. Beside them was a typed note that read:

To: my best friend
From: Sir.

"I'll leave you gentlemen to it," Mary said as she smiled and backed out of the room.

Horace picked up the bottle of whiskey and twisted the cap off it. "This is the good stuff, Sir...um, D'Quandray. Sorry."

"Either is fine." D'Quandray stood, walked over to the tray, and put a hand on his shoulder. He grabbed one of the apples from the tray and bit into it as Horace poured them each a glass of whiskey. "Mm, they taste even sweeter when you're free."

"They do, don't they?"

For hours, they talked, laughed, cried, drank whiskey, and smoked cigars. They enjoyed one another's company. When it got late, Horace insisted that D'Quandray stay the night. He did not want him to drive while he was under the influence of alcohol. D'Quandray agreed. After he and Horace bade one another a good night, Mary showed D'Quandray to his room.

The guest room rivaled any 5-star hotel suite in which D'Quandray had ever stayed. Not only did it have its own bathroom, but it also had a desk, a computer, and a fully stocked mini refrigerator. D'Quandray showered and went to bed. As he lay there, his heart rate quickened, and he knew exactly why. He was confident that his days in Jamestown were over, but something embedded in his psyche simply would not let it go. He understood just how far trauma could reach to wrap its wicked arms around its victim. Despite that, he closed his eyes anyway. He felt a variety of emotions, but fear was not one of them—or so he thought.

Chapter 19

Brunch Tales

"No!"

D'Quandray sat straight up in bed. The bed sheets were soaked and so was his back. He wiped the moisture away from his forehead as he stared into the darkness. The bed was too comfortable to be the palate in his Jamestown loft and too unfamiliar to be his own. As his eyes adjusted to the darkness and his surroundings became clearer, he remembered that he was in Horace's guest room. A quick glance at the digital clock on the dresser told him that it was 2 o'clock in the morning. Aside from the ambient noises of the home, everything was silent.

D'Quandray had not considered how he would react to lucid dreams in the aftermath of his event. He had been too concerned about whether he would return to Jamestown. That concern had been allayed by sleep that did not result in time travel, so he felt the experience was truly over. He removed his tee shirt and slid his body to the dry side of the bed. Then, he pulled the covers up to his neck and made himself comfortable. As hard as he tried, he could not stop himself from thinking about Jamestown. He had left an entire family there, and he wondered how they had fared in the aftermath of the uprising.

No longer shackled by his fear of being influenced by information that he otherwise should not have known, he got out of bed and logged onto the computer. As he opened the browser, he was determined to research everything he could about the Lester plantation. He made several queries about the plantation and some of the families of the white men who had worked it when he was there. Outside of the Lester family ancestry, and information on what products the plantation primarily produced, he found nothing. There was no mention of the 1810 uprising or the murders of ten innocent Black men.

He also researched Joseph Freeman's name. According to the information he found, he had been a minister. The truth was he had been an abolitionist. It also said that he had died of natural causes in 1740, which was also untrue. Joseph had lived as a free man prior to coming to the Lester plantation, thus the surname Freeman. The reason his death was listed as natural causes was to cover up the crime committed by John Lester. D'Quandray felt his lips tighten and his nostrils flare.

"Predictable. How many men like Joseph Freeman have been forgotten throughout time?" As he spoke those words, he also wondered how many men like John Lester had been hidden from the history books.

He decided that any further research would only anger him more. What he needed to know, he had learned first-hand in Jamestown, and nothing he found on a computer could dispel what he already knew to be true. Slavery happened, and it was ugly. He got back into bed and quickly fell asleep.

When he woke the next morning, he could hear voices throughout the house, and he smelled breakfast cooking. It was 7 o'clock. He got out of bed, brushed his teeth, and showered. After he got dressed, he hurried downstairs to the kitchen. Horace was sitting alone at the dining room table. Breakfast had not yet been served.

"Good morning," he said as he walked in.

"Good morning, Sir." Horace looked directly into his eyes. "How'd you sleep?"

D'Quandray had been an overnight guest in several homes over the years, and despite how he had actually slept, the canned response he had always given to that question was "good," because he knew he would not be there for an extended stay, and it did not matter. The important thing had always been to show appreciation for the host's hospitality. But when he saw the intensity in Horace's gaze, he knew that answer would not suffice. Horace wanted to hear the truth, and that had nothing to do with how comfortable D'Quandray found the room to be.

"The room is amazing, but I did not sleep well at all. I had a terrible dream." He smiled. "But it was just a dream." He sat beside Horace. "Was it that way for you, too?"

"It was for a while. I had to get over the fear of going to sleep." He leaned forward in his chair and looked around to make sure no one else was in earshot of their conversation. "Instead of traveling through time, I dreamed *about* traveling through time. But mostly, I dreamed about those sentries that came after us. Our friend, Daniel, never made it off those grounds."

D'Quandray put a forearm on the table, leaned close to Horace, and studied his face. "Did you see them?"

Horace nodded. "They could've killed me, but they didn't."

D'Quandray leaned back and folded his arms across his chest, keeping his eyes fixed on Horace. "Interesting. The same thing happened to me. I was the only one from my group who saw them. They fired at me, but in retrospect it feels like that was more to get my attention than it was to do me any harm. Why'd they let us live?"

"The question that has bothered me all these years is why did Daniel have to die? What did he live through that they didn't want us to know about?"

On that point, D'Quandray paused to reflect. Miles Jackson had communicated with them and had lived to tell others about it, but that still did not explain what it was they were trying to protect. He then began to wonder if he should have run toward them instead of running away from them.

"I know what you're thinking," Horace said. "I thought the same thing for a while, but, make no mistake about it, they would've killed you. At least I believe so anyway. One can never be too sure about these things."

"Have you ever tried to look up anyone from our time in Jamestown?"

"I have, but you must realize that most of our history is told from the perspective of the victors. Then, if you consider the fact that they burned nearly every courthouse in existence in eighteen sixty-five to get rid of the evidence of the atrocities they committed, it becomes nearly impossible to find the truth. You have to read between the lines—see what's not on the pages and put yourself in the place of those who were involved. You can make assumptions and educated guesses based on that, and we certainly have been educated."

"Why'd you choose that time and place?"

"Likely for the same reason you did. I'm sure we had different motives, but our reasons were the same. We wanted to witness the origin of our trauma, and we sure as hell did."

D'Quandray leaned forward to look at the screen on his phone as it lit up. He had set it to silent mode so he would not be disturbed while he slept. The alert was a message from Elijah. He unlocked his phone so he could read it. "Looks like I have a brunch date with my other friends," he said as he set the phone back on the table. "We decided to meet up to discuss everything today."

"That's wise. We didn't get that opportunity—not right away anyway, and definitely not together. He stood and extended his hand. "These last few hours have been amazing; it was well worth the wait. I believe there are great things in store for you, Sir."

D'Quandray shook Horace's hand. "Maliq told me it was possible, and now I believe him, and I believe you." They embraced. "You have my number and I have your address; this is only the beginning. I'll see you around."

***

D'Quandray was the last to arrive at the brunch location. Still, he was on time. He had stopped by his house to change clothes before coming. As Elijah had indicated earlier, the restaurant was Marissa's choice. It was small, and it was in an area of the city called Old Town. Its exterior blended seamlessly into the store fronts of the quaint shops that surrounded it. From the outside, he could see that there was barely anyone inside. From that, he surmised that the food was either subpar, and people liked to eat there because it was convenient, or it was too expensive for blue-collar people, or that the restaurant was simply a well-kept secret.

The door chimed as he walked into the restaurant, and the lone waitress on the floor smiled at him as she looked away from the table that was occupied by his friends.

"Hi! Welcome to *Shady's*, D'Quandray. My name is Haley."

D'Quandray smiled. "Hi, Haley, nice to meet you."

Bradley, Elijah, and Marissa all stood to welcome him as Haley walked away from the table. They were all smiling.

"It's only been a few days, but I feel like I haven't seen you guys in years," he said as he pulled out a chair. When he sat, they sat. The square table was in the center of the floor and each of them had a side of their own.

"Well, in a way, that's true," Bradley said.

"I know. I was joking, BG. How's everybody feeling?"

"Couldn't be better," Elijah said.

"Same," Bradley said. "In fact, I think it's possible that I'm better than that. How about you?"

D'Quandray forced a smile and shrugged. "I'm here. How's the food in this place, Marissa?"

She sat up, widened her eyes, and flashed a toothy smile. "It's so good. They make the most amazing waffles you'll ever have, and the mimosas are absolutely to die for."

"And the omelets?"

"Even better."

D'Quandray observed that she had a shoulder leaning toward the corner of the table she shared with Elijah, and she was wearing one of the pro basketball camp tee shirts that he had given to him. Elijah was also leaning toward her. Bradley was across from Marissa and had both forearms on the table as he sat on the edge of his seat. His lips were rolled inward, and he was drumming his fingers on the table.

For his part, D'Quandray felt calm. The major psychological hurdle that had him apprehensive about his post-Jamestown life had already been jumped—achieved by a night of sleep in which he went nowhere. As he looked at Bradley, he was reminded that he was also familiar with who Horace was, just not to the same degree that he had become. Until D'Quandray traveled to Jamestown, Bradley had been, for the longest amount of time, his best friend. That was not the case anymore, and he wondered how Bradley was going to react to that information.

Haley returned with glasses of water for each of them, and she took their orders. D'Quandray noticed that Bradley had not changed his body posture the entire time and that his fingers were even more active. He had rearranged his silverware several times, moved the napkin around, and needlessly pushed his plate forward and backward an inch or two several times.

"Listen, guys, I can't wait anymore," Bradley said as Haley walked away from the table.

"Then go ahead." Elijah waved his hand across his plate with a sweeping motion. "The floor is yours."

"I went to Sapien."

Elijah placed his hands flat on the table and widened his eyes. "You went *where*?"

"That's right, the Sapien solar system. It exists. Seth Tolliver, the old crazy guy we saw at *Lord Leopold's* that day, was a general in a gang there. That's how he knew my name. I worked for him."

"You were a gang member?" Marissa said.

"Well, it wasn't a gang by our definition, but it wasn't quite the military, and it sure as hell wasn't the police."

"So, what was your job in this *organization*?" D'Quandray asked.

Bradley nodded in his direction and smiled. "Good word. I was a low-level worker. They called us squaddies. That's kind of like a soldier with no rank." He paused and brought his hands up to shoulder level with his palms facing them. "That's not what I'm excited about, though. The tech in that place was unbelievable, not like anything I've seen here."

"You mean it was more advanced, or was it just different?" Elijah asked.

"Way more advanced, even from a conceptual standpoint."

"Such as?" Marissa asked.

Bradley flashed a sheepish grin. "Ha. Nice try. I can't tell you right now. What I *can* tell you is that we're going to be rich."

"We?" D'Quandray asked.

"Yes, *we*. I'm going to need investors, and because you guys are my friends, I'm going to allow you to get in on the ground level. I'm telling you this is a can't miss."

Elijah's shoulders slumped, and he sighed heavily. "That was not what I was expecting to hear. I'm thinking you went on some transformational journey and here you are pushing a get-rich-quick scheme."

"I was gone for ten days, Elijah. There's nothing *transformational* happening in that amount of time. Seth warned me to pay attention to the tech, so that's exactly what I did, and I'm glad I did. You will be, too."

Elijah sighed. "Is that all you got?"

"Well, yeah. I'm sorry I didn't get an opportunity to spend decades away like you guys did, but I had to make the most of what I had to work with. By the way, I got murdered by some sociopath named Onin Gesh. That wasn't any fun."

"You took a chance there," Elijah said. "Have you considered what would've happened to you if that place didn't exist? You could've disappeared into thin air or something like that."

"Or he could've just stood still for sixty seconds and not gone anywhere," D'Quandray said. "As strange as all of this is, it's hard to believe that you went to an entirely different planet."

"Make that *three* different planets."

"In ten days?" Elijah was incredulous. "How is that even possible?"

"You just traveled through time and you're asking me how something like that could have happened?"

"Touché. It was really more of a rhetorical question anyway." He looked at Bradley, then D'Quandray, then back at Bradley. After taking a quick glance at Marissa and receiving a head nod that seemed to grant him permission to speak, he continued. "I guess it's my turn now, huh? Have either of you noticed anything different about me?"

"Yeah, you and Marissa are a couple," D'Quandray said.

"Besides that."

D'Quandray looked him over for a few seconds, then leaned across the table to get a closer look. "Where's your cross?"

Elijah smiled and nodded his head. "You're very observant. I'm not going to be wearing that anymore."

"Are you saying that you're no longer religious?" Bradley asked.

"That's exactly what I'm saying."

"What happened to you that you don't believe in God all of a sudden?"

"I didn't say that, BG. You asked me if I was religious. I will no longer be practicing a religion, but I absolutely believe in a higher power. How could I not after what we've just experienced? In fact, I'm more certain that there is a higher power now than I have ever been in my life. What I do not subscribe to is any biblical explanation of what that higher power is."

"I'm at a loss for words," Bradley said. "What happened? Where'd you go? The suspense is killing me."

"I traveled to ancient Rome. I went to the Council of Nicaea. You know what they say about seeing sausage being made? It's true. Once you know all the dirty details and get a look behind the curtain, it changes you. Religion is a business, and it's a dirty one at that. I no longer want any part of it."

"Wow, I'm shocked," Bradley said.

"I'm not," D'Quandray said.

Elijah cast a knowing glance his way—a look that was mirrored by Marissa's expression. "Where'd you go, D'Quandray?"

"Jamestown, Virginia, from seventeen-forty to eighteen-ten."

Marissa's eyes widened and she brought a hand to her mouth. "Dear God, that's slavery."

"Yeah, it was slavery." He turned to face Bradley. "You know that old man that has been following me to every single game I've played since I was thirteen years old?"

Bradley narrowed his eyes and recoiled slightly. "Yes?"

"Well, there's a good reason for that. He and I have been friends for over seventy years. He was there with me in Jamestown. I went to see him yesterday."

"Wait, does he know Seth?"

"Yes; they're friends. They traveled together like we did. Horace—that's his name—was the missing guy they wouldn't speak of. They protected his identity all these years."

"You must hate us now?" Marissa said.

"Why would I hate you guys? You haven't done anything to me, and I haven't seen any indication that you are racists. I will not be answering to 'the stud' anymore, though. That's almost as nasty as the n-word."

"But..."

"Do not, in any way, try to defend it, BG. I'm telling you it's offensive *to me*, and that's all that should matter. Please respect that."

"Okay. Sorry."

D'Quandray placed his elbows on the table and brought the palms of his hands to his forehead. "It's alright, man. To be honest, all of this is still hard for me to adjust to." He leaned back, folded his arms, and looked at the empty plate in front of him. And as he felt Bradley's hand on his shoulder, he got angry at himself for feeling bad about offending his friend when he was only protecting his own peace of mind. He looked at Bradley and nodded. "Thanks, BG."

As subtle as the moment was, D'Quandray knew that it was a microcosm of what was to come. The whole nation recognized him as The Stud, even though his circle of friends—the ones who would grant him a reprieve from the slur—was small. He would have to deal with microscopic cuts to his psyche with each utterance of it, and each time he would be presented with the decision to correct it or to simply let it go. He was frustrated because he knew it was going to be hard finding the line that he would forbid people to cross, but that line had to be drawn. If not, his peace would forever be disturbed. For now, he decided, he would only take the time to correct those who knew him personally. For now.

Haley brought their food to the table, and as they ate D'Quandray thought of some of the surnames of the people the universe had placed in his path—Goodman, Godson, and Freeman. Those names were descriptive of the men who possessed them, and his experience with the events that led him to Jamestown taught him that in life there were no coincidences. Tyson was a name that had likely been handed down from slave masters, and he was going to change it.

Chapter 20

Tension

As he lay in bed, D'Quandray sensed brightness in his room. He opened his eyes, sprang up to a seated position, and immediately looked for his clock. It was forty-five minutes past the time he normally woke up, and he was going to be late for work—much later than usual. He shook his head as he recalled the verbiage that he had used to adjust his house alarm to play on weekends. He had unwittingly negated the weekday alarms. He sighed.

"Housemate, set my wake-up alarm to play *every day*."

"Initiated. Alarm with sound at 6 o'clock a.m. each day. Good morning, D'Quandray."

D'Quandray got out of bed with an absence of haste. His bosses rarely got to work before an hour or two after start time, so he still had time. He showered, ate breakfast, got dressed, and left his home. He waved at Albert as he drove by the guard shack, but he noticed that the dutiful attendant took a moment to check his watch after he returned his greeting. He continued down the main road and past the bus stop, which now had yellow, concrete bollard posts separating it from the roadway and a new sign. The tire tracks were gone.

When he got to work, it took him longer than usual to find a parking space—ten minutes, in fact. A bad feeling came over him when he finally walked into the office. As usual, Maliq was already there but so was Jason, and so were Victor Wainwright and Greg.

"Good morning, everyone."

"Look here, stud..." Victor began.

He stopped walking and looked directly into the CEO's eyes. "My name is D'Quandray."

Maliq stood, placed his hands on his hips, and stared at D'Quandray and Victor as they stared at one another.

"You're late, D'Quandray," Greg said.

"I apologize. There was a mix-up with my wake-up alarm. It won't happen again."

D'Quandray walked to his desk and turned on his computer as all eyes in the room remained on him. The conversation that had been taking place prior to his arrival had ceased. He sat in his chair and faced the rest of the room. The expressions on the faces of each of his colleagues told a different tale. He saw anger in Victor's eyes, disbelief in Greg's, and sheer delight on Jason's face, but on Maliq's face he saw a mixture of approval and disappointment. Not one of the reactions came as a surprise to him. As he took inventory of them, he knew his days at *Turbo Boost Sports Agency* were numbered.

Victor and Greg walked into their respective offices without saying another word, leaving the three members of the department to finish the office meeting that D'Quandray had somehow overlooked on his calendar. When he checked his emails, he saw that the one about the mandatory meeting had been sent five minutes before the close of business on Friday. By the time it had been sent, he had already left and so had Jason. It stated that the start time would be the start of business on Monday morning, which, by now, was more than an hour ago.

D'Quandray swiveled his chair around to face his coworkers. "Who told you about this morning's meeting, Jason?" Maliq smiled and Jason's face turned red.

"I got an email."

"We both got an email, and we both were gone when it arrived. The question I asked you was *who* told you about the meeting?"

Maliq swiveled his chair around to face Jason.

"I don't have to answer that."

"You just did. Thanks." And just like that, he had validation for his belief that Victor and Greg would try to seek some form of retribution against him for what had occurred on Friday. They knew he would not see the email. They also knew that Maliq would be on time for work because he always was. But more than anything, the smile he had seen on Jason's face when he walked into the office told the story, even more so than his actual presence.

Also included in the email was the notification that there would be an afternoon golf outing with a potential client. The timing of the message managed to accomplish the proverbial killing of two birds with one stone, D'Quandray noted. They had embarrassed him by taking advantage of the fact that he was not punctual, but at the same time, they had given him enough notice to prepare for the song and dance routine that went along with wooing their clients. By that time, he would have recovered from any bad feelings he had resulting from the former. If he was correct in his assumption, the attitudes and demeanors of his bosses would be completely different when he saw them again. They needed to be upset with him for being late, but they would also need to treat him well so that he would put on a happy face for their client. The former had already come to pass. If the latter occurred, he would have confirmation of their suspected motives.

Jason's face was still red as he stared at his computer screen. Maliq was typing away on his computer as he worked on yet another project, likely *Exum Industry's*. D'Quandray opened a project he had been working on prior to his leave of absence and started working on it as well.

"Listen, gentlemen," Greg said as he opened his door, a smile on his face. "Lunch is on the company today. You've all been working hard, and we just want to show our appreciation."

"Thanks, Greg," D'Quandray said, making sure that he was the first to respond. He would not make the mistake of showing his hand the way Greg and Victor had, and Jamestown had taught him that moving quickly in that situation was a good way to disarm the person who possessed the power.

Greg smiled and stepped back into his office, closing the door behind him. A text message from Maliq flashed on D'Quandray's phone. It read: *One fake smile deserves another. Well played.* He looked away from his phone and gave a subdued thumbs-up to Maliq, which Jason did not see.

***

They reached the par four ninth hole tied at two under. D'Quandray had purposely missed chip shot birdies on the seventh and eighth holes to keep it close. His ball was on the fringe of the putting green, where he would play for birdie on his next stroke. Their client, who had been very gracious and polite to that point, was standing over a two-foot putt for par. He sank the putt, retrieved his golf ball, and smiled.

"Well, stud, looks like there will be no heroics today. That's a two-putter you've got in front of you, and you haven't exactly been draining birdies today."

Though he did not look their way, D'Quandray could feel Greg and Victor staring at him, trying to gauge his temperament. He forced a smile. "You're right, Mr. Knowles. Why don't I just concede? Great game." He walked toward him with his hand extended.

"Oh no, boy. No way. I'm going to beat you fair and square." His smile was at war with every other aspect of his expression, and his face was turning red. Perhaps, D'Quandray thought, he was slightly embarrassed for letting his true self bubble to the surface in a moment of self-induced pressure. He wondered how he had missed all of that beneath his thin veneer of kindness earlier. "Be a good sport and play it out."

Boy? Asshole. D'Quandray dropped his hand and walked toward his ball. "If you insist." He kneeled to study the lay of the green between his ball and the hole. Then, he stood over the ball and immediately delivered a confident stroke. Immediately afterward, he walked toward his opponent with his hand extended, not even watching the ball as it traveled. "Like I said, great game."

His opponent was still watching the ball while D'Quandray was watching him. He heard the tell-tale sound of it dropping into the cup, and he smiled as he watched the cockiness and color leave his opponent's face. When he looked at D'Quandray, he frowned, shook his hand, and got onto his golf cart with his team. They drove away without saying a word.

D'Quandray looked back at Victor and Greg and shrugged. Like synchronized swimmers flawlessly executing an Olympic routine they had worked on for weeks, they both dropped their heads and shook them from side to side. D'Quandray walked to their golf cart and sat behind the steering wheel.

"Are you two going to get in, or are you walking back?"

The ride to the clubhouse was as silent as their opponent's departure from the putting green, but D'Quandray did not care. Being called stud by a stranger was, at this stage, forgivable, but being called boy was something he would no longer tolerate under any circumstance. He did not have to travel back in time to know that that was a pejorative that had always been weaponized in exactly the way that Mr. Knowles had just used it. Only now, attempts at subtle racism were louder than an operatic crescendo, and it was impossible for him to ignore them.

They walked into the clubhouse in time for Greg and Victor to catch up to Mr. Knowles before he walked out the front door. They were able to engage him in conversation, and a few minutes later, a smiling Victor summoned D'Quandray to join them.

"Mr. Knowles has an important meeting to get to, but he wants to know if you'll be gracious enough to take a few pictures with him and his team."

D'Quandray smiled. "I'd be honored." He walked over to him and put his arm around Mr. Knowles's shoulder as they posed for the first picture.

"Tell the truth, that putt was luck," the client said through a frozen smile.

"It sure was, Mr. Knowles. First time I've ever sunk one that long in my life." That was the compromise D'Quandray was willing to make. Victor and Greg were good at what they did and had effectively diffused a potentially volatile situation. He felt it was his duty to take the baton across the finish line for them. If asked about it later, he would say that it was his opponent's challenge of his competitive fire that motivated him to make the putt, nothing more.

***

Four hours after he left work, D'Quandray walked into his home. He had stopped by Horace's house on the way there and spent time with him. He would have stayed longer, but his friend had started to get sleepy after they ate dinner, and he could tell he was only staying awake because he was there. He wondered if Horace had been driven to be that successful before he traveled through time to Jamestown or if that experience had given him more focus and a greater sense of urgency about life. The advantage D'Quandray felt that he now had was one that Horace had already exploited. He had all the youthful exuberance necessary to do the difficult things that needed to be done and all the wisdom to do them as intelligently and as efficiently as possible.

On his way to Horace's house, he had spoken to Bradley. Their entire conversation was about him investing in *Bradley Gates, Inc.*, or *BGI*, and him possibly becoming a limited partner. To D'Quandray's surprise, Bradley had also said that he would be resigning from his job to focus on his own company. He had never seen him so serious about anything, and he considered his pitch to be a strong one—so strong, in fact, that he even discussed it with Horace.

"Housemate, what time is my wake-up alarm set for?" The artificial intelligence responded with the correct time, to his relief. He did not want to be late for that reason again. His phone rang. It was a call from the *USA National Team*. "Coach Stone, good evening. To what do I owe this pleasure?"

"We're going to need you earlier than we thought. Can you join us for practice this Wednesday?"

"That shouldn't be a problem; I have pre-approved leave for this from my bosses."

"Awesome. We'll fly you out. I'll email the details to you shortly. By the way, they want to kick things off with you being interviewed by Dick Rogers in New York on Sunday. They think it'll generate some excitement about the team and help to sell merchandise."

"So, they want me in New York on Sunday, then the team on Wednesday?"

"Yes, that's exactly right. You can either go back home for Monday and Tuesday, or you can join us early. It's up to you."

"Sounds good to me. In fact, I can't wait. See you soon, coach." He ended the call, but a few seconds later, he received another one. It was from Tiffany. "Hello, Tiff," he said as he answered.

"Hi, stranger. How are you? I haven't heard from you."

"I'm well. I've been super busy. Things have been crazy since I saw you." As he spoke those words, he tried to think of a way to tell her that he would not be able to see her the way he had in the past. Casual sex no longer appealed to him. He had been in too many encounters that involved no emotional attachment and had had his fill of them.

"Please don't be upset with me, but I have to tell you something." His body went numb, and he held his breath. "Are you still there?"

"I am. Go ahead; I'm sorry."

"Good, I thought I lost you. The reason I'm calling you is my boyfriend and I have decided to get back together. We're going to work things out. If I led you on in any way, or anything like that, I apologize. That was not my intention. From my perspective, we were just having fun."

"That's the way I saw it, too. Trust me, there are no hard feelings. I wish you both the best." He had often heard the phrase "fair exchange is no robbery," and for the most part, he had believed it to be true, but now he thought differently. He knew that every time you had an intimate exchange with someone, you gave a little of yourself that could never be emotionally redeemed, only physically reciprocated. Those days were over.

"I hope we can remain friends."

"Of course, we can. Thanks for being honest with me. Goodbye, Tiff."

"Goodbye, stud."

A conquest and nothing more. That was what he had been to her. Only his celebrity status was attractive to her. If he had been a regular person, she probably would not have paid him any attention whatsoever. He laughed as he looked at the blank screen, realizing then that he should have thanked her for helping him to salvage his self-respect. She could think whatever she wanted to think, and he would remain cordial to her if he encountered her in social settings, but they could no longer be friends.

Chapter 21

Better Days

D'Quandray walked into the office twenty minutes before work was scheduled to begin. Maliq was already there. After they greeted one another, D'Quandray went to the break room to get coffee. When he got back, it was officially time for his workday to begin, but Jason was still not there. A few minutes later, Greg walked into the office. He greeted D'Quandray and Maliq, but his eyes focused for more than an instant on Jason's work area. He walked into his office and closed the door behind him.

"We're off to a good start this morning," Maliq said.

"Well, it's about to get better. I just sent him an email requesting a leave of absence for the *National Team*."

Maliq raised an eyebrow. "That's going to be a tough sell. They aren't exactly happy with you right now."

"I know, but I think they'll look at the big picture. Any exposure *Turbo* can get is positive, and what better than a national stage like the *World Tournament*?

Jason walked into the office. "Good morning, guys. Are Greg and Victor here yet?"

"Good morning, Jason," D'Quandray said. "Greg is here but Victor isn't."

Jason winced, looked at his watch, then looked at Greg's door. "Did he seem upset?"

He and Maliq both chuckled sheepishly after he asked that question. "Seemed normal to me," D'Quandray said. "Why would he be upset?"

Jason narrowed his eyes as he looked at D'Quandray. "No reason, just curious," was his tight-lipped response. He sat at his desk and turned his computer on. "Oh crap." He put his elbows on his desk and his face in the palms of his hands. After remaining motionless for a few seconds, he shook his head and started to type on his keyboard.

A few seconds later, Greg opened his door and stood in the threshold. "Step into my office, Jason." He bladed his body sideways to allow enough room for Jason to walk by him. Then, he put his hands on his hips and stared at him the entire way as he did.

"This should be interesting," Maliq said after Greg closed the door behind them.

"If by interesting you mean he's going to give him a piece of his mind for making him look bad, you're absolutely right."

"You know, D'Quandray, I don't know what's gotten into you, but I like it." He pointed toward Greg's and Victor's offices. "They don't like it, but I sure do. I feel like I have an ally around here now."

"You're a standup guy, Maliq. Values like yours travel, and they travel well. After our little *conversation* the other day, I got immersed into some of the history around slavery, and it was eye-opening. Everything you said was right." His cell phone rang, and he furrowed his brow when he looked at the screen. "BG knows I'm at work; I'll call him back later." As he turned his attention back to Maliq, the phone on his desk rang. He answered it. *"Turbo Boost Sports Agency,* where we supercharge your profile. D'Quandray Tyson speaking. How may I help you?"

"D'Quandray, this is BG. Sorry to bother you at work. I went by *Lord Leopold's* to visit Seth Tolliver this morning. He's dead."

"Well, he was pretty old; there's really nothing peculiar about that. Did something happen to him?"

"No. The staff said he died of natural causes, whatever that means. The medical examiner was wheeling him out when I got there. For some reason, I'm a little spooked by it."

"Why so?"

"The timing. It was because of him that we got involved in all of this in the first place. Each domino fell exactly when it was supposed to fall, but this one makes no sense at all. I don't know, maybe I'm just being super paranoid. I just felt like I should tell you about it."

"I understand. Try not to let it get to you, man. Call me back if you need to talk." As he hung up his phone, he wondered if he should call Horace to tell him about it. Then, his cell phone rang again; it was a call from Horace. D'Quandray sighed. "He already knows." As he pressed the answer button, he tried to think of the words to comfort his dear friend about his loss. "Good morning, Horace. I'm so sorry…"

"This is Janice."

***

Life is a practical joker who simply keeps on performing well after the punchline has been delivered. When Mary opened the front door, and he heard Horace's family members grieving, D'Quandray fell to his knees. He had held it together to that point, but the atmosphere was just too much. Mary put a comforting hand on his shoulder as tears rolled down his cheeks. Neither the police cars parked out front nor the news van on the other side of the street had elicited that response from him—it was the grieving.

He pulled himself up from the floor. As much pain as he was in, Horace's family was in even more, so he consciously made the decision to suppress his own emotions so he could play the role of the comforter. Janice needed him. He wiped away his tears and allowed Mary to lead him into the study where the rest of the family had assembled.

"He just sat there at that table and went to sleep," Janice said as D'Quandray grabbed her hand. She was sitting in the same chair Horace had sat in when he had visited him on Saturday and Monday. She wrapped an arm around D'Quandray's waist and rested her head against his hip. He placed an arm around her shoulders. "I think he was just trying to live long enough to get you here. It took him all that time to get the family together. He wanted you to meet everyone." She looked up at his face and smiled. "Thank you."

"It was my pleasure, Mrs. Goodman."

"There must be something special about you. Horace had a lot of friends, but you're the only one he allowed in our home."

That surprised D'Quandray. He had always viewed Horace as someone who had an accommodating personality, so he figured that it transferred to everyone he knew. The fact that he was the only one who had gotten to know him on that level seemed unfair to everyone else he had known, but he felt fortunate to be the beneficiary of the exception. He looked toward the hallway when some police officers walked by. As they continued to the foyer, one of them stopped in the threshold of the door that led to the study.

"On behalf of the mayor, our city, and our police department, I would like to offer my deepest condolences to your family. We have completed our portion of the investigation, and we have contacted the medical examiner's office. As a courtesy to you, we will leave an officer outside until the morticians have come and gone." He handed a card to Janice. "If you have any questions, or if we may be of assistance to you in any way, do not hesitate to reach out to us." He nodded and backed out of the room.

It then occurred to D'Quandray that Horace's body was still in the house. He needed to see it, even though he understood that what made the man who he was had already left. Before he could finish the thought, the rest of the family began to move from the study to the dining room, where Horace had drifted into his eternal sleep at the table and, in front of Janice, departed from the earthly realm. He followed them.

Horace's body lay on the dining room floor where the paramedics had worked on him as they attempted lifesaving measures. His pajama top had been ripped open, leaving his bare chest exposed. As D'Quandray looked down on the lifeless body of his best friend, he reflected on what Horace had said about their earthly bodies being nothing more than vessels that contained their souls. He believed him, and the thought of that brought him a sense of peace. He also thought back to the video of Richard Chester they had watched at Marissa's house, and it occurred to him that everything that they had yet to do had already been done. Horace had also said that there was no such thing as time, that it simply did not exist. That, now more than ever, was clear to D'Quandray. He knew that wherever in the universe Horace was, he would be waiting for him to arrive. Just like in his last moments in Jamestown, D'Quandray no longer feared death, and he promised himself that he would live accordingly from that day forward.

The morticians came about an hour later and removed Horace's body. One of Horace's grandchildren had already provided a statement to the media personnel who had assembled outside. After getting the obligatory shot of his covered body being wheeled from the house, the press left as well. Only the family and D'Quandray remained. He decided that he should go, too. The family needed time to themselves. After he said his goodbyes, Janice asked him to join her in the study for a moment.

She handed him an envelope with his name on it. "Horace left this in the place where he kept his primary care physician's information. I guess he knew I'd have to look there if something happened to him." Her eyes were filled with tears, yet she smiled. "I have no idea what's in it—that's between you and him—but if you would do the family one favor..."

"Anything, Mrs. Goodman. Just name it."

"I would like for you to eulogize him. You're the closest friend he had, and I think that would make him happy. The funeral will be this Saturday."

He hugged her. "It would be my pleasure. Thank you for allowing me this honor."

***

D'Quandray left the Goodman residence and went straight to the county courthouse. Once inside, he logged into their secure system to access the name change and driver's license update forms. He filled them out and submitted them. He had entertained the idea of changing his first and last names, but D'Quandray now held a different meaning for him. It was the one thing that linked the lives of him and his best friend from Jamestown to the present. He would keep it, but Tyson did not belong to him.

He walked into the courthouse as D'Quandray Tyson, but he left it, two hours later, as D'Quandray Free. As he stepped into his new life, he wanted to embrace a new identity—to live unapologetically, for his people and for himself. There was power in a name. Far too often to overlook, he had seen that those people who had carried surnames of substance had conformed to them. Somehow, the descriptions within them had shaped the character of those who possessed them, and those names told the rest of the world who those people were.

Horace's letter was on his passenger seat, yet unopened. He decided he would do that once he got home. Things would be different now, and with that thought in mind, he made a detour from his drive home and headed for the gym. Seeing Imani on Saturday had made him think of the women he had encountered in the village on the Lester plantation. She possessed the same type of beauty that they had. It was born of inner strength and expressed through her confidence in her outer presentation, regardless of what anyone else may have thought. He understood now. He had once jokingly called her 'super sister,' but nothing could be truer. When he got there, he parked, walked inside, and went straight to the service desk. Her eyes were red, and he saw sorrow in them. The smile she presented to him looked as if it was the hardest thing she had ever had to do, but she did it anyway.

"I suppose you've heard?" he said as he nestled up to the counter.

She nodded and wiped the corner of one of her eyes with the back of her hand, catching a teardrop before it could fall. She looked at the television monitor overhead. "It was on the news. He was beloved around here. We hated to hear about it."

"So did I." As he looked at her, he realized that she would not be the one to fill the silence with conversation. Why would she? It was he who had come for her, after all.

She narrowed her gaze. "Is there something you need, D'Quandray?"

"Um...maybe this is a bad time." He lightly tapped the counter with the palm of his hand. "I knew you and Horace were kind of close. I just wanted to make sure you knew he had passed. I'll...I'll be in touch." He turned to walk away. "By the way, the funeral is Saturday. His wife is going to forward me the details of the service when she gets them."

"Thanks. Will you forward them to me?"

"How?"

"You can either call here, email me, or call my personal phone."

"I only have one of those."

She pulled a sheet of paper from the notepad on the counter, wrote her contact information on it, and handed it to him. "Now, you have all three. The sooner, the better."

D'Quandray smiled. "Noted. Have a better day, Imani. I'll talk to you soon."

She raised her hand and wiggled her fingers as if she was tickling the stomach of an imaginary child. "Bye now."

D'Quandray winced as he turned away from her. Part of him wanted to apologize to her for being awkward, and part of him wanted to congratulate himself for taking a chance. When he got to the exit, he looked back at the service desk. Imani was already busy with another member, but right before D'Quandray turned to leave, she looked at him and smiled—a smile that was in no way coerced. Free, he noted. He smiled back and walked out.

He did not remember Imani being so nice. In fact, the last time he had spoken to her before Saturday, he sensed an attitude, like she did not want to be bothered. Despite it, she had been cordial, but there had been underlying tension. Definitely.

As D'Quandray got into his car, another thought occurred to him. The universe had, once again, spoken loud and clear. Seth Tolliver and Horace Goodman were taken from this realm on the same day and, likely, at the same time. He was beyond wondering if coincidences were possible. They were not. The universe was playing chess, and each second of each day consisted of millions of calculated moves. If life had already been predetermined, then he would go boldly as he navigated his way through it, and he would do his part with conviction.

"Your move, D'Quandray Free. Your move."

He started his car and drove home. By the time he got there, it was much later than the normal time he would have gotten home from work. After he showered and changed into his pajamas, he went into his office to work on Horace's eulogy. Before he started, he opened the envelope that Janice had given to him.

Dear Sir,

I know neither the time nor day that I will leave this place, but I sense the hour is coming soon. I have always believed that we are kept in our reality until that time and place no longer has a use for us, or, to put it more politely, we have served our purpose. I feel I have served my purpose. The meaning of our connection will be revealed by the way you live your life moving forward. No pressure, right? I assure you that you are capable of doing what is necessary. I imagine that you have had that epiphany already.

In this life, I have amassed more wealth than I have needed. My family is taken care of. Wise investments and frugal habits in my youth guaranteed that. That having been said, I see potential in what your friend, Bradley, has started. Invest heartily; it will pay dividends. I am also investing, through you, two hundred thousand dollars of my own money. All I ask is that my great grandchildren be taken care of if this turns out to be as lucrative as I suspect it will be.

I love you, brother, and I will see you again. Wherever the universe decides to place me, I'll take solace in the fact that I will one day be joined there by my best friend, perhaps for eternity. For now, goodbye.

Your friend,
Horace.

Also inside the envelope were a debit card, pin number, a bank account number, and a password.

Chapter 22

Primal Man

Saturday morning.

As D'Quandray lay in bed listening to his wake-up music, he thought about Horace and what he meant to him. He had already transferred his generous investment into Bradley's business account, and he had matched it in full, giving Bradley a nearly half million-dollar head start to his career as an entrepreneur and, in the process, securing his position as a junior partner in *Bradley Gates Incorporated*. He was certain that he would not have made that move prior to recent events. Bradley had lamented that nothing transformational could have occurred in the ten days that he had been away, but D'Quandray did see a change in him. Bradley was confident, so much so, in fact, that it seemed it would be impossible for him to fail. That is why he invested in him so robustly.

    D'Quandray had made it to work on time each day for the rest of the week after the missed email debacle that had led to him being late on Monday, and each day he stayed there until it was time for him to leave. He had also worked diligently on his assignments the whole time, taking minimal breaks in between. As a result, their department finished the *Exum Industries* project ahead of schedule.

    He rolled out of bed to prepare for a day that was sure to be an emotional one. Even though the song stopped when he placed his feet on the floor, he continued to sing the chorus as he walked into his closet. He pulled out his black suit, which was still wrapped in the dry cleaner's plastic, and placed it on his bed. He grabbed a white button-down, dress shirt, his best cufflinks, and a black necktie—which was accented with specs of gray—and promptly tied it into a half-Windsor knot. He folded a gray handkerchief into the pocket of the suit jacket.

After he ate breakfast and showered, D'Quandray drove to the Goodman residence. Janice had requested that he take the limousine ride to the venue with her and their two living sons. When they arrived at the Kelser auditorium, it was already near capacity. He blended into the long line of family members who were already there waiting. A short time later, they all marched in together and filled the first few rows in the center section of the auditorium.

The funeral service felt more like a celebration than a sad occasion. When it was time for D'Quandray to speak, he did so with the family in mind. He had prepared a speech that he felt was worthy of the man he had come to know. Unable to give details of the events that had made them bond with one another, he spoke in superlatives about the man and spoke anecdotally about his specific personality traits, which garnered laughs and applause on several occasions. He left the stage to a standing ovation. Only when he walked back to his seat did he see that Imani was in the section next to the one in which he was seated. She smiled and nodded as he walked by, continuing her applause—like everyone else—until he was seated.

When the pallbearers removed the casket, the family filed out behind it. When it was D'Quandray's turn to enter the aisle, he reached across to the other side and grabbed Imani's hand. She offered no resistance as he pulled her along with him.

"Horace would want you with us," he said to her over the loud processional music. She simply smiled, and he held her hand tighter. He smiled back at her and looked forward as they followed the casket out of the auditorium.

The limousine ride to the gravesite was a quiet one. There were many things D'Quandray wanted to say to Imani, but he respectfully mirrored the mood of Horace's family while he was in their presence. She was quiet as well. They did, however, sit side by side, and she had yet to release his hand. The transfer of energy between them, he felt, conveyed everything he needed to say; it at least conveyed the feeling. The awkwardness he should have felt was nowhere to be found, and the only barrier between them was one that had to be conquered by time and effort, not some magical, imaginary relationship key that one could simply insert and twist. He was okay with that.

They stood behind the family, who were under a canopy and seated beside the grave, as the pastor recited the last rights. As his casket was lowered into the ground, returning his remains to the earth, Horace's family wept. D'Quandray did not. He placed an arm around Imani's shoulder, and she wrapped an arm around his waist and put her head on his chest.

As the mortician announced the conclusion of the ceremony, the family rose to their feet and walked to their respective modes of transportation. D'Quandray and Imani, once again, joined the immediate family in the limousine. The ride back to the Goodman residence from the gravesite produced a much lighter mood. Janice and her sons talked openly and seemingly went out of their way to include D'Quandray and Imani in their conversation, much to his relief.

They arrived at a house that was already overflowing with people. When they got out of the limousine, Imani let go of his hand—with a smile—so that he could offer an elbow to Janice, which he did and which she accepted. After stopping several times for people to offer Janice special condolences, he escorted her to the study. She was greeted with a warm embrace by Mary before taking a seat in one of the comfortable chairs.

Several tents had been constructed in the large back yard of the residence to accommodate the people who were there for the repast, but Janice asked D'Quandray and Imani to remain in the study with her, so they did. As he sat there listening to Janice tell stories about Horace's youthful exploits, D'Quandray found himself focusing more and more on Imani. He was seeing a side of her that simply had not been available to him all those times he had seen her at the gym. Like the woman standing at the bus stop, Albert's wife, he had prejudged her. He equated that to how the bosses at the company had treated Maliq compared to how they treated him and Jason. Bias was a dangerous thing, and it thrived between skepticism and the benefit of the doubt. He had been so cynical about who he thought she was all that time that he had failed to recognize all the positive attributes she possessed—her kindness, her gentle nature, her thoughtfulness, and her confidence. If Elizabeth had a spiritual doppelganger, it was Imani.

After spending a few hours with the Goodman family, D'Quandray felt he had held Imani hostage long enough. He said goodbye to everyone and walked her to his car to take her home. She patiently waited with her hands clasped together in front of her as he opened the passenger side door. After she got inside, he closed the door behind her and got into the car. He immediately reached for the radio dial to turn to a different station. He figured she would want to listen to music, so he thought he would find something neutral. He had muted the podcast station he had liked to listen to a few days back. In fact, he now found the content infuriating and the various hosts to be devoid of empathy.

"You can leave it there," she said.

He looked away from the radio and at her. "Excuse me? You listen to *that*?"

"I do," she said as she fastened her seatbelt.

D'Quandray put the car in drive, checked his mirrors, and entered the roadway. "That's a surprise."

"You're telling me you're surprised that I listen to them when it's on *your* radio?" She laughed—not a condescending laugh but one that seemed to denote pure amusement. It was no different than the way a mother would laugh at a toddler who fell on his butt after trying to walk for the first time. "That's funny."

He expected her to ask him why he listened to the program. In fact, he hoped she would so he could explain why he no longer liked it. He was concerned that she may have drawn an unfavorable conclusion about him, especially since he had attempted to change the station.

"May I ask why you listen to it?" He decided to put the proverbial ball in her court.

She looked directly at him. "You're an athlete. In all your years of practicing for opponents, have you ever practiced your defense against your own offensive sets or your offense against your own defensive sets in preparation to face them?"

"No, that wouldn't make sense. We practice against what our opponents are going to run. That way we can…" Then it dawned on him exactly what she meant. "Oh." He looked at her and smiled. "I see what you mean."

"Keep your eyes on the road," she said as she continued to look forward.

D'Quandray looked away from her and back to the road. Then, he applied his brakes, bringing his car to a screeching halt mere inches away from the rear bumper of the car stopped at the stop sign in front of him.

She looked at him and smiled. "Thank you. As much as I'm enjoying your company, I don't want to spend the rest of the night in the ER with you."

At that, he smiled. Then, he realized he was driving to the gym. "Wait, I don't know where you live."

"I was wondering when you were going to figure that out." She leaned forward and programmed her address into his car's mapping system.

He furrowed his brow as he looked at it. "That's on the southside."

"Last I checked," she said. "By the way, my car is still at the Kelser auditorium. That's where I need to go."

He tapped his forehead with the palm of his hand. "Right, how forgetful of me." Then, it occurred to him that she had given him her address, even though she knew he would not be taking her there. "Listen, Imani." He drummed his fingers on the steering wheel as he tried to find the right words. "Starting Wednesday, I'll be away with the *National Team* for a few weeks. As a matter of fact, they're flying me to New York tomorrow to be on the *Dick Rogers Show*. I'd like to take you out when I get back."

"Why do we have to wait until then? I've never been to New York."

He pulled the car to the side of the road and shifted it into park. "Are you serious?"

She faced him, leaned back against the door, and wrapped her hands around the transverse strap of the seatbelt. On her face was a look that was somewhat flirtatious but mostly sheepish. "That's, of course, if none of your other girlfriends mind," she said with playful sass.

"Very funny." He delivered the line with a deadpan expression as he shifted his car into drive. "You know, for a long time I thought you didn't like me."

She corrected her body position in the seat. "Why should I have liked you when *you* didn't even like you?"

Her words were so spot on that they nearly took his breath away. After a few seconds of silence, he recovered enough to pose a question. "What makes you think I don't have a 'girlfriend' now? All jokes aside, you don't seem like the type to share a man."

"If you were in a serious relationship with someone, she would've been by your side when you eulogized your friend today. It means a lot when someone wants to stand with you in difficult times." She paused. "On the other hand, when you choose to pull someone along with you, it means you feel a need for them on a primal level. If you think my offer to go to New York with you is about sex, you're mistaken. It's about what you said to me without speaking, when you were reduced to your basic self."

"What time should I pick you up tomorrow?"

***

D'Quandray arrived at Imani's house at 8 o'clock the next morning. She was already packed and ready to go, even though their flight was at noon. They were an hour drive away from the regional airport. He had booked her a ticket on the same flight, downgrading his first-class ticket so that they could sit next to one another in coach. She invited him into the modest three-bedroom home.

"It smells good in here; what are you cooking?"

"I'm not cooking, mom is. She insisted on making us breakfast."

He looked at his watch. "Well, we certainly have time."

"I thought you'd see it that way. Have a seat. Make yourself comfortable."

He sat on the living room couch as Imani went into the kitchen, presumably to help her mother prepare breakfast. He focused his eyes on a framed picture on top of the console table in the foyer. There were unlit candles around it and multiple cards of sympathy interspersed between them. The image was of a man who appeared to be about twenty years old. As he scooted to the edge of the couch to get a better look, Imani walked back into the living room with her mother. D'Quandray stood to greet her.

"My goodness, he *is* tall," her mother said as she opened her arms to invite D'Quandray into a hug. As she wrapped her arms around him, she looked at Imani. "But you didn't tell me he was so handsome."

When D'Quandray looked at Imani, she scrunched her nose and playfully rolled her eyes. "Thank you, Mrs. Colson," he said, blushing. "And she didn't tell me you were so beautiful. Breakfast smells delicious."

"Oh, thank you, and you can call me Claire. Breakfast will be ready in about two minutes. I just wanted to come in and say hello. I didn't want you to think I was rude or anything."

"It's a pleasure to meet you, Claire. Thank you for your hospitality."

"The pleasure's all mine, honey," she said as she walked back into the kitchen.

"She is one sweet lady."

"She's my heart and soul. I don't know what I'd do without her."

"I bet." He nodded to the picture. "Who's that young man right there?"

"That's my brother," she said, pain surfacing on her face. "We just buried him on June 22nd."

"Wait, didn't I see you at the gym that day?"

"Yes, as a matter of fact, you did." She narrowed her eyes. "You have a really good memory. We were short staffed, so I came in after the funeral. That's why we opened late that day."

"Oh, that's right, we did get a late start that day." He remembered complaining to Bradley about how unprofessional she had been for showing up late, and he had also complained that her demeanor was unpleasant when she finally arrived. He shook his head. *I was a real piece of work.* "If you don't mind me asking, what happened to him?"

"He was murdered. It was a robbery gone bad. He didn't have anything, but they didn't believe him."

"I didn't hear about that on the news." She looked at him with an expression that seemed to ask if she really needed to explain to him why that was the case. "Silly me. I'm sorry that happened to him and to your family. That must be painful. What was his name?"

"Darius. Everybody called him DC."

He was about to ask her more about Darius when Claire walked back into the living room. He decided to hold any further questions for the hour-long drive they had to the airport.

"Breakfast is ready, you two. I hope you like scrapple, grits, and eggs, D'Quandray."

He smiled because Ms. Sarah had prepared something similar for them in Jamestown on an almost daily basis. "I love scrapple." Not only did he enjoy the meal, but he had two helpings, much to Claire's delight. D'Quandray offered to help with the dishes when he was done eating but was quickly booted out of the kitchen by Claire. She hugged him and Imani and wished them safe travels. They loaded her luggage into his car and left for the airport shortly thereafter.

Chapter 23

Showtime!

D'Quandray and Imani arrived in New York City three hours before the show was scheduled to start. The five-star hotel the network had booked for him was a block away from the Manhattan studio. D'Quandray had long ago gotten accustomed to amenities like the ones the hotel provided, but he noticed that Imani had used her cell phone to take pictures of the bed, the living room, and the bathroom. She had also made several comments about how luxurious it was.

On their journey to New York, they had discussed multiple topics. He had told her that he had changed his last name to Free, which sparked a deeper conversation between them about the significance of names. He had also talked about his plans to be more active in the Black community, something that seemed to please her. He learned that Imani had been an excellent student in school but had chosen to delay going to college so she could help her mother with bills. Darius was going to be a doctor, and he had been on his way home from the community college when he was accosted by his assailant.

Imani showered first. As she got dressed, D'Quandray showered and shaved. He had brought his favorite designer suit to wear on the show. It was cerulean, and he brought his whiskey-colored shoes and belt to go with it. He also had an expensive watch with a band that matched the rest of his attire. He chose to forgo a tie and wore his white, button-down shirt with the top button undone. Imani was dressed in a black camisole dress that stopped just above the knee, with spaghetti shoulder straps. They left the hotel an hour before the show was scheduled to start. They had asked the concierge to order them a taxi, but he convinced them to walk, as that was the tradition of the talk show guests who stayed there, so that is what they did. He held Imani's hand as they walked down the busy sidewalk. She smiled and held her smartphone high as she videotaped the entire way. Within a half block walk, D'Quandray had been called The Stud no less than fifteen times.

When they got to the building, he saw D'Quandray "The Stud" Tyson in bold letters on the marquis. He forced a smile as they approached the line of soon to be audience members who were standing outside. Several of them recognized D'Quandray. He paused to take pictures with a few of them and signed autographs for others as Imani waited.

Once inside, they were greeted by a friendly, gregarious production assistant who was dressed in black from head to toe and had an earpiece in her ear. She handed them both lanyards with access badges, which they each put around their neck, and promptly led them to a green room. She handed him the show line-up and told him what time she would be back to get him. Then, she turned on the television, which was already tuned to the show, and left them alone. The warm-up act was already entertaining the studio audience.

"You act like you've done this a hundred times."

D'Quandray smiled. "Just a few. They do a really good job of taking care of the talent with shows like this." He grabbed two bottles of water from the craft service table and handed one of them to Imani. "You look very nice. I'm glad you came here with me. This trip is already ten times better than any I've taken in the past."

"Thank you. I'm enjoying myself, too. Is all that food for us?"

"It sure is. I wouldn't eat too much of it, though, if I were you. I have reservations at a five-star restaurant. We're going there when we leave here. The food is incredible. You'll be mad if you spoil your appetite."

"I don't know; I can eat a lot."

When she sat back, inhaled deeply, and smiled as she exhaled, D'Quandray felt the hard work had been done. In fact, he felt the universe had given him an assist on the biggest shot he was ever going to take, and it was a perfect pass. Before July 28th, he would have considered that luck. He knew better now. There was a knock on the door.

"Twenty minutes, Mr. Tyson."

"You're not going to respond?" Imani asked.

"To whom? There's no one there waiting. They don't have time. They've already moved on to the next task. They know exactly how loud to knock and speak for you to hear them. And they'll be back in exactly twenty minutes, believe me. Do you want to stay here and watch it on television, or do you want to stand backstage?" He stood and walked to the mirror to take one last look at himself. Hearing no response, he thought he would further explain each option. "If you stay here, you'll have peace and quiet, and you'll be able to hear the interview clearly. If you go out there, you'll get to see all the things that make a show happen and possibly run into a celebrity or two."

"In that case, I think I want to stand backstage. We can always catch the replay later."

He turned to her and smiled. "Wise decision." He began to pace the floor after the warm-up act was done and Dick Rogers began his opening monologue. As Imani looked herself over in the mirror, he meditated on what he wanted to say, thinking of pertinent facts that related to the *US National Team* and how he was going to announce to the world that he was now D'Quandray Free.

There was another knock at the door. "It's time, Mr. Tyson."

He looked at Imani. "It's showtime." They walked toward the door, and he grabbed her by the hand as they walked into the hallway.

As soon as the production assistant made eye contact with D'Quandray, she smiled and walked toward his mark. He followed her. Seconds later, they were backstage, watching and waiting for D'Quandray to be introduced. The production assistant attached a small microphone to his lapel and was off to her next task.

"Ladies and gentlemen," Dick Rogers said, "without further ado, I present to you D'Quandray 'The Stud' Tyson."

As the audience roared with applause, he turned to Imani. "Wish me luck." He walked from behind the curtain, made a few between-the-leg dribbles with an imaginary ball, and pantomimed a jump-shot. Then, much to the crowd's delight, he did his signature "get off me" celebration, which they all yelled in unison at the right time. He sat in the chair beside the host's desk and smiled as he waited for the applause to die down.

"Wow, you look like you can still play," the host said after the crowd quieted.

He smiled and said playfully, "I'm a resilient guy, Dick; they don't make them like me anymore." The audience laughed.

"It's good to see you again, D'Quandray. Welcome to the show."

"Thank you for having me. I think the last time we talked was the postgame interview after I hit the shot." The crowd applauded. He smiled, nodded, and put a hand over his heart. "Yes, thank you. Thank you very much."

"Things have changed quite a bit for you since then, haven't they?"

"They have. It's been a whirlwind situation. I got drafted in the first round by my favorite team, which was a dream come true." The crowd applauded. "Thank you. But then life happened. I blew out my knee in camp." As the crowd groaned in unison, he brought his hand to the corner of his eye and playfully pretended to wipe a tear away. "It's okay. I'm fine. I made some wise investments that set me up for life. I graduated college." The crowd applauded again. "Yes, thank you," he said as he clapped with them. "My parents were very happy about that; it got me off their couch." The crowd laughed. "That put me in position to work for an amazing company, *Turbo Boost Sports Agency*, where we supercharge your profile. Through them I've made some wonderful connections, and we've been able to do some amazing things.

"Another thing is I've been invited to travel with the *US National Team* as an alternate. They are, or we're, currently involved in pool play here in America, and they wanted a little more depth at my position."

"So, we're going to get to see you on the court again? This is huge."

"Not likely. Things would have to get pretty bad for me to be needed. I'm there just in case. We have a capable team. As you know, they have Grayson Randolph, and he's been playing lights-out so far."

"Well, to tell you the truth, I haven't been watching it, but now that you're on the team, I'm sure everyone will be interested." The audience applauded. "I will, however, be in Ghana for the championship game to do the play-by-play commentary for the American broadcast. So, if you make it to the big game, we'll see each other again. And maybe we can create another magical moment or two."

"That would be amazing, Dick." D'Quandray moved to the edge of his seat. "There is something very important that I want to say." He looked at the host. "Which way is my camera?"

Dick Rogers pointed at a waving cameraman just beyond the set. "That's yours right there."

"Thank you," D'Quandray said as he oriented himself toward that camera. "My last name is no longer Tyson; it's Free. I've legally changed it. Also, from this day forward, I will no longer respond to 'The Stud.'" He faced the host. "I know it's a moniker you coined in the heat of the moment, and you said it with the best of intentions, but I think it no longer applies. It just doesn't align with my sensibilities."

"Well, I must say that this comes as a surprise." He gave a hand gesture to someone off set. "I'll tell you what, we'll go to a commercial break, and we'll come back with more from D'Quandray um..." He looked at him for confirmation.

"Free."

"Yes, D'Quandray Free. We'll be back." As the band played them into the commercial break, he pressed the earpiece in his ear. "Goddamit, didn't I tell you people I don't like on-air surprises? Which one of you simpletons dropped the ball?"

Two producers rushed onto the set. One of them approached D'Quandray while the other went to Dick Rogers.

"D'Quandray, our entire next segment is built around him showing you videos of men doing stupid things and asking you if each guy is a stud or a dud. It's good natured and harmless. We put a lot of time into it, and it would help us out tremendously if you would just go along with it."

While she begged him to participate, he could hear the other producer telling the host that they were expediting the next guest and not to worry if D'Quandray would not remain on the show.

D'Quandray looked directly into his producer's eyes. "No, I'm not going to do it."

The color left her face. Then, she looked at the host, whose face was completely red. "Well, we're going to have to...um...could you..."

"No worries." D'Quandray stood and removed the microphone from his lapel. "I'll just leave." He extended a hand to Dick Rogers.

"Thank you for having me on your show." When the host looked away from him and flicked his hand dismissively without saying a word, D'Quandray knew he had made the right decision. He walked backstage and grabbed Imani by the hand. "Come on; let's go."

"Is everything okay?"

"They're a little upset with me right now, but I don't care. They'll be alright."

After taking a few minutes to find the exit, they were back on the bustling sidewalk in front of the building. It took five failed attempts before he was able to successfully hail a taxi. The driver had recognized him and chose to drive past another Black man who had his hand raised to pick him up. After telling him his destination, D'Quandray made sure to engage Imani in conversation for the entire trip there, so that he could avoid mindless banter with the driver. He had contemplated not tipping him well but believed that the driver would simply take that out on the next Black person who needed a ride. He begrudgingly gave him something that was on the low end of good and got out of his taxi.

D'Quandray recognized that his mood had degraded since their walk from the hotel to the studio. As he walked through the front door of the restaurant, he made sure to smile at Imani. He thought it was important to compartmentalize his frustration and not transfer any of it to her. They approached the maître d,' a well-dressed, slender Black man who was standing behind a podium with an electronic ledger in front of him.

"Good evening, and welcome to *Mason's*, may I have the name on the reservation please?"

"That would be D'Quandray Free."

"Thank you." He scrolled through the tablet. "Ah, here you are." The phone rang just as he was about to seat them. He held up a finger. "Please excuse me for a moment. Yes," he said as he answered the phone. He closed his eyes and sighed. "Yes, I see. I understand, sir." He shook his head as if he did not agree with what he had just been told. "I'll inform him." He hung the phone up. "That was the owner." He stilled his face to maintain a professional appearance but whispered his next words. "He's a friend of Dick Rogers. Word travels fast around here. I'm sorry."

"I understand, brother. It's not your fault." D'Quandray put his hand in the small of Imani's back. "Come on. Let's find somewhere else."

"Wait," the maître d' said. "There's no chance you'll get a cab any time soon. I'm calling someone." He picked up the phone and dialed out. He put his hand over the receiver and looked at D'Quandray. "Do you like soul food and jazz?"

"Yes, we do," he replied after first looking at Imani for confirmation.

"Good. My driver is five minutes away. He's taking you to Harlem. He'll wait for you to finish dining, then he'll bring you back to your hotel. Sorry for the inconvenience."

D'Quandray pulled out his phone. "What's your number?" As the maître d' recited it to him, he punched it into his phone. Then, he showed it to him for verification. "Is that it?"

"Yes, that's it."

D'Quandray then transferred five hundred dollars into his account. "Thanks, Black man. Come on, Imani."

The maître d' smiled and nodded. "This is quite generous. The car is black, and the driver's name is Jerome; I'll split this with him. Enjoy your night."

And they did enjoy their night. In fact, it turned out to be one of the best nights of D'Quandray's life. Instead of focusing on all the things that had gone wrong, he focused on doing what he could to make Imani's first trip to New York City a memorable one. The result was a night of laughter, discovery, and good food, all made easy by the backdrop of great music. Imani described their time at the jazz club as amazing, much to his relief. The fact was that he had enjoyed it, too, even though his expectations were not that high, especially given the fact that he had never heard of the establishment on any of his previous trips to the city. It was now designated a required stop for all his future visits to New York.

From the back seat of Jerome's luxury car, he watched the city lights blend into a blurred kaleidoscope as Imani rested her head on his chest. She was wearing his suit jacket. It was late, and they had stayed longer than they had anticipated they would, but the night had dictated the terms, and they simply obeyed its commands. He gave her a gentle nudge as Jerome stopped his car in front of the hotel. She craned her neck above the doors to see their surroundings, squinting as her eyes absorbed the bright lights that shined through the car window. Jerome opened the door from the outside and they stepped out.

"What time is checkout for you, Mr. Free?"

"It's officially noon, but my flight is at one o'clock, so we'll be leaving here at ten."

"Good. I'll be downstairs waiting for you at nine forty-five. It was a pleasure to serve you. Enjoy the rest of your night."

"Thank you, Jerome." He grabbed Imani's hand and led her through the lobby of the hotel and up to their suite.

D'Quandray's phone rang as they walked through the door. As he closed the door behind them, Imani curled up on the couch and pulled his jacket closed around her. "What's up, BG?" he said as he answered the phone.

"What the heck happened between you and Dick Rogers?"

"Oh that. He didn't take too well to the news that I wasn't going to respond to his nickname anymore. I think he took it personally."

"Yeah well, he roasted you pretty good after you left the set. They ran a blooper reel of all your bad plays from SSU."

"BG, as much as I'd love to hear about how I was clowned on national television, I'm kind of tired. I'll give you a call when I get back. I'll talk to you later."

"Okay, man. I hope you had fun otherwise. Talk to you soon. Bye now."

D'Quandray placed his phone on the dresser and sat beside Imani on the couch. He placed his arm around her as she readjusted her body to accommodate him. Then, she wrapped her arms around his waist and put her head on his chest. When he looked down at her, she was already looking up at him. Their words had all been used up, and their emotions synched. The need to touch one another more intimately became too much to resist. They kissed.

She placed her head back on his chest, squeezed him tighter, and released a long sigh. At that very moment, he knew he would never live another day without her playing a significant role in his life, and he felt that she knew it, too. In that position they remained for five more minutes.

"I guess I should get up and shower," she said finally.

D'Quandray raised his arm so that she could move. She stood, but she held onto his hand as she did. He stood and leaned down to kiss her once more. She smiled and pulled herself away from him. Then, she gathered her things and went into the bathroom. After showering, she walked out wearing pajamas.

"Your turn. I tried to leave some hot water for you."

"Yeah, that was only thirty minutes," he said sarcastically as he walked toward the bathroom.

"You're lucky; I was being considerate."

He leaned out of the bathroom door, looked at her, and raised an eyebrow.

"Just kidding. Enjoy your shower."

Imani was already under the covers with her eyes closed when he came out of the bathroom. He turned the television and lights off and got into bed. As he settled in, she snuggled up to him and put her arm over his torso. He kissed her on the forehead, and they fell asleep in each other's arms.

Chapter 24

Free

As D'Quandray approached the guard shack, Albert stepped out of it and flagged him down. He lowered his window to hear what he had to say.

"Good morning, Mr. D'Quandray. You're early today."

"Good morning, Albert. What's going on?"

"There's a bad accident on the main road, and they have everything blocked off. I think you should use the south gate today."

"Thank you, Albert. I'll do that. Have a nice day." He powered his window up as Albert walked back into the guard shack. He drove around it and headed toward the south gate of his community, thankful that he had decided to leave home early. The alternate route would add about ten more minutes to his commute.

As he entered the main road, he drove faster to compensate for the time he was going to lose. It was Tuesday morning. After dropping Imani off at her house, he had spent the rest of Monday resting up and preparing for the tour with the *US National Team*, which he was scheduled to join on Wednesday. He was excited and ready for what the upcoming weeks had in store for him.

When D'Quandray got close to the billboard, he slowed. Workers on a scaffold were removing the *Exum Industries* advertisement that featured him. He knew how long billboard ads typically ran and how much they cost. Someone had made a conscious decision to take it down early. A horn blew behind him, which made him realize he was impeding traffic. He sped up, and when he did, the other car passed him. Then, a police cruiser sped from behind the sign with its red and blue lights on.

D'Quandray pulled over to the side of the road to allow room for the police officer to pass him and catch the speeder, thankful that he had slowed to look at the sign. To his surprise, the officer positioned the police cruiser behind him instead of pursuing the other vehicle and got out of his car. Using his sideview mirror, he saw that it was Officer Roberts approaching. He breathed a sigh of relief and powered his window down.

"Good morning, Officer Roberts. To what do I owe this pleasure?"

"License and registration."

"Oh. Okay. Did I do something wrong? I know I was under the speed limit." He opened his center console to retrieve his driver's license and registration.

"Slowly."

D'Quandray took his hands away from the center console and placed them on the steering wheel. He looked forward and took a few calming breaths before turning his head to look at the officer. "I'm going to keep my left hand on the steering wheel while I retrieve the items that *you requested* with my right hand. Is that okay?"

The officer squared his body to the window and put his hand on the backstrap of his holstered weapon. "Like I said, slowly."

D'Quandray took his time getting the requested items and handed them to him. As the officer examined the license and registration, D'Quandray powered his window up. Then, he called Maliq.

"Good morning, Black man."

"Maliq, I've been pulled over by an Officer P. Roberts, badge number 9381, and I need you to be a witness."

"No problem. I'll stay on the line. Just keep your hands where he can see them. Do I need to come to you?"

"No; just stay on the line for me. Thanks." When the officer walked back to his police cruiser, D'Quandray placed the phone on his passenger seat.

Five minutes later, the officer walked back up to D'Quandray's car and tapped on his driver side window. D'Quandray powered it down about two inches. "Yes?"

"I clocked you doing thirty-five miles an hour."

"It's a forty mile per hour zone!"

"That's when it's not a construction zone. Today the speed limit is twenty-five. Here's your ticket." He slid the paper through the small space in the window that D'Quandray had created. Afterward, he handed him his license and registration. "I warned you once before to slow d—"

D'Quandray drove away before he could finish his sentence. "I don't have to listen to that shit." Through his rearview mirror he could see the officer still standing in the middle of the roadway with his hands on his hips.

"Is it over?" Maliq asked.

"Yeah, I'll see you soon. Thanks."

"No problem. See you when you get here."

D'Quandray ended the call with Maliq. As he continued down the road, there was no question in his mind why that had occurred. The same thing that had denied him access to the restaurant in New York City got him pulled over in his own city, and it was likely the reason his face was no longer plastered on the billboard. He surmised that they would say it was the disrespect he had allegedly shown toward Dick Rogers they did not like, but he knew that it was his rejection of their definition of who he was that had gotten everyone upset. He no longer fit into the box they had created for him, just like Maliq never fit into who *Turbo Boost Sports Agency* thought he should be. He got it now. He understood fully.

Despite his encounter with the police officer, D'Quandray got to work on time. Victor, Greg, and Maliq were already there.

He checked his watch as he walked into the office. "Good morning, everyone."

Victor, who was standing in front of D'Quandray's desk with his arms folded, sighed heavily, his eyebrows pointing downward. "Good morning, D'Quandray."

"Is there something wrong?"

"I wouldn't say there's anything *wrong* per se, but there is something that needs to be fixed."

D'Quandray put his hands flat on his desk, looked at the floor, and shook his head. Then, he looked up at Victor and Greg. "Is this about the Dick Rogers interview?"

"Dick's a heavyweight in our industry," Greg said. "He has a lot of influence, and we don't want to upset him."

"He's a sports personality."

"He's a sports personality with a high-profile platform," Victor said through clenched teeth, his voice slightly elevated. He paused and put his hands in front of him in a pushing motion. "Look, this could very easily go away," he said in a lower, more measured tone. "Our clients are spooked. They think you're all woke now. I've assured them that that's not the case. You have the right to be called what you want. The compromise is..."

"There's no compromise necessary, Victor. I've done nothing wrong."

"It's not that simple, D'Quandray," Greg said.

"How complicated can it be, Greg? My name is D'Quandray Free, not Tyson, not stud, and not boy."

"You see, that's what we mean by woke," Victor said. "Just hear us out. I promise you it won't be something you can't stomach."

"I'm listening."

"Okay. We'll send out a presser saying you've been suspended without pay. Of course, we'll still be paying you, but it'll be a lay-low situation. We'll draft an apology statement and attribute it to you. That way everybody's happy."

D'Quandray laughed. "You have my resignation." He pulled his company identification from his pocket, placed it on his desk, and turned to leave.

"We have your *what*? Are you serious?" Victor turned to Maliq. "Talk to him! Tell him not to leave!"

Maliq frowned. "Do I look like the personnel department? He's not my responsibility."

Victor followed D'Quandray into the hallway. "Rethink this. It's not that big of a deal. All we're asking is..."

D'Quandray stopped and turned to face him. "I'm done, Victor. I'm not bluffing. I no longer work for *Turbo*. Find you another boy. Good luck getting Jason to pick up the slack until you do." He walked to the elevator and got on. The ride to the lobby seemed to take longer than usual. As he walked out of the building, Jason was walking inside. "Good morning. The bosses were just talking about how important you are to the company. They're up there waiting for you."

Jason stopped and narrowed his eyes. "Are they upset with me?"

"No, not at all. See you around."

"Where are you going?"

"To find my purpose, because it sure as hell isn't to be here."

The closer D'Quandray got to his car, the more liberated he felt. By the time he grabbed his door handle, he was smiling. He had never needed the company; they needed him. He had enough money to sustain him for life if he lived modestly, and his experience in Jamestown showed him that he was more than capable of doing that. Besides, if Bradley was confident enough in himself to step out on faith that he would succeed, then he could do the same.

As he got into his car, his phone rang. "This is D'Quandray," he said as he answered it.

"This is Victor. We've reconsidered. Come back and we'll fix everything ourselves. You've become the face of our company, and we can't afford to lose you."

"My mind is made up, Victor. Donate my last check to charity." He ended the call without saying goodbye.

D'Quandray decided to sit still and meditate before moving his car. Though he felt he was in control of his emotions, he wanted to make sure he was calm before he drove. He started the engine and reclined his seat slightly, making sure the air coming through the vents was hitting his body just right.

It was still early, but he decided he would treat himself to a free day. He had earned it, and he needed to cleanse his mind of all the negativity that surrounded his awakening. He thought that America, in a lot of ways, was just like Dick Rogers. In fact, the old school sportscaster embodied its spirit. Black people would only be accepted on white America's terms, not in the way Blacks chose to present themselves. America liked Big Bartholomew and One-hand Moses, not Joseph Freeman, or George, or Isiah. It also liked D'Quandray Tyson—The-coon-dray, as Maliq had once informed him—but D'Quandray Free was already too much of a problem for them. In a way, he pitied

America, because the man they had seen so far was only a child in the chronology of what was to come. His appearance on the Dick Rogers show was a rude awakening, but the rest of his life was going to be a sustained assault on their fragile psyches.

On the Tuesday after his first night of time travel, he had gone to the park, so that seemed like a good place for him to start today. He backed out of the parking space and started to drive. As he pulled into the park, he thought about the state of mind he had been in the last time he was there. His entire world had been flipped upside down. He had just learned that all the things he thought he knew about life had been based on a lie and that reality for Black people was closer to what Maliq was seeing through his lens. He had been ignorant his entire life. As he thought more deeply, he started to believe that he had always known it. Of all the women he had dated, he had never thought enough of one of them to bring her home to meet his parents. On draft night, it was his mother and father who had sat with him as he waited for his name to be called, not the girl he had been dating at the time. *The girl.* He had to concentrate for a moment to remember who she was.

D'Quandray removed his necktie, tossed it onto the passenger seat, and unbuttoned his collar. Then, he got out and walked to the same bench he had sat on the last time he was there. Same bench, different perspective. Things had changed. *Everything* had changed, his name, his life, and—most importantly—his perspective. He also looked at women differently. His definition of beauty had been redefined, and all the things he now appreciated—kindness, sensitivity, compassion, understanding of self, and, yes, outer beauty—could be found in one woman: Imani. He unlocked his phone and called her.

When she answered the phone, he heard excitement in her voice. It reminded him of the way his mother had sounded the first time he called home from college. He had sensed warmth and affection then. He had also felt appreciated by her. His mother had known all about the things a young man had at his disposal in a college environment. She had remembered how big-time athletes had been treated on major college campuses when she had attended, especially since her then boyfriend—her husband for three years prior to D'Quandray being born—had been a star football player on that level. For him to find the time to call his mother despite it, showed respect, and for that she showed appreciation. Imani sounded the same way. He had just spent all of Sunday and part of Monday with her. She was aware of everything he had to do in preparation for his upcoming trip, and he had told her about everything he was dealing with at his job. Her tone conveyed appreciation and understanding. She agreed to have lunch with him later and said that she would be ready when he got there to pick her up.

When D'Quandray walked into the gym at noon, Imani had already stepped away from the service desk and was waiting by the door.

"I'm ready when you are." She smiled and raised up on her tiptoes to meet him halfway when he leaned down to kiss her.

D'Quandray grabbed her by the hand, and they walked out to his car. When he got back inside, he saw that he had a missed call from Bradley. Before he could call him back, the phone rang again.

"What's up, BG?"

"Are you okay? I just called your job, and they said you don't work there anymore. Is that true?"

"Yep."

"What happened?"

"I quit. What's going on with you?" He pulled the phone away from his ear and leaned toward Imani after seeing a concerned look on her face. "I'll explain later. It's nothing to worry about." Then, he continued to listen to Bradley. A few seconds later, they ended the call. "Bradley wants me to meet him at a park. Do you have a few extra minutes?"

"I have as long as you need."

D'Quandray smiled as he put the car into drive. "Good."

"What does your friend want?"

"He wants to do some sort of demonstration. He mentioned a prototype. I'm interested to see what he has."

"I always found him a little weird, that guy."

D'Quandray smiled. "BG's a good guy. He's just a tad awkward around women. I don't think I know anyone smarter, though. He has got to be a genius."

"Well, maybe that's it. They say when you excel to certain levels in one area, it makes you deficient somewhere else."

He cast a thoughtful glance at her. "There may be some truth to that. I never thought of it that way."

As they continued toward the park, they both got silent, but not uncomfortably so. D'Quandray was too immersed in the positive feelings that came with sharing her space to entertain any negative energy. When he looked at her face, he saw an expression that hovered between curiosity and concern, as if she was poised to ask a question but could not find the words to pose it.

"What's up?"

His question appeared to hit her like an alarm. When Imani snapped her eyes toward him, she smiled as if she was trying to conceal her surprise. She also appeared to be somewhat embarrassed that he had observed her in that state. She looked forward and overtly commanded her expression to one that conveyed peace. She grabbed the transverse strap of the seatbelt with both hands—something he noticed she would do whenever she was going to venture into unfamiliar territory—and turned her body toward him. "I've been around you for at least parts of three days now, and you've not once mentioned your parents. Please don't take that as criticism. It's merely an observation."

D'Quandray now knew that whenever she grabbed the seatbelt that way, it meant she was nervous about something. *Noted.* He turned into the park from the main road and pulled into a parking space. "They're in Florida," he said as he scanned the park for Bradley. "There he is." He looked at her. "Let's go; I'll tell you the rest later."

Bradley was holding a basketball in his hand, but he was nowhere near the basketball court, which D'Quandray thought was strange. He was standing near the woods that surrounded the park. Even more peculiar was the fact that he was not close to any of the trails. But he kept an open mind. He was eager to see what Bradley had to show him.

When they were close enough, Bradley threw a chest pass at him with the basketball, which he instinctively caught with both hands. As Bradley and Imani said hello to one another, D'Quandray kept his eyes focused on the basketball. It had an odd texture. When he looked closer, he saw that it was wrapped in a clear material, almost as if it was covered by an invisible spider web. He also noticed that it had a solid patch on it about the size of a quarter, which was also transparent.

"Bring it here," Bradley said.

D'Quandray walked over to where he was standing and handed the basketball to him. Bradley plucked a blade of grass from the ground and carefully tucked it into the quarter-sized patch on the ball. Then, he set the ball down. In a matter of seconds, the basketball disappeared. It had blended into the grass.

"That's incredible!"

"That's what's going to make us rich," Bradley said. "I'm calling it the chameleon project. I've already submitted my patent paperwork, and I'm meeting with the Department of Defense in a few days. They're *very* interested in it. My plan is to integrate the polymer into the host material instead of having it on the surface like this one. That way, you won't even know it's there. It can be put into anything solid. They'll be able to hide entire tanks in plain sight."

He almost asked him if that was something he had learned about in Sapien. Almost. Instead, he consciously kept his eyes focused on where he thought the ball was.

"And what are you and Imani doing hanging out together?"

With that, D'Quandray's question had been answered. The fact that Bradley's mind had stopped on Imani meant that he had cycled through the same thought process and stopped at the same obstacle. He looked up and smiled. "I'm sorry, BG, but she's my new best friend."

"Wow, I've been replaced twice in one week."

Whether Bradley's thinly veiled reference to Horace was a slip up or not, D'Quandray decided to change the subject. They were playing too closely to the edge of the cliff, and he could not afford any missteps. "What's your next move, BG?"

"I need to assemble a staff. I have other products I'm going to be working on and rolling out. I'll need engineers," He gestured toward D'Quandray with an open hand, "and a marketing department. Do you know anyone who could use a job?"

D'Quandray chuckled. "I might, but I think he's going to be on a hiatus for a while. He's definitely willing to help out though." He squatted and reached for the ball, grabbing nothing but air. Then, he slowly waved his hand horizontally over the ground about four inches high until he contacted it. When he picked it up, he gathered the material that surrounded it with his fingertips and pulled it off the ball, marveling at it as the retracting green revealed the bright orange basketball.

"What are you two about to do?" Bradley asked.

"We're about to get lunch. Would you like to join us?" He handed the mesh material to Bradley but kept the basketball under his arm.

Bradley found the solid patch on the mesh material and removed the blade of grass. The polymer reverted to its transparent state. "I was actually supposed to meet up with Elijah and Marissa next to show them this."

When D'Quandray looked at Imani, she shrugged. Then he looked at Bradley. "Why don't you just have them meet us for lunch? It'll be nice to see everyone, especially since I'm leaving tomorrow."

"I'll do that," Bradley said as he started to walk. "Are we going to the diner?"

D'Quandray shook his head as he thought about Katy, the waitress he had slept with. He hoped that Bradley would properly infer from his reticence that he was romantically interested in Imani and did not want to jeopardize his chances with her. "No, let's go somewhere different. *The Ultimate American Grill* has good food. I think we should meet there."

At that, Bradley furrowed his brow. Then, his mouth fell open as if he had had an epiphany at that moment, but the mechanism that vetted his thoughts before they were spoken quickly failed. "Are you an Imani dating?"

Imani stepped close to D'Quandray and wrapped her hand around his upper arm. "Yes, we are."

D'Quandray looked down at her smiling face, removed his arm from her grasp, and placed it around her shoulders. Bradley's awkwardness had finally worked in his favor, as it helped to confirm what he had hoped would soon be the case. "Any more questions?"

"Um, no. I guess not. Welcome to the family, Imani."

"Thank you, Bradley. I'm happy to be a part of it."

And with that, they were officially a couple.

Chapter 25

Get Off Me

Location: Accra, Ghana
Championship game, 13 October 2211

The horn sounded to end the intermission, and D'Quandray made his way to the end of the bench. As the coach gathered the starters to give them a few last second instructions before they took the court to start the second half of play, D'Quandray turned around to wave at Imani, who was two rows back from the bench. She had arrived in Ghana that morning, but they had not yet had an opportunity to spend time together. They had made plans to spend a week in the African country after the tournament was over.

The first half had been a competitive one. The *US National Team* had attacked the *African Coalition Team* in several ways offensively, and Grayson Randolph had scored twenty points already. Kofi Boateng, his African counterpart, had scored twenty-five points and was personally keeping the coalition team in the game. At present, the coalition was down ten points.

D'Quandray sat on the edge of his seat as play began. He had a towel around his head to keep in the warmth he had generated during the shoot-around at the half. His left knee felt good. The team trainers had done an excellent job of keeping him stretched, and he had done his part by making every physical therapy appointment throughout training. His role had been reduced to that of an offensive specialist for the team. Coach Stone had designed a few plays for the shooting guard to get open shots from the corner of the court, top of the key, and from the elbow area of the court.

The coalition team scored the first three baskets to open the half, prompting Coach Stone to call a quick timeout. They had deployed a strategy of double-teaming Grayson Randolph, even when he did not have the ball, a move that disrupted the *US National Team's* offensive flow. As D'Quandray watched the coaches draw up plays on the dry-erase clipboard, an uneasy feeling came over him. When he looked across the court at the coalition team, the body language of those players sent a different signal than what he was seeing from the players on his sideline. He got up and joined the starters in the huddle, placing his hands on the shoulders of the players in front of him.

"Come on, guys. Stay locked in. If we can just weather this storm, we'll be okay." He looked into his teammates' eyes, searching for any hint that one of them lacked confidence. As the huddle broke, he walked up to Grayson Randolph. "Listen, if they're going to continue to double you like that, make them pay. Stand out by the five second line so the rest of the court can open for your teammates. That way they'll have to defend four of our players with only three of theirs."

Grayson nodded as he walked on to the court. On their next two offensive possessions, the *US National Team* scored consecutive baskets, a fastbreak layup by Grayson Randolph and a three-pointer by another player. The coalition team had managed to score one two-point basket in between. The next few times down the floor, Grayson stood by the five-second line as D'Quandray had suggested. On each possession, the *US National Team* scored easily. When the coalition team finally called a timeout to adjust, The *US National Team* held a precarious six-point lead.

After their timeout, the coalition team abandoned their tactic of doubling Grayson Randolph. As a result, he immediately continued his scoring barrage. The game quickly turned into a shootout between him and Kofi Boateng, much to the crowd's delight. At the five-minute mark the contest was all tied up. An errant pass by the coalition point guard led to a break-away layup attempt by Grayson Randolph. As he went airborne, the coalition point guard, who had hustled back to stop him, chose to run by him instead of jumping to contest the shot. As he did, his shoulder bumped Grayson's forward knee and caused him to lose balance. The ball flew out of bounds as Grayson flailed his arms to maintain equilibrium. He fell flat on his back and was knocked unconscious when the back of his head hit the court.

The coaches and referees cleared the players from the court as the trainers and medical staff attended to Grayson. Eventually, he regained consciousness and was brought to a seated position, eliciting applause from the audience and both teams. As Grayson was helped off the court and taken to the locker room to be treated, it was apparent that he would not be returning to the game. He left having scored forty points in thirty-five minutes of play.

When play resumed, the coalition team built a six-point lead. With three minutes to go, Coach Stone called their final timeout. D'Quandray sat back in his chair and folded his arms as he watched the jubilant players on the other side of the court. The *US National Team* was about to experience a rare defeat in a championship situation. As he sat there shaking his head, he thought he heard his name. When he looked toward the huddle, he saw his wild-eyed head coach coming toward him.

"Free, check in!"

D'Quandray immediately got off the bench and took off his sweats. There was no need for him to get extra instructions from the coaches; he knew all the plays. He had also been mentally involved in the game throughout the contest. As he walked onto the court, he visualized each situation. Then, he looked up at the scoreboard. There was time. They needed offense, and he knew the plays would be run through him. There was no other reason for him to be on the court.

D'Quandray settled into the corner as the point guard brought the ball up the court, waiting for his time to move. He took a step toward the baseline to influence his defender, then reversed his direction and sprinted toward the elbow area of the court as one of his teammates set a pick on the player who was guarding him. The moment he was open, the point guard passed him the ball. As D'Quandray raised up to shoot it, his teammates raised their hands. The ball swished through the net, cutting the coalition lead to four. As he ran down the court to play defense, D'Quandray checked the time. They had less than two minutes to play.

On the defensive end of the court, D'Quandray was tasked with guarding one of the less offensive minded players, a small forward who was primarily a defensive specialist. The coalition team's offensive possession ended with a shot clock violation. As the *US National Team* converted to offense, the point guard called a different play for D'Quandray. When he crossed half court, he passed the ball to D'Quandray on the wing and D'Quandray quickly passed it back to him. Then, D'Quandray jogged toward the baseline. Once he was there, he sprinted toward the opposite corner. As the center and power forward stood shoulder to shoulder on the baseline to block the trailing defender's path, D'Quandray settled in the corner with his hands ready to receive the pass from the point guard. As soon as it touched his hands, he raised up to shoot the three-pointer. As he released it, the Americans in the stadium yelled "Free, Free, Free." Again, the ball swished through the hoop. The crowd roared and the coalition team called its last timeout.

When D'Quandray got to the sideline, he went straight to the head coach. "They're going to try to do to me what they did to Grayson. Right now, they're spending their entire timeout on a defensive set to stop me. If I were you, I'd hold me out until the next dead ball. There's no way they'd anticipate that."

After taking a moment to ponder it, the coach made the decision to replace D'Quandray with David Lang, a highly skilled defensive player. It was Lang who had shown D'Quandray just how far off he had fallen when he reported to camp to join the team. When guarded by the specialist, D'Quandray had been unable to dribble past him, and getting a shot off on him had proven to be even more difficult. But it was D'Quandray's ability to shoot the basketball with a high degree of proficiency that made him an asset to the team still, so on it he remained. They waited until the whistle to resume play was blown before making the substitution. As the *US National Team* walked back onto the court, the entire coalition team had their eyes on D'Quandray, who was seated at the end of the bench. As play resumed, Lang guarded Kofi Boateng, and the coalition team's offensive possession ended with him blocking Boateng's shot. The Americans hurried up the court, but their possession ended with them missing a shot and the coalition team rebounding the ball.

The coalition team brought the ball up the court with less than thirty seconds to play. They were up by one point. Boateng aggressively drove to the basket, but Lang swiped down on the ball causing it to hit his leg and bounce out of bounds with ten seconds left on the clock. It was the *US National Team's* ball, and everyone in the arena was standing. D'Quandray re-entered the game as the American fans applauded Lang's defensive efforts.

The *US National Team* had only three plays that were specifically designed for D'Quandray to score, and the coalition players had already seen two of them. As the power forward accepted the ball from the referee to inbound from the coalition baseline, D'Quandray set up in the far corner on the American side of the court. When the referee blew the whistle to start play, the power forward threw the inbound pass to the speedy point guard. He quickly dribbled past half court. D'Quandray sprinted toward the top of the key. When he reached his spot, the point guard passed the ball to him and moved out of the way. The crowd yelled, "Free, Free, Free!" The trailing defender crouched in front of D'Quandray with his hand extended and touching his midsection. The seconds were ticking away.

The defender was too close for D'Quandray to attempt a three-point shot, so that option was gone. Out of the corner of his eye, he saw the center flashing toward them. When the big man set a pick on the defender's right side, D'Quandray dribbled the ball to the left of the screen but quickly had to dribble forward and off the three-point-line as the defender who had been guarding the center switched to guard him. D'Quandray's teammate released himself from the pick, rolled toward the basket, and raised his hand. With one defender to beat, D'Quandray dribbled the ball aggressively toward him, drawing the defender in. When the defender committed to stop the ball, D'Quandray threw a bounce-pass to the center, who then exploded up from the floor and dunked the ball with two hands as time expired. The *US National Team* won the game by one point.

The stadium erupted with applause and screams as the heavy contingent of spectators from America rejoiced. D'Quandray and the rest of his teammates ran toward their center and hugged him, sending him crashing to the floor under an avalanche of bodies as camera crews surrounded them. As the players celebrated, the half of the basketball court they were on was cordoned off for the media by the event staff. The players eventually extracted themselves from the pile and went to shake hands with the other team. Kofi Boateng approached D'Quandray with a broad smile on his face.

"My brother, it was a pleasure to share the basketball court with you once again," Boateng said. The Ghana native had tallied sixty points, a championship game record.

"The pleasure was all mine. You're..." D'Quandray paused to compose himself. He almost called him a stud. "You're an amazing player. The league is going to love you."

"Thank you. Do you mind if we pose for a picture?"

"Not at all." He stood beside the African star and placed an arm around him.

They posed for several pictures as people from various networks approached to interview them and the other players. Among the crowd of media personnel was Dick Rogers. The smile on his face reminded D'Quandray of those he had seen on the faces of the people in the hostage videos the team had been shown as a precaution in preparation for international travel. He wrapped his arm around D'Quandray's shoulder as the cameraman centered himself on them and started a countdown.

"Be nice," Dick Rogers said through his frozen smile. When the cameraman's countdown got to one and he turned his camera light on, Dick Rogers' eyes lit up, and he transformed to interview mode as he raised the microphone to his mouth. "We are *live* with one of the stars of..."

D'Quandray forcefully removed the two-faced analyst's hand from his shoulder, turned his back to him, and walked toward several news crews from the Ghanaian press corps. "I'm available for an interview if anybody wants one," he said as he approached them.

Dick Rogers made a slashing gesture across his neck with his hand. "Cut the camera." The cameraman, instead, turned his lens away from the legendary sportscaster and continued to film D'Quandray. "I said cut the goddamn camera, you shithead!"

As the American media scrambled to recover from the on-air slight, D'Quandray was surrounded by the host country's press, and he proceeded to answer every question they asked him with enthusiasm and respect.

***

Though it was far below the quality of the rooms in the five-star hotels in which D'Quandray was accustomed to staying, the one he found himself in was clean and spacious. He winced as he hoisted his left leg onto the ottoman, making sure to keep the ice pack in place as he did. Imani wrapped an elastic bandage around it. When she was done, she sat on the arm of the chair he was sitting in, wrapped her arm around his shoulders, and kissed him on his forehead.

"I'm proud of you, D'Quandray. What you did was amazing."

"What I did comes naturally to me. I'm an athlete, and I just happen to be one who performs best when the stakes are high. I consider it a gift."

She put her hand under his chin and tilted his face upward toward hers. Then, she planted a gentle kiss on his lips and tapped his chest lightly with her hand. The smile she showed him told him that he had somehow missed her point entirely.

He furrowed his brow as he looked up at her. "What?"

"I'm not talking about the game. I'm talking about how you put that sports guy in his place. Stuff like that needs to happen to them more often. Maybe then they won't be so passive aggressive."

"Oh, *that*. You saw that?"

"We all did. We were watching the live feed on our phones. He's in a lot of trouble. There was a hot mic situation after you walked away from him, and I'll be surprised if he still has a job."

"I don't know what he was thinking."

"I do. You've got to understand that they're so used to getting their way—even against your will—that it flusters them when it doesn't happen. Think of the audacity it took for him to try to get an interview with you after he did *you* wrong, especially when he didn't even have leverage. It's one thing if you needed him or if it was a mutually beneficial situation, but that wasn't the case. He felt he was entitled to your time and that you were obligated to be there—for *him*. That's why what you did was so important. Our first step to achieving freedom, *Mr. Free*, is to take ownership of ourselves."

And there she was, the "Super Sista" he had seen every time he had looked at Imani in the past. And just like a superhero, she arrived at exactly the right time. He raised his leg from the ottoman with a groan and placed his foot flat on the floor. As Imani shifted her body to allow space for him to move freely, he wrapped his arms around her waist and pulled her into his lap. She, in turn, wrapped her arms around his neck. They kissed. But unlike all the other times in the past, they did not stop.

D'Quandray Tyson had been a womanizer disguised as a lady's man his entire life. For him, sex had been easier to get than food, and he had often craved it more. His experience had become such that the mere act meant nothing to him emotionally, especially after Jamestown. But for the first time in his life, he made love, and D'Quandray Free made a promise to himself with his heart, and a promise to Imani with his body and soul, that for as long as the universe allowed him to live, he would never touch another woman in that way again.

Chapter 26

The Golden Jubilee House

D'Quandray had no idea that Kofi Boateng was also the nephew of Ghana's President until he was told the next morning. He learned that through an official request for him and Imani to join his family at the presidential palace for dinner. The family had also sent a driver to take them around the city of Accra until the time came. Two hours before the scheduled time of the dinner, they were brought back to their hotel to freshen up. When the driver pulled up to the front of the hotel, there was a crowd assembled outside.

"I wonder what's going on here," D'Quandray said as he looked out from the backseat window.

The driver looked back and smiled. "They love celebrities here, sir."

"Oh really? Who's here?"

"You are, Mr. Free. They're here to see you." He got out of the car, walked to the back door, and opened it. "I'll be here when you return. Take all the time you need."

When D'Quandray grabbed Imani by the hand, she mouthed the word "wow" without speaking it. As they walked toward the crowd, chants of "Free, Free, Free" filled the air. He estimated there to be about one hundred people. He greeted and signed autographs for as many of them as he could. After about thirty minutes, he pulled himself away from the crowd, dragging Imani along with him. As much as he wanted to accommodate each fan, he was more concerned about being on time for the President's dinner.

After taking an hour to get showered and dressed, D'Quandray and Imani were back inside the car. They both sat up as they arrived at the presidential palace. The driver stopped in front of the massive black gate while it retracted. The guards used mirrors that were attached to long poles to look underneath his car. When the gate was open, the guards stepped back and gave the driver permission to proceed.

The driver stopped the car with the passenger side facing a woman who was standing with her hands behind her back and smiling. She was dressed in traditional Ghanaian attire, with vibrant colors and a matching headdress. "This is the *Golden Jubilee House*," he said, "home of our beloved President. Amma will be your host. Welcome."

"Thank you," D'Quandray said.

As the driver opened the back door to let D'Quandray and Imani out, Amma greeted them warmly. She then asked them to follow her. Once inside the palace, they were met by security personnel—two men who were dressed in white suits and wearing earpieces. Amma advised D'Quandray and Imani that it was both customary and respectful for visitors to wear traditional Ghanaian clothing when they were guests of the President. They quickly agreed to comply with the custom and were taken to separate dressing rooms by the security personnel.

When he walked into his dressing room, D'Quandray heard a beep from the vertical sensor that was embedded into the door frame. He quickly changed into the clothing he was given. As he looked into the mirror inside the dressing room, he was amazed by how well the outfit fit him. He wondered if the base color being cerulean was a coincidence or if they had known that he was an alumnus of SSU and had chosen to honor him with clothing that featured his school colors. He hung his own clothing on the rack on the wall and walked toward the exit. He decided to leave his watch in the dressing room, not wanting to wear anything that could possibly trigger the metal detector as he left. When he pressed the door handle, he heard a buzz. The door lock demagnetized, allowing him to leave.

"This way," the security officer said with a sweeping hand gesture as soon as D'Quandray exited the room.

The security officer escorted him to a part of the house that was different from the way they had entered. They rounded the corner into a corridor that led to several rooms. Imani was already there. To his surprise, her outfit matched his—a nice touch, he thought. She smiled, and so did he. He grabbed her by the hand. Amma rejoined them and led them through two large wooden doors and into a waiting room that resembled some of the better family rooms D'Quandray had seen when he had visited homes in the American South. Far from ornate, the room had been furnished with the comfort of its guests in mind.

Still basking in the afterglow of their magical night together, D'Quandray and Imani snuggled together on the comfortable couch. They were alone, and, despite their appreciation of the whirlwind of activity that surrounded them, they enjoyed the quiet. Moments later, Kofi Boateng walked into the room. He was accompanied by a tall, slender woman who was about his age, and they were both attired in traditional garb. She had the looks and physique of a supermodel. D'Quandray and Imani both stood to greet them.

"Welcome, D'Quandray." Kofi walked over to Imani and grabbed one of her hands, covering it with his massive hands—one underneath and one over top of it. "And whom might this be?"

"Thank you for inviting us. Imani Colson is the lady in my life."

"And a wise selection she is." He gestured to the woman behind him. "This is my wife, Naomi."

D'Quandray nodded. "It's a pleasure to meet you. It appears that Kofi is even more talented off the court than he is on it." She smiled and nodded, acknowledging his compliment. "Thank you for inviting us. We are honored."

"The honor is ours. My uncle cannot wait to meet you. He has been a fan of yours for some time now."

"I'm speechless. The fact that the President of your country even knows who I am is simply mind boggling to me. I look forward to meeting him, too."

Kofi brought his hand to his chin, concentrated for a moment, then gestured toward D'Quandray with his open hand. "You know, it was not what you did in the game last night that made this country love you." He shook his finger from side to side at chest level. "No indeed. It was the time you spent with our media—the respect you showed. *That* had never happened before. There is such a thing as the ugly American in the rest of the world. You were anything but. And you were just as gracious when I visited your town. Speaking of that, how is your friend Maliq?"

"You have an excellent memory. Maliq is doing quite well. I'll tell him you asked about him. He's a great man. I wish he was here."

"Perhaps, I will invite him someday. We play exhibition games here often, and it would be nice to have some American players participate in them. He is one I would welcome with open arms, and so would my country."

"He'd like that, I'm sure. That also sounds like something I'd be interested in playing in as well. Just let me know ahead of time, and I'll make myself available. By the way, what are your plans for the league?"

"I've only worked out for four teams, the franchises in New York, Los Angeles, Miami, and Washington, D.C. I will join one of those teams as a free agent." He frowned and shook his head. "I'll not subject myself to that draft. I want to control my own destiny, and I fear that the lottery selection process is not as arbitrary as they wish for us to believe it is. In fact, I think it's farcical."

D'Quandray smiled. "That's not the first time I've heard that." He furrowed his brow. "The franchises you mentioned are stacked with talent and have maxed out salary caps…"

"My family has more money than I would be able to spend in three lifetimes. There, I would play for the minimum. It's more important for my people to see me play and play well among the best in the world than it is for me to languish on a team that has no chance of winning, only for me to gain personal wealth. That's why they weren't heartbroken when we didn't win last night; they got what they came to see. They know we belong."

"That's a beautiful perspective," Imani said.

The host opened the double doors behind them. "Pardon the intrusion. It's time."

Kofi nodded. "Thank you, Amma." He turned back to D'Quandray and Imani, then extended an elbow to Naomi. "Let us go. We will continue our discussion later."

They walked into a grand dining hall, in the center of which was a rectangular table with ten place settings. The colors inside the room were breathtaking. The table was sturdy and constructed from quality wood that complemented the marble floor. On top of each plate was a card with the name of the person whose seat it was. Naomi's and Kofi's seats were across from D'Quandray's and Imani's. Following the lead of their hosts, they stood behind their seats instead of sitting.

"I present to you," a loud, booming voice announced, "the President of our great nation, Ike Boateng, and our First Lady, Priscilla."

Everyone stood still as Kofi's uncle walked to the head of the table and stood behind his chair. Priscilla stood behind the first chair to his right, on the same side of the table as Kofi and Naomi. Amma sat in the unoccupied seat beside D'Quandray, which was on the President's immediate left and directly across from the First Lady. The other chairs were occupied by dignitaries to whom D'Quandray had not been introduced.

"Guests, we are honored to have you here," the President said with a smile. "We hope that this will be as memorable for you as it promises to be for us. Please, introduce yourselves and be seated."

"Thank you, Mr. President," the man standing at the other end of the table said. The Liberian dignitary introduced himself and sat. The others—a woman and another man, who were from other African countries—did the same.

So that she would not have to face the pressure of being last, D'Quandray nodded to Imani to introduce herself before he introduced himself.

"Good evening, Mr. President, madam First Lady, and special guests. I am Imani Colson of the United States of America, and I consider it an honor to be here. Thank you for having me." She nodded and sat.

"Greetings," D'Quandray said, channeling Maliq to speak on his behalf. "I am D'Quandray Free. Thank you, Mr. President, for honoring me with such an amazing experience. It is one that I will remember and cherish for the rest of my life." He placed his right hand over his heart, nodded, and sat. As the President began his pleasantries, D'Quandray continued to scan the room, awestruck by the beauty contained within it.

"I hope you have brought your appetites," Ike said. "Our cooks have prepared for you some authentic Ghanaian dishes that are sure to titillate your palates." He placed his hands flat on the table and looked at D'Quandray.

After being nudged by Imani, D'Quandray snapped out of his daze and looked at his smiling face.

"Mr. Free, there is a lot I would like to discuss with you."

"I'm open to discussing anything you like, Mr. President."

"Very good. I have always been a fan of the way you play." His smile faded from his face and his expression transitioned into one that indicated something serious was about to be addressed. "I've also followed your progression as a man. I must admit, I was concerned for a while. However, I sense an awakening in you. Am I wrong?"

For a moment, D'Quandray simply looked at him. He was embarrassed that someone, who was so important on the world stage, had been aware of who he had been before he came to his senses. Then, he narrowed his eyes as he studied the President's face, wondering if, by chance, Ike Boateng had been one of the ten men who had been tied to a post in that death clock in Jamestown. He quickly realized that he did not recognize him from there. However, the fact that the President of an African country had recognized *what* he had been only months ago brought him back to Maliq's assertion that he did not realize how important he was.

"You're *not* wrong, Mr. President. In fact, you're spot on. Some amazing people have come into my life recently, and I've been educated. I assume you're referring to the idiotic comments I've made in the past about social issues I had absolutely no business talking about. I look back and get angry at the way I was used and taken advantage of by people with far more life experience than I had. Not anymore. I'm wide awake now."

Ike smiled and pointed at D'Quandray with a poking gesture. "Exactly. What changed? I want to hear about it."

If not for what he had experienced with Ms. Sarah in Jamestown, D'Quandray would have considered the President's line of questions aggressive, rude, and possibly inappropriate, but now he knew better. Ike Boateng was direct, and D'Quandray appreciated that.

"I started listening to people who care about me. Once I did that, I started to see how much the people who were using me to push their agendas did not. I started to read between the lines, to listen to the silences in conversations. Then, I started to see the evil behind the fake smiles."

The President smiled and applauded. "Yes." He looked to the other end of the table at the dignitary from the country of Liberia. "Do you know, Mr. Free, whose idea it was to combine the African teams into one?"

D'Quandray knew as the President continued to stare at the Liberian national that that had been a topic of discussion between the two of them in the past, the degree to which he was about to find out. "I don't, sir."

The President looked away from the Liberian and back at D'Quandray. "It was my idea. Tell me, Mr. Free, why would I involve myself so heavily in something as trivial as sports?"

"I would say it's because sports are a metaphor for life." He paused. "Better yet, they're a microcosm of it. They bring out the true nature of men and women in ways that few things can."

"What about war?" the Liberian national asked. His voice cut through the air like a cannonball fired down the middle of a busy Manhattan street. All eyes turned toward him.

And D'Quandray looked directly at him. "With all due respect, war is different, and men can—and probably should—be excused for what they are forced to do there." He turned back toward the President. "Sporting events, like normal life, are wrapped in artificial pressures that we create. Nobody dies if I don't hit the last shot, but that doesn't mean the moment isn't real *to me*. People can take things from that and directly apply them to their lives. Wars are savagery; that's why they're relegated to battlefields as much as possible. No one needs to witness them. They should only be experienced."

The Liberian national rattled the silverware on the table when he placed his elbow on it. His face was even more serious now. "What do you mean when you say, 'artificial pressures' in regard to actual life, Mr. Free?"

"I mean..." Again, he paused to gather his thoughts. "Just look around the world. Think about how resources are allocated. In America, one decision made today by one CEO of one top corporation can cause a seismic shift in our stock market. That affects everyone in our country, and that's because we're capitalists. Now, that's not an argument for or against capitalism; it's just a statement of fact. Likewise, people who live under socialist and communist economic structures enjoy the advantages and endure the disadvantages of doing so. That is artificial pressure in that it can be changed with the decision of whoever is in charge. By the same token, games are dictated by the rules of their governors. If something became impossible to accomplish, one would only need to change the rules. In that way, sports are a microcosm of life. War could never be. War is the consequence of someone looking at the rules we've collectively decided to play by and arbitrarily deciding that they simply do not apply to them."

"You are wise beyond your years," the President said. He looked back at the Liberian national. "It matters not that our coalition team lost the game. What matters is the rules have been changed to include us in our present form. It is only a matter of time before we dominate. African boys and girls all over this great continent saw what was once considered the impossible. On the grandest stage imaginable, we almost did the unthinkable. We almost beat the American team. Before now, no team from an African country had ever made it to tournament play. The message is that we are stronger together."

Stronger together. Their conversation went on to cover many other topics, from sports to other social issues, but that was the part D'Quandray knew he would never forget. Two men from different worlds had arrived at the same conclusion, and each was making sure to do what he could do at his level to bring black people in Africa together and Black Americans together in their respective lands. He had wondered if the Liberian national was a foe or an ally at the beginning of their conversation. D'Quandray determined that the Liberian was the latter and that Ike Boateng had welcomed discourse and had even used those passionately expressed differences of opinion to strengthen his own position.

After dinner, they all migrated to a more formal lounging room, where they listened to soft music and continued to talk. Drinks were served and the mood was light. D'Quandray had finally gotten comfortable in the environment, and as he soaked it in, he began to see it as a place in which he belonged.

"Mr. Free, I'd like for you to come with me," Ike said as he tapped him lightly on his elbow.

D'Quandray set his glass of wine on a nearby table. "Excuse me for a minute," he said to Imani. She nodded, and he followed the President out of the room.

Accompanied by two members of the President's security detail, they walked across the hall and into another room that looked to be part office and part library—a study. It reminded him of the one in Horace's house. In the center of the room was a desk, and on top of it was a piece of paper with an official government seal on it.

"I would be honored, Mr. Free, if you agreed to become a citizen of Ghana. This will not affect your status as an American in any way. You would have dual citizenship, and you would be able to live among us as one of us. Would you be so kind?"

D'Quandray felt tears forming in his eyes and found it difficult to speak. Of the many words he wanted to say, "thank you" were the only ones he could get out. He grabbed the official pen from its holder and signed the document. Then, the President signed it and handed him the pen.

"This is yours, to commemorate the moment. Congratulations, you are now a citizen of Ghana. When you marry Imani, she will automatically become a citizen as well, by my decree—and so will your children." Ike stepped forward and hugged him. Then, he moved D'Quandray out to arm's length by his shoulders. "You will do great things, Mr. Free; I am certain of it."

It was the perfect ending to a great night. And on that night, D'Quandray decided that he would propose to Imani one day soon. They spent the rest of the week getting to know the city of Accra and becoming great friends with Kofi and Naomi. The events of their visit, which started with what had occurred at the *Jubilee House*, dictated a change in his travel plans. So, instead of flying home from Ghana, he chose to fly to Florida to visit his parents. For the first time in his life, he was going to introduce them to a woman he was dating.

Chapter 27

Meet the Parents

It was upon Imani's insistence that D'Quandray did not check them into a hotel prior to going to his parents' home. He gave in to her demand after she convinced him that it could possibly cast her in a negative light in the eyes of his parents and that the proper thing to do was to allow them the opportunity to host. She informed him that a lot could be gleaned from a person's willingness to stay or eagerness to leave after having been in someone's home. She told him that she wanted them to see her beyond the formalities of an introduction—without pretense. D'Quandray suspected that Imani wanted to see them in the same way.

They held hands as they stood on the front doorstep of the ranch style home. Their suitcases were behind them.

"Stop squeezing my hand so hard," Imani said. "I'm the one who should be nervous; I look a mess."

"You look just fine." He sighed and pressed the doorbell. The door immediately opened.

"We were wondering how long you two were going to stand there?" his mother said. "Hi, sweetheart. My name is Tamara, and this is my husband, Rashon."

"Hello, I'm Imani." She covered her mouth with her hand to hide her laughter as D'Quandray rolled his eyes. She stepped aside as he pulled his mother into an embrace and then hugged his father. Then, D'Quandray stepped aside as they both greeted and hugged Imani in the same sequence.

D'Quandray grabbed Imani's bags as his parents turned to go inside.

"I told you she was Black," his father said to his mother. "White folks don't name their kids Imani." Despite the loose-fitting tee shirt that he was wearing, his musculature was evident, and his vascular forearms looked like they had been carved from granite.

"Child, hush," his mother replied. "It's about time you were right about something."

This time Imani could not hide her laughter. "Do they know I can hear them?"

D'Quandray shook his head. "They don't care. Come on, let's get inside."

As D'Quandray and Imani walked into the house, Rashon grabbed some of the suitcases from him. "I'm assuming these little pretty ones belong to her," he said as he walked toward one of the bedrooms. He stopped and turned to look at D'Quandray. "You do know y'all are sleeping in separate bedrooms while you're here, right?"

"Of course," D'Quandray said. "I wouldn't have it any other way."

"Okay, just checking. You never know with you youngsters. Imani, you have your own bathroom, and there's a linen closet with fresh towels and washcloths in there. Son, you know where your room is."

"Thank you, Mr. Tyson," Imani said as she followed him into the room.

"Oh no, if you're going to be sleeping in my home, you're going to call me by my first name."

D'Quandray chuckled to himself as he listened to them talk from the hallway outside the room. He was tired, and as he stood there, he started to regret not getting a hotel room prior to coming to his parents' home. He wanted more alone time with Imani. He was also hungry. It was still early afternoon, however, and he knew his mother had not yet started to prepare dinner. He walked outside and brought the other suitcases into the house. Then, he closed the front door behind him.

As Imani and Rashon continued to banter inside the room, he walked into the living room, where he was instantly overtaken by nostalgia. Several of his trophies were displayed throughout the room, as well as his father's, and there were also little league pictures of him on the walls. D'Quandray smiled as he imagined how Imani was going to react to seeing those. He sat on the couch, leaned back, and closed his eyes.

"There you are," Tamara said. "Get up and go take a nap. We're going out for dinner tonight. You have time."

"Where's Imani?" He had dozed off and did not know how long he had been asleep.

"I think she's taking a shower. I had to pull Rashon out of there so she could. He was about to talk her ears off. I like her, son. Where'd you meet her?"

"She works at the gym where I play basketball every Saturday. I've known her for a while now."

"Well, you must be serious about her if you brought her here."

He smiled. "I am—very serious."

D'Quandray grabbed his suitcases and carried them into the third bedroom. Unlike the one Imani was in, his room did not have its own bathroom. He would have to use the guest bathroom in the common area of the home.

"We'll talk about why you changed your last name later," she said from the other side of his bedroom door.

D'Quandray winced. He had anticipated having to explain that to his parents, knowing full well the explanation he had given to Dick Rogers and to others simply would not be enough. After showering, he lay down and took a nap.

***

The two couples walked into a family-style restaurant three hours later, having been driven there by Rashon. D'Quandray felt rested, and he thought that Imani looked amazing, even though she was dressed more for comfort than style. All her years of working at the gym had resulted in her being fit, and everything she wore looked good on her. Tamara had even complimented her on her looks. That was after Imani had whispered to D'Quandray that his parents looked amazing.

Even after being married for close to thirty years, his parents still held hands—something that had made Imani gush over them a few times already.

They were seated in a corner booth a short time after arriving. D'Quandray and Rashon both occupied the end seats while his mother and Imani were nearly side by side in the booth interior. They made small talk with one another as they looked at their menus and waited for their orders to be taken.

A brunette waitress approached a short time later with an electronic device in hand, ready to take their orders. "Oh my God," she began, "you're..."

"D'Quandray Free. It's nice to meet you." When she winced, he knew he had saved her from an embarrassing mistake. "And you are?"

"My name is Lauren. It's nice to meet you all. Do we know what we're having tonight?"

Crisis averted. D'Quandray deferred to his father to place their orders, which is what his dad had always done when they had gone out to eat in the past. Everyone had told him what they wanted prior to the waitress's arrival. Rashon placed their orders accurately, including all their special requests, and sent the waitress on her way.

"So, that's where D'Quandray gets his excellent memory from," Imani said. "I'm impressed."

"Thank you, young lady. I've had a lot of practice." He leaned over and kissed Tamara on her cheek, bringing a broad smile to her face.

"Aw," Imani said.

"Don't get them started; they do that all the time. Dad, how are you liking retirement?"

"I'm loving it. You'll never be able to beat me in golf now—not that you ever had a chance to in the first place. Your mother and I get to spend a lot more time doing stuff around the house, too."

"Yeah? Like what?"

"Like watching him sleep." Tamara playfully rolled her eyes. He could write a how-to manual on that. He has several techniques." Imani laughed as Rashon looked at his wife in mock disbelief. D'Quandray also found it funny. "Don't look at me that way; you know it's true."

"Anyway," he said, turning away from her, "Imani, how'd this lucky joker manage to get you?"

Imani shot a sideways glance at D'Quandray. "He always had a chance. I just had to wait until he was done with whatever *phase* he was going through." She smiled. It was D'Quandray's turn to look at her in mock disbelief, although his expression was not as manufactured as his father's. "Don't look at me that way; you know it's true." She looked at Tamara and winked.

"Oh, I like her already," Tamara said. "I finally have a teammate against you men."

"I bet you do like her," Rashon said. "What about you, D'Quandray? How's the job coming?"

"I quit."

"You did *what*? Why?"

"The condensed version of the story is they didn't respect me."

"No, I kind of want to hear the long version. They had to be pretty disrespectful to make you leave your job without having something else lined up."

"Now, I didn't say that. I do have something in the works. It's a grassroots type of operation, but it looks promising."

"Listen, son, I know they paid you a nice settlement for the injury, but you can't just rest on your laurels. You have to stay active. Young men aren't meant to be stagnant."

"I hear you loud and clear, dad. Trust me, the last thing I want is to be poor."

"Well, that's good to hear." Rashon listened to D'Quandray talk about his involvement in *BGI* and other plans he had to keep money coming in. He sat erect as the waitress returned pushing a cart with their food on top of it. Once everyone had their food and drinks, she left. Rashon looked down at his plate as he carved his steak. "D'Quandray, your mother and I would like to know why you changed your name." He looked up, put a piece into his mouth, and started chewing it as he awaited the answer.

Oh boy, here we go. "Well," he sighed, "it goes like this. I've come to realize that there's more to a name than appears, especially for us Black folks. Have you noticed how different our first and last names usually are? D'Quandray and Tyson don't even seem like they belong to the same person. D'Quandray is culturally Black American. Now, I don't know where Tyson comes from, but it sure isn't Black American, and it ain't African. Through a little bit of research, I learned that surnames were historically created to describe what an individual did for a living or what he was known for. Johnson, for instance, came about because somebody was John's son."

He took his hands away from his plate and sat up. "I chose to name myself Free for two reasons. One, it describes how I feel and what I believe myself to be. We can get into all the ways I feel free later. Two, it *frees* me from the slave name Tyson. I don't feel like it belongs to me or to our family, for that matter."

Rashon sat back and folded his arms across his chest. "So, why did you stick with D'Quandray?"

"D'Quandray is important to me." As he thought about Horace and Jamestown, he almost teared up. He knew he had failed to hide his emotions when Imani put a comforting hand on his back. "I've never heard of another person named D'Quandray. It's unique. It was given to me by you, my parents, and though I hated it as a child, I've come to appreciate it. It defines me."

"I hated that name, too," Tamara said, "but *your father* insisted on you having it. He said it represented strength and bravery, but when I looked it up, I couldn't find it anywhere. I'll let him tell you why he named you that."

"I'll be happy to tell him." He leaned forward and put an elbow on the table. "See, the history books don't tell you everything, especially when it comes to Blacks. The story goes that in the early eighteen hundreds, in Jamestown, Virginia, there was a brutal slave plantation. On it, there was an enslaved man who, for all his life, refused to tell his masters his name. He pretended to be dumb, but behind their backs he was a protector. He was big and strong, and he was an upright man. Then, one second before they killed him, he screamed his name out in pure defiance of them, almost taunting them, and his name was D'Quandray."

A chill went through D'Quandray's body. "That's an amazing story." He forced a chuckle. "It's probably not true, but I'll take it. Thanks, dad." And as his father shrugged his shoulders and casually went back to carving his steak, it took all the restraint D'Quandray had not to get up and hug him.

"'Thanks' for the story or for the name?" He asked the question without looking up from his plate of food.

"For both. I love the name, and you'll never have to worry about me changing it."

His father looked up, smiled, and looked back at his plate of food.

For the rest of the meal, they talked about D'Quandray's performance in the *World Tournament* championship game, his and Imani's experience in Ghana, and about Imani's family. The longer they stayed there, the friendlier Imani and Tamara got with one another. By the end of the night, the women were laughing and joking as if they had known each other all their lives.

D'Quandray had always viewed his father as a physically powerful man, but he had never realized until that conversation that his strength permeated every aspect of his being. He looked forward to having more conversations with him in the future. He regretted all the times he had mindlessly squandered opportunities to pick his brain in the past. He now viewed him through a different lens. Rashon had made sure that D'Quandray had never been physically hungry a day in his life, but now he was starving for all the information his father could give him, and he could not wait for his next helping.

Chapter 28

We Are Family

D'Quandray loved his parents more than anything else in the world. He was happy that he had gotten a chance to see them, and even happier that they had gotten to meet Imani, but he was glad to be home. They had never discussed it beforehand, but he did not take Imani to her house after they got back to their city, and she never requested to be taken there. She simply walked into his house and started putting her things away, a move to which D'Quandray offered absolutely no resistance or protest. When she got into the shower, he went into the *Housemate's* settings from his office computer and reconfigured them to accept her as a resident. It was officially their home.

He texted Bradley, Elijah, and Maliq to let them know that he was back in town. He immediately received responses from all three; however, Bradley's included a request to meet up to talk business. D'Quandray was, after all, a junior partner at *BGI*. When Imani got out of the shower, she called her mother to tell her that she had made it back. He could hear her laughing as she talked to her. He also heard her tell her that she would be by later to get her car and more of her things. That made D'Quandray smile.

While she talked to her mother, he went through the pages of emails that had been sent to him while he was away. One caught his eye. It was from the apparel company that had supplied him with free athletic gear in exchange for him wearing their stuff in public. After a formal greeting, which was addressed to D'Quandray Free, the message began, "We regret to inform you that..." He did not need to read the rest of the email. The date and time showed that it had been sent to him a short time after the *US National Team's* victory over the coalition team. That, and the fact that he had not received any free merchandise since his appearance on the *Dick Rogers Show*, told him everything he needed to know. He sighed and shook his head. He fought his urge to logout of his computer, and he went through the rest of his emails.

"Don't let them upset you, babe."

He looked away from the screen and toward the sound of Imani's voice. She was leaning against the door frame, wearing a white, terry cloth robe, and holding a cup of coffee. "How long have you been standing there?"

"About ten minutes." She lowered her nearly empty cup so he could see inside it. "This was full when I got here."

"Well, where's my cup?" She tilted her head to one side and raised an eyebrow. "Noted; I'll get it myself."

"You are as perceptive as you are handsome."

He laughed. "Touché." He swiveled his chair around to face her. "What time are we going to your mother's house to get your things?"

She lowered her coffee cup from her mouth and raised an eyebrow. "What time do I need to go?"

"That's a great question. I say we have a little fun first."

"That's an even better answer. I'll be in the bedroom." She winked at him and turned away, leaving her robe in the place she had been standing.

***

By the time Saturday came, Imani had completely moved into their home. She had been back to work at the gym for a few days already, having exhausted her leave while traveling with D'Quandray. She had already been gone for an hour. As he got ready to go there himself, he texted Bradley to confirm that he would be there as well. It had been months since they played basketball together, and he was looking forward to getting back to it. He had spoken to Maliq the previous day, so he knew that his former coworker, and now friend, would be there as well.

D'Quandray put on a tee shirt, some basketball shorts, one of his SSU sweatsuits, and a pair of basketball shoes made by the chief rival of the company that used to provide him free apparel. His phone buzzed with a message. It was from Bradley, and it stated that he would be there and on time. That did not come as a surprise to D'Quandray. Bradley had been hard at work as he tried to get *BGI* off the ground. In fact, D'Quandray had received several email reports on the status of the company, which already had a staff of fifteen employees—largely consisting of engineering students from SSU and Kelser University—while he had been away. If anyone needed to blow off some steam, it was Bradley.

When D'Quandray pulled up to the gym, he saw Bradley standing outside by the front door with his arms folded and frowning. As he pulled into the parking space, he kept his eyes on him. Bradley had never waited outside the gym for him before. The fact that he did today, seemed strange, especially since D'Quandray had encountered heavier than usual Saturday morning traffic on the way and was late getting there. He got out of his car but stopped when Imani came storming out of the front door with her phone to her ear. His phone buzzed in his pocket.

"I'm right here, Imani," he said. "What's going on?"

She pulled the phone away from her ear and pressed the button to end the call. "They took away your free membership."

"*What?*"

"Yes. When we scanned Bradley's membership, it didn't work. Since he had been allowed access as your guest, I checked your status to see if it was still active."

D'Quandray simply stared at the front door. He wanted to ask why, but he already knew the answer. Even though the man who owned the gym was an SSU alumnus, he was also a sports booster who was friends with Dick Rogers and many others of his ilk. He shook his head. "Score one for the bad guys." Then, he noticed that Imani was wearing her jacket and had all her personal belongings from inside with her. "Where are you going?"

"Home. I quit. I know exactly what this is about, and you do, too."

D'Quandray sighed. He walked up to her, took some of the items she was carrying from her hands, and kissed her on the forehead. "I'm sorry, babe." He saw tears beginning to form in her eyes, but as he looked at her, he knew exactly what kind they were—angry tears. They were tears of a person who had had enough—not with her job, but with the system that allowed what had just occurred to take place. She was fed up. He hugged her. "They won't win. I won't let them." When she wrapped her arms around his waist and started to cry, he knew that he had read her correctly.

D'Quandray cradled the back of Imani's head as she pressed her face into his chest. As he consoled her, he looked at Bradley and nodded. Bradley nodded back, and nothing needed to be said. Suddenly, Maliq barged out of the gym.

"They must be crazy!" he said before noticing D'Quandray, Imani, and Bradley standing there. He stopped. "I heard what happened, Black man. I just canceled my membership. I can play somewhere else. *Southside Athletics*, here I come."

Before D'Quandray could respond, the doors opened again, and out walked a few more disgruntled members. Word had traveled fast, and they were all complaining about D'Quandray's membership being revoked. "Don't they know the only reason I signed up here was because he was a member?" one of them said.

D'Quandray extended a hand to Maliq. "Thanks, man; that means more than you know, seriously."

"Don't mention it. That could just as easily have been me. I refuse to stand by and act like that's not possible."

And he was right. The thing that D'Quandray admired most about Maliq was his selflessness. He had always had a village-first mentality. He thought that he would have been an asset to the enslaved people in Jamestown, but he also realized that it was slavery that had spawned the likes of him. The evil that existed in those times caused those enslaved people to evolve into who he saw at that moment, a man who could never be subjugated in any way. He could very easily have been the progeny of either George or Isiah, spiritually if not physically. Yes, he would absolutely have been a problem for the Lesters.

"I guess I'll be finding another gym, too," Bradley said as Maliq walked away. "I can't believe they're being so petty."

"I can." D'Quandray rubbed Imani's back, gently kissed her lips, and used his thumb to wipe away her tears. "You okay, babe?"

"I'm okay. Can we leave before I burn this place to the ground?"

***

Eight months later.

Imani was scheduled to begin work in her new role as general manager of the *Goodman Sports Complex*, which happened to be in the exact same location as the gym she had ceased to work at several months earlier, in two weeks. In fact, it was at the same address. Only this time it was under the ownership of *BGI*. But today, she and D'Quandray had more important things to do.

As Imani walked out of the back door of Janice's home with a bouquet of flowers in her hands, D'Quandray turned to face her. *Canon in D major* was the selection played by the keyboard player and violinist as the attendees stood to salute her. Behind him, and dressed in black tuxedos, were Bradley, Elijah, and Maliq. He smiled when his father winked at him from the front row of the groom's side. *He* was dressed in a white tuxedo that matched D'Quandray's. Then, he looked at the other side and chuckled when Imani's mother, Claire, smiled and wiggled her fingers at him. He wiggled his back at her.

They had been blessed with perfect weather for the event, and he had been blessed with a perfect partner for his life. As he refocused on his approaching bride, his emotions began to overwhelm him. Everything he had been through—every argument with Maliq, every conversation with Horace, and every whipping he had endured in Jamestown—had led to this moment. The tears that rolled down his cheeks carried with them the pain that had formed the man he had become, and the smile he wore on his face freed him from that pain. He was a man reborn and a *boy* no more.

The ceremony unfolded as eloquently as any others before it had, no less beautiful than the most beautiful and no less touching than the most touching—poignant. The aftermath saw a reception that was full of love and happiness. From the first dance to the last picture taken,

D'Quandray and Imani Free enjoyed it all. At the end, Kofi and Naomi Boateng presented gifts from President Ike Boateng to the loving couple in a way so grandiose and full of pageantry that it wowed the people in attendance, culminating with the presentation of citizenship papers to Imani. The President of Ghana had fulfilled his promise to D'Quandray at the earliest possible opportunity. After Imani viewed the papers, she turned around and raised her hands in triumph, which, much to the delight of the Boateng's, brought forth cheers from the guests.

Perfection was a concept D'Quandray had always had a difficult time grasping. He had spent too many days in the gym trying, unsuccessfully, to achieve it. But as he looked at Imani's smiling face, he understood just how imperfect his life had been before the universe had compelled him to grab her hand at Horace's funeral.

When everything was over, only D'Quandray and Imani's closest friends and family remained. They had all migrated from the back yard to the study, where D'Quandray used to visit with Horace. The women were now all in flats and the men were sans bowties. Present were Janice, Claire; Tamara and Rashon Tyson; the Boateng's; Elijah and Marissa; Bradley and his supermodel girlfriend; and the Frees, D'Quandray and Imani. The remainder of their night together consisted of light conversation, wine, and jazz music. D'Quandray wanted to stay there as long as he could. He felt it was the best way to include Horace in the occasion. It was only his consideration of Janice's age that brought the night to a conclusion.

Chapter 29

Bradley's Big Day

Claire had moved into the Free residence at the beginning of Imani's second trimester. Her pregnancy had been a difficult one to that point, and her doctor had prescribed her bed rest as a precautionary measure. Meanwhile, D'Quandray had gotten heavily involved in the day-to-day operations of *BGI*. Bradley had sold his patent to the government prior to their marriage, which had made them all instant millionaires and catapulted his company into the fray as a major player in the tech entertainment industry. Bradley's plan was to take advantage of the momentum of his company's good start and use it in a way that would make each of their families wealthy for generations to come. That meant he had to make *BGI* the best it could be.

D'Quandray, Bradley, and Elijah stood beside the bed, looking down on Imani as she held the newest edition to their family in her arms.

"What's his name?" Bradley asked.

"Manis Tobe Free." D'Quandray replied with the last words that Horace had said to him in Jamestown—words that lived in his soul from that moment forward. Though his friend was no longer there in the flesh, D'Quandray's son, the newest addition to the Free family, would be the embodiment of Horace's spirit.

"He's beautiful," Elijah said, "and that is a *great* name."

"Thank you." He leaned over and kissed Imani on her forehead, then kissed his sleeping son on his cheek. "Come on, guys, let's go to my office."

"Congratulations again, Imani," Bradley whispered.

She simply smiled. Claire entered the converted nursery as they walked out. When they got to his office, D'Quandray sat in the chair behind his desk as Bradley and Elijah sat on the futon.

"Can you believe it?" Elijah asked as they made themselves comfortable. "Look what July 28, 2211 did to our lives."

"And to think, I had to beg you to come along, D'Quandray. You have a family now."

He shook his head as he thought back to what his life had been prior to the event. "I'm glad you did, BG. I'm not even the same person anymore."

"None of us are," Elijah, the former clean-cut, cross wearing religious zealot, who was now sporting shoulder-length hair and a scraggly beard, said. "How could we be?"

"We can't," Bradley said. "It's not possible after what we've been through. Everything has changed for us, literally and figuratively, but the biggest change is I don't fear anything anymore."

"I feel the same way," D'Quandray said. "It's amazing how your mindset changes when you realize you're not in control and that everything is part of a grand design. Being *away* taught me some things—about life and, more importantly, about myself." He shook his head. "I was a bad person, and I didn't even know it." He sighed. "BG, I'm going to take a step back from my role in our company. I think my time would be better spent speaking directly to my people."

"I need marketing, D'Quandray, especially now. Can you give me a little time?"

"Not necessary. I've already spoken to my replacement. I can promise you one thing; the company will be better off for it."

"And whom might that be?"

"Maliq. Trust me, he's the best. He will do things in that position that you've never even dreamed of. He's a marketing guru." He frowned as thoughts of Greg and Victor entered his mind. "They don't appreciate him at *Turbo*."

"When can he start?"

"Immediately."

"Then tell him he's hired. I'll pay him double what he was getting over there."

"Thanks, BG. You won't regret it."

"What are your plans, D'Quandray?" Elijah asked. "How are you going to speak directly to the people?"

"The same way I always have, except this time it'll be from my own show. I'll control the narrative, not them. It's going to be controversial, which is another reason I need to take a step back from *BGI*, but I feel it's necessary. My athletic gifts have given me a platform, and I intend to use it for good. When you see life for what it is—when you've been through what we've been through—you realize how precious these moments are."

"Marissa says the same thing," Elijah said. "She's been haunted by the fact that she couldn't see her grandfather since the day we watched that video."

"Speaking of Marissa..." Bradley began.

"I love her more than anything or anyone else in this world."

"Do I hear wedding bells?" Bradley asked.

"No; we don't believe in it. Our bond goes beyond what any document can define. We're committed to one another in ways that defy description, but we understand it, and that's all that matters."

D'Quandray almost voiced his disbelief at what he had just heard from Elijah, a man who had, before the event, taken every word written in the Bible as law. Now, he was defying one of its clearest mandates—for love. As he marveled at the change in his friend, he accepted it fully, knowing what a profound effect his own experience had had on him. It would have been naive to think the same would not be true for Bradley and Elijah. "I guess you have Bradley to thank, too."

"You guys give me too much credit," Bradley said before Elijah could respond. "We should all know it had nothing to do with me by now. It was the universe. I accept it. I *embrace* it. I think we all do."

And Bradley was right. Everything that had happened to them before and after the event was due to circumstances beyond their control. They were simply chess pieces being moved by a master player, or grains of sand so small they lacked the perspective it took to realize their importance to the desert. Or maybe they were humans who played their roles in the snippet of time they were allotted by simply staying here—as Horace once said—until their purpose was fulfilled.

***

Five years later.

Turbo Boost Sports Agency folded. The losses of Maliq Godson and D'Quandray Free were simply too much for them to overcome. Majority of its marketing department—who were not Greg, Victor, or Jason—were now working for *BGI* and were under the leadership and guidance of Maliq Godson, who was now the company's marketing director. Presently, the entire executive staff gathered in the lounge of *BGI's* downtown headquarters—a converted industrial warehouse with wall-to-wall windows that overlooked the city—to film a commercial, one they thought was going to radically change the way people visually consumed home entertainment. Also in attendance were executives from the major retail electronic stores, all of whom had been promised a breakthrough.

Bradley called it the *Cathedral View*. He had also applied a short sequence of numbers and letters to its name to identify the model. In the center of the room was a two-foot tall, three foot in diameter black circle with a shiny top—the prototype. It resembled an Avant Garde furniture piece. Around the walls, cameras no bigger than a dime were evenly spaced at the top, center, and base, creating three hundred sixty degrees of coverage of the room.

The demonstration would be centered on coverage of the *World Tournament*. For the third time in five years, the championship game was going to feature the *US National Team* against the *African Coalition Team*. The US National Team had won the previous two meetings against the coalition team—the first being a close game that went down to the last second and the following, a blowout—and four of the last five championships, missing one that was played in a communist state for political reasons.

This year's championship game was back in Accra, Ghana. Government officials had allowed *BGI* to outfit the arena with the same camera configuration that they now had at their headquarters. So, as *BGI's* guests prepared to watch the game on Bradley's new *Cathedral View* television, the commercial crew prepared to film their experience, which was also Maliq's idea.

D'Quandray, Bradley, and Elijah stood together in a corner of the room and sipped wine. They watched closely as Maliq stood near the *Cathedral View* and explained the features of the appliance to their select guests. Partially for comparison sake and partially to keep the guests entertained, pregame footage was being shown on the large flat screen televisions that were mounted on the walls.

"Who do you guys think will win the game?" D'Quandray asked.

"*BGI*, that's who," Bradley said with a smile. The black, two-button suit he was wearing was perfectly tailored, and his two-hundred-dollar haircut almost made him look like a model. He had come a long way from the off-the-rack suits he had worn to work each day five years ago. "In all seriousness, though, I think this is the year the coalition team breaks through. They have a lot of firepower. I don't see anyone stopping Boateng now. He's too experienced and too good."

"I agree," D'Quandray said. "This will be historic, and when the rest of the world sees this commercial, people are going to go nuts."

Bradley smiled and took a sip of wine from his glass. "That's the plan."

D'Quandray looked down and around. Then, he looked up and scanned the room. "Man T, get back over here." He smiled as the five-year-old stomped back over to where he and his friends were standing.

"You, too, Stacy." Elijah kneeled and opened his arms to his three-year-old daughter. "Come to daddy. I don't want to have to hear Marissa's mouth if something happens to you."

"You guys are so lucky," Bradley said as he watched Elijah scoop his child up into his arms.

"When are you going to settle down and start a family?" Elijah asked.

"Me?" Bradley laughed. "No time soon. I'm having way too much fun for that. Plus, these supermodels can't be trusted." They all laughed at that.

"May I have everyone's attention, please?" Maliq said aloud. Once all eyes were on him, he held the *Cathedral View* remote control high above his head. "It's time. Bradley Gates, the man of the hour, would you please step forward and do the honors?"

As everyone in the room applauded, and as the commercial crew focused their cameras on him, Bradley set his glass of wine on a nearby bar table and walked toward Maliq. He grabbed the remote control from him and thanked him. As Maliq joined the rest of the crowd, Bradley put his back to the *Cathedral View* and faced his audience. "First of all, I'd like to thank you all for coming. This, my friends, has been a labor of love." He waved his hand around the room. "Look at those beautiful televisions on the wall. After today, you'll probably have no desire to do so again." He turned to face his appliance and pointed the remote control at it. "Without further ado, I present to you the *Cathedral View* experience. Enjoy!" He pressed the power button and stepped away from the set.

Audible gasps escaped the mouths of all in the room as they looked at the miniature basketball players who were suddenly moving around on the basketball court on top of the *Cathedral View's* surface. Instinctively, they formed a circle around it after having been standing together on one side to listen to Maliq and Bradley speak. The three-dimensional, holographic images looked so real that one of the CEOs waved his hand over the appliance to see if he could touch them, much to the amusement of everyone else in the room. They all got closer, equally engrossed in the game that was being played and the way that it was being presented to them.

Before long, it was only the game that mattered. Kofi Boateng was performing to standard, but, unfortunately for the *US National Team*, his teammates had raised their level of play. They were not equal to the Americans, they were better. With ten minutes to go in the game, the outcome was already a foregone conclusion. When it was all said and done, the coalition team walked away with a ten-point victory. Kofi Boateng was named the tournament's most valuable player.

When the broadcast ended, the people who were there to film the commercial shut down their operation. They had gotten the footage they needed, and they promised Bradley that it would be edited and ready to go by the next evening. The executives from the companies lined up to thank Bradley for inviting them. They knew that once the commercial ran, demand would be high, so most of them were already in communication with their people to make sure they could accommodate the orders they were going to receive. Bradley sent them on their way with the knowledge that they would each be given their first *Cathedral View* and that it would come with footage of their evening already downloaded onto it. That was another suggestion given to him by Maliq.

Two hours after the game ended, D'Quandray, Bradley, and Elijah were still in the room. It was late, and they were tired. The children had been taken home by one of Bradley's drivers at the start of the game. The televisions on the wall had been turned off and the surface of the *Cathedral View* was clear, the game having been the only program it was equipped to show. The way regular programming was filmed simply was not compatible with the *Cathedral View's* hardware and software. A bit of serendipity was the behind-the-scenes footage they had gotten to see while the rest of the world watched commercials. Everyone in the room got to look at what the people inside the arena were seeing, which added an unexpected aspect of entertainment to the experience.

Their night ended with a lengthy video call from Kofi Boateng. They all congratulated him on his brilliant performance and the coalition team on their long-sought victory—one that would, according to former President Ike Boateng, "change the world." D'Quandray was curious to see what the long-term ramifications of the victory would be. As for *BGI*, the best still lay ahead of it.

Chapter 30

See You Next Lifetime

15 years later

D'Quandray Free had completely reinvented himself as the voice of his people and the conscience of the world. As he had predicted it would be, his *Free Your Mind* podcast—which he broadcasted from his home office—was controversial, but it was also highly rated. It had been configured to support being viewed on Bradley's *Cathedral View* television—which was now on its tenth model—immediately after they had run their commercial to introduce it to the world. Because it was one of only a few programs that were compatible with the *Cathedral View*, once the new viewing option was available and it became widely used, D'Quandray's show was heavily watched. Movies, sporting events, the news, regular tv shows, and everything else that had been consumed on standard television, had to be reformatted to accommodate the new technology, relegating the old systems they had used before to relics.

His in-studio guest was Ghana's ambassador to the United States, Kofi Boateng. He and his wife, Naomi, had spent the previous night at the Free residence. Boateng's godson, Manis T. Free, was home from college, where he was Kelser University's leading scorer. Boateng was five years removed from a stellar professional career in the United States, one that started after the coalition team's first loss to the *US National Team* in 2211. Playing his entire professional career in

Washington, D. C. had given him the thirst to get involved in politics, and he had also collected four championship rings along the way.

"Are you ready?" D'Quandray asked as he looked across the room at his guest and longtime friend.

Kofi nodded. "I am."

D'Quandray gave a signal to his engineer, and they began the show. "Welcome to the *Free Your Mind* podcast. I'm your host, D'Quandray Free, the purveyor of truth, and today I have a special guest. He is Ghana's ambassador to the United States, Kofi Boateng. Welcome, Ambassador Boateng."

"Thank you, Mr. Free. It is a pleasure to be here."

"I assure you that the pleasure is all mine. We first met when we played a pickup game against one another way back in 2211. I remember a few things about you from that day. One, you were very good. Two, you were ultra-competitive, and finally, you comported yourself as a gentleman the whole time. As I think about that, it makes perfect sense that you would become an ambassador."

"I am what I am, Mr. Free. I like to think that these things are preordained and that I am simply playing my role."

"I definitely understand that. Also, let me pause to offer my condolences to you and your family on what can only be described as the brutal assassination of your former President, Ike Boateng. We felt it here."

"Thank you. It rocked the continent of Africa. My uncle was a visionary, and those who sought to silence him have only amplified his message."

"And what is that message?"

"His message was, or is, that we need to unite the continent under one flag, the banner of Alkebulan. One thing we—the coalition team—showed Mother Africa during our historic run of three consecutive *World Tournament Championship* victories was that we could do amazing things together."

"Why was there resistance?"

"Our continent is full of kings and princes. The idea that they all would fall under one leader did not sit well with some of them. They feared that their power would be diminished, although that was far from true. They also feared that my uncle wanted to be the ruler of

Alkebulan, even though he stated on numerous occasions that he had no desire to do such a thing." He paused to compose himself. "I think it was his popularity that frightened them. As you know, he was a very charismatic man."

"Indeed. Are you concerned that continuing his message could be harmful to you and your family?"

"There is always that chance, but I am governed by the Most-High, not fear. If death comes, I will embrace it as I would a relative." He smiled. "But I will not tell death my address or when my visiting hours are."

D'Quandray laughed. "You are wise, my friend."

For the remainder of the two-hour long interview, they went on to cover a variety of topics, while leaving the details of their personal relationship up to speculation. At the conclusion of the show, they quickly transitioned back to their friendship. Naomi and Imani had been in the living room the entire time. Manis T. Free had been in a corner of the room as the podcast was being filmed. He would appear in the footage once it aired, but his role would be of no significance other than to mark the fact that he was in the room, for posterity.

The Frees agreed that Man T would spend the summer in Ghana with his godparents after his junior year of college was over. He was a lock to make it to the professional league, but D'Quandray and Imani thought that it was important for him to continue his yearly trips there for his personal enrichment, and they thought it would likely be his last opportunity to do so for a while. Manis T. Free had been considered a top prospect his entire college career, but D'Quandray had made him promise to get his degree before moving to the next level. His own personal experience with injury, and with life, had taught him that it was important.

***

2286

D'Quandray sat in his rocking chair on the front porch of his country home, looking out over his land. It was evening, and the summer breeze was just strong enough to ruffle the sleeve of his loose-fitting tee shirt and just cool enough to keep him outside instead of inside his air-conditioned home. The slow-moving ceiling fans spaced evenly underneath the overhang of his wrap-around porch were a nice complement to the gift offered to him by mother nature.

For the first time in some time, he and Imani were alone. He could not remember the last time he had no grandchildren or great grandchildren there to show him some new game they had learned to play or to ask him all the questions that curious little children liked to ask. Having been retired for thirty years, he had given up his suburban home for rural living. His move to the country had coincided with his departure from public life, a place where his only son had become a giant. The tranquility suited him, and, more importantly, it made Imani happy.

He was waiting for his wife to join him on the porch, where they would watch the sunset together, as they always did. His ears perked up when he heard her talking on the phone on the other side of the door. For a time, her voice was loud, then it faded to a point where he could barely hear her talking, reaching varying levels of clarity as she walked back and forth from the front door to other parts of the house.

During one of the lulls, he suddenly felt sleepy, but it was not the type of sleepiness to which he had become accustomed. Afternoon naps had been a part of his daily routine for the better part of thirty years now. Today, he was sluggish and lethargic, and he felt like each breath he took lacked the amount of oxygen he needed. He sat erect and took a deep breath but could not pull in enough air to alleviate the stress he was feeling. He placed his hand over his heart and grabbed his chest—no pain, just discomfort.

"Bradley *and* Elijah?" Because she was now hard of hearing, Imani spoke loudly, and her voice carried. "Oh no, this is going to crush him. My goodness. Thank you for calling me, Stacy. You have my condolences."

For most people, living to be one hundred years old would be a dream, but for D'Quandray Free, it had simply been enough. As the screen door opened behind him, his head lowered, and his eyes closed.

"That was Stacy Chester. D'Quandray?"

He stopped breathing, and, for a moment, he thought nothing, heard nothing, and felt nothing. Then, his body began to tingle, summoning him from the absence. That familiar tinge of electricity, that he had first felt on July 28, 2211, had returned. As it surged through his body, he raised his head, opened his eyes, and stared into the distance. Then, he stood. A portal appeared. And just like what happened the last time he had seen it, he felt an irresistible urge to walk toward it. He started to move, and he immediately felt his bare feet on the porch. When he looked down at his body, he saw that he was naked. When he looked back, he saw that Imani was attempting to bring the body of the man she had loved for years back to consciousness, but he, the soul of that man, was looking back at them. Then, he knew.

He turned away, exhaled, and continued toward the portal. Within two steps, his breathing was back to normal. After ten steps, he was moving faster and with less body pain. He stopped and extended his arms out in front of him. They were fuller and had greater muscle density, and he felt stronger. The pull of the portal tugged at him more now, so he started to walk again, feeling stronger with each step. By the time he reached the threshold, D'Quandray was standing fully erect. His youth had been restored. He stepped through the portal as the same twenty-five-year-old man who had entered it seventy-five years before.

D'Quandray turned to look back at the porch and felt his heart break when he saw Imani hugging the shell that once possessed his soul. As she wiped tears from her face, he held his own; and as much as he wanted to go back, he could not.

"Don't worry, Sir, you'll see her again."

The voice startled him, but it was friendly, and it was familiar. D'Quandray pivoted around to confirm that it was who he thought it was. "Horace?" He was wearing a white, body-length, cowl, and he was the same age he had been when D'Quandray first encountered him in Jamestown, only this time he was clean shaven. But he still wore that signature smile upon his face.

Horace opened his arms. "Yes. Welcome, my friend."

Behind him stood two sentries. They looked like the ones D'Quandray had seen that night, and they were every bit as imposing as he remembered. But unlike the last time, he sensed that they were no threat to him, that they meant him no harm. He looked at his own body, and he was now dressed in a garment like the one Horace was wearing. He knew not to question the universe, so, without fear or reservation, he fully accepted their current version of reality. As he hugged Horace, the sentries' bodies phased, and they were suddenly facing in the opposite direction. They remained there for only a moment. Every time their bodies disappeared and reappeared, they were further away. When D'Quandray let go of him, Horace followed the sentries. As much as his eyes were fixated on Horace and the sentries, D'Quandray's heart was still attached to Imani. He turned around so he could look at her one last time, but the portal had already closed.

THE END

About the Author

T.O. Burnett is, in many ways, a typical inner-city man. Having moved to the southeast section of Washington, D.C. by the age of one with his single mother, he spent his adolescent years learning in the school of hard knocks. He grew up in the Barry Farms community where he developed his tenacious spirit.

Despite not having much, T.O. managed to do well academically. Always inquisitive, he quenched his thirst for knowledge with after school programs—such as the *Higher Achievement Program (HAP)*—and public television. He prided himself with acquiring trivial knowledge and learning from everything and everyone he encountered. That helped him to become a first-place regional winner of the *IT'S ACADEMIC CLUBS* competition while he was an eighth grader at Douglass Junior High School.

After moving South to rural Alabama to start high school, T.O. began to explore writing, which came naturally to him. His literary skills and overall writing talent were cultivated by his father, who was a respected educator and dedicated public servant. A short stint in the United States Marine Corps, and a career in law enforcement helped him to develop a well-rounded perspective on life. In addition to being a patrol officer, he also taught at the police academy—where he was a firearms instructor, defensive tactics instructor, and senior drill instructor—for over seventeen years. He was named MPCTC instructor of the year in 2011.

As a science fiction author, T.O. has been heavily influenced by space operas, science fiction shows of the 1970s, kung fu movies, and numerous sci-fi authors. The author of the *Sapien* series hopes that he, too, will one day be recognized as an influential writer in the science fiction genre. T.O. has never been married and does not have children.

Made in the USA
Middletown, DE
26 April 2023

29506611R00156